A VICKY HILL
Exclusive!

HANNAH
DENNISON

ROBINSON

Constable & Robinson Ltd
55–56 Russell Square
London WC1B 4HP
www.constablerobinson.com

Published in the US by The Berkley Publishing Group,
a division of Penguin Group (USA) Inc., New York, 2008

First published in the UK by Robinson,
an imprint of Constable & Robinson Ltd, 2012

A copy of the British Library Cataloguing in
Publication data is available from the British Library

ISBN: 978-1-78033-059-4 (paperback)
ISBN: 978-1-78033-060-0 (ebook)

Printed and bound in the UK

1 3 5 7 9 10 8 6 4 2

For Pose

Acknowledgements

I wish to extend my heartfelt gratitude to:

Claire Carmichael: instructor extraordinaire, Australian guru, and wonderful friend. Thank you for your irrepressible humour, genius suggestions, and endless support. I hope to repay your many services one day with the gift of a small island.

Mark Davis: chairman of Davis Elen Advertising and amazing boss. Thank you for supporting my dreams and embracing them as your own.

Linda Palmer: fellow author, kindred spirit, and sister-in-crime. Thank you for your selfless advice, kindness, and infinite generosity in sharing your publishing experiences.

Kerry Madden: author and teacher who discovered the character of Vicky Hill and insisted I bring her to life.

Sarah Smith, aka Pose: my daughter, who never stopped believing in me.

The Dennisons: with special thanks to my parents for passing on their sense of humour and for sharing their unusual and often intriguing insights on life and love. Happily, they have never been wanted criminals.

Readers and well-wishers: James Ward, Kevin Butterworth, Cam Galano, Andra Berkholds, Rob Nau, Gavin Reardon, the

Elen clan, Giles Instone, and Tamara Sobel. An extra-special thank-you to Mark Durel, who has enthusiastically read every incarnation of Vicky from day one.

Natalee Rosenstein: editor at Berkley Prime Crime. Thank you, not just for taking a leap of faith, but also for the brilliant suggestions without which Vicky might still be languishing in a bottom drawer. Thanks also to Michelle Vega, assistant editor at Berkley Prime Crime, who does everything with a smile and is the most efficient person I know.

My agent, Betsy Amster: for taking a chance on an unknown writer.

The UCLA Writers Program: For enabling me to transition from amateur writer to professional author.

And, last but by no means least, Jason Elen: my husband, who willingly took on the roles of nursemaid, drill sergeant, cheerleader, therapist, cook, launderer, man Friday, and without whose love and support this book could never have been finished. You are my hero.

1

The brown envelope addressed to Annabel Lake sat on her empty chair.

Of course, it was marked *confidential,* but given that Annabel was home, suffering from a severe case of food poisoning, I thought it prudent to open it. After all, it could be urgent and what was in a name, anyway? Weren't we journalists all seeking truth and justice?

The note bore today's date but was tantalizingly unsigned. I felt a thrill of excitement. Apparently, something 'macabre' had been discovered at Gipping County Council Rubbish Tip, and 'could Annabel Lake go there straight away.'

Within minutes, I had my headline: RUBBISH REVEALS ROTTING REMAINS: A VICKY HILL EXCLUSIVE! Or, should the discovery prove really grisly: GIPPING TIP TORSO TERROR.

All I had to do was persuade Pete Chambers, my boss and chief reporter of the *Gipping Gazette,* to give me the story.

I tapped on Pete's office door and braced myself for the usual barrage of obscenities.

'Who the hell is it?' he shouted.

1

'It's Vicky.' I opened the door a crack and waved the note and envelope at him. 'Just got this in. Could be a big one.'

'That'll be the day.' Pete sneered, gesturing for me to step through a wall of cigarette smoke into his cramped office. 'You'll soon learn, luv.'

I felt sorry for Pete. Somewhere along the line, he'd grown disillusioned. Apparently, this happened to a lot of middle-aged journalists who saw too much of life's cruelties. It would never happen to me.

Pete scanned the note with a frown. 'This is addressed to Annabel. Where the bloody hell is she?'

'She's got diarrhoea.' I tried to sound sympathetic. 'It's really bad. Every five minutes—'

'This is marked *confidential*, Vicky.'

'I thought it looked urgent. Diarrhoea could go on for days. I'd never have opened it otherwise – honestly.'

'Where is everyone?'

'Tony has a cold – flu, actually – and Edward's covering that abused sheep love-triangle case in court that could go on all week.' I smiled. 'But I can—'

'No you bloody can't.' Pete flicked ash onto the floor. 'You're reporting Trewallyn's funeral. Christ! Why did Annabel do this to me? She knew today was important.'

I wanted to point out that Annabel had not deliberately chosen to eat a dicey curry, but thought it wise to keep quiet. Besides, I knew exactly the reason for Pete's angst – though I would never let on. He and Annabel were secretly working on something important. I'd caught snatches of 'Biggest story Gipping has ever had,' and 'The report will confirm it all.'

Then, yesterday, when I brought their afternoon tea and made an innocent remark about Sir Hugh Trewallyn's funeral, Annabel had become flustered. She'd quickly hit 'sleep' on her computer keyboard so I couldn't see the screen. Honestly! How immature! Didn't she know I was aiming to become a famous international correspondent like Christiane Amanpour? It was only a matter of time until I would find out what was going on.

'I thought I could go via the rubbish tip on my way to the funeral,' I ventured.

'No.' Pete drummed his fingers on the desk. 'It's Annabel's lead, Vicky. Not yours.'

I longed to shout aloud, 'It isn't! It isn't! I was here before her. It's not fair!' but instead, I gave a bright smile and said, 'Just trying to help.'

'Well, don't.' Pete angrily stubbed one cigarette out and lit another.

I knew this so-called report was due to be delivered today and, judging from Pete's reaction, I guessed one of his informers would be slipping it to him on the quiet.

'Why don't you go? I'll wait here for that special *report*,' I said, with wide-eyed innocence.

'Report?' Pete snapped. 'Did Annabel tell you?'

'Oh, you know how she is,' I said, airily. Annabel hadn't said a word to me.

'I've got no bloody choice, have I? My balls are in a vice.'

I pushed that image firmly to the back of my mind. Before Pete could change his, I put on my beige safari jacket – Christiane wears hers in the field all the time – and headed for the door. 'You won't regret it,' I said.

'Wait!' Pete took a key out of his pocket, unlocked the bottom drawer of his desk, and retrieved a Nikon digital camera. 'You'd better borrow this. Annabel tells me you don't have one.'

'Of course, I do! It's being repaired,' I said mentally cursing Annabel who always loved to make me look incompetent. Dad had given me a Canon Digital Rebel before they left for Spain, but the batch had turned out to have a faulty flash. Thanks to the barcode tracking system, I couldn't even use the guarantee to get a replacement. It was most annoying.

'I hope you didn't take it to Ken's Kamera,' Pete said. 'He's worse than bloody useless.'

'No,' I said quickly. Of course, I had.

3

'No reporter should ever be without a camera these days,' Pete scolded, 'Especially if it's for the front page.'

Front page! This could be it – my lucky break! 'What do you think I'll find at the dump?'

'How would I know?' Pete snarled. 'That's your job.'

'Right. Sorry.'

Pete handed me the camera. 'Know what to ask?'

'Who-what-when-where-how-and-why,' I recited crisply, automatically giving Pete a nautical salute.

I hurried out of his office. With Annabel out of action, this was my long-awaited chance to prove my mettle and escape from what seemed like the never-ending world of funeral reporting.

When my parents fled the country four months ago, I moved from northern England to begin an apprenticeship with the *Gipping Gazette* in Devon. I imagined I'd be working on the crime desk – or recording gruesome murders at the local Magistrates' Court. I was sorely disappointed.

Gipping-on-Plym had to be the most boring town in all of England. Divided by the River Plym, Upper Gipping, to the north, was home to toffs, wealthy farmers, and the nouveau riche – the sort of place where Dad would do a lot of business. By comparison, Lower Gipping, to the south, resembled a mining slum from a D. H. Lawrence novel. Once a bustling community that took pride in working for Trewallyn Wool and Textiles, the old factory had long closed down leaving the residents disillusioned and unemployed.

The most gripping front-page scoops from the past twenty years were framed and mounted on the walls in reception: THE FLOOD OF '93 that closed Withybottom for two whole days; THE STAMPEDE OF '80 when twenty-five cows escaped from a neighbouring farm and thundered through town in the dead of night; and, most exciting of all, last week's PLYM VALLEY TOWER TRAGEDY, the latest bungle by eco-activists trying to stop Devon Satellite Bell from erecting a mobile phone transmitter on top of St Andrew's church tower. Adopting the name 'Eco-Warriors,' this rogue band of troublemakers are convinced that electromagnetic waves could expose the community to dangerous radiation. Unfortunately, their candlelit protest ended when a bird's nest caught fire, engulfing the fifteenth-century belfry in flames.

I yearned to cover real news but up to this point had done nothing other than stand outside church doors taking names of local mourners, paying particular attention to correct spelling.

The *Gazette* was famous for being one of the few remaining newspapers in the country to record the names of all the bereaved. It was very proud of its reputation for accuracy and attention to detail. According to my funeral log, I had attended 157 so far. It astonished me just how many old people lived – or should I say, died – in the area. I concluded it must be the countryside. Most people imagined a staple diet of fresh air and open spaces was marvellous for one's constitution. I disagreed. As an expert on death, I believed it was the endless farmyard smells – raw pig manure being the worst – that eventually overwhelmed the elderly.

Downstairs in reception, I grabbed an umbrella from Barbara Meadows, our plump receptionist who was proud of the fact she started work here, 'when the Beatles released "A Hard Day's Night"' and thrived on local gossip. It was threatening to rain – again.

'You're off early,' she said. 'Trewallyn's funeral doesn't start until eleven.'

'I'm off to the rubbish tip,' I said, unable to contain my excitement. 'Big story down there.'

'Oh! You don't want to take any notice of Ronnie Binns, dear,' Barbara said dismissively.

'Ronnie Binns?'

'The dustman! Such a smelly little man.' She laughed. Barbara may think she knows everything but she doesn't have a reporter's instinct for hard-boiled news.

'Always dropping in with his silly *anonymous* notes for Annabel. Always crying wolf. I told Annabel, if she had wanted a reliable informer, I could have listed a dozen lusty, virile men who would—'

'Maybe this time it's for real,' I said, trying to ignore the unwelcome news that Annabel had her own personal informer. 'Anyway, Pete seems to think it's worth investigating.'

'Suit yourself.' Barbara shrugged. 'Frankly, you've got to take anyone born in Lower Gipping with a pinch of salt.' She dropped her voice – not that she needed to, reception was empty. 'Such an *untrustworthy* sort.' Barbara lived in The Marshes – a small section of swampland reclaimed from the River Plym and highly susceptible to flooding.

'I'll bear that in mind. Bye.' I felt instantly deflated. Surely, if Pete had been aware of the note's origins, wouldn't he have told me not to bother? Unless he just wanted me out of the way when the report arrived?

Out in the High Street, rain fell in sharp, windy gusts. I set off at a brisk pace. The walk to the rubbish tip would take approximately twenty minutes. It was already nine thirty. Sir Hugh's funeral was on the other side of town, so I'd have to get a move on. If only I could afford a car.

Annabel drove a new silver BMW 328i, yet we both earned the same paltry trainee salary. I suspected she had wealthy, generous parents. Perhaps her father was a banker, rather like my dad who also dealt in money – albeit somewhat unconventionally.

Unlike myself, Annabel could always afford the latest fashions. I remembered her first day at the *Gazette* when she turned up dressed in Dolce & Gabbana low-rider jeans exposing a naked, perfectly toned midriff with pierced navel. A cropped, matching jacket accentuated her voluptuous figure. Pete was so shocked he nearly swallowed his cigarette. Even Wilf Veysey, our reclusive editor, made a rare appearance from his corner office to see what all the fuss was about. He declared it was unprofessional to expose so much flesh in public despite Annabel's protests that she'd always found her choice of attire a journalistic asset. Much to Pete's sorrow, Annabel was sent home to change.

As I splashed through the puddled streets of the small market town, greeting everyone I passed with a smile – a reporter could never have too many contacts – it was hard not to dwell on my rival. Initially, I'd been looking forward to making a friend. We'd talk about boyfriends – even though I'd never really had one. We'd spend our free time getting drunk at The Three Tuns on Friday nights or going clubbing in Plymouth.

The moment Annabel arrived I realized friendship was the furthest thing from her mind. From the start, she made it clear she did not see me as her equal, even though we were the same age. She repeatedly rejected my suggestions that we eat our sandwiches together in the park, preferring to hang around Pete and reapply her lipstick.

I never wore makeup. There was no time for vanity in the front line. I favoured warm clothes and comfortable shoes. As an ex-Girl Guide, I always liked to be prepared. Tucked in one of my safari jacket pockets, I carried a Swiss Army knife, a flashlight, and a whistle.

It made no difference to Annabel that I started at the newspaper months before she had. As the most junior, it should have been *her* responsibility to make the tea for all of us. Instead, I was still doing it. Annabel had claimed it was too dangerous for her to go down the steep, rickety stairs to the basement where our makeshift kitchenette harboured a cracked porcelain sink, gas water heater, and small refrigerator.

Announcing she was allergic to gas fumes, Annabel had insisted that Pete accompany her to check the equipment for leaks. They were gone for at least half an hour and, when they did reappear, Annabel looked smug and claimed making tea would be a health risk for her lungs. Pete, red in the face, held a copy of a newspaper in front of his crotch. The headline read UNEXPECTED HEAT WAVE CAUSES RUPTURE IN TANK, which I thought highly apt under the circumstances.

Of course, I realized what had gone on in the basement! The birds and the bees were no mystery to me. My mum had warned me how men, confined in small spaces with big-breasted girls, could rarely control themselves. Promptly, I pushed the image of Pete and Annabel away. I was finally embarking on my first real reporting job and, until it turned out to be a hoax, refused to dwell on such frivolities.

The note said the discovery was 'macabre'. This was a strange word. It conjured up horrible scenes from *Voodoo Vixens,* the thriller I finished reading late last night. In the book, the word *macabre* is used to describe the grotesque voodoo dolls and mutilated chickens that littered the jungle floor. Perhaps one had made its way from darkest Africa to Lower Gipping? I really hoped so.

As I turned onto Refuse Dump Drive, my stomach filled with butterflies. No doubt the place would be seething with ill-mannered onlookers, anxious to enjoy other people's tragedies. I suspected the police would have cordoned off the area with blue and white tape, like they did on telly.

I steadied myself for what horrors lay ahead. To my annoyance, the tip showed no sign of any activity at all. It looked like Barbara was right.

The giant, iron gates were closed and padlocked, though frankly, the broken, rusty fence surrounding the tip would never deter a determined trespasser. Other than a muddy dustcart – emblazoned with the logo, GIPPING COUNTY COUNCIL: REFUSE WE WON'T REFUSE – parked alongside a trailer, the place was deserted. I felt a stab of disappointment, but reminded myself that I still had a job to do. I headed for the trailer – a soulless box on wheels, which I presumed to be the site office.

'*Gipping Gazette*!' I called out, feeling a sudden thrill of importance. I knocked smartly on the door. 'Press!'

'Won't be a moment,' shouted a male voice from inside.

I waited for what seemed like aeons.

The door flew open. 'Morning,' said a wiry, balding man in

his early sixties. He was dressed in dirty gabardine overalls and thigh-high rubber boots that looked too snug for comfort.

'Ronnie Binns?' I asked, trying not to gag as a vision of Ronnie and Annabel passionately kissing flashed before my eyes.

'Who are you?' Ronnie's voice was edged with suspicion. 'Where's Annabel Lake?'

'Vicky Hill,' I said, offering my hand and swiftly withdrawing it again as I was practically poleaxed by a boiled-cabbage like stench that surrounded him like atmosphere. Barbara was right again.

'Annabel's ill,' I said pleasantly. 'The *Gazette* sent me instead.' This was perfectly true.

'Oh, aye.' Ronnie wiped his nose with the back of his hand and looked me up and down with what seemed like ill-disguised lust. 'I suppose you'll do. Same arrangement?'

I felt my face grow hot. There was no question of any form of payment, bodily or otherwise, with this revolting little person.

Dad had told me a lot about handling informers, particularly those who seemed too cocky: first, never feel intimidated; second, never pay up front; and third, be willing to walk away.

'I'm afraid not,' I said firmly. 'The deal has changed.'

'A deal's a deal,' Ronnie said flatly. 'No money. No story. Good day to you.' Ronnie neatly stepped back inside and tried to shut the door. I slipped my foot into the crack.

'Let's not be hasty, Mr Binns!' I said, immensely cheered by the knowledge that sex was off the menu. 'As you can imagine, we have a lot of loyal readers willing to tip off their favourite newspaper. For *free*.' This was probably true. 'In exchange, they get a special thanks for looking out for the community. Sometimes, their name even gets in the paper.'

'That's their lookout.' Ronnie pushed the door hard against my foot. 'Excuse me, but I've a phone call to make.'

God! He's going to call Annabel. 'I wouldn't do that,' I said quickly. 'She's very ill. She might even be in a coma.'

9

'I wasn't going to call *her*,' Ronnie said. 'I'm sure another newspaper will be interested in what I found yesterday. It's your loss.'

Blast! What an infuriating little man, I thought, but instead gave an indulgent chuckle. 'Oh, Mr Binns, I haven't come about whatever you found at the tip.'

'You haven't?' Ronnie blinked. 'What do you want, then?'

I paused trying to think up another reason. 'I'm afraid it's come to our editor's notice that some of the stories you have brought to our attention are a load of codswallop.'

'Who said that?'

'Who do you think?'

Ronnie's eyes flashed. 'She told me what passed between us was private.'

'Ah, well, Annabel's new and overenthusiastic,' I said cheerfully. 'Just take this visit as a friendly warning, Mr Binns. We love the public to tip us off, but one can cry wolf too many times! Nice to meet you. Must be off. Bye.' I turned to go, one ear ready for the inevitable.

'Wait! Come back here!' Ronnie shouted, hurrying after me. 'Cry wolf! No one calls me a liar.'

I stopped. 'Mr Binns, you're wasting *Gazette* time. I'm afraid I just can't pay you.'

'It's not about the money! It's about *respect*!' Ronnie seemed genuinely upset. 'No one insults the Binns's family name and gets away with it!'

'If you feel you really want to tell me, then go ahead. I'm all ears.' I whipped out my reporter notebook and mentally prepared my routine list of questions.

'And no cops. This is between you and me.'

I heartily agreed with that remark, having heard my father say countless times, 'The only good copper is a dead copper.' Personally, I wouldn't go quite that far, but I did view the police with somewhat of a jaundiced eye.

'Where exactly is it now?'

'Like I said, in there.' He gestured towards the locked gates.

'When did it happen?'

'Like I said, yesterday.'

'What is it?'

Ronnie paused, and gave me a strange look. 'It's the work of the devil. That's what it is.'

Blast! What a complete waste of time. These country folk saw the devil everywhere. I went on with my next question out of pure habit. 'How did you find it?'

'Like I said, picking up at The Grange.'

'Trewallyn's place?' What a small world, I thought, considering my next port of call was Sir Hugh's funeral. Rumours were flying about Sir Hugh's body being found mysteriously spread-eagled in the middle of a yew hedge on the estate. I thought the idea of foul play rather far-fetched.

Sir Hugh was seventy-five, which was a perfectly acceptable age to go. He was a notorious hedge-jumper – the local pastime – and probably suffered a heart attack whilst attempting a jump at a particularly challenging, large yew. I reminded myself it was important for a reporter not to make assumptions until I'd gathered all the facts, which I would have following the service later today.

'Do you want to see it?' Ronnie whispered as he extracted a key from his pocket and gestured for me to follow him.

I shrugged. 'If we're quick.'

We stopped outside the padlocked gates.

BEEP! BEEP! BEEEEEP!

The car horn startled me. I spun around, momentarily blinded as a pair of flashing headlights filled my vision.

Ronnie stood transfixed as a silver BMW barrelled towards us. He spun to face me, his expression filled with accusation. 'You told me she was at death's door!'

Blast! It was Annabel.

2

'Thank God you're alive!' I said, opening Annabel's car door. 'She's alive! It's a miracle!' I yelled out to Ronnie who was standing over by the open gates with a face like thunder.

'For heaven's sake, Vicky, you're such a hypochondriac!' Annabel sneered. 'It was just a touch of food poisoning. You'll never survive out in the field if you're worried about little things like that.'

'I'm not—'

'I'll take over now.' Annabel checked her reflection in the rear view mirror. With her auburn hair (Nice 'n Easy Natural Copper Red), she looked pale and beautiful. She was wearing another new outfit – an indecently short, denim miniskirt and leather bomber jacket – obviously for Ronnie Binns's benefit. 'Is there a loo around here?'

'I think there's one in the office.' I know it sounded uncharitable, but I couldn't help hoping she'd suffer a hideous relapse.

'Haven't you got a funeral to go to?' Annabel opened the glove box and retrieved an envelope that, to my practised eye, looked thick with banknotes.

'You don't have to pay Mr Binns,' I declared. Ronnie was

striding towards us flushed with self-righteous indignation. 'He says he's happy to give us information for free.'

'Nothing is for free, Vicky.' Lowering her voice, she added in a voice heavy with menace, 'And if you ever try to steal one of my stories again, I'll make sure you're fired.'

'Pete sent me. He thought you'd be on your back for days,' I said. Pointing to the office camera swinging around my neck, I added, 'He even loaned me the Nikon digital.'

'Well, really!' Annabel seemed annoyed but switched to full-blown charm as Ronnie – and his fragrance of boiled cabbages – joined us. 'Ronnie darling! How lovely to see you.' I noted her effusive greeting did not extend to a warm embrace.

Ronnie's eyes zeroed in on the envelope clutched in Annabel's hand. He threw me a look of triumph, 'Is that for—?'

'Excellent. You remembered.' I snatched the envelope from Annabel's grasp, thrust it into my pocket, and drew her to one side. 'You do realize that everyone at the *Gazette* knows his tips are pure invention,' I whispered.

Annabel didn't answer. No doubt she was feeling foolish for paying for the old man's ramblings.

'I feel a bit peculiar.' Annabel started doing little bunny hops on the spot.

'Don't. We all make mistakes. He's not worth it.' I glanced over at Ronnie who was glowering at me. If looks could kill, I'd be six feet under.

'I haven't got all day,' he shouted. 'Do you want to see it or not?'

'Be right there!' I cried. Turning back to Annabel, I shared one of Dad's pieces of wisdom. 'You're far too trusting. Never pay for information first.'

'You don't know what you're . . .' Annabel trailed off and closed her eyes tightly. A grimace spread over her face.

Good grief! Had the woman no spine? If she were intimidated by the likes of Ronnie Binns, she'd never be able to deal with squealers from organized crime.

13

'Don't worry,' I said, 'I won't tell Pete about your financial arrangement with the dustman.'

'You silly *cow*.' Annabel clenched her fists and suddenly froze. 'Toilet. Got to . . . oh God . . .' and darted in the direction of the trailer. She wrenched open the door and disappeared inside.

'Is she going to be long?' grumbled Ronnie as he adjusted his thigh-high waders with a pained groan. 'I was up at four and still have Cowley Street to do.'

How I yearned to leave them both to it, but Ronnie was bound to tell Annabel I'd told him he was off the payroll. She'd be furious with me for interfering. I felt the envelope in my pocket, half tempted to give it to him anyway and be done with it. But, of course, I couldn't do that. Family principles ran deep. The Hills never paid for information without proof first.

'Better wait for Annabel.'

We lapsed into an uncomfortable silence. I could feel Ronnie's eyes boring into me.

'I know who you are,' he suddenly announced. 'You're the young lass lodging at Mrs Poultry's place in Rumble Lane!'

'Yes,' I said, warily, happy to change the subject but wondering what my landlady had been saying about me. 'Why?'

'She's a good sort.'

'Mrs Poultry *is* wonderful, isn't she?' I wondered if we were talking about the same person. 'Heart of gold.'

'Generous.'

I let that one go. Clearly, our definitions of *generous* were worlds apart. I recalled the weak tea at breakfast with one slice of toast; the 'kitchen closed after 6.00 p.m. rule', which meant I rarely had the chance to make myself a hot meal at night.

To add insult to injury, Mrs Poultry ran a special event agency called Cradle to Coffin Catering. One of the few perks I enjoyed after working a funeral was being invited back to the house for cold cuts and fruitcake. Given that my landlady usually supplied these delicacies, she always complained I was eating her profits.

'Her dustbins are a joy to empty,' Ronnie said. 'You can tell a lot about a person by the way they treat their rubbish.'

'Mrs Poultry certainly loves a clean dustbin,' I agreed.

'Does she ever . . . like . . . talk about me?' he asked shyly. Surely he didn't fancy that dour old battle-axe? Yet who am I to cast judgment? My mum always says, 'There's someone for everyone.'

'Mrs Poultry says you're reliable,' I said.

'*Reliable,* see?' Ronnie thumped his chest. '*She'd* never accuse me of crying wolf! *She'd* believe me!' With that, he spun on his heel and stormed back to the open gates shouting, 'The devil's at work here in Gipping, and I'm going to prove it!'

What if he was right? I couldn't risk Annabel snagging a front-page scoop beneath my very eyes. I trotted after Ronnie, positive that Christiane Amanpour would have done the same in similar circumstances.

The stench of rotting garbage was overpowering. How could anyone work here? The rain of the past few weeks had turned the narrow muddy paths between the towering stacks of rubbish into a quagmire.

We sloshed past piles of abandoned household articles – mattresses, dozens of rusting prams, and old refrigerators.

'Over there,' said Ronnie, pointing to a rough clearing among the debris. I could make out a small shape under a piece of black plastic.

My heart began to pound faster with the wildest hope that even if it wasn't a body, it could be part of one. I steeled myself. A head, though shocking, would look terrific on page one.

'Wait!' I heard a shout and looked around. Annabel was attempting to catch up in kitten-heel shoes. Mud was spattering up her bare legs and she was slipping all over the place.

'Vicky! Wait for me!' she screamed. 'This is *my* story.'

Ronnie bent down and whipped off the plastic.

Three white fluffy birds lay in a heap.

'Chickens.' I felt a stab of disappointment. All that fuss for nothing. 'Just chickens.'

'They're not just any old chickens.' Ronnie poked at the pile with the toe of his boot and flipped one of the unfortunate creatures over. 'Blood's been completely drained out, see?'

I knelt down to take a closer look. The hairs on the back of my neck prickled.

'Their throats have been cut, see?' said Ronnie. 'Usually you just chop their heads off, but someone's gone to a lot of trouble here. If you ask me, that's not normal.'

He was right. Each fragile neck had a neat slice, yet there wasn't even a speck of blood on their snowy white feathers.

Apparently, Ronnie Binns had some expertise in chicken killing. 'First, you take your chicken,' he began, 'and you string it up by the legs—'

'Where *are* their legs?' I said alarmed. Each chicken was minus vital limbs. Ronnie was right to describe this spectacle as macabre. It reminded me of the curse scene in chapter four of *Voodoo Vixens* – with one vital ingredient missing: a voodoo doll. The Vixens's trademark signature.

'You're right to bring this to our attention, Mr Binns.' I reached for my camera.

'No, stop!' Annabel stumbled towards us and stood staring at the pathetic wretches in silence.

At last, she gestured for Ronnie to replace the plastic. 'Sorry to waste your time, Mr Binns.'

'What?' I was astonished.

Ronnie scratched his head – he seemed to often do this – dandruff, possibly, or worse. Head lice? '*She* doesn't think so.'

'Vicky doesn't know what she's talking about.' Annabel's tone was crisp. 'The *Gazette* appreciates you calling, but there is no story here.' Annabel turned on her heel and began to slosh her way back towards the car. 'Come along, Vicky.'

'I'll walk,' I said, anxious to have another word with Ronnie. Obviously Annabel had not read *Voodoo Vixens*.

'Nonsense, it's going to rain. I'll give you a lift,' she demanded, adding darkly, 'And besides, I want a word with you.'

The last thing I wanted to do was be trapped in Annabel's car getting a lecture. But a glance at my watch – Dad said it was a genuine Christian Dior – told me I needed a lift back to Middle Gipping.

'I'll be back later,' I whispered to Ronnie, fighting the urge to give him the money, after all. 'Please don't go to another paper. I believe you.'

He rewarded me with a gap-toothed smile, 'Tell your lovely landlady I said hello.'

Back at the car, I found Annabel carefully rearranging the dealership paper in both foot wells.

'Keep your feet on this,' she said. 'The carpet's new.'

We drove up the muddy lane, slick with garbage residue. Annabel, cursing under her breath, did her best to steer around numerous, rain-filled potholes.

After some minutes, she heaved a big sigh. 'Vicky, Vicky, *Vicky*. What *am* I going to do with you?'

'Pete told me to come.' I felt six years old.

'You had no business opening a confidential letter,' Annabel scolded. 'Ronnie's not always a reliable informer, but he still belongs to me.'

'The money—'

'Is mine. Pete gives me a small allowance for these little incidentals.'

I felt jealous. Annabel had an expense account. I didn't.

'Which reminds me, the envelope, please.' Annabel took one hand off the steering wheel and held it out, palm side up. 'I wouldn't want Pete to think you've been stealing money as well as stories from me.'

Her insult left me speechless. I may have inherited many Hill traits, but theft was not one of them.

'I suggest you forget all about Ronnie Binns and the chickens.' Annabel laughed. 'I mean, the countryside is full of them – dead or otherwise.'

I glanced over at my rival. A complacent smile was on her

face. She thought she had me fooled. Fat chance! It was clear to me that whatever the chickens meant to Annabel, she was determined not to share her theories with me.

It was nearly ten fifteen. 'Do you mind dropping me off at the church?' If I walked from the *Gazette,* I'd never make Sir Hugh's funeral in time.

'No can do. I've got to get back to the office.' Annabel pulled a face. 'You really must learn to manage your time.'

'If it's for Pete,' I said, adding pointedly, 'there's no rush. He's going to wait for that *special* report.'

'What are you talking about?' Annabel turned pink.

I yawned, feigning indifference. 'He told me everything.'

'Pete told *you* about the coroner's report?'

This was an interesting piece of information. A coroner's report put a completely different slant on matters. 'Why *wouldn't* he tell me?'

'I don't believe it!' she snorted. 'Typical man.'

'I've never seen Pete so agitated,' I said, warming to my theme.

'Well, who wouldn't be?' Annabel said with a sniff. 'If anyone found out, it could cost him his job.'

The plot was thickening! Getting access to a coroner's report before the inquest was illegal. 'Bit risky, isn't it?' I said.

'Of course it is, but this is a very special circumstance.'

I did a mental check of who had died recently and could only conclude it had something to do with Sir Hugh.

'Poor old Trewallyn.' I bluffed. 'It'll be good for us to know the truth.'

Annabel's look was pure spite. 'Pete gave this story to *me,* Vicky.'

So it *was* connected to Sir Hugh! My hunch was spot on. It seems I have a natural gift for getting information out of people without having to resort to bribery, blackmail, or physical torture.

'Of course it's your story,' I said, savouring the rare moment that Annabel's feathers were so decisively ruffled. 'I'll keep my eyes peeled when I go to The Grange after the service and interview the family.'

'Change of plan.' Annabel shot me a triumphant look and tossed her hair. 'His wife didn't want press at the after-service reception, so Pete and I are going tomorrow morning – once we've studied the report, of course.'

I felt as if she had punched me in the stomach. All efforts at being civil vanished. 'You? Why? *I* do all the funerals. In fact, stop the car. I can walk from here.' I needed to be alone. 'Stop the car, *now*.'

'Don't be childish. It's going to rain.'

'It's only drizzling.' The heavens opened, and rain thundered onto the windscreen. I bit my lip in frustration. This was a serious downpour.

Annabel reached over and gave my knee a condescending pat. 'I'll take you to the church, you silly thing.'

I was livid. Pete should be taking *me* to the interview. Funerals were my speciality. *I* went to the church; *I* took the names at the door and waited for the service to end; and *I* trooped back to the house for tea and fruitcake, mingled with the mourners, and got the obituary interview. Funerals were *my* kingdom.

It just wasn't fair. Suddenly I hated Gipping. I hated the dreariness of country life. I felt trapped and depressed.

'Come on, don't sulk,' Annabel said. 'Which church is it?'

'St Peter's the *Martyr*,' I said, easily identifying with said saint's character trait. 'Turn left here.'

Annabel swung the BMW down a narrow lane flanked by towering yew hedgerows that marked the church boundary. We pulled into an empty gravel car park in front of a twelfth-century, grey stone, Norman church.

St Peter's the Martyr was in Upper Gipping. It boasted the largest cemetery in South East Devon and was jammed with medieval memorials, lichen-covered headstones dating from the seventeenth century, and marble family crypts. Quite simply, it was *the* place to be buried.

The rain ceased as quickly as it had begun. Annabel stopped in front of the wooden lych-gate. 'There, you see – plenty of time. All that worrying for nothing,' she said. 'Are you sure it's the right place? There's no one here.'

'*Yet*,' I snapped. 'No one here, *yet*. It's important to be early.'

'Oh God, look!' Annabel's mouth dropped open in awe. 'Over there!'

A sleek black Porsche was parked farther up the lane in the shadow of the hedge.

'Exactly my point,' I said. 'That car could belong to a mourner.'

'I would do anything for a ride in a car like that,' gushed Annabel. 'Be an angel and make sure you find out whose it is.'

'Don't get too excited,' I said, opening the door. 'They won't be from round here.'

'Vicky, wait.' Annabel grabbed my arm, digging her scarlet painted nails into my safari jacket. 'Look, I know you started at the *Gazette* ages before me—'

'Three months, actually—'

'Oh! Is it really as long as that?' Annabel's look of surprise did not fool me for a minute. 'What I am trying to say is that journalism is a tough world. Tough, tough, *tough*! We have to look out for number one, but we can still be friends. Hmmm?'

'Absolutely.' I gave her a brittle, totally insincere smile and shook her hand off my arm. 'Thanks for the lift.'

'And don't forget about the driver of that Porsche.' Annabel gave a seductive wriggle. 'I can't *resist* a man who drives a sports car.'

'Must go now. Hope the diarrhoea clears up.' I slammed the door hard, pushed open the gate, and stormed up the brick herringbone pathway towards the church vestibule. I was sick of hearing about Annabel's obsession with sports cars – or rather, their drivers.

20

I, too, was curious about who owned the Porsche. Gipping rarely attracted flashy visitors. The town had its fair share of tourists, but most came from the East End of London or from the industrial cities of the north. I wondered what had brought the driver to such a remote corner of rural England out of season. Perhaps he was a long-lost relative of Sir Hugh's, come to claim his inheritance?

I cast around for a glimpse of the mysterious driver. Perhaps he was already in the church, praying to the Lord Our Saviour? I peeped inside, inhaling the comforting smell of musty prayer books and brass cleaner, but, apart from the floral tributes that lined the aisle from font to pulpit, the place was empty.

Outside, I scanned the churchyard. Funerals could be harrowing at the best of times. Perhaps he had sneaked off for a soothing cigarette?

My instincts were spot on. Lurking by the hedge, a man stood smoking. Dressed in a long black trench coat, he had short black hair and wore sunglasses. It was hard to tell from this distance but he bore a striking resemblance to Pierce Brosnan.

After a moment's hesitation, I decided to walk over and get his name – not to satisfy Annabel's curiosity, but to get a head start on my mourner list. If strangers were expected to attend, it could get busy. Retrieving my reporter notebook from my jacket pocket, I gave him a cheery wave and set off across the damp grass. To my surprise, he turned abruptly on his heel and disappeared through a hole in the hedge.

How unbelievably rude! Hadn't anyone any idea how much skill was involved in recording these names? Spelling was vital. The integrity of the newspaper was at stake. Many a time the *Gazette* had to print embarrassing apologies for a misspelling or omitted participant or – far more heinous – a participant who had been recorded as present but who turned out to have a long-standing feud with the deceased, and, declared he or she, 'Wouldn't be seen dead at old Johnson's funeral.'

Gipping-on-Plym was rife with petty grudges – usually over

cattle or wayward second cousins, caught *en flagrante* in semi-public places. I felt frustrated. This was destined to be a very trying morning – especially as the appearance of the man in black suggested there could be mourners from all around the country attending who would be unfamiliar with funeral format.

Cars started to arrive in the car park to disgorge occupants dressed in sombre shades of grey, black, and dark navy. They trickled up the path towards the church where I eagerly waited, pen in hand and notebook flipped open. My expression was a nice blend, I hoped, of attentive, yet respectful, professionalism.

Fortunately, the local mourners knew the drill. They helped those who were visiting to carefully spell their names for me. In the few moments when I was not wrestling with some extraordinary spelling, my thoughts returned to those poor, mutilated chickens. Why were they found at The Grange? My mum always says, 'There is no such thing as coincidence.'

As the belfry clock struck eleven, the funeral motorcade arrived.

'Hello, young Vicky,' boomed the Reverend Whittler, whose habit of materializing from thin air I always found unnerving. 'We really must stop meeting like this. People will talk!'

I smiled weakly and caught a waft of pear drops and whisky on his bream. Whittler's attempts at being racy always made me uncomfortable. Tall and thin, with his hawk like nose and long, black hooded cape, he reminded me more of the Grim Reaper than a man of God.

Clapping his hands sharply, Whittler shouted, 'Come along, come along, ladies and gentlemen. Please take your seats.'

Obediently, the mourners trooped up the path and entered the church.

Whittler turned to me with a hopeful smile. 'Are you joining us for the service today?'

Pierce Brosnan had still not passed by. 'Can't afford to miss any last-minute stragglers,' I said. 'But I'll be with you in spirit.'

Pallbearers dressed in pinstriped trousers, black mourning coats, and top hats carefully dragged the coffin, laden with white chrysanthemums, out of the back of the hearse.

Lady Trewallyn rose majestically from one of the sedans. I'd heard that Sir Hugh's second wife was younger, but had not expected someone in her early thirties.

She was wearing an elegant black designer suit with jaunty hat and veil. Even from this distance, I could see the scarlet slash of lipstick through the net fabric, and thought she resembled a film star from the forties.

A handful of fawning locals fussed around the widow, in preparation for the slow procession up the path and into the church.

Whittler retrieved a small silver whistle from a hidden pocket, and blew three sharp peeps. On cue, the ancient pipe organ lumbered into life and began the dour opening chords of Chopin's Funeral March.

I scanned the churchyard once more – still no sign of Pierce Brosnan. Then, to my astonishment, I caught a glimpse of a familiar figure emerging from the shadows close to where I'd first spotted my mystery man.

I'd recognize that brown tweed coat and matching cloche hat anywhere.

It was my landlady, Mrs Poultry.

Her appearance was puzzling. Not only was she a self-proclaimed atheist, she should have been at The Grange laying out the finger buffet.

To my surprise, Mrs Poultry did not even look in the direction of the church. Instead, she crept stealthily alongside the hedge towards the ornate iron railings that enclosed a small, domed mausoleum – the Trewallyn family crypt.

Flanked by granite pillars, the bronze door stood invitingly open. Engraved above the doorway was the family motto: HOMO PROPONIT, SED DEUS DISPONIT – 'Man proposes, God disposes'. For a ghastly moment, I thought she was actually going to go

23

inside, but instead, she headed over to a large hawthorn bush a few feet away.

Mesmerized, I watched Mrs Poultry drop to her knees. With lightning speed – all the more extraordinary given her advanced years and chronic arthritis – she crawled beneath its branches and vanished from sight.

3

Half an hour and two hymns later, I realized Mrs Poultry was not coming out. At one point I considered the wisdom of going over to the bush to say a friendly hello but, recalling the surreptitious approach to her hiding place, I guessed she wanted to remain unseen. Everyone grieves differently.

There was no sign of Pierce Brosnan, either. It was relatively easy to watch both hedge and bush from inside the church vestibule, which also afforded an excellent view of the mausoleum.

I stamped my feet to keep warm and mused over my landlady. What on earth she was doing under there was anyone's guess. Our paths only crossed at breakfast – served between 7.45 and 8.15 a.m. – and occasionally in the evening, when I was using the bathroom and bumped into her on the landing.

I had found the furnished room in Rumble Lane via the classifieds in the *Gazette*. It was on the outskirts of Middle Gipping, a convenient fifteen-minute walk to the office.

As with most attic rooms, the eaves sloped from ceiling to floor. Light came from a tiny dormer window above a built-in wooden cupboard, which housed a noisy water tank. I had a narrow iron bed; child-size desk, small chair, and a metal dress rack on wheels that served as a wardrobe. Behind the door was a plastic chest of drawers in a hideous shade of salmon pink. I kept telling myself it was a temporary arrangement until I could afford my own flat.

My mind drifted to Ronnie Binns and his odd comment that Mrs Poultry was always clean and that her dustbins were a joy to empty. It didn't surprise me. Mrs Poultry's house was sparsely furnished. There were no knickknacks or mementos. My landlady was meticulous about her appearance and never had a grey hair out of place, making her foray into the mud and under the bush so out of character.

Why *did* Mrs Poultry mention me to the dustman? For a ghastly moment I wondered if news of my parents' exile had got out and she'd heard of the reward for their arrest. Perhaps she'd found the waterproof plastic box I had hidden in the water tank, and discovered the two postcards from Mum in Spain? My stomach began to churn at the implications.

I gave myself a sharp slap to the forehead with my notebook. *Pull yourself together, Vicky!* Perhaps I was right about Ronnie being infatuated with Mrs Poultry? Just because you reach a certain age doesn't mean the heart is not capable of great passions. He'd certainly been praising my landlady's virtues with unexpected enthusiasm. I didn't know anything about her past, but assumed she had been married – though I could be wrong. Spinsters are notoriously defensive about being left on the shelf and dying a virgin. Why not invent a dead husband?

I turned my speculations to Pierce Brosnan. It seemed he was not going to reappear, either. Clearly, he could not be a mourner, after all. Unless he was some kind of funeral pervert who enjoyed witnessing other people's grief. As I grew older, the more I saw of the world and the more funerals I attended, I realized how fleeting life really was. With global warming, viral pandemics, and biological warfare an all-too-real threat, who knew when the end would come? This chilling thought made me realize even *I* could die an old maid if I didn't get a move on.

I could only think of one eligible man to do the deed – Dave Randall, the hedge-jumping champion, whom I met last Sunday. I was just about to dwell on his manly virtues when an extraordinary thought struck me. Wasn't Sir Hugh's body discovered in a hedge? Wasn't he a passionate jumper? Surely, hedge-jumping was a relatively small world. Why wasn't Dave present, right now, paying his respects to one of his kinfolk?

It was an interesting lead, and one of which Annabel was totally unaware. Dave would become my personal informer. If Annabel had one, why shouldn't I? If Dave and I ended up in the bedroom, so be it – to say nothing of killing two birds with one stone.

The hymn, 'Blessed Are the Pure in Heart,' signalled the end of the service. In a few minutes, the mourners would emerge. I took one last look at the bush and decided Mrs Poultry was either prostrate with grief or had taken a morning nap.

Positioning myself outside behind a stone buttress, I watched Whittler lead the procession towards the Trewallyn crypt tucked in the corner of the churchyard.

I scanned the grounds, startled to see Pierce Brosnan again, lurking in the shadows of the hedge.

To my annoyance, he made his way there, too. I knew it was inappropriate for me to tear over and get his name at such a late stage. Any further thoughts vanished as I watched the man barge through the crowd. Bold as brass, he positioned himself mere inches in front of Lady Trewallyn's face. She froze, caught off guard. The man calmly lifted her veil.

There was a deathly pause. Neither of them moved. You could have heard the proverbial pin drop. The mourners seemed flabbergasted at such an appalling lack of propriety.

Suddenly, Pierce Brosnan cupped Lady Trewallyn's chin and kissed her violently on the mouth. The onlookers gasped with disbelief and horrified delight. I felt a familiar tingle in my loins – though not for long. Lady Trewallyn abruptly came

27

to her senses. She pushed him away roughly and began to scream.

The astonished spectators did nothing but gawk as the man turned away and sauntered back towards the hedge. Lady Trewallyn, screeching like a banshee, kicked off her high heels and sprinted after him. Her athleticism was staggering. Within seconds, she'd caught up, whereupon she launched herself at his retreating back, flinging her arms around his neck and lifting her feet off the ground – probably hoping her weight would topple them both into the mud.

Lady Trewallyn might be fleet of foot, but he was definitely stronger. In one fluid motion, the man grabbed her hands from around his neck. He did a little jump and splayed his legs, then tossed her over his right shoulder. She landed hard on her bottom without so much as a cry. It was an excellent judo move.

The mourners remained in total shock as the man melted through the hedge and disappeared. Then, all chaos broke loose. Everyone, except the vicar, ran towards Lady Trewallyn, who had already got to her feet. Dismissing all efforts of assistance, she simply adjusted her hat, gave no more than a cursory glance at the mud stains on her skirt, and limped back towards the crypt where Whittler – who ran a strict timetable – had been continuing with the service alone.

I tore down the path and into the lane just as an engine's throaty roar indicated the mystery man was making his getaway. I thought my heart was going to burst with excitement as the black Porsche – with tinted windows and no licence plate – sped past.

The Porsche stopped briefly at the main road before turning left towards the wilds of Dartmoor and disappearing from sight.

As I returned to the churchyard, I had an epiphany. Lady Trewallyn – young, beautiful, and fit – had killed her elderly husband for his money. Pierce Brosnan was her lover and accomplice.

Predictably, now the old man was dead, she no longer needed

her paramour's services, and – typical man – he wasn't going to take rejection lying down.

In a town where everyone knew everything, it shouldn't be too difficult to find out Pierce Brosnan's true identity.

As my mum would say, strike while the iron is hot, which is exactly what I proposed to do.

4

'Does anyone know the driver of a black car?' I asked the mourners as they filtered out of the churchyard. Most seemed excited by the extraordinary graveyard scrap, others gave Lady Trewallyn a wide berth. It was only when a pale-faced woman with a lavender-coloured perm turned to glower at me that I realized my faux pas. The hearse, of course, was black.

'Sorry, I mean a black Porsche. You know, a sports car?' I adopted my most friendly expression and cast around the crowd for a flicker of recognition. All I got were blank, hostile stares.

'Typical press,' snapped lavender perm. 'Poor Sir Hugh not even cold, and already they're sniffing around for dirty laundry.' She gave me a venomous glare. 'Vultures.'

'Now, now, Mrs Pratt,' said old Coroner Sharpe, 'Vicky is only trying to do her job.' Lavender perm scowled and walked off.

I liked the old coroner. With his immense belly, white bushy eyebrows and beard, he reminded me of Santa Claus. Next to Whittler, Sharpe attended as many funerals as I did. I thought it touching he liked to see a job through, literally, to the bitter end.

'Thank you, Mr Sharpe.' I gave him a grateful smile. 'I'm glad someone understands.'

'Only too well, dear,' he said. 'We both serve the public in our own way.'

Seeing Sharpe reminded me of the imminent arrival of his report. I felt uncomfortable. Was he aware there was a traitor in his morgue? Shouldn't I hint that something underhanded was afoot?

Sharpe muttered something about Lady Trewallyn and headed over to where she stood leaning against one of the black sedans. The unfairness of not being present for the interview tomorrow at The Grange hit me afresh. Why couldn't I ask Lady Trewallyn who her young friend was? Right now. This minute. I hurried towards them.

Lady Trewallyn's smart suit was caked with mud – as were her knees. To my surprise, Sharpe promptly took out his handkerchief, spat on it, and began to rub them vigorously. Lady Trewallyn seemed indifferent to his feverish efforts. In fact, she seemed lost in some private world of her own.

'Lady Trewallyn!' I said. 'May I talk to you for a moment?'

Lady Trewallyn snapped out of her reverie, pushed Sharpe away, jumped into the sedan, and locked the car door. The engine burst into life and peeled out of the car park.

Sharpe chuckled. 'Katherine doesn't like the press.'

I had never before been so patently rebuffed, but supposed I had better get used to it. I was the press. The *paparazzi*. Perhaps, even someone to be feared?

Sharpe had called Lady Trewallyn by her first name. Perhaps he knew who the Porsche driver was?

'Sorry, Vicky.' Sharpe had read my mind. 'No questions.' And with that, he turned on his heel, got into his new black Mercedes CL550 Coupé, and drove away.

I had to lay my hands on that coroner's report. No wonder Pete and Annabel were so desperate to get it. As far as I was concerned, Lady Trewallyn's flight had confirmed her guilt.

Perhaps Sharpe was involved, too? What was the significance of the mutilated chickens? And why had Mrs Poultry decided to watch the funeral proceedings from under a hawthorn bush?

It was time to do some serious investigating.

5

As I crawled beneath the branches of the sprawling hawthorn, admiration for my landlady's nimbleness soared. Prickly burs caught in my hair and, twice, my safari jacket got snagged on thorns.

Needless to say, Mrs Poultry had gone. I wriggled into the interior and managed to manoeuvre into a sitting position. Through a small gap in the foliage, I could see the Trewallyn crypt – now sealed shut. Perhaps Mrs Poultry had merely decided to pay her respects to the dead man in private?

I scrambled out, determined to broach the subject of Sir Hugh's funeral next time our paths crossed. I'd definitely mention Ronnie's high regard for her clean dustbins. I quite liked the idea of playing Cupid to the elderly.

Glancing at my watch, I realized I might still catch Ronnie at Cowley Street. I was sure he'd share his chicken theories with me if we were alone.

I was in luck. Ronnie was emptying the very last dustbin when I caught up with him.

'Mr Binns!' I called out with a cheery wave.

Ronnie finished tossing the contents into the rear of the truck, and put the bin back on the pavement.

'Remember me? Vicky Hill,' I said warmly. 'We met this morning at the tip?'

Ronnie, flushed from his exertions, shook his head and frowned. 'No. Can't say I do.'

'Mrs Poultry's lodger?' Good lord, I thought. It was only two hours ago. What was wrong with the man? 'You remarked on her clean dustbins always being a joy to empty?'

Ronnie's expression remained blank. Had my appearance altered that much since my foray under the hedge?

Self-consciously, I patted my hair, yanking out several small brown prickles. 'I had a question about the chickens.'

'Chickens?'

'The chickens you showed me at the tip?' I said, adding helpfully, 'The white fluffy ones? You know, the ones with their throats cut?'

'I don't know what you're talking about,' he mumbled, looking down at his green rubber waders.

Reminding myself that journalism was all about persistence, I pressed on. 'They were under a piece of black plastic.'

Ronnie shook his head. 'No. Sorry. Good day to you.' And with a curt salute, he clambered into the cab and drove off.

Flabbergasted, I watched the truck disappear from view. Naturally he was lying. In the short time since we last spoke, someone had got to him. I knew the signs – the lack of eye contact, the fascination with footwear, and of course, a convenient attack of Alzheimer's.

Ronnie's denial confirmed my suspicions of foul play – no pun intended. What's more, I knew who had warned him off. Annabel must have double-backed to the tip after dropping me at the church. Her money had bought his story and his silence.

Blast Annabel! I thought back to her clumsy attempt at throwing me off the scent: her feigned disinterest in the chicken corpses and how she dismissed Ronnie as a time waster. Annabel may have won this battle, but that did not mean she had won the war. I wasn't quite done with Ronnie Binns, yet.

6

When I reached the High Street, a huge commotion was taking place outside the *Gazette* office. Raised, angry voices, car horns blaring, and the inevitable group of curious bystanders, who seemed to emerge from the ether at any sign of trouble, were present.

Annabel had obviously stolen the one remaining parking space on this congested one-way street – much to the fury of an elderly woman in a brown woollen hat. Hurling obscenities, the old lady was showing considerable strength as she leaned against Annabel's driver door, supposedly to prevent her from getting out. I had to admire Annabel's sangfroid. It would seem her intestines had calmed down. She seemed indifferent to the verbal attack, being far more concerned with touching up her lipstick in the rear-view mirror.

An old red Mini, presumably the outraged pensioner's, remained in the middle of the street, holding up the traffic, which had backed up all the way to the public library. The last thing I wanted was for Annabel to notice me, or even worse, drag me into the melee. I darted across the road and into the sanctuary of The Copper Kettle.

Despite the fact that the cafe was opposite the office, I'd never been inside. It was a bit of a disappointment.

The Copper Kettle was part of a row of Queen Anne terraced houses that flanked the High Street. The tearoom was obviously a former shop of some description. Copper kettles were arranged along the length of the old counter. Cheap prints of dead game hung from shabby walls. The whole place had a neglected air. There wasn't a customer in sight.

I took a table by the window, which afforded an excellent view of Annabel and the High Street. A quick glimpse outside revealed the traffic warden had arrived and was attempting to act as a mediator between the old lady – still gesticulating wildly – and Annabel, who had refused to get out of the car and was looking bored with all the palaver.

A young, pasty-faced waitress in heavy black eyeliner, wearing an olive-green serge medieval dress, and lace mob cap, hurried over to greet me. 'I'm frightfully sorry,' she said, 'that table is reserved.'

I looked around the cafe. 'There's no one else in here.'

'I like to keep this one vacant. You never know . . .' The waitress frowned, then brightened considerably. 'You work for the newspaper, don't you?'

'Yes. Why?' I said warily. People will do anything to get their names in print.

'You're Vicky Hill!' she said, giving me a brilliant smile exposing acres of gums.

Should I be flattered or alarmed? My mother despised nosy neighbours, and had insisted the Hill family keep themselves to themselves. What later transpired with the police and Dad's nocturnal activities more than explained her caution.

The waitress pulled out a chair and flopped down. 'I *knew* I recognized you. I'm Topaz Potter.'

'Good for you,' I said, feeling more than a little affronted by the waitress's overfamiliarity. 'I'd like a cup of tea and a slice of fruitcake.'

'I want to be a reporter,' she gushed, ignoring my request.

'Actually, I'd really like a cup of tea,' I said, deeply resenting the impulse that put me in this position. So far, today had been filled with lunacy: Ronnie and the devil chickens, Lady Trewallyn's bizarre behaviour with the mysterious Porsche driver, my landlady hiding under a bush – and now this.

'I'd make a really good reporter. I see everything that goes on around here.' Topaz tapped the side of her nose. 'That's why I like to keep this table free.'

'It's not easy to break into journalism.'

'I'm not afraid of hard work and danger,' Topaz said, adding eagerly, 'You won't be disappointed.'

A part of me felt boosted by her obvious admiration – the other resolved never to venture into the cafe again. I glanced out the window. Traffic was once again moving. The BMW remained, but there was no sign of Annabel.

I got to my feet. 'On second thought, I'd better get back. Really busy—'

'I'll get your tea right away.' Topaz sprang up. 'Work *here*. Do! It's lovely and quiet.'

Before I had a chance to protest, Topaz disappeared through a red and white plastic fringe, which presumably led to the kitchen.

It was true. The cafe was as silent as the grave. Topaz could be right. It was hard to think straight at the *Gazette* when everyone was on constant high alert, anticipating the next big scoop.

I sat back down and opened my reporter notebook. Finding the driver of the black Porsche should be fairly easy. A car like that in these parts was rare. With regards to the *ménage à trois* – well, it was understandable really, Lady Trewallyn was young and Sir Hugh, seventy-five. It seemed logical to assume Pierce Brosnan and Lady Trewallyn were lovers, despite her outburst at the cemetery. Adultery was a well-known country pursuit. Yet, true blue-blooded gentility tended to avoid public outcry like the plague.

I scribbled down: *Was Lady Trewallyn born into money, or did she marry it?*

Topaz returned with a floral tray bearing a pot of tea, chipped cup and saucer, and a sliver of fruitcake. 'Milk and sugar are on the table,' she said. 'I won't disturb your important work.'

'Thanks.'

'I'll wait over there. Just nod if you need anything.'

Topaz promptly sat down at the very next table – dead opposite. Playing with a stray strand of dark brown hair dangling from her mob cap, she stared at me. It was most unnerving. I shifted my chair around so my back was to her.

Pouring the greyish liquid into the cup, I took one look at the fruitcake and knew instantly it was going to be a disappointment. It had the waxy, glazed appearance seen in British Rail buffet cars. I took a bite. I was right. It was totally inedible.

Somehow the fruitcake emphasized for me the wretched fact that Annabel would be savouring one of Mrs Poultry's leftover slices at The Grange tomorrow morning. Annabel was doing the interview. Annabel would be asking inciting questions. Annabel would have read the coroner's report and know everything. Annabel would *shine. Blast Annabel!*

Conscious of Topaz's intense gaze boring into the back of my skull, I flipped through my notebook with assumed professionalism, scribbling down any words that came into my head – *sex, death, devil, chickens.*

I came across the notes I made for the hedge-jumping feature that I'd written in my free time. I'd actually slipped a copy onto Pete's desk, but had not heard from him, yet. It appeared the newspaper did not go in for features. Presumably, they felt their readers did not want to broaden their minds and were happy with the staple fare of funerals, flower shows, and excruciatingly embarrassing theatre productions performed by the Gipping Bards.

However, with Sir Hugh's death and this new hedge-jumping connection, my feature on Dave Randall might just hold some weight. I reread my notes. My face grew red when I realized I'd drawn a heart around Dave's name with an arrow through it and written, *Dave Randall is HOT and I should know.*

I had hoped Dave would like my story about his triumphs – enough to ask me out on a date, perhaps take me back to Cricket Lodge where he lived like Mellors, the gamekeeper in *Lady Chatterley's Lover.* Unbeknown to Dave, I had earmarked him as the lucky man to take my virginity. Suppressing a shiver of anticipation, the tearoom faded as I thought back to last weekend when we first met.

Hedge-jumping was still a controversial sport in the West Country because environmentalists claimed it was barbaric. When I first saw signs leading to the showground, I presumed it was a regular horse-jumping event. You can imagine my surprise when I realized there wasn't a horse to be seen. Dozens of men dressed in heavy commando-style jackets and gabardine trousers reinforced with serge gaiters limbered up in an open field bordered by a pristine seven-foot-high prickly hawthorn hedge.

The hedge was sectioned off in slices with blue ribbon and numbered. Each competitor drew a number and headed over towards his section, where a line judge marked the ground with white chalk two feet away from the hedge base.

Spectators had congregated in groups here and there. Some held flasks of coffee or cherry brandy; some were there just to cheer on their favourite jumper – others to enjoy the possible arrival of an ambulance.

I soon discerned the rules. The jumper was allowed to back up to a maximum of twenty-five feet, marked with an orange traffic cone, and then, under the starter's gun, would run full speed towards his fate. On the chalk baseline, he would leap off the ground using his preferred style of jump and, hopefully, land safely on the other side.

The trophy was awarded to the man, or woman, who cleared the hedge without damage to Mother Nature's glory or vital body parts. Points were awarded for style – of which there were many. The Fosbury Flop, the Belly Roll, or the Straddle.

The first time I watched Dave attempt the Fosbury Flop, I feared he was attempting a bizarre form of suicide and would break his neck. Dave charged towards the hedge with a gait that resembled a lame duck. At the last moment, he swerved to the right, stomped one foot down on the chalk line, and twisted his body round so his back was to the brush. Looking over his shoulder, Dave launched up and over, legs pointing skyward, and soared over the hedge with his back barely skimming the top before disappearing headfirst from view. Fortunately, a burst of applause from the other side signalled that he was in one piece.

For me, it had been love at first sight. I tried to think of a way to force an introduction and came up with the feature idea. He was *very* happy to talk to the press – even promised to drop into the office with some professional photographs, especially for me.

Truthfully, Tony was the sports reporter – presumably hedge-jumping was a sport – but when I broached the subject, he dismissed it, saying the newspaper didn't want to cater to maniacs; that to 'Report it, would be to support it.'

Pushing Dave firmly out of my mind, I finished my weak, watery tea and closed my notebook. Topaz fluttered over and handed me the bill. 'Did you finish your story?'

'Not quite,' I said.

'What's it about?'

'It's secret.'

Topaz clasped her hands together and went into raptures. 'I just love secrets! I'm frightfully good at keeping them, too. *Do* tell!'

'If I did, it wouldn't really be a secret, would it?' I said, hoping she'd get the hint and shut up. I counted the exact amount in small change, and left it on the table. 'Thanks for the tea.'

I got to my feet and headed towards the door. Topaz followed me with doglike devotion. 'I say – do you want to go out for a drink tomorrow night?'

'Tomorrow?' I said, mentally preparing my standard list of excuses, although I did feel a pang of guilt. Could Topaz be as lonely as me?

'Please?' Topaz beamed, then her expression changed. 'Wait! What's this?'

She reached over and gently disentangled a prickly bur from my hair. 'Goodness. Have you been playing in hedges?' she said, adding suspiciously, 'A hawthorn hedge – to be precise.'

'No.' Her question caught me by surprise. It was curiously specific. She did not look the gardening type.

Topaz pocketed the bur, her expression stony. 'Do you know Dave Randall?'

I paused, unsure how to answer. How odd that she would connect the bur with Dave. Topaz had already revealed she wanted to be a reporter. My hedge-jumping idea was unique. Plagiarism was everywhere – even in High Street cafes. How did I know that she hadn't quietly stood over my shoulder and read my work! What would stop her submitting the story herself? Most important – who *was* Topaz? She sounded too posh to be a waitress, and she definitely couldn't make a decent cup of tea.

'Dave who?'

'Randall,' she said coldly. 'The hedge-jumping champion.'

'I've heard of him, of course.' It wasn't a lie. I didn't know Dave personally – although I intended to. 'Is he a friend of yours?'

Topaz shook her head and looked glumly out the window. 'There are some nasty things going on in Gipping. *Nasty* things.'

My heart skipped a beat. Topaz might be a useful person to know, after all – especially with her penchant for blatant spying.

'Tomorrow night sounds great,' I said.

'Just the two of us.' Topaz grabbed my arm. 'Don't tell that awful Annabel Lake, will you?'

'Of course not.' I nodded in complete agreement. 'Just you and me.'

I crossed the road with a skip in my step. Today was turning out quite well, after all. Without so much as a whisper about money for services rendered, I'd just recruited my very first informer.

7

Annabel was waiting for me in reception. 'There you are!' she called out, perched on the counter that separated Barbara's filing cabinets from the rest of the room.

'Here I am,' I said, dismayed at her miraculous recovery from food poisoning. 'Has the report—?'

'Sssh!' Annabel nimbly sprang off the counter with catlike grace and grabbed my arm. 'Quickly, let's talk in the nook.'

The nook was an in-house joke. Back in the early seventies, a flimsy plywood wall had been crudely erected to partition off the far corner of reception into a temporary interview area that would supposedly guarantee privacy and comfort. Privacy was debatable, since the walls were paper thin. A brown and cream spangled curtain that closely resembled the entrance to a fortune-teller's grotto guarded the entrance.

Annabel pushed me inside and pulled the curtain closed with a flourish. The nook was gloomy and smelled of the stale cigarettes that overfilled the ashtray on a small, circular plastic table. Annabel pushed me down onto one of the two green plastic chairs.

'How was the funeral?' she whispered, pointing dramatically in Barbara's direction. 'Don't let her hear. She's a nosy cow.'

'Did you get the report?' I said in a low voice.

'Did you get the Porsche driver's name?'

How typical! Annabel was bartering one piece of information for another. 'Not yet but I *did* find out he isn't a Trewallyn.'

'Not local and not family, either?' Annabel frowned. 'How odd . . .'

I stole a quick glance, wondering if news of the graveyard scrap had already reached her ears. 'Why? Did you hear something different?'

'I should have gone to the church, obviously.'

'It was just another funeral.' I stifled a yawn, aware that my heart had begun to thump in a disconcertingly erratic manner. 'Why the sudden interest?'

'Oh, you know. Details. Little giveaways. Behaviour slipups.'

'You've read the coroner's report, obviously.' I tried to keep the envy out of my voice.

'Sssh! For heaven's sake, Vicky, keep your voice down,' Annabel hissed. 'It's not here yet. Pete is going demented. He's even gone to find Brian himself.'

'What a bore.' I had no idea who Brian was.

'Pete's terrified it will get into the wrong hands.'

My mind was going a mile a minute. Unless Annabel was deliberately misleading me, she had not gone to grill Ronnie Binns, after all. Perhaps his staunch denial about the chickens meant someone else had got to him first – or had he taken his story elsewhere?

Casually, I asked, 'Did you think any more about those dead chickens?'

'Honestly, Vicky! What are you – a vegetarian or something?'

'I just don't like cruelty to animals,' I retorted.

'You'll never be a good journalist if you let sentiment get in the way of professionalism.'

I marvelled at how Annabel always managed to turn anything I said into an insult.

Suddenly, she fell silent – her expression fixed in an unnatural frown. I could see she wanted to ask me something. 'Vicky, will you do me a little favour?'

'It depends,' I said, mentally cursing her if she asked me to make the tea. With Pete gone, Tony and Edward out – I was damned if I was going to make someone my junior a cuppa.

'I've got to go to the loo. Right now, actually.' I realized the grimace was one of pain. 'Can you wait here in case Brian, that messenger, comes?' Before I had a chance to answer, she had darted out of the nook.

I trooped back into reception and slumped into one of the brown leatherette chairs, which was as uncomfortable as it looked.

Barbara emerged from behind the counter. 'Your hedge-jumping man will be here in a minute.'

'Dave Randall?' My heart went over. 'Today?'

'He has some photographs for you and was going to drop them off but I told him to come back later.'

Barbara produced the tortoiseshell mirror and matching comb that she always kept handy. 'Oh dear, I *must* do something with your hair.'

She ducked under the counter and, with a critical air, began to comb through my dark brown bob. 'You really should grow it long, like Annabel,' Barbara said. 'Men like long hair. It brings out their caveman instincts.'

Barbara's iron grey hair was pulled back in a tight bun. I tried not to think of her clad in animal skins.

I peered at my reflection in the mirror. Mum had described my looks as *handsome* and *natural*. I supposed I did have flawless skin – that was something to be grateful for. People had even remarked that I must wear tinted contact lenses because my eyes were such an unusual sapphire blue.

'Dave's *hot*, isn't he?' Barbara cooed. 'Isn't that what you young girls call it?'

Abruptly, Barbara hid the comb and mirror behind her back

45

as the door opened and Dave walked in holding a large brown envelope. I caught my breath. I'd forgotten how gorgeous he was. I only prayed Annabel's diarrhoea would keep her captive for some time. I wouldn't stand a chance with Dave if she turned up with her buoyant breasts.

Dave was a little older than me, dressed in thick trousers, a navy fisherman's jersey, and woollen hat under which escaped dark wavy curls. I longed to run my fingers through those curls and explore his hairy chest – I hoped he had one. Mum always said chest hair was a sign of virility.

'Vicky, why don't you take Mr Randall into the nook?' Barbara suggested with a meaningful wink.

'No, we're just fine here.' I was afraid that being in an enclosed space would have the predictable effect on Dave. The memory of Pete emerging from the basement with Annabel still fascinated, yet repelled me at the same time. Besides, I wanted my first experience to be romantic. Flowers, chocolates, Celine Dion singing, 'My Heart Will Go On', not some grope in a dingy nook smelling faintly of mildew and old cigarettes.

Of course, there was another reason, too. If Brian arrived and we were in the nook, he would have to deal with Barbara's insatiable curiosity. The cat would be out of the bag. Barbara may well be a gossip but she was a conscientious worker. The newspaper was her life. If she suspected any illegal dealings, she was sure to report them to the editor.

Conscious of the fact that Annabel could surface at any moment, I turned my attention to Dave who was looking bored. It was best to get the photographs and whisk him away as soon as possible. At least I knew where he lived. It would be easy to invent some vital last-minute story detail that would entail a visit to Chez Randall.

'Thanks for coming by, Dave.' I gave him one of my best smiles. 'I'm on a bit of a deadline this afternoon, so don't have a lot of time to chat.'

I ignored Barbara's surprised look. She seemed let down. No

doubt planning to live vicariously through me.

I sat in one of the leatherette chairs and gestured for Dave to take the other. He grunted something unintelligible. I felt a twinge of disappointment. Where was the man I remembered on the field? There, he had been overexcited in a there-will-be-tears-before-bedtime kind of way, no doubt heady from his triumphant win. Celebrities were like that. They shone when the camera was on them, but take them out of the limelight and they were as dull as ditch water. If it weren't for the lack of alternative suitors, I would have moved on to pastures new.

'Here.' Dave opened the brown envelope. With a shy smile, he pulled out two eight-by-ten colour photographs. 'Can the paper use them, like?'

I'd forgotten how much his country brogue sounded like Mellors the gamekeeper. I gave myself a mental slap. This was no time to daydream.

I looked at the pictures. 'Wow. This is amazing,' I gushed, masking my dismay. The first photograph appeared to be nothing but a collage of green leaves.

Dave pointed to the centre of the photograph. 'That's me.'

Much to my relief, a faint form began to take shape. 'Good Lord. So it is!'

Dave's entire outfit was moss green, including a jaunty peaked cap. His face was smothered in brown boot polish, which didn't help much, either.

Dave lay spread-eagled in the middle of razor-sharp fronds – his expression, not one of ecstasy, but agony.

'That must have hurt.' I wondered if he was one of those men who enjoyed pain and frequented dubious establishments run by Asians with names like Madame Spankee.

'I've got my moleskins,' said Dave grimly, giving his thigh a brisk slap. 'No good wearing cavalry twill. Won't last five minutes in hawthorn. It's okay with yew.'

I tried to look interested. 'Do tell me more.'

'*Taxus baccata* or yew, to the common man, is a difficult

jump,' Dave enthused. 'It's all about getting enough lift on the approach.'

Unwilling to dwell on the pros and cons of hedges, I pointed to the second photograph featuring Dave holding what could only be described as a round stick about one foot long. 'That's my trophy.'

Dave held the trophy-stick as if it were the Olympic torch. Behind him, a decimated hedgerow looked as if an entire Panzer tank division had merrily bulldozed through it.

There was a ghastly silence. 'That hedge put up quite a fight,' I said at last.

Frankly, I was shocked at the carnage. Perhaps Tony's staunch objection to this barbaric sport was actually justified.

'She was reluctant at first, but we prevailed,' Dave said. 'We jumpers are always on a quest for the perfect hedge. Sometimes,' he continued dreamily, 'I get so excited when I see a neatly trimmed privet, I'd sell my grandmother to have first go.'

'Wasn't Sir Hugh Trewallyn a jumper?' I said, seizing the chance to turn the conversation around. Though I could not visualize the septuagenarian, hampered by a walker, able to get up enough lift to soar over a hedge.

I slipped the photographs back into the envelope. 'Hedge-jumping is a small world, I'm sure you knew him well.'

'Aye. He was a good man.'

'You must have spent a lot of time at The Grange?'

Dave blushed. 'What's that supposed to mean?'

'When you were practising,' I said. 'I expect you met the chappy in the black Porsche?'

Fascinatingly, his face turned quite pale. 'No. Why would I?'

'Some acquaintance of Lady Trewallyn's gate crashed the funeral,' I said. 'Looked just like Pierce Brosnan.'

'I have to get back for the pheasants.' Dave leapt to his feet and headed for the exit. 'Didn't realize the time.'

The door from the inner hallway flew open.

'At last!' yelled Annabel. 'I say! Wait!'

How typical of Annabel to show up at the crucial moment. She seemed to have a gift for ruining my life.

'Thanks for the photos. I'll call you later,' I said, bundling Dave out the front door.

Annabel pointed to the envelope I was holding. 'I'll take that.'

I clutched it to my chest. 'It's *mine*.'

'Give it to me,' Annabel commanded.

'It's not what you think,' I said, beginning to panic. What if she put two and two together and realized Sir Hugh and Dave were avid jumpers? She'd steal my only lead.

'I know what you are up to, Vicky Hill.' Annabel's eyes flashed with accusation – she'd obviously had a lot of time to think on the loo. 'You've wanted to steal this story from me from the beginning.'

'That's not true!' Annabel believed Dave was *Brian*! She must think the envelope contained the coroner's report.

'Girls! Girls! Really!' Barbara's face popped up from behind the counter. 'What are you two arguing about?'

Annabel and I froze instantly. How much had our nosy receptionist overheard?

Barbara chuckled. 'I expect it was about men. Well. Let me tell you—'

'Actually, we were discussing your ingrown toenail,' I said quickly. 'Annabel said you weren't in pain and I said that wasn't true.'

'Yes, that's right, Barbara. You seem so brave.' Annabel snatched the envelope out of my hand, adding pointedly, 'So brave that I think I'll tell *Pete* about it.'

'Oh goodness.' Barbara turned pink. 'There's no need to bother Pete.'

'I'm sure Pete likes to know *everything,* don't you, Vicky?' Annabel glared at me. 'Must dash. Why don't you be a dear and make me some tea. I'm utterly *parched.*' With that, Annabel sauntered out of reception, leaving me speechless.

49

'Well, that's a turn up for the books.' Barbara beamed. 'Annabel has never asked after my toe before.'

There was no point disagreeing. I flopped into one of the chairs.

'Can you hold the fort while I nip to the loo?' Barbara said.

I suppressed my impulse to growl that it seemed that the only role I was good for was covering loo breaks and making tea.

No sooner had Barbara left the room, the front door opened. A young acne-faced youth dressed in black motorcycle leathers and clutching a sky blue helmet wandered in. He looked around nervously before hurrying to the empty nook and swishing the curtain closed behind him.

Puzzled by his odd behaviour, especially as he did not reappear, I tiptoed over and drew back a corner of the curtain. 'Can I help you?'

'Don't want to be seen,' he whispered, eyes darting left and right. He bent down and peered under the plastic table as if expecting Scotland Yard to suddenly spring out and arrest him. 'You can never be too careful.'

I slipped into the nook beside him. 'You must be Brian.'

'Annabel, right? Got this for you,' the youth replied, scratching a ripe pimple on his chin.

Brian opened his leather jacket a crack and whisked out a brown envelope, whispering urgently, 'You *are* Annabel Lake, aren't you?'

'Actually—'

'Do you wear tinted contacts?' Brian stared at me.

'No, these are my own eyes.'

'They're cool.' He thrust the envelope into my hands. 'Sorry I was late. Liquid chromatography. Old Sharpe is getting slow.'

I had no idea what *liquid chromatography* meant but it sounded important.

'Well, I'll be off then,' said Brian, making no effort to move. There was an ugly pause. The thought occurred to me perhaps he was waiting for payment.

'Didn't Pete—?'

'Oh yes, but . . .' He fingered his overripe spot again. 'I usually get a tip.'

A tip! How awkward. I could hardly ask Barbara for some petty cash. I pulled out the tattered nylon wallet from my jeans and opened it. There was just one ten pound note inside. I'd have to ask for change. In a flash, Brian had whisked it out of my hands and, with an appreciative nod, vanished through the curtain. I stared mournfully after him. That ten pounds was supposed to last until Friday.

I looked at the envelope weighted with so much promise. Never had I had such an overwhelming urge to rip something open and devour the contents. I fought with my conscience. I really should give it to Annabel straightaway. Yet, surely, this information could be crucial to my own investigation? What's more, hadn't I just paid ten pounds for the privilege?

The envelope was sealed, but luckily, not tamperproof. When I was a child, my mum had shown me how to steam open envelopes. She claimed that married couples should have no secrets and swore me not to tell my father. Mum said it was just bills and that by her knowing how much he owed made her a better and more frugal wife. As I grew older, I realized Mum was tracking Dad's affair with Pamela Dingles via this method.

Barbara appeared in the nook entrance. Startled, I hid the envelope behind my back.

'Ooh, that feels better.' She gave a little wriggle and adjusted her underwear. 'It's always such an effort to go. Just you wait until you're my age.'

'Excuse me, must get on.' I sidled past her, wrenched open the door, and disappeared into the hallway, promptly knocking Barbara's wretched pink bicycle over. It fell to the ground with a resounding crash. *Blast!* Why did the old biddy insist on keeping it indoors? One day, someone would really get hurt.

'Vicky, is that you?' shouted Annabel from the upstairs landing. 'What are you doing?' There was a note of panic in her voice. 'You *must* wait in reception! Brian will be here any moment.'

To my horror, she started towards me, down the stairs.

Wildly, I looked around for somewhere to hide the envelope. I wasn't going to steal it. I was merely borrowing it. 'You told me to make the tea!'

Swiftly, I shoved it down the back of the iron radiator. A searing pain shot through my hand. The metal was blisteringly hot.

Seconds later, Annabel paused at the door to reception. 'Bring my tea in here. I'll wait for Brian. By the way, I put those photographs back on your desk. You *do* realize that any new ideas have to go through me now, don't you?'

I didn't. It was another blow to my self-esteem. Clearly Annabel's rise in the newspaper hierarchy was far more meteoric than I realized. The thought of Annabel officially my superior was too much to bear. Yet, I was marginally comforted that she had no idea of the significance of those photographs and couldn't resist making a comment.

'I did try to tell you it was the wrong envelope,' I said.

'You should learn to speak up.' With a toss of her head, she pushed past me and opened the door into reception.

Alone again, I turned my efforts back to the radiator. Somehow, I had to get the report out. I tried to slide my fingers down the back of it but only succeeded in burning my hand.

I needed something long and thin. I clattered down the basement steps and picked up a stick used for unblocking the drain. I put the kettle on to boil, then tore back upstairs.

I tried to pry the envelope out of its hiding place, but all I succeeded in doing was pushing it farther down. Exasperated, I got on my knees and attempted to reach the envelope from the bottom up. It was hopeless, as the skirting board was flush with the radiator base. The most awful thought struck me. It could become a fire hazard. The whole place could go up in flames. I could even be imprisoned for arson!

Stifling a cry of frustration, I stomped back down to the basement to make the tea. Tea was always a good salve in situations such as these.

As I waited for the kettle to boil, I actually had an inspirational flash. Wasn't the central heating turned off at night? I'd just have to come back later on. If I could put the report on Pete's desk by morning, surely no one would care how it got there?

A few minutes later I returned to reception bearing two mugs of tea. Annabel was sitting in the brown leatherette chair, leafing through a magazine on tractors.

'Still no sign of Brian?' I said, handing her a mug with a sympathetic smile. 'What a bore!'

She shook her head. 'Barbara's locking up at five. I suppose something must have happened to him.'

'Goes with the territory, doesn't it?' I said. 'Perhaps he thought he was being followed?'

'Pete's going to be furious.' Annabel looked worried. 'He specifically told me to get it today.'

'Have you tried to phone him?'

Annabel shook her head. 'We only have his mobile.'

'The hazards of living in a valley,' I said, glad of Gipping's non-existent mobile phone reception. 'Never mind. Once Devon Satellite Bell finds a new site for that transmitter, our lives will be much easier.'

'Which is hardly relevant now, is it?' Annabel sneered.

'Surely it can't be *that* important.'

'Actually, Vicky, it really is.' Annabel swallowed hard and inspected her fingernails. Clearly that was as forthcoming as she was prepared to be.

'Anyone would think it was a matter of life and death,' I said lightly.

'You really don't know what you're talking about,' Annabel snapped.

Her patronizing tone stung. 'Perhaps not,' I said. 'But aren't we supposed to be a team?'

Annabel peered into her mug of tea. 'I can't drink this. You've made it too strong.'

How ungrateful! Who on earth did she think she was? Why should I retrieve the coroner's report just to save Annabel's hide? Lord knows I had tried to offer the olive branch enough times, but not anymore. From now on, it was each woman for herself.

8

It was nearly 1.00 a.m. when I finally sneaked out of Rumble Lane. Mrs Poultry's routine was like clockwork. She was a night owl and never went to bed before midnight.

Whilst my landlady was awake, it was hopeless to even attempt to leave the house unseen. She had acute hearing and kept the sitting room door ajar. It gave her a good view of the hallway and kitchen. I made the mistake once of trying to slip in for a late-night snack, but the moment my toe touched the floral linoleum, a voice materialized from the void, 'Victoria! Out of bounds.' I loathed being called by my full name. It always made me feel like a naughty child.

Earlier in the evening, I had tentatively broached Sir Hugh's funeral when we had run into each other on the landing. I mentioned there had been a good turnout, taking care to watch her expression for any sign that she had actually been there under that bush.

Mrs Poultry, sucking slowly on her favourite Coff-Off cough drop, stared at me in silence. Then, turned on her heel and entered her bedroom without a word. I began to think I really had imagined it all, until I donned my outdoor clothes.

An Edwardian coat and hat stand stood against the wall to the right of the front door. As I searched for my scarf, I came across Mrs Poultry's cloche hat stuck on a peg. To my delight, a tiny bur was caught under the brim. It was proof that she had been there in the church grounds, but why remained a mystery I resolved to look into later.

Soundlessly, I let myself out of the front door; Dad had showed me how to turn a lock so it wouldn't click. I set off for the office at a brisk walk. Patches of fog sank down on my shoulders, filling the air with an oppressive heaviness that, just as quickly, lifted to reveal a cold, starry night and half-moon.

I shivered. Pulling my woollen scarf up around my face to keep warm, glad this was Gipping in the twenty-first century and not London in 1888. This eerie kind of weather would have provided fertile ground for Jack the Ripper's stabbing sprees.

Oddly enough, I wasn't afraid of the dark. I liked the stillness of night when I felt I was the only person awake in the whole world. I felt no fear taking the shortcut past the ruins of Gipping Castle and through the narrow alleyways.

In no time at all I was standing outside the *Gazette*. The three-story building loomed above me, seeming much larger in the dark. Even though the High Street was empty, Dad's voice in my head insisted, '*Success in an undetected, forced entry centres on one's ability to look as if you have every right to be there.*' It was the main reason why I had carefully selected a brightly coloured purple and green striped scarf to wear with my safari jacket and jeans, as opposed to dressing all in black – complete with a black knitted balaclava – so favoured by burglars. If I were spotted, I would simply be doing some late-night research.

The front door was locked and bolted. Barbara was always overzealous when it came to security. I took the cobbled path alongside the building to the rear, which backed onto a narrow lane.

This rarely used entrance to the *Gazette* was via an old wooden gate, half off its hinges and wedged into a four-foot-high slate wall. I'd have to vault over it. Backing up a few paces,

I launched myself into a pretty impressive straddle without so much as touching the surface. What a perfect couple Dave and I would make. We could hedge-jump together.

Safely over the wall, I was faced with never-ending piles of sodden, disused newspapers that, for decades, were tossed out of the basement door and left to rot.

Swiftly, I cast an appraising eye over the job, mentally running through Dad's checklist:

1. *Assess the situation.*
2. *Check for hazards.*
3. *Proceed with caution.*

Above the basement door, about four feet to the right, was a corroded burglar alarm. Pete had given up persuading Wilf to get a high-tech security system installed. He said it was an unnecessary expense.

Like many foolish property owners, he believed just the sight of an alarm bell, or a sign reading BEWARE OF DOG was an effective deterrent. Dad and I always laughed about that, but in this case, I couldn't afford to take any chances.

Needless to say, there was no ladder of any kind for me to take a closer look at the alarm. Reminding myself that every obstacle built character, I cast around for an alternative and, literally five seconds later, had a brilliant idea.

I began to stack the old newspapers into a tower against the wall under the alarm. It was jolly hot work as they were heavy with moisture. Many had disintegrated, most were soggy masses of mulch, but I pressed on regardless.

After ten minutes of heavy lifting, I was boiling and had to take off my matching scarf and gloves, which I carefully folded and put to one side.

Half an hour of backbreaking labour later, the newspaper stack was almost as tall as me. I felt chuffed and stepped back to admire my handiwork. True, it leaned horribly to the left, but would have to do. I was utterly exhausted. As I wiped my hands across my brow, I realized I was sweating buckets.

It was time to put my efforts to the test. Using the hedge-jumper run-up again, I backed up several feet, sprinted a few steps, then threw myself into the climb with gusto.

For about one minute, I stood on top of the heap, breathless, but triumphant. When, to my horror, the pile slowly began to sink beneath my weight. I grappled for a handhold but was instantly pitched face-first against the rough brick wall.

My arms were splayed out like Jesus on the cross, legs spread, quivering with the effort of keeping upright. Although the ground was only a few feet away, it may as well have been fifty. I was stuck – but, alas, not for long. With a sickening jolt, the lopsided tower collapsed, catapulting me sideways and forward straight onto the basement door. It flew open at impact.

I tumbled, head over heels onto the sticky tiled floor, and sat there, dazed, bracing myself for the shriek of the burglar alarm. Never had I felt so close to Dad. Somehow, knowing he must have experienced these moments, too, gave me the courage not to panic. The basement smelled of mould and dampness but it was comfortingly familiar.

There was no sound. Just silence. I counted to one hundred and got to my feet, ignoring the stabbing pain in my elbow from the fall. My God! I'd done it!

Taking a flashlight from the kitchenette – kept handy for regular power outages – I took the stairs up to the inner hallway. It was cold, meaning the radiator would be, too. Removing the coroner's report should be a piece of cake.

A sliver of moonlight peeped through the skylight above, enough to see what I was doing. Abandoning the flashlight, I plunged my hand down the back of the radiator but only my fingertips touched the envelope. It was still beyond my grasp.

Returning to the kitchen, I retrieved a knife from the drawer and scurried back upstairs. Carefully, I pierced the knife tip into the envelope and dragged it slowly upward.

The moment I saw the top of the envelope, I grabbed it and pulled hard.

The envelope ripped and emerged, scorched and torn. *Blast!* My heart sank. I'd been overeager, horribly careless. It must have caught on a loose screw or piece of metal. I could never casually leave it on Pete's desk now. I'd be lucky if I could read it myself.

I heard a floorboard creak behind me, and froze. My heart was pounding. Someone was in the building. Slowly, I turned to face the closed reception door where a pool of light crept under the door towards me – the tell-tale signs of an intruder.

I darted upstairs on tiptoe, slipping into the reporters' room, which was never locked. There had to be *somewhere* I could hide. Annabel's kneehole desk was ideal. It was pushed against an old fireplace that provided a handy cranny for me to curl into.

Moments later, the door opened and heavy footsteps followed the flashlight beam. My stomach was in knots. All I could think about was that I should never have had that last cup of tea. Nerves were making me desperate to go to the loo.

The footsteps approached Annabel's desk, then turned away and stopped in front of mine. All I could see were expensive black leather shoes peeping from beneath a long, black trench coat. This was no local dressed in corduroys and Dr Martens.

I wriggled forward to get a better look and was startled to recognize Pierce Brosnan. Seen close at hand, he really did resemble James Bond – in an Italian godfather kind of way.

Still cowering in my hiding place, I saw him don latex gloves and begin to search systematically through my desk – a true professional! With a jolt of excitement, I realized he must be looking for the coroner's report! Pierce Brosnan must be Trewallyn's murderer. He was out to destroy evidence, and nothing would get in his way.

I clutched the torn and crumpled envelope tighter to my chest, aware that he wouldn't hesitate to kill me, too, if he knew I had it. Somehow, I had to stay alive to tell the truth to the world: MAFIA MOBSTER'S MISTRESS IN MURDER MYSTERY: A VICKY HILL EXCLUSIVE!

Mesmerized, I watched Pierce Brosnan flip through my reporter notebook. I thought I would expire altogether when he actually copied down some information gleaned from within. Other than a list of mourners at the church, I couldn't understand what would interest him – other than my address.

Why would he want to know where I lived? A more horrible thought occurred: what if this *wasn't* about the Trewallyn family at all? What if – I could hardly dare think – it was connected to *my dad*!?

All further theories stopped when Pierce Brosnan found the envelope containing Dave's hedge-jumping photographs and tipped them out. He scrutinized both by flashlight, before slipping them into his top inside pocket. I was stunned. What on earth could he want with Dave's photographs?

Recalling Dave's hasty exit at the mention of the Porsche, it was obvious the two men were connected. Could Lady Trewallyn have *already* taken a new lover? The woman must be a shameless nymphomaniac – poor Sir Hugh was not even cold in his grave – to say nothing of her selfishness in snapping up what looked like the only eligible bachelor in Gipping.

Suddenly, Pierce Brosnan froze. I'd seen a fox do that once, ears pricked, sniffing the air for danger.

I shrank from sight, curling myself into the smallest ball possible – and promptly dropped the envelope. In my heightened sensitive state, I may as well have dropped an atom bomb.

Pierce Brosnan swung the flashlight in my direction. I closed my eyes, hoping in some childish way that if they were shut, I couldn't see him, so he couldn't see me. He took a step towards me, playing the beam on my face. I was caught in the spotlight. My jaw ached from clenching my teeth. Any moment now he would be hauling me out from my hiding place by my hair.

I took a shallow breath to stave off unconsciousness and began to pray silently to God, hoping that the changes I suggested in my behaviour might instil His mercy. I promised I wouldn't read the coroner's report because deep down, I knew it did not belong to me. I vowed to be nicer to Annabel, because research showed that overachievers generally had hard, unfeeling parents. I'd buy Topaz a drink because she was lonely and it was a nice thing to do. And finally, the biggest sacrifice of all, I'd be content to remain a virgin for the rest of my life – even enter a convent if necessary. Resigned in the knowledge that I had done all I could in my power, I sat back to see if my prayers would be heard and only hoped death would be quick.

To my astonishment, my would-be attacker suddenly snapped off the flashlight, turned on his heel, and left the room. I listened as his footsteps went downstairs and faded away to silence. His reaction was so unexpected that it took me a few moments to realize I'd got away with it.

How extraordinary! There really *was* something to this religion lark, after all.

As I crawled out of my hiding place, I wondered if Pierce Brosnan was still in the building. I assumed he had what he wanted but perhaps he was merely luring me into a false sense of security? Yet, I could hardly stay here all night without admitting to the break-in.

Stiffly, I got to my feet and straightened my shoulders. *Courage Vicky!* What was a girl to do? First, I must go to the loo.

Thankfully, my would-be attacker was not on the landing, as I had feared. I crept downstairs and into the tiny bathroom, next to the door that led down to the basement. There was no sign of him there, either. He had gone.

After my trip to the loo, I felt considerably better and wondered if much of my anxiety had been connected to my waterworks. It's hard to concentrate on anything if one has to go. As I washed my hands, I caught my reflection in the mirror above the washbasin, and gasped. I couldn't believe it! The face that stared back at me was blackened with *newsprint*! It must have come off on my hands when I was stacking the newspapers.

Obviously, I had some subconscious instinct for survival. My confidence soared. I had a natural flair for espionage. It was in my genes! Pierce Brosnan hadn't seen me at all.

A new dilemma arose. I had made that rash deal with God. Wouldn't the fact that I had been, unwittingly, camouflaged all the time cancel our arrangement? Anyway, wasn't God all-seeing and all-knowing? No doubt He'd been highly amused by my behaviour and took my promises in the manner in which I made them – as a bit of a joke. Surely He didn't think I was serious about the virgin-convent deal?

Returning to my desk, my euphoria evaporated. My reporter notebook lay open, prominently displaying the heart-shaped doodle with *Dave Randall Is HOT and I Should Know* in purple felt-tip. Dave's address was conveniently – and childishly – noted alongside: *Cricket Lodge, Old Road, Upper Gipping, Devon, Great Britain, The World, The Galaxy, The Universe, The Solar System.*

Since Pierce Brosnan stole Dave's photographs, it was logical to assume the bit of scribbling he'd been doing had involved copying out Dave's address, not mine. I had, inadvertently, signed Dave's death warrant.

Without wanting to appear heartless, there wasn't much I could do for Dave at this precise moment. Cricket Lodge was at least a three-mile walk from the office, and, with no phone reception, his mobile was useless.

I settled into my chair and switched on my banker's desk lamp. The green shade cast a ghoulish light over the damaged papers. The good news was that only the title page was scorched. The bad news was that I didn't understand the legal jargon and lofty, incomprehensible sentences. It may as well have been written in Russian. I skimmed through, looking for anything that looked remotely decipherable.

Halfway down on the third page, a familiar phrase leapt out: *Gas Chromatography-Mass Spectroscopy* or GCMS. *This* was the test old Sharpe had been waiting for. It had to be significant.

I turned on my ancient computer and typed in my password. I couldn't wait until I was a full-fledged reporter and was given a snazzy high-powered laptop. Even Annabel wasn't allowed one of those.

Google described GCMS as 'A separation technique that can positively identify a substance narcotic, poison, or similar.'

Returning to the coroner's report, I read on. 'Traces of digitalis purpurea found in victim's stomach. Probable Cause of Death: Digitalis Intoxication.'

Poison! According to the report, Lady Trewallyn had discovered her husband at five minutes to midnight, sprawled in the middle of a yew hedge on the estate. No wonder Pete and Annabel had wanted to get their hands on this before the obituary interview tomorrow. They'd be in the perfect position to ask incriminating questions.

I could imagine Lady Trewallyn preparing the deadly concoction and slipping it into Sir Hugh's brandy and milk nightcap. He'd watch her with eyes filled with trust and love, unaware that she had been planning to get her hands on his millions since the day they met. She'd kiss him goodnight, gently smoothing back the hair on his head – if he had any, I personally had never met Sir Hugh – and lurk somewhere out of sight but within earshot. He'd stay in the library, reflecting on his luck at having such an attentive young wife.

A little later, there would be an anguished cry and the sound of a body falling to the floor. Lady Trewallyn would hurry to his side to check that he was stone-cold dead. From behind the curtains, her accomplice – and lover – Pierce Brosnan would emerge.

The two heartless killers would drag the dead man out of the house into the night and artistically arrange his body in the yew hedge. Sir Hugh would *appear* to have been out jumping alone. It would look as if he had misjudged a leap and fallen forward with his mouth wide open in surprise. Just as the yew branches cushioned his fall, he would have accidentally swallowed a sprig of scarlet yew berries, which everyone knows are deadly poisonous.

But I was puzzled. Thanks to Dave's lesson on the merits of the English yew, I knew *taxus baccata* was not *digitalis purpurea.*

On searching Google for *digitalis purpurea,* I was even more puzzled to find it was the common purple foxglove, which when ingested can cause 'uncoordinated contractions of the heart leading to cardiac arrest and finally death'. The article went on cheerfully, 'Thus, the *digitalis purpurea* has earned several more sinister monikers: "Dead Man's Bells" and "Witches Gloves".'

No doubt Dave was out doing some late-night jumping and witnessed the disposal of the body, hence his terror of the man in the black Porsche.

Satisfied with my findings, I couldn't help but feel a bit smug. These murders were quite simple to solve if one had a logical mind.

As I switched off my computer and put the report back into the envelope, I spotted something that chilled me to the bone.

Written on the back page under *Miscellaneous Observations* was the following: 'Deceased's mouth contained six chicken legs complete with feet, claws, and feathers bound by a black silk cord, placed after death.'

I felt hot and cold all at the same time. It didn't require a brain surgeon to realize there was a connection between these limbs and the three corpses Ronnie had found at the local tip.

Tucking the coroner's report into my safari jacket, I wondered if I'd been wrong about Annabel. Perhaps *she* hadn't silenced Ronnie with money – someone else had. What if Ronnie had tried to alert us to evil goings-on in Gipping but we'd shot him down? Was Lady Trewallyn dabbling in the occult?

There were dark forces at work here in Gipping and it was my duty to the townsfolk to expose them all.

9

Adrenaline surged through my body as I hurried down the stairs towards the basement. For the first time, I didn't relish the walk home alone through those dark alleys.

Should I have a chat with Whittler? Though I doubted his eagerness to get involved with the devil. The more I thought about my brief conversations with him over these past few months, the more I wondered if he was all that bothered about good versus evil. Whittler was probably one of those fair-weather vicars. As long as things ran along smoothly, and people died from natural causes, he was everybody's best friend. But just hint at the dark forces, and he was gone.

In the basement kitchenette, I was surprised to see the outside door closed. I could have sworn I'd left it ajar. Pierce Brosnan must have exited the building this way. The moment I opened the door, I practically had a heart attack.

An earth shattering clanging erupted from the bowels of the building. The alarm worked, after all! It went on and on, seemingly growing louder by the second.

What a stupid oversight! Thank God Dad was not here to witness my faux pas. Obviously, Pierce Brosnan had disabled the alarm *before* I arrived, then switched it back on when he left.

The shrill ring continued. My heart was beating so rapidly I feared I'd become hysterical if I didn't take action. In five minutes, the police would arrive. I tore outside, grabbed a handful of stones, and flung them haphazardly at the ringing bell. Even though most hit their mark, they made no difference at all.

Ducking back into the basement, I grabbed a wooden long-handled mop and raced back. I thrust the pole, mop end first – to muffle the sound – into the belly of the alarm, praying it would jam. The bell gamely shuddered to a halt and expired altogether with a pathetic *phut!* There, the mop stayed, providing ample evidence of my guilt. *Blast!* I couldn't reach it, and my newspaper tower had long collapsed. I'd have to leave the mop there.

I bolted out of the alley and into the High Street. Stopped dead. *Blast!* I'd left my scarf and gloves outside the basement door. They weren't exactly run-of-the-mill, either, being a fluorescent lime green and vivid purple stripe. I may as well have left my name and address, too. How could I even *think* I was my father's daughter?

Paralysed, I stood outside The Copper Kettle as a police car, siren blaring, blue and red lights flashing, barrelled towards me up the High Street. My God, the cops were on the ball tonight. It couldn't have been more than two minutes since the bell went off.

Suddenly, firm hands grabbed my shoulders. I struggled to escape, but a hand clamped firmly over my nose and mouth. 'Quickly. In here!' cried Topaz, dragging me backwards through the door of the tearoom. With surprising strength, she threw me facedown onto the floor and hurled herself on top of me.

Winded, I took in deep gulps of air, utterly confused by the turn of events and my unexpected rescuer.

'Don't move,' Topaz said.

I refrained from telling her I couldn't. She was actually heavy. Her breath was hot on my neck, and her body moulded into the contours of my back.

'We'll wait until the coast is clear,' she whispered into my ear.

Luckily, Topaz could not see my horrified expression. How much had she seen and why rescue me?

'I can't breathe, Topaz,' I groaned, trying to jostle her off. 'Please!'

'I've got an idea,' she said, rolling onto her knees. 'Follow me, but keep down!'

Topaz crawled, leopard-style, beneath the window over to the table where I had sat only hours earlier. 'Good view from here.'

I duly followed, noting she was wearing her mob cap and wondering if she slept in it.

We both knelt by the window, peeping over the sill as another panda car screamed to a halt, ejecting two more coppers, who swarmed all over the *Gazette* as if there'd been a bank robbery. I felt sick. No doubt they'd find the mop – covered in my fingerprints – and my scarf and gloves. As the old saying goes, it's a 'fair cop'.

Mesmerized, we watched the *Gazette* office windows light up, one by one. The police were methodically combing the building.

Topaz turned towards me, her gaze steady. 'What do you think happened?'

Did she really not know, or was she testing me?

Dad always maintained it was best to stay as close to the truth as possible when telling a lie. I shrugged, noncommittally. 'Looks like a break-in to me.'

'That's what I thought.' Topaz paused, before adding darkly, 'I saw him, you know.'

'Who?' A horrible lump stuck in my throat.

'The American.'

'*American?*' I was astonished! Pierce Brosnan was a *foreigner?*

I tried to keep calm. 'Is he one of your regulars at the cafe?'

67

'Oh *no*! He's not a customer,' she said in a mysterious voice. 'Most definitely not.'

'Who is he, then?' I could hardly contain my curiosity. How strange and convenient that the very identity of the man I wanted to know was about to be unwittingly revealed by a waitress!

Topaz nodded. 'I know who he is, all right.'

My patience was beginning to fray. 'Well, *who*?' I demanded. 'Why would he want to break into the *Gazette*?'

'Why does anyone do anything?' She turned to stare at me again. I hadn't noticed before how her deep green eyes reminded me of Kaa, the snake from Disney's *Jungle Book.*

'Topaz—'

'The funny thing is,' she continued wistfully, 'I thought you were in there, too. A midnight lover's tryst, perhaps?'

'You must be joking.' I was just about to add that Pierce Brosnan had to be forty, when three policemen emerged from the alley.

'Goody!' Topaz gave a little squeal. 'They've found something.'

I felt ill. A young policeman brought up the rear, holding the floor mop aloft as if he'd discovered the Holy Grail. His colleagues surged around him, offering congratulations, along with hearty backslaps. I forced myself to keep calm. Surely, if they found my fingerprints I could easily explain them away – after all, I worked at the *Gazette*. However, my scarf and gloves were another matter. Had they found those, too?

After some initial difficulty, the coppers managed to tie the incriminating evidence onto a panda roof rack with orange baling twine. They piled into their respective cars and sped off.

'How frightfully exciting!' Topaz got to her feet. 'I expect they'll be questioning all the neighbours in the area tomorrow morning.'

Would my nightmare never end? 'Gosh. It's late. Really must go.' I stood up and headed towards the front door.

Topaz darted in front and beat me to it. 'Vicky, you still

haven't told me what *you* were doing over there in the middle of the night.' She leant her back against the door, covering the handle with her body.

I felt more than a little alarmed. The cafe ceased to be a friendly refuge. Topaz was scantily clad in a short cotton nightdress at odds with her mob cap. Immediately, my eyes were drawn to a silver Victorian locket she wore around her neck.

Seeing the direction of my gaze, Topaz defiantly stuck out her chest. I could feel myself blush and hastily looked away. Surely she hadn't thought I was looking at her *breasts?*

'Please tell me, *please?*' she said coyly.

Recalling another of Dad's favourite sayings, *'Keep your friends close, but your enemies closer,'* I forced myself to stay calm. 'Topaz, you and I are kindred spirits . . .' I began, taking care to cross my fingers behind my back. I wasn't really lying. 'I've not been sleeping recently. My mind is always working on stories . . . thinking up new ideas. You know how it is?'

Topaz's expression remained blank. She didn't say a word, just stood there with her hands on her hips. I rambled on. 'I couldn't sleep so I decided to come to the office and work there rather than disturb my landlady. And, wouldn't you know it! No sooner had I got to the *front* door, the alarm went off and—'

'You got scared,' said Topaz, her disappointment plain.

'That's it!' I was relieved. 'Scared to death actually. Then you came outside and . . . you know the rest. Must go. Really tired.'

Topaz nodded her head slowly. 'So, let me see. When the police question me, do I say that I saw you, or not?'

'I'm sorry?' I was confused. What was wrong with the stupid girl? She wore a strange expression on her face that I didn't like one bit.

'Of course, you saw me. Why lie?' I said, all wide-eyed innocence. 'I'm not hiding anything.'

'Is that what you want me to say?' said Topaz. 'You really, *really* want me to?'

'Why ever not?' I didn't feel so sure now. Topaz was a peculiar creature. What had she been doing up all hours of the night spying on the unsuspecting public? Was she looking for material for future blackmail?

With a sigh, Topaz opened the front door of the cafe. She stepped outside and peered up and down the High Street. 'The coast is clear. Everyone's gone home.'

'Which is exactly where I am heading.'

Topaz quickly put her hand on my arm and leaned in closer. For an awful moment, I thought she was going to try to kiss me. 'I'm looking forward to our drink tomorrow. Oh! It *is* tomorrow already.'

'Me too,' I said, anxious to get away and wishing I hadn't been so forthcoming in accepting her invitation.

At last I headed for home. It had been an extraordinary night, albeit disturbing. What if Pete found out I'd taken the coroner's report and fired me? Even worse, what if I were arrested for breaking and entering? Oh God! The repercussions could be *huge.*

When my parents fled to Spain, I had strict instructions never to call them in case Interpol traced the phone number. If I were interrogated, it would only be a matter of time until the cops found out the truth – unless I pretended to be an orphan. No one knew about my family here in Devon. An orphan, alone in the world, wasn't such a bad idea. Of course, I'd have to think of a way to kill my parents off – a car accident would do nicely. I wasn't superstitious. Naturally it would have happened a long time ago – somewhere they couldn't check, like Africa.

That decided, I turned my attentions to the night's revelations. Topaz knew who Pierce Brosnan was. Perhaps she had inside information on his relationship to Lady Trewallyn. Better still, maybe she knew why he was so interested in Dave Randall and his photographs.

It was probably a good idea to keep our drinks arrangement. Alcohol was good for loosening up inhibitions. I could ply her with cheap sherry – she looked the type – though I wondered if I could trust her. Who was Topaz Potter and how did she know so much? Why take so much interest in my American?

Glancing at my watch, I realized it was almost 3.30 a.m. but, like Christiane Amanpour, I never gave in to tiredness. It took a certain kind of person to be a successful investigative journalist.

I was on the brink of a great discovery and even beginning to look forward to the evening ahead with Topaz. But first, another busy day at the *Gazette* beckoned. I was ready.

10

Even though I expected the police to pay the *Gazette* a morning visit, the sight of the panda parked outside the office with its flashing blue lights still made me feel quite ill. A crowd of nosy bystanders had already begun to assemble in the High Street. How typical of the cops to make a mountain out of a molehill, unless Topaz had already talked and they realized they had a real crime on their hands – breaking and entering. Over at The Copper Kettle the sign on the door said CLOSED.

I gritted my teeth and eased my way to the *Gazette* entrance through the jostling mob where Barbara, pale and anxious, was holding the door open a crack. I only hoped if I were arrested and taken down to the station, the cops would have mercy and cover my face with a black hood.

The memory of my poor dad's sentencing at the Old Bailey came flooding back. How he must have suffered! I was only ten at the time and not allowed to attend the trial. Mum and I watched Dad being taken away on *News at Six*. I was so excited to see him on the telly, unaware that this kind of notoriety was not something to brag about. School the following day had been particularly gruesome.

Slipping through the glass front door, Barbara slammed and locked it behind me. I forced myself to adopt a devil-may-care attitude. 'What are those little boys in blue doing here?'

'That rusty old alarm went off last night.' Barbara pulled the door blind down. 'Someone tried to break in.'

'Anything stolen?'

'I don't think so.' Barbara's usual bright-eyed curiosity was replaced with an expression I'd seen on my mother's face every time the police paid us a visit. Fear. Could Barbara be hiding something?

'Vicky,' shouted Pete. 'Over here.'

Everyone was present. Pete, Tony, and Edward, along with two policemen who seemed to be talking to someone – obviously Annabel – seated in one of the brown leatherette chairs.

I approached the group with my chin held high. There was nothing to worry about. These men were country coppers, not hardened veterans from Scotland Yard.

My bravado evaporated the moment I realized it wasn't Annabel in the chair. It was Topaz – and what's more, she was wearing my *scarf*! She must have taken it when I was inside the building. I felt dizzy with the implications.

She also had my gloves, which she waved cheerfully in my direction. 'Vicky! Come and join us!'

I gave a sick smile just as Topaz stood up and engulfed me in a huge embrace. 'I was just telling everyone what fun we had last night. I've told them everything.'

There was a deathly hush, apart from a snigger, presumably from Pete, who saw sex in any situation – Topaz's insinuation must be making his day. Why hadn't I seen it before? Topaz must be a lesbian. Last night, or rather early this morning, she had mistakenly believed I'd been scrutinizing her breasts and not the silver locket around her neck.

Hadn't she jumped on top of me in the cafe and stayed there far longer than necessary in her flimsy nightdress? Hadn't she appeared to want to kiss me when we bade each other goodnight?

73

I found myself gawping at Topaz who, grinning like a Cheshire cat, seemed to be revelling in the attention. Why was she tormenting me? I hardly knew her, and to my knowledge, had never done her any harm. True, I had not left her a tip yesterday, but surely she couldn't be that petty?

Thank God Annabel was not there to enjoy my embarrassment. Perhaps she had suffered another attack of diarrhoea.

'Ms Hill?' said the younger of the two policemen. 'I'm Detective Constable Probes.' I recognized him as the one who carried the mop from the alley last night. Up close he looked barely older than me. Tall, with bright red hair and a forest of freckles spattered all over his face, he was actually quite attractive. It was a pity he was a copper.

'And I'm Detective Inspector Stalk,' barked his partner, idly tapping his truncheon against the back of Topaz's chair. Stalk was a bearded thug. His reputation in Gipping was legendary, as he regularly hauled innocent kids in off the streets to accuse them of 'casing a joint' or 'behaving in a way that threatened society'. Nine times out of ten, the kids were released and Stalk's dream of a promotion to Plymouth remained just that – a dream.

My heart sank. With Stalk heading the inquiry, I was as good as guilty. Then I remembered I actually *was* in fact guilty.

'Well, now we all know who we are, I'll be off,' boomed Stalk. 'DC Probes will conduct the inquiry. I've got bigger fish to fry.'

Thank God. Probes looked wet behind the ears. I could easily handle him.

Pete stepped forward. 'Why don't we all go into the nook?' he suggested. 'It's bad publicity for the *Gazette* to see cops swarming around in reception.'

Topaz bounded to her feet. 'Where's the nook?' she said, grabbing my hand. I shrank from her touch. 'It sounds so cosy.'

'You've got ten minutes of my time, officer,' said Pete, who was clearly edgy, having one cigarette on the go, and another already lit. 'Vicky and I have some business to attend to this morning.'

'We do?' My heart sank. Pete never included me in any of his *business*.

'No point you hanging around, Topaz,' Pete said. 'I'm sure the officer wants to talk to us alone,'

'No. I just need Ms Hill.' Probes gave me a pleasant smile. His teeth were small and reminded me of a shark's.

'I'm the bloody chief reporter. I should be there.' Pete mouthed something incomprehensible at me and wiggled his eyebrows – probably scared I'd mention his illegal arrangement with Brian.

'Well, *I* think *I* should stay in case you have any more questions.' Topaz flopped down on the leatherette chair and pointedly began to play with the tassels on my scarf.

Pete squeezed Topaz's shoulder. 'Come on, luv, if you're needed, DC Probes knows where to find you.'

It was clear from Pete's authoritative tone he meant business and had experience with children. His words were a mix of cajoling, underlined with the unspoken threat of a jolly hard smack should his command be ignored.

Topaz reluctantly got to her feet and actually *winked* at Probes. His face remained impassive but I knew what was going on. She'd already sold me up the river. What lay ahead in the nook was pure formality.

Barbara whisked up the blind and unlocked the front door. One woman dressed in a red headscarf had her nose pressed against the glass. These locals were like vultures.

As Topaz sauntered towards the exit, she blew me a kiss. 'Don't forget our date tonight. Seven o'clock sharp!'

I was speechless. Date? I was not a lesbian! Fortunately Pete missed the sexual innuendo, being too preoccupied with picking up his lighter that he'd dropped on the floor. Nerves, obviously.

Topaz paused at the door. 'Oh! And one more thing, Vicky, don't forget to tell the nice policeman about your American friend who drives that lovely black Porsche.'

Horrified, I glanced quickly over at Probes, who was studying the framed scoops hanging on the wall. He seemed not to hear.

Barbara bundled Topaz off the premises, where she was promptly engulfed by a bloodthirsty mob, shouting hopefully, 'Has someone been stabbed? Is anyone dead?'

'Tony! Edward!' Pete barked. 'Get back upstairs. Christ! You've already wasted half the bloody morning.'

Probes waited patiently as the others dutifully trooped out of reception.

Pete turned to me. 'Vicky, take the officer into the nook. It's private.'

I let that one go. The walls were as thin as a sheet. No doubt he wanted to eavesdrop on my conversation. He needn't have worried. I had far bigger problems at the moment than Pete's shady business deals – my freedom, for one.

'Please follow me.' I led the way. My knees felt like jelly.

We entered the nook. Even though the ashtray had been emptied, the smell of stale cigarettes remained a permanent aroma. I pulled the star-spangled curtain closed behind me and gestured for Probes to take a seat. My mouth felt dry. No doubt Dad must have felt like this each time the police dragged him off for questioning. I had no idea what Topaz had said about me before I arrived. It was little wonder that suspected criminals demanded a solicitor be present during interrogations. Someone had to field the awkward questions. Someone had to know when it was timely to use a standard catchphrase, such as 'You don't have to answer that.' Luckily, one of my favourite after-dinner games as a child had been Quiz the Copper. As long as I controlled the interview, all would be well.

I regarded my young opponent shrewdly. With any luck he could still be in that idealistic phase – common to new policemen – eager to believe all were innocent, until proven guilty.

I began with my first question. 'Can I make you some tea?'

'No thanks. I'm on duty.' Probes removed his helmet and carefully put it on the table. His hair was a brilliant shock of copper curls. I wondered what he looked like naked.

I perched on the corner of the desk so I'd sit higher than he

– another psychological power strategy. 'You're new to the area, aren't you?'

'New to Gipping but not new to the force, Ms Hill,' Probes said firmly. He took a pencil out of his top pocket and flipped open his notebook. 'Shall we start?'

'Great!' I tried to sound enthusiastic. 'What time did the alarm go off?'

Probes regarded me with surprise. No doubt my chutzpah had thrown him off balance. 'We got the call just after two-oh-five a.m. Why?'

'Good. Was there any sign of a break-in? Damaged locks? Broken windows?'

He flipped through his notebook. 'No, but—'

'Excellent. So no harm done?'

'Someone had thrust a mop in the old workings.'

'Amateurs. Interesting.' I gave a knowing nod. 'Probably a childish prank.'

'I hadn't considered—'

'Anyone see the Barker brothers run off?' It was a safe bet. Their names appeared often enough in the newspaper. The three young teenagers were always in trouble for vandalism and petty theft.

'Barker brothers?' Probes tapped the end of his pencil on his front teeth. 'Barker . . . Barker . . . name rings a bell.'

'Live on The Marshes housing estate. Call themselves the Swamp Dogs,' I said dismissively. 'Don't worry. You'll hear about them soon enough once you've lived—'

'I *have* heard of them.' Probes frowned. 'They're serving time in Plymouth for stealing a tractor.'

Blast! Probes seemed more in the know than I realized. 'Oh, you mean the *ringleaders.*' I lowered my voice. 'Actually, officer, word on the street is that the Dogs have a couple of new recruits. Could be one of them cutting their teeth.' This was distinctly possible. The youth of Gipping were an unemployed, angry bunch.

'Gipping Constabulary is looking for someone with . . . street knowledge, Ms Hill.' Probes looked hopeful. 'Perhaps you'd like to act as our informer?'

'Of course. Be delighted.' I blanched. *Over my dead body!*

'Going back to last night,' Probes continued. 'Topaz Potter, the young lady from the cafe, described the offender quite clearly.'

I felt light-headed. Who had Topaz identified running from the building – the American, or me? The wretched copper's bland expression gave nothing away.

Surreptitiously, I pinched the inside of my thigh – pain never failed to induce clear thinking. I couldn't allow Probes to gain the upper hand.

'Dear little Topaz.' I chuckled. 'Such a vivid imagination. With all due respect, you should take everything she says with a pinch of salt.'

'Really?' Probes inspected his notebook again. 'Are you saying you *weren't* with her?'

'What day are we talking about? I pop in and out of the cafe all the time.'

'Miss Potter said the alarm was keeping you both awake. I quote . . .' He referred to his notebook, reading in a monotone voice. '*Vicky and I are frightfully modern girls, officer. We like to experiment, and the loud ringing was putting us off!*'

Topaz's nerve and imagination were staggering! She was clearly infatuated with me. I'd have to let her down gently. But right now, her schoolgirl crush could save my bacon.

'Naughty Topaz,' I said, lowering my voice. 'To be honest, officer, I'm new at this girl-to-girl frolicking. I'm not quite sure it's for me – yet – so I'd rather keep it quiet, if you don't mind.'

Probes's cool demeanour was finally rattled by my brazen admission. He turned a lurid shade of beetroot and dropped his pencil under the table. Emerging moments later, he gave me an appraising glance that implied more than a passing interest in lesbian scuffles. Men! Mum was right. They were all perverted voyeurs.

He cleared his throat, struggling to regain his composure. 'Was it your idea to use the mop?'

In all the excitement of portraying myself as Topaz's lover, I'd forgotten the entire point of the lie. Had it all been for nothing? Had I just pandered to Probes's fantasies at my own expense?

'Yes.' I shrugged. 'The alarm went off unexpectedly. It put us completely off our stride. I didn't know what else to do.'

Probes bit his lip in anguish – or restrained lust. 'Tell me what happened.'

'I got the mop from Topaz's kitchen. I ran across the street and thrust the mop into the bell ringer. It stopped. The police arrived. *We* went back to bed.'

Probes silently scribbled my confession into his notebook. He shut it and got to his feet. 'Tampering with an alarm could be seen as a criminal offence,' he said sternly. 'But we'll overlook it this time.'

I was euphoric. Topaz's predatory designs had given me a cast-iron alibi.

'Those old workings occasionally go off, and it's hell to disconnect them.' Probes picked up his helmet and tucked it under his arm. 'Pretty clever idea, using that mop. I'll be off.'

I shook his outstretched hand – glad that Dad wasn't there to see me touching a copper. Probes's grip was firm, sending an unexpected and delicious tingle straight to my nether regions. I couldn't help reassessing his sexual potential – policeman or not. Could this seemingly emotionless young copper be an insatiable lion in the bedroom?

'Oh! Just one more thing.' Probes frowned. 'That American friend of yours? The one Ms Potter mentioned? The one with the Porsche?'

'Friend? Porsche?' I suppressed a moment of panic. I *knew* it was too good to be true. I was a victim of a *Columbo* moment.

Columbo was Dad's favourite TV show from the seventies. He'd downloaded the entire series onto DVD – pirated, obviously – and encouraged Mum and I to study Lieutenant Columbo's psychological approach to questioning. It was astounding just how Columbo got his suspects to confess to their crimes using the casual afterthought of 'just one more thing'.

Probes's right eye blinked rapidly, several times. Was he even affecting Peter Falk's signature optical affliction? 'Ms Potter said you knew him.'

'Me? A friend with a Porsche?' I laughed rather too loudly. 'Do *I* look like someone who has a friend with a Porsche? I don't even have a car.'

Probes's stare was so intense I had to look away. 'Ms Potter was most insistent—'

'In fact, I don't even have *parents*!' With a whimper of grief, I sat down and buried my face into my hands.

The curtain flew open, startling us both. Pete hurried to my side. 'Goddamit! What's going on? Have you upset her?' He flung his arm around my shoulder, supposedly in an attempt to give comfort. His breath stank of cigarettes.

'Jesus, Vicky! Are you an orphan?' Pete glared at Probes, who seemed genuinely mortified. 'I had no idea.'

'I'm sorry. I didn't know.' Probes looked miserable.

'Well, you know now,' Pete barked.

'It's not his fault,' I said. 'I don't like to talk about it.'

'You'd better go.' Pete nodded at Probes.

Probes opened his mouth as if to reply, then snapped it shut. He slipped out through the open curtain, looking crestfallen. For a fleeting moment, I even felt a bit sorry for him.

Pete sat down and pulled me roughly to his chest. His arm crushed my left breast. 'Poor Vicky,' he crooned, deliberately rubbing his elbow across my bosom. 'You should have told me.'

'I'm all right, really.' I pushed him away. 'It was a long time ago.'

'The cops are insensitive jerks,' Pete exploded. 'Come on. Let's get out of here.'

Pete gripped my arm and propelled me out of the nook. I was grateful to be back in the safe fluorescent glare of reception. The nook was claustrophobic and gave me the creeps – especially when I was actually in the presence of one.

Pete looked at his watch. 'Bugger! We're going to be late! Meet you out front in five minutes. I'll get the wheels.'

'Meet me? Why? Where are we going?' I was alarmed. There was no way I wanted to be alone with Pete, especially not in his old van. 'I've got an awful lot to do today.'

'It'll have to wait.' He hurried out of reception. Frankly, I was nervous. Probes's questions were child's play compared to Pete's volatile temper.

Where was Annabel? Weren't she and Pete supposed to be at The Grange conducting the obituary interview today? What if she had found Brian and he had told her he'd given the coroner's report to me – the girl with *cool* eyes.

As I waited for Pete outside, it was hard not to reflect on life's ironies. I had escaped interrogation and arrest by the Gipping Constabulary, only to face probable molestation by my boss and the very real possibility of being fired.

I was at a crossroads. There must be some way to turn this tricky situation around to my advantage. Would I be forced to consider sacrificing my body to keep my job? Or even worse, sleep my way to a front-page placement line by line? Up until now, I had never fully understood the temptations that Annabel faced in her quest for fame and fortune. It seemed so easy to acquiesce and be done with it. Mum said it only took ten minutes of pandering to make a man happy. I could do that, couldn't I?

Pete's van appeared around the corner and screeched to a halt in front of me. He threw open the passenger door. 'Hop in, luv!' Decision made, I got in.

11

The front seat of Pete's old blue van was littered with discarded food cartons from Mr Chinkie's Chow and various parts of a Mr Potato Head toy.

'Kids!' he grumbled, sweeping the debris into the foot well.

I gingerly sat down and pulled on my seat belt. I assumed Pete had children although he never mentioned them. It made the ordeal ahead even more sickening.

Pete slammed into gear and we sped off down the High Street in the direction of the moors. I felt nauseous, although I was unsure if it was Pete's driving – he drove like a lunatic – my nerves, or the fact that the car was rapidly filling up with cigarette smoke.

I grabbed the door handle. 'Can I open a window?'

'Doesn't work, luv,' said Pete.

Too late. The handle came off in my hand. I dropped it on the floor and kicked it under an empty take-away carton.

'Well, what do you make of it all?' Pete slipped his hand onto my knee and gave it a squeeze.

I froze, unsure how to reply – or even what he meant. There were so many possible answers.

'It's a total screw-up,' Pete continued, taking a deep drag on his cigarette. 'I *knew* I should have got that report myself.'

'My mum always says, "If you want a job done, you should do it yourself."'

'I thought your mum was dead?'

'She is. They are.' I blushed. 'Her sayings are so vivid, it sometimes feels like she's still alive.'

'Well, your mum – God bless her soul – was right.' He gave an emphatic nod. 'I shouldn't have given Annabel such a big responsibility.'

'I'm sure she did her best.' I felt uncomfortable. Not just cringing at my remark about my parents' demise, but for getting Annabel into trouble.

The van left the comforting confines of Gipping and zoomed into open country.

'How did Brian get hold of that report in the first place?' I said.

'Helps with odd jobs up at the morgue.'

I couldn't think of anything worse. What kind of odd jobs would those be? Filing away internal organs?

'Tips us off if anything suspicious comes in,' Pete went on.

'And Sir Hugh's death was definitely suspicious,' I said.

'How do you know?' Pete looked annoyed. 'Did Annabel tell you?'

'Of course not.' This was true. She hadn't. 'It's just a hunch.'

'I bet that's why Brian didn't show up,' Pete muttered to himself. 'Someone probably warned him off. Maybe we should go by his flat and check?'

'No!' I said quickly. 'Informers get paid for taking risks.'

'Yeah, but I know Brian. He would have called if he couldn't deliver,' Pete said.

'Not if he's only got a mobile phone,' I pointed out.

Pete was only half listening. 'We'll go to the morgue first after we're done with this just to check.'

This? The van slowed down, bringing me back to matters in hand. To my surprise, we were not in a desolated spot on the moors conducive to seduction. We had stopped outside a pair of formidable wrought-iron gates, flanked by Victorian gatehouses.

'Where are we?'

'The Grange, of course.'

'For the Trewallyn interview?' I couldn't believe it. It was as if I'd finally won the lottery! All this time I'd been imagining the worst for nothing. God truly worked in mysterious ways. This was my chance of a lifetime. I could now impress Pete with my broad range of verbal expertise and inciting questions. 'So, it's just you and me?'

'Yep. You and me, luv.'

We turned into the driveway, bordered by acres of parkland that seemed to stretch for miles.

'If you really believe there was foul play . . .' I trailed off. My use of the word *foul* reminded me of another kind of fowl. Hadn't Ronnie Binns said he had found those poor little fluffy chickens at The Grange? What a perfect opportunity to case the joint.

'You were saying?' Pete said.

'Just that it's a good chance for us to infiltrate the Trewallyn household and look for clues.' My confidence was increasing by the minute. 'Perhaps study Lady Trewallyn? She was much younger than him, you know.'

'Yeah,' leered Pete. 'I've seen her a few times in the town. She's got great tits. What do you think she saw in the old geezer? I've got my theories.'

'Money,' I stated flatly. 'Obviously.'

'Ah, that's where you're wrong,' said Pete with a smirk. 'Trewallyn was broke.'

'What do you mean?' I was shocked. If that were true, my theory of young wife marries rich dinosaur was completely off track.

'Trewallyn lost the family fortune betting on horses,' Pete continued. 'Old Trewallyn's first wife was loaded, but he soon went through her money.'

'What happened to her?'

'Heart attack.'

Pete was so naive. Obviously, he did not understand women. Lady Trewallyn saw an elderly man, stricken with grief. She believed him as rich as Croesus and married him on the rebound. Months later, she realized the truth and killed him in a fit of pique. He probably had a hefty life insurance policy.

As we approached The Grange, just visible among tall pine trees in the distance, the fence changed into a thick, ten-foot-high yew hedge.

'Christ!' Pete exclaimed as he slammed on the brakes. The van skidded in a cloud of dust. 'What the hell happened here?' The hedge was peppered with gaping holes.

'Hedge-jumpers,' I declared. 'They train on The Grange estate.'

'There's a bloody story here, my girl.'

My heart leapt. 'As a matter of fact, there is and I've written one.' Today was turning out to be better than I dreamed.

'Angle?'

'Men pit themselves against—'

'Man against nature!' Pete was exuberant. 'Yeah! I like it. Where's the copy?'

'Apparently, Annabel has to clear any—'

'Screw her. Got any photos?'

'Absolutely.'

I was thrilled. At last I'd been drafted into the *Gazette*'s, inner circle of power. Hopefully, it wouldn't be long before Annabel was down in the basement making the tea for *me*!

Pete turned to face me, his expression hopeful. 'Can you work in a sexual angle?'

'A what?' I said, hiding my dismay. The hedge-jumpers had been heavily padded for protection against nature's wrath. Even a determined groper's efforts would have little effect penetrating clothes as thick as a rhino skin.

Pete eased the car into gear and we drove on. 'Sex sells newspapers,' he said cheerfully. '*That's* what readers want.'

'You mean, like the *Plymouth Bugle*?' Founded by two sailors in Plymouth docks, the *Bugle* was our rival newspaper. It was supposed to provide educational material for navy personnel away at sea. I'd flipped through it once, shocked to find pages devoted to topless strippers with lurid headlines like, ORGIES AHOY! and HORNPIPE HARLOTS!

'Yeah. That's what I'm talking about.'

I wondered what our old-fashioned editor thought about blatant pornography.

As if reading my mind, Pete continued, 'Wilf is stuck in the dark ages. But, a sex scandal on page one—'

'Would increase circulation,' I said with a nod.

'Hell yeah! The old codger would see we were right,' Pete enthused. 'You and I make a good team, Vicky.'

A team? Had I misunderstood him? All earlier suspicions as to Pete's sexual motives vanished. No doubt he had a frigid wife. A nag. Someone who spent all his hard-earned money buying clothes. According to women's magazines, men who felt unappreciated in the home were forced to find solace elsewhere.

We passed under a brick archway – topped by a rather grand Victorian clock tower splattered with bird droppings – and emerged into the cobbled courtyard of The Grange. Stables with green painted doors flanked the yard. Grimy dormer windows above indicated former living quarters for the servants and grooms of a bygone age. Although I felt a pang of nostalgia for the glory days of the British Empire, I was aware the likes of me would be slaving away below stairs in the scullery, never up with the toffs.

As we drove on through, the cobbled stones were strewn with weeds. Paintwork was chipped, and the stone water trough carried a film of green slime. I could understand why Dad felt little guilt in dealing with his upper-class clients who so casually allowed their possessions to fall into disrepair. In many ways, he was a modern-day Robin Hood. Why not take from the rich – who don't care – and sell to the poor at bargain prices?

We exited the courtyard through a second, matching archway and arrived at the rear entrance to The Grange.

'Oh no,' I whispered, stunned.

Annabel's BMW was parked alongside a bank of derelict outbuildings. She sat perched on the bonnet, snuggled in a fake fur bomber jacket to keep out the autumnal chill. In her hand, she waved a brown manila envelope. It *had* to be the coroner's report. Annabel must have found Brian, after all. No doubt, he would have remembered my *cool* eyes and the cat would be out of the bag. My heart sank. My career was finished.

'Thank God she's got it.' Pete wiped away what looked like a tear. 'Bloody hell! That was a close shave. Good old Annabel. She's the best.'

'Yes, isn't she wonderful,' I said bleakly.

Pete stopped the van next to Annabel's car and got out to engulf her in a highly unprofessional embrace. That same hand that had spent most of the last twenty minutes on my knee was now clamped firmly on Annabel's left buttock. I noted she made no attempt to move away from his touch. My earlier feelings of compassion towards Pete and his marriage evaporated. Didn't the man have any control?

The two of them spoke in low, secret voices. They looked over in my direction. I braced myself for an angry shout or reprimand from my soon-to-be ex-boss.

'Vicky!' Pete called out. 'We don't need you now. You can wait there for us.'

'We'll be an hour or so,' Annabel shouted, pulling Pete towards her to whisper into his ear. They laughed. I knew it was about me – or sex.

'Annabel says if you get bored, you can clean out my van!' Pete sniggered.

'Good idea!' I shouted back, suppressing my fury as I watched them link arms and head towards the short flight of stone steps leading up to the back entrance.

Clean out the *van*? Who did they think I was? The charlady?

Yet, how little they knew me! Hadn't Dad said, *'Opportunity knocks when you least expect it'*?

Hadn't Ronnie Binns said you could tell a lot about a person by the state of their dustbins? Pete and Annabel had unwittingly played into my hands. It was time to investigate Lady Trewallyn's rubbish.

12

Pete was right when he said Sir Hugh was penniless. The rear of the house was distinctly run-down, too. A row of ramshackle outbuildings revealed an old tractor with no wheels and an assortment of rusty farmyard machinery.

Two metal dustbins stood on the far side of the courtyard, which was littered with broken glass and empty beer cans. Recalling Dad's advice, I double-checked the area for any sign of activity. Given the general state of decay, it was unlikely that a stray gardener or handyman would appear, but one could never be too careful. I felt very exposed and wondered what reason I could give should I be spotted foraging through the Trewallyn rubbish.

Suddenly, I was struck by an idea so clever that even *I* couldn't help but be impressed by my own ingenuity.

I returned to the van to retrieve one of Pete's empty Chinese take-away cartons. Ignoring the sweet-and-sour sauce dripping from the bottom of the box and onto my shoe, I strolled leisurely across the courtyard.

The dustbins were located below the cobwebbed window of a stone pigsty. To the right, a five-bar gate opened onto a narrow rutted cart track that presumably looped back to the tradesman entrance and from there, on to the main drive.

As I drew closer, a strange, prickling sensation swept all over my body, and my heart began to pound. Someone was watching me.

Suppressing the urge to dash back to the van, I held my cardboard alibi on high and began to hum my favourite hymn, 'Jerusalem', for courage.

The first dustbin was empty – not even a stray potato peel left behind. Ronnie had done a thorough job. I lifted the second lid and stifled a scream.

In the bottom of the metal bin lay the corpse of *another* fluffy white chicken – throat neatly cut and legs removed. I felt a rush of elation. Frankly, I hadn't really expected to find anything at all. Yet something irked me. Ronnie claimed he'd found the other three chickens at The Grange, so why leave one behind? The coroner's report stated Sir Hugh had been discovered with six chicken legs stuffed in his mouth – where were this little chap's feet?

Was it possible – my stomach churned at the implications – that Lady Trewallyn was planning a *second* murder? How careless to leave the evidence behind for the dustman!

The sensation of being watched hit me anew. I looked over my shoulder, but the courtyard was empty. Turning back to the pigsty, I practically had a heart attack.

Pierce Brosnan's face was peering through the cobwebbed window, his nose pressed against the glass. Our eyes met. Although blind panic consumed me, *this* time I was determined to keep my head. Nonchalantly, I looked away, tossed the leaky carton into the dustbin on top of the chicken and replaced the lid. Brushing my hands with a flourish I said loudly, 'Must keep Britain tidy,' and turned on my heel.

Pierce Brosnan rapped sharply on the window. 'Hey! Wait up!'

I pretended I hadn't heard and set off at a brisk walk.

Planning to return to the front of the house, I hurried through the gate and down the track.

'Stop!' Pierce Brosnan yelled. I didn't look round. He was gaining on me. I wasn't surprised. His judo moves in the churchyard showed him to be a fit man. I broke into a jog.

To my dismay, the track led *away* from The Grange, and safety. In fact, it fizzled into a narrow corridor, flanked by tall fir trees. I ran down the path and darted through a gap where I came face-to-face with Hugh's Folly.

Standing thirty feet high and with a tiny window up top, it looked like Rapunzel's tower from Grimms' *Fairy Tales*. There wasn't time to pick the heavily padlocked door. Instead, I circled the thick yew hedge at the tower's base, and dived into a convenient hole.

My safari jacket sleeve tore on the inner branches as I wriggled as far as I could to the back – Dave was right about moleskins and the importance of being properly dressed.

There was no way Pierce Brosnan would think of looking for me in here. I felt safe in this cocoon, buffered from the outside world.

Slowly, I managed to catch my breath and take in these new surroundings. There was far more room than I had imagined and it would actually make a terrific den.

As my heart regained its natural rhythm, I wondered why I hadn't stood my ground and waited to see what the American had wanted. Better yet, I should have turned the tables and demanded what on earth he was doing lurking in the old pigsty. I had acted unprofessionally and sternly resolved never to do that again. I was quite certain that Christiane Amanpour would never have scurried back to the tent at the sound of the first little bang.

I glanced at my watch. Time was ticking on. Pete and Annabel could even be back at the car, wondering where I was. Apart from a few birds twittering and the rustle of the wind through the leaves, the coast seemed clear.

I'd no sooner crawled a foot back towards the entrance, when my heart flipped over. Familiar black shoes blocked the only escape route. The American had been as silent as a fox. How foolish of me! Dad always said in situations like this, it was vital to wait until dusk before making any move – not a mere ten minutes. I'd been careless and it could cost me my life.

People disappeared every day. No one knew where I was. What's more, Pete and the entire police force thought I was an orphan – and, with my parents hiding out in Spain, let's face it, I practically *was*.

Only God could help me now and frankly, even I was tiring of asking Him favours. Much as it's handy to have the Almighty in my corner, I realized I was quite resourceful and had – so far – managed to solve my own problems.

This time, I would work alone.

13

It's amazing how inventive the mind can be when faced with annihilation. I decided to be a hedge-jumper.

Drawing myself up into a crouching position, I lunged left and right yelling, 'Yay! Yay! Yahooooo!'

I thrashed around in a frenzy of athletic leaps, much to the annoyance of a flock of pigeons who flew off at high speed.

'Ma'am? Ma'am? Hello?' The American sounded concerned.

I stopped, took a deep breath, and, adopting an angry tone, shouted, 'What the *hell* . . . ?

'Are you okay?' The shoes disappeared to be replaced by Pierce Brosnan's face peering into the gap. He removed his sunglasses to reveal piercing blue eyes. 'I thought you were being murdered.'

Very funny, I thought – a killer with a sense of humour. I crawled towards him. 'I'm perfectly fine, thank you. I was doing some exercises.'

'Is that so?' his eyes twinkled. To my surprise, they did not seem to be those of a dangerous man.

'Let me help you up.' Gallantly, he extended a black-gloved hand.

'No need. All part of my *hedge*-jumping training,' I said pointedly. Scrambling out, I got stiffly to my feet.

Elegant and distinguished, the American was dressed in a long black cashmere coat. His hair was jet-black, too – dyed. I recognized the bluish tinge from Dad's efforts at knocking off a decade or two.

The American frowned. 'Did you say you were a *hedge*-jumper?'

'Oh! Do you jump, too?' I asked, as if talking about the merits of fishing. 'It's fun, isn't it?'

'I was forgetting my manners. Name's Chester Forbes.'

We shook hands. His fingers lingered over my palm for a second longer than necessary, sending an unexpected tingle to the soles of my feet. Really, he was quite an attractive man despite his age.

'Pleased to meet you,' I said, conscious of a new dilemma. The slightest whisper of me being press could be disastrous. I was fairly confident he hadn't recognized me in the churchyard and I was sure my accidental newsprint camouflage last night had rendered me invisible beneath Annabel's desk. So far, Chester Forbes had no idea who I was, and I was determined to keep it that way.

'My hedge-jumping friends just call me Vicky,' I said, casually.

'In that case you must know Dave Randall.'

Blast! Chester had stolen Dave's photographs so naturally he was going to ask about him.

'Everyone knows Dave,' I said with false enthusiasm. 'He's famous for the Fosbury Flop.'

'Wouldn't you think, as a friend of Sir Hugh's' – he paused – 'Mr Randall would have *flopped* into his funeral?'

Clearly, this was a trick question. Thinking quickly, I said, 'Dave? I heard he was prostrate with grief. Couldn't leave his bed.'

'Is that so?' Chester's expression indicated some doubt. He looked at me keenly. 'I feel we've met before.'

I pretended to give this some thought. 'I can't imagine where.'

'I saw you in the churchyard yesterday.'

'You were there, too?' I gushed. 'I thought you looked a bit familiar. Wonderful funeral, wasn't it?' I gave a nervous cough and fell silent. Checking my watch, I exclaimed, 'Good God! Is that the time? I really must go.'

Chester took my elbow and pulled me towards him. 'So you saw what happened?'

'Oh, that!' I said, dismissively. 'A new widow lashing out at random. Happens a lot in the country.'

'Yeah. She *was* pretty mad.' Did I detect a glint of amusement in Chester's blue eyes?

I felt it safe to add a comment to show I was on his side. 'I thought you handled it very well.'

'Kandi's always been a firecracker.'

'Kandi?' Switching deftly into my reporter mode, I inquired, 'Katherine's nickname, obviously.'

'*Katherine* now, is it?' Chester shook his head with a sigh.

'She's American. You're American.' I launched into my reporter routine. 'Where did you meet?'

'In America,' he said sourly.

I wished I had a pen and paper. 'How did you meet?'

'Why all the questions?' Chester's expression darkened. Suddenly, he seized my hand again and turned it over. Alarmed, I tried to slip from his grasp but he held tight.

'Too soft,' he said, studying my palm.

I felt my face grow hot. 'What do you mean?'

'Your hands are too soft for hedge-jumping.' He stared deep into my eyes. 'Who are you really, Vicky the hedge-jumper?'

'I just told you. Honest.' I snatched my hand away, burning with embarrassment. 'The reason my skin is so soft is because . . . I usually wear gloves. I go to bed with my hands wrapped in oil, actually.'

I felt myself go a bit redder. Why would I talk about *bed* to this man, not to mention oiled hands?

95

'Don't worry, honey,' he said with a soft laugh. 'Sooner or later, you'll tell me the real reason you ran away from me and hid in a hedge.'

'Ran away?' I said scornfully. 'What a funny thing to say! I was practising my sprint-and-dive technique. I've enjoyed our chat but I really must be going.' I tried to dodge past him but he blocked my way.

'Why don't I escort you to your car?'

'I walked here.' The last thing I wanted was to bump into Pete and Annabel. 'Hedge-jumping is a gruelling sport. Fitness is everything.' I demonstrated with energetic squats and lunges.

Chester stood back, his hands on his hips. When I stopped – panting heavily – he said, 'Allow me to give you a ride back to town.'

'Are you *sure* you don't mind?' I enthused, praying my face did not betray the sudden wave of terror I felt inside. After all, Annabel might be in the house getting the interview, but I was out in the cold, with the killer.

Chester offered me his arm. 'Well, Vicky? Shall we?'

From this moment onward, I was not Victoria Brenda Hill, cub reporter on the world's most boring newspaper, I was Vicky Hill, sharp and cunning private investigator and I was going undercover.

Slipping my arm through Chester's, I gave him my best smile. 'Lead the way.'

14

The Porsche was partially hidden under a bank of low-hanging trees. The moment Chester shut the passenger door I knew I'd made a foolish mistake. Not only was I getting into a car with a perfect stranger, I had broken the cardinal rule of safe reporting by not telling anyone my whereabouts.

Was I going to be another Peggy Fowler? I had been six years old when my school friend disappeared one hot summer afternoon. Peggy's body had been unearthed months later, buried under a pile of leaves in a ditch by the side of the road. Martin Whelks, the postman, had done it. He'd lured Peggy into his van with a bag of sherbet pips. A few weeks before Peggy's disappearance, Martin had offered the very same sweets to me. I preferred chocolate. It just goes to show that life is all about choices. Because of the cocoa bean, my life had been spared. Yet today, who knew if I would cheat death a second time?

With a grin I could only describe as wolfish, Chester slid into the driver's seat and slammed the door. He turned towards me, fingers outstretched towards my throat. Good God! Was he going to attempt to strangle me straight away? Before I could lunge for the door handle, Chester reached for the seat belt behind my shoulder.

'I like to drive fast,' he said, drawing it over my body and fastening it with a snap. 'Wouldn't want you disappearing through the windshield and ruining that pretty little face.'

'Ready?' Chester asked as he turned the ignition.

The Porsche's throaty engine exploded into life, sending a thrilling vibration straight through my body. There was something predatory about the sleek black car crouched low over the ground like a stalking panther. I couldn't help thinking how jealous Annabel would be if she could see me now.

Chester reversed the car out from its hiding place and gently eased into the grassy track that led back to the main drive. His touch on the gear stick was a caress, so different from Pete's awkward grope. I couldn't help imagining Chester's hand on my knee, then, perhaps, slowly making its way up my leg. I shuddered, instinctively clenching my thighs tightly together.

I glanced over at the man, reminding myself he was a creepy American who was nearly as old as Dad. Still, he seemed to possess a sophisticated James Bond aura, which I found attractive and unsettling. If I were to be seduced by Chester, surely he would be experienced in matters of love? I might even enjoy it!

'Look at that!' Chester said in an angry voice, putting a stop to my virginal musings.

He slowed the Porsche down to crawl alongside several yards of the decimated hedgerow bordering the drive.

'Sheer butchery,' he snarled, turning to me. 'Why would you want to be a part of such a barbaric hobby? Don't you have any respect for nature?'

Blast! I had no defence. How was I to know my claim to hedge-jumping would backfire so horribly? All my valiant efforts at forging a friendship – and therefore securing a confession – seemed to dissolve in Chester's contempt.

'It's taken decades to cultivate hedges like these,' he raged on, his face flushed.

'I suppose—'

'Some of these country homes have hedges that date back to the seventeenth century—!'

'I didn't—'

'It's enough to force a man to take the law into his own hands!'

Bloody hell! This was the third time Chester had practically confessed to murder.

Fuelled by Chester's fury, the Porsche picked up speed once more. His face set in severe lines, he said, 'Dave Randall and I need to have a little chat and *you're* going to arrange it.'

We had reached the Victorian gatehouses where, to my relief, the car turned towards the safety of Gipping, not in the direction of the desolate moors.

'I don't really know Dave all that well,' I said, suddenly hating Dave Randall and his stupid hobby.

The Porsche was going faster and faster. I cleared my throat. 'Excuse me, but I think it's a thirty-mile limit here.'

'You said you *did* know him.' Chester deliberately pushed his foot down on the accelerator to increase the speed. Any suggestion of friendliness had evaporated. I gripped the edges of the bucket seat and glanced over at the speedometer. We were doing over sixty-five miles an hour! Oncoming cars flashed their lights and sounded their horns. At any other time, this would have been exhilarating.

'If you want to know about Dave, you should buy the local paper,' I said, calculating how many limbs I would break if I threw myself from the moving car. 'There's a really good feature on him in it. I bet it would answer any questions you have and – whoa!'

The car swerved over to the side of the road and stopped with a jerk. My heart was pounding.

Chester turned to me, eyes narrowed. 'I know you're lying,' he snapped. 'If you are covering up for Dave Randall, you're making a very dangerous mistake.'

I had to get out of the car. 'I think I'm going to be sick,' I announced. It was my favourite childhood technique for long car journeys and very effective. Surely, the last thing Chester wanted was someone vomiting in his immaculate Porsche.

'Got to have fresh air.' I gave two, very convincing dry heaves. 'Going to throw up.'

'Get out then,' said Chester, coldly. 'I'm not stopping you.'

With one hand clasped over my mouth, I undid the seat belt and scrambled out.

'Good-bye, Vicky,' he said, adding with a touch of sarcasm, 'I hope you feel better soon.'

'Thanks,' I mumbled, scrambling out, surprised to find my knees *were* shaking and I *did* feel nauseous.

The Porsche roared off. I glared after the car. No real gentleman would have abandoned a sick woman on a deserted road. Unless, of course, he'd not believed me.

Apart from a herd of Jersey cows in a field, I was alone. There were no houses in sight, just a dreary string of telegraph poles stretching into the distance. It was too far to return to The Grange. I'd have to trek back to the office.

I plodded along. The walk seemed endless. As if to add insult to injury, a light sprinkling of rain began to fall of the variety famed in the West Country – it looked deceptively harmless but, in fact, soaked right through even the thickest raincoats.

Over and over again, I replayed my conversation with Chester, kicking myself for lost opportunities. What was he doing in Gipping skulking in pigsties? He had warned me about Dave Randall but I hadn't asked why. Why did he call Lady Trewallyn 'Kandi' and why was she so afraid of him? Was he really involved in Sir Hugh's murder?

Then, from behind, I heard wet tyres on the road. A car was approaching. A horn blasted two loud beeps. My heart turned over. It had to be Chester! With head held high, I turned around to confront my fate, with dignity.

15

Annabel's silver BMW burst into view. Never had I felt so happy to see her – though relief was mixed with anxiety. Annabel was bound to tell Pete the truth about the missing coroner's report. I'd rather have risked a run-in with the killer than with my boss. Yet, surely wouldn't my little faux pas prove insignificant compared to the fabulous truth that Sir Hugh had been brutally murdered?

As the car drew alongside, it splattered my already sodden jeans liberally with muddy water that looked suspiciously like liquid cow manure. Even that indignity – to say nothing of the stench – failed to suppress my joy at her arrival.

I yanked open the passenger door. 'Blimey! Am I glad to see you.'

'Stop!' Annabel said, pinching her nose. 'Absolutely not. You smell like a sewer.'

'For heaven's sake. It's only farmyard muck.'

Annabel shook her head decisively. 'This car is six weeks old. You'll have to walk.' Clearly, Good Samaritan skills were not one of her attributes.

I peered into the rear. 'You've still got the dealer's plastic stuff on the back seat.'

'I have to keep it clean.'

'I'll sit on that.' I opened the back door and slithered in feeling like a naughty child.

Annabel swivelled round to check I was following her instructions. Satisfied, she thrust the BMW into gear and we sped off.

'Why on earth didn't you wait for Pete and me?' Annabel said, via the rear-view mirror.

I leaned forward, resting my hand on the top of her seat. 'I decided—'

'Sit back!' she commanded, slapping at my fingers.

I slumped against the seat. All gratitude for my rescue vanished. How dare she speak to me in such a scathing and patronizing way! After all, I was four months older than her.

'How unprofessional of you not to tell us you'd decided to go off on your own,' Annabel continued. 'Didn't you—?'

'What's it to you? It's a free country, isn't it?' I felt inexplicably close to tears. My encounter with Chester had upset me more than I realized.

'Pete and I were concerned about you, that's all.'

'Well, don't be.' My eyes stung. For an awful moment, I thought I might actually cry.

Annabel studied me in the rear-view mirror. 'Are you all right?'

'Jeez! Have I grown two horns or something?' I retorted hotly, and turned away from her to stare dismally out of the car window.

'You just look a bit pale. You really should wear makeup.'

'I do, as a matter of fact – I just don't wear it plastered over my face like war paint.'

There was a ghastly silence. Feeling slightly guilty, I made a supreme effort to be civil. 'How did everything go at The Grange?'

'It didn't exactly go anywhere,' Annabel said sourly.

'No magical secrets in the coroner's report?' I said, leaning forward. 'No death in suspicious circumstances?'

This time Annabel did not order me to sit back. 'Sir Hugh Trewallyn had a heart attack.'

'*What?*' I was astonished. 'That's not possible.'

She shrugged. 'Apparently Lady Trewallyn discovered him in the library.'

'The *library*!' I cried. 'And you're telling me the verdict was death by *natural* causes?'

Annabel's voice quavered then broke into a sob. ' Oh Vicky, I had *so* wanted Sir Hugh to be murdered.'

So did I. 'Poor you.' I gave her shoulder an awkward pat, thoroughly puzzled by this turn of events.

'Yes, poor me.' Annabel snatched a tissue from a handy snap-on pouch under the dashboard and blew her nose.

'It's not the end of the world,' I said briskly. 'It's only a funeral and there'll be plenty more before the year is out.'

'You are sweet to say so, but it was going to be my big break.' Annabel sighed. 'Can you keep a secret?'

'Maybe,' I said warily.

'I've got a deal with the *Bugle,*' she said, watching me through the rear-view mirror. 'My murder story would have made the front page.'

I was miffed. By rights, any murder story should belong to me. And then there was the question of company loyalty! 'What about the *Gazette*?' I demanded.

'The *Gazette*!' Annabel said scornfully. 'It's so boring, Vicky. The *Bugle* wants a crime reporter—'

'But you're still training,' I broke in, jealousy rearing its ugly head. I'd heard about that job, too, but had dismissed it as too senior. 'You have to have experience – contacts in the police world. *Reliable* professional informers, not someone like the local dustman.'

'Oh Vicky.' Annabel sneered. 'Surely you don't think old Binns is my *only* informer?'

'Of course I don't!' A fresh jolt of envy hit me anew. 'Who else?'

'No can do. Got to protect my sources.' Annabel smirked, adding, 'You and I are so different, Vicky. You're happy in this fleapit. You don't have my ambition. I'm suffocating here. I really am.'

I was about to tell her that I, too, was dying of boredom but didn't trust her not to tell Pete.

'Is my mascara running?'

Annabel's face resembled a panda's. 'Not really.'

'I'll just drop you off.' Annabel pulled up outside the *Gazette,* oblivious to the building traffic behind us. 'I've got to see someone.'

'I expect Mr Binns will be back at the tip by now,' I said, wondering if she was going to chastise him for the false lead about the chickens.

'Oh him,' said Annabel dismissively. 'I've moved on. Pete needs a new front page, and I'm going to get it.'

I was just about to mention Pete had approved the hedge-jumping story, when my stomach turned over. Outside the post office, tucked in between a pale yellow VW Bug and an ancient Reliant Robin – a death trap on wheels if ever there was one – crouched the unmistakable shape of the black Porsche. I tried to keep calm. Perhaps Chester had gone to buy stamps?

'Are you going to sit here all day?' Annabel said as the motorist behind sounded his horn three times. 'Hurry, Vicky, I've got a lot to do.'

I scanned the area. There was no sign of the American. Reluctantly, I got out. The BMW moved off. As I turned to give the impatient motorist an apologetic smile, he wound down his window and swore obscenities at me. To my annoyance, several pedestrians turned round to stare. It was hardly my fault.

'Yoo-hoo!' called out a familiar voice. Topaz, *still* wearing my scarf, was standing in the doorway of The Copper Kettle.

I had a bone to pick with Topaz, and at least I could spy on the Porsche from inside the cafe. After our heated conversation, the last thing I wanted was to bump into Chester in the High Street.

Even though it was only four thirty, Topaz flipped the CLOSED sign across the door. 'Shall I put the kettle on?'

'I didn't come for tea.' I pushed past her, headed for the table next to the window, and sat down. The Porsche was in plain sight.

Topaz hurried after me. She slowly unwound my scarf, then gently draped it around my neck.

'Oh, is that mine?' I tried to sound unconcerned. She'd obviously decided to keep my gloves. 'I must have left it here.'

'Not exactly *here*.' Topaz pulled out a chair and sat down. Cupping her chin in her hands, she looked at me intensely. 'I think one good turn deserves another, don't you?'

'I've no idea what you're talking about.' I looked away and glanced out of the window. To my utter horror, Chester was leaving the *Gazette*! The fact that we could have met each other *there* was too much to handle. I felt quite faint. Surely, he couldn't have guessed my true identity when I'd been so careful?

'Are you all right?' Topaz reached over to stroke my hand. 'You've gone as white as a sheet.'

I couldn't risk her spotting Chester. I had to distract her attention. Impulsively, I grabbed her hand and pulled her towards me. 'Topaz—'

'Goodness, Vicky!' she gasped with wide-eyed wonder. 'Of course, I was hoping, but truly, I had no idea.'

I was aware of Topaz's body scent – a mixture of Elizabeth Arden's Blue Grass and stale kitchen. If I could smell Topaz, I was certain she could smell me – especially as the warmth from the cafe was heating up my damp clothing.

I was right. She sniffed, and then grimaced. 'If you don't mind me saying, you pong a bit.'

'I got caught in the rain.'

Topaz raised her eyebrows invitingly. 'Do you want to get

105

out of those wet clothes? Our size is identical.' She had the same peculiar glint in her eye that I'd noticed in Pete's when he asked if I had a boyfriend.

I looked away embarrassed just in time to see a flash of black streak past the window. The roar of the Porsche engine was unmistakable. Thankfully, Chester had gone.

The cafe was closed. If Topaz were to make a lunge at me, no one would hear my cries for help. I scrambled to my feet. 'Tell you what, why don't we go for that drink now?'

'I can't go out dressed like this,' Topaz declared, pointing at her mob cap. 'Why don't we get changed together?'

'My clothes are almost dry, but, please, you carry on.' I headed for the cafe door. 'Meet me at the office in ten minutes.'

Outside, I gulped down fresh air, trying to clear my head. I could handle Topaz as long as we were in a public place. I was more worried about the American. Why had he returned to the *Gazette*? With a jolt, I realized my mistake. I'd told Chester there was a newspaper article on Dave. He must have come to buy a copy. But, there was a problem. The article had not been published. In fact, it was still sitting on Pete's desk.

As I crossed the street, I prayed that Chester had not asked Barbara too many questions. If he found out my true identity, my cover was blown.

16

'Goodness, Vicky. You look like a drowned rat.' Barbara wrinkled her nose with distaste. 'That smell—'

'What did that American want?' I was not in the mood to discuss cow manure when my very existence was at stake. In the short time it had taken me to cross the street, Chester had grown into a mass murderer with me as his next victim.

'What a handsome man!' Barbara's eyes sparkled. 'So polite. He wanted to know about a hedge-jumping article.'

'There isn't one.'

'That's what I told him, but he insisted there was.'

Blast! 'Did he mention me, by any chance?'

'Oh yes, you lucky girl,' she said wistfully. 'If I was twenty years younger—'

'What were his *exact* words?'

'I told him he was misinformed. Then he said, "Can I speak to Vicky Hill" and I said, "She's out, but will be back later."'

This was far worse than I feared as I'd distinctly made a point of only giving him my first name.

'Then, he asked if I knew the hedge-jumping chappy. I told him he should definitely talk to you as you knew Dave extremely well.' Barbara gave a tinkling laugh. 'The Yanks are so charming. I had a little tryst in the war with a GI—'

'Jimmy Kitchen, I know.' I was getting a headache. Barbara was so indiscreet! She was typical of spinsters who fell to pieces the moment an attractive man entered their orbit. Chester must have guessed who I was from the very beginning. How humiliating! And to think I'd pretended to be a hedge-jumper!

'Such a lovely man,' Barbara gushed. 'He told me I had a "pretty little face".'

Chester had said the very same thing to me. Men! Maybe Topaz had a point in preferring girls. At least they weren't as fickle.

Barbara pointed towards the door. 'Is she waiting for you?' Speak of the devil. Topaz, holding an armful of clothes, stood with her nose pressed against the glass.

'It's open!' Barbara waved her inside and turned to me. 'Goodness me. Is she wearing a wig?'

Topaz was, indeed, wearing a wig – a long, platinum blond one to be precise. She'd also made an effort with the rest of her appearance. Gone was the drab serge uniform of The Copper Kettle fame. Instead, she wore an orange tartan miniskirt, orange fringe poncho, and white plastic knee-high boots. Even her lipstick was orange.

'I brought you some clothes.' She dumped the pile on one of the leatherette chairs and turned to Barbara. 'Hello, I'm Topaz Potter from The Copper Kettle, across the road.'

'Barbara Meadows,' Barbara enthused. 'I have a little skirt just like yours. Sometimes I think I really *should* wear it again.'

'Oh! Please give it to me!' Topaz rewarded Barbara with a gum-toothed smile and gushed, 'I just adore vintage clothes, don't you?' She picked up a pair of turquoise and green striped hot pants. 'A sixties, Mary Quant original – perfect for Vicky. She's got such a nice little bottom, don't you agree?'

Barbara's eyebrows shot up so high they disappeared under her fringe. I picked a lemon fuzzy sweater and a mustard-coloured plastic raincoat.

'I'll just borrow these,' I said, hoping the raincoat would cover my 'nice little bottom'.

'Change in the hall, dear,' said Barbara. 'But mind my bicycle.'

Topaz flopped on top of the pile of clothes, exposing a large expanse of naked thigh. 'I'll wait here and chat to your friend.'

I did not want her talking to Barbara or vice versa. Who knew what they'd say. 'To save time, why don't you take that stuff back to your place? I'll be over in a tick.'

'Okay,' Topaz smiled. 'By the way, what happened to that handsome American? Wasn't he here earlier?'

Barbara beamed. 'Isn't he charming—?'

'Off you go.' I shooed Topaz towards the door, suppressing the urge to throttle her into silence.

'Vicky and I are going out on our first date tonight,' Topaz announced.

'Date? Don't be silly.' I gave a nervous laugh.

'Goodness.' Barbara gave an embarrassed cough and suddenly found something very interesting to look at on her desk.

'It's purely business,' I said quickly.

'Business?' Topaz's face lit up. 'You mean you want me to work for the *Gazette*?'

Blast! 'Something like that,' I mumbled.

'Oh God, Vicky. That's my *dream*!' Topaz squealed and did several bunny hops on the spot. 'You won't regret it.'

'Congratulations, dear,' said Barbara, clearly confused. 'When do you start?'

Gathering the clothes from the chair, I pushed them into Topaz's arms. 'Now. See you in a minute.'

As Topaz swept out the door, I turned to face Barbara. Her expression was etched with concern.

'Does Pete know?' she inquired.

'He doesn't need to. It's a private arrangement.'

Barbara regarded me shrewdly. 'I think that girl's in love

with you. I recognize the signs. You know, I went to an all-girls school. Once, in the dorm—'

'Just going to pop this top on in the downstairs loo.' I'd heard Barbara's boarding school stories dozens of times – naked midnight feasts, naked pillow fights, and naked squashed sardines. 'Got to rush.'

'Don't forget to—'

'Mind your bicycle, I know.'

I clambered over Barbara's ancient, pink bike with its wicker pannier and into the loo. As I changed into Topaz's clothes, I wondered what on earth I was thinking. My entire day had been a nightmare – and the evening ahead promised more drama. I had to get a grip. I reassured myself. This was what being an investigative reporter was all about. Risk. Danger. Living on the edge.

Topaz could prove useful. It was vital I discovered what she and Probes had discussed this morning in my absence. Topaz clearly knew more about Chester Forbes than she was prepared to admit. I could only hope the alcohol would not inflame her passion for me.

17

'You seemed to get on well with that copper this morning,' I said, taking a sip of shandy. Although it wasn't quite six o'clock, The Three Tuns was bustling with activity – mostly farmers on their way home from the livestock market in nearby Newton Abbot.

Topaz had snagged a cosy corner table next to the large inglenook fireplace in the public bar, where a fire blazed. The intense heat had forced me to sit on the wooden bench beside her, which was a bit too intimate for my liking.

Topaz fastidiously removed the glacé cherry from her Babycham and put it in an ashtray. No one drinks Babycham these days. Her fussy fake-champagne drink with its trademark baby deer logo cost three times the price of my half-pint. I was paying and she was already on her third.

Topaz put her hand on my knee and squeezed it hard. Oh God, Barbara had been right.

'Don't worry,' she said. 'I just told the police officer what you ordered me to say.'

Not quite true, but there was no point arguing. Now that she believed we were working together Topaz had relaxed. I wasn't sure quite how to tell her there was no job at the *Gazette,* but resolved to tackle that problem another day.

Topaz withdrew her hand to pull a strand of hair over one eye, which unfortunately shifted her wig a fraction. Presumably she thought it sexy. 'Isn't this nice? I'm *so* glad you asked me out.'

I wanted to point out that suggesting a friendly drink and asking for a lesbian date were two different things, but didn't want to distract her from the issue at hand.

'Come on, Topaz, tell me what you said' – I lowered my voice – 'girl to girl.'

I flinched as she leaned her head on my shoulder. 'Of course, now that we're a team, it's different.'

'It shouldn't be,' I said firmly. 'You only had to tell Probes the truth.'

'Remember, I asked you what I should say and you told me to go ahead, and say exactly what I saw.'

'Which was?' My head began to pound again. God! Not *another* headache. I'd never had so many before. The deafening sound of the Rolling Stones' 'Brown Sugar' blaring from the jukebox didn't help much.

She turned and looked brazenly into my eyes. 'You. And the American.'

So Topaz Potter had seen us. The question was, where? Was it out in the alley or inside the *Gazette*? Her flat was directly opposite the reporters' room. There were no curtains or blinds on the windows. Chester had moved around with a flashlight, and I had stupidly switched on the light when he had left, conveniently illuminating the entire area.

I adopted an expression of outrage. 'Surely you don't mean you saw us . . . *together*?'

'Don't be silly.' Topaz polished off her third Babycham and held out the empty glass to me. 'And some cheese and onion crisps. I'm starving.'

I took it but made no move to get up. 'Tell me the details – and I'll buy you a packet of peanuts as well.'

Topaz sighed. 'The American walked out of the alley first. Then I saw you—'

'Outside. *Not* inside, surely.'

'Whatever you say. I just told the policeman about the American and . . .' She batted her eyelashes. 'And . . . us.'

'Us? *Us*? Why would you say that?' What the hell was she playing at? Why would she insinuate we had a relationship to Probes – I recalled the furtive way she winked at him before leaving reception.

Topaz gazed adoringly at me with her big green eyes. 'I saw the way you looked at . . .' She dropped her voice to a whisper. 'At . . . my breasts.'

'I most certainly did not.' Recalling her flimsy nightdress, I felt my face redden. 'I was admiring your silver locket, actually.'

'It's all right to be shy.' Topaz took my hand. I snatched it back. 'You *did* like them, didn't you?'

'I liked the necklace,' I said firmly. 'Probably early Victorian. Definitely silver, inlaid with mother-of-pearl.' Naturally, with my upbringing, I knew a valuable piece of jewellery when I saw it. 'There should be a photograph of the dead owner inside with a lock of their hair.'

'You're right. There is.' Topaz's eyes began to fill with tears. 'The locket belonged to my aunt.' Topaz pulled a red handkerchief from under her poncho and dabbed at her eyes. 'It's all I have left of her now.'

'For heaven's sake, I'm sorry about your aunt, but people are staring.' Three farmers dressed in tweed caps, jackets, and thick twill trousers broke off their conversation to turn and gawk. They probably thought we were having a romantic tiff.

Topaz blew her nose furiously. 'Tell me about the American.'

'Chester Forbes?'

'I thought you didn't know his name,' she said accusingly, all grief forgotten.

'I don't.' *Blast!* Topaz's unexpected tears, following on the

113

heels of blatant flirting, had totally thrown me off guard. 'I made up the name. We can't keep calling him "the American", can we?'

'Oh, I just thought . . .' A lone tear trickled down her cheek. 'I thought you knew something.' She took a deep breath. 'Have you ever been in love?'

It was hard to keep up with Topaz's mood swings, but I was happy to change the subject. 'Yes. With a man.'

'I went out with this chappy for six months,' Topaz said.

'Chappy? But—'

'Oh, I know what you are thinking.' She twisted her handkerchief in despair. 'He broke my heart and I decided never to go out with men again. Ever.'

'That's a bit drastic, isn't it?'

'All men are cheaters. They're weak and easily led astray.' She wiped another tear away, smudging her eyeliner.

I couldn't really argue with that. Topaz sounded just like Mum. I'd seen Pamela Dingles showing her stocking tops under her micro-mini. Poor Dad had been powerless to resist.

'I really love him,' Topaz blabbered on. 'Then *she* turned up, determined to have him. Dave didn't stand a chance.'

'Dave? Not Dave Randall?' I was stunned. Not *my* Dave Randall.

Topaz nodded, her face tragic. 'I could never be as exciting as *her*. I'm not rich and I don't drive a fancy car.'

Nausea swept over me. Surely Annabel was not the *she* implied? Was there no justice? She'd even had the nerve to pretend there was nothing between them when they met in reception last Wednesday.

'I thought it was you to begin with,' Topaz continued, which gave some consolation to my fragile ego. 'But then I realized whoever it was had bewitched him. It was as if someone had cast a spell.'

My mind was spinning. 'You think Dave is the victim of *witchcraft*?'

Topaz looked at me, forlorn. 'Everyone knows she does it. But we're all too scared to say.'

The alcohol was working on Topaz like a charm. 'Let me get you another drink. Stay there. Don't move.'

'Don't forget the crisps and peanuts.'

As I waited at the bar, my confidence began to waver. Perhaps I had been wrong all the time. It was Annabel, not Lady Trewallyn, who was the ringleader. Maybe Annabel was caught up in some sordid sex game that involved chickens. No wonder she had denied their significance at the tip. Maybe she had also seduced Sir Hugh, killed him, and tried to cover it up with a fake report?

Although this prospect was disturbing, no one could deny what an amazing front-page scoop it would make with all Pete's favourite ingredients: FOWL PLAY LINKED TO NYMPHO'S LUST FOR LOVIN': A VICKY HILL EXCLUSIVE!

Returning to the corner table, Topaz had brightened up. 'Remember you owe me a favour?'

'I do?'

'The scarf, silly,' she said with a giggle. 'Of course, I kept the gloves as a sort of security.'

I gave a nervous laugh. 'Topaz, there is no need for bribery. We're friends as well as teammates.'

'Good.' She beamed. 'Because I want Dave back, and *you're* going to help me!'

'Honestly, I don't see how—'

'I read a magazine about how men are turned on by the idea of two women doing it.'

'What are you saying?'

Topaz looked at me intensely. 'I mean, I haven't done *it* with a woman before but . . . do you want to give it a go?'

I almost choked on my shandy. 'You want to have sex with me in order to win Dave back?'

I had kissed a girl once when I was seven and it wasn't too disgusting. I'd kissed boys, too, of course, but not since leaving school. For a moment, the vision of Annabel's devastated look on making such a tawdry discovery was quite tempting. She'd walk in on us, writhing around in ecstasy in Dave's bed at Cricket Lodge whilst he looked on panting with lust – for me, obviously.

'We'd have to practise a bit first,' said Topaz. 'Maybe after I've finished my drink?'

'Practise?' I was appalled. 'Now?'

'We've got to look convincing,' she said, sliding her hand up my leg under the table. 'I've got a book with diagrams.'

'I'm not really in the mood.'

'It won't take long. Fifteen minutes, tops.'

I was stumped. On the one hand, I was desperate to lose my virginity and had pretty well got to the point where it didn't really matter who it was with. Although, I suspected, doing it with a girl wouldn't really count. Topaz seemed a nice sort – a bit high strung, but at least she looked clean. How unexpected that tonight could be the night I became a woman. So why was I hesitating?

What if Dave and Topaz discovered they enjoyed orgies and invited Annabel to join us? There was no question of me frolicking naked with my rival. No, it was a bad idea.

I glanced over at Topaz, who had downed her Babycham in one fell swoop. I'd have to let her down gently. Taking her hand in mine, I gave it a squeeze. 'I'm sorry, Topaz, I don't think I could.'

She scowled. 'Why?'

'The problem is, Annabel and I work together—'

'Annabel?' said Topaz, scornfully. 'That tramp in the flashy BMW? All hair and lipstick?'

I nodded. 'She's a frightful tart,' Topaz continued. 'Did you know that car isn't even hers?'

I began to feel a little dizzy. 'I thought you meant *Annabel* stole Dave from you.'

'Oh *no*. Annabel's too busy sleeping with the local bigwig.'

116

'Good Lord! Who?' I wondered if Pete knew he wasn't the only one. I did a quick mental run-through of important Gipping men – bank manager, postmaster, Rotary club president – none were under fifty.

'I'm talking about bloody Lady Trewallyn.'

For a moment, I was speechless. Perhaps that was why Dave had turned pale when I mentioned the black Porsche? He'd trodden on old Chester's toes.

Topaz grabbed my hands and pulled me towards her. 'You've *got* to help me get him back, Vicky. You've *got* to.'

Worried that she might lapse into another crying fit, I decided placating her was best for now. 'All right. Let me think of something.'

My thoughts no longer dwelled on a steamy *ménage à trois*. There was no question of me obliging Topaz if Lady Trewallyn were involved. The woman had terrified me the first time I saw her at her husband's funeral. It wasn't just the scarlet lipstick or the speed with which she attacked Chester. There was something menacing about her. The more I thought about it, the more I realized Lady Trewallyn would make an ideal High Priestess. Good God! Dave might be involved, too! Devil worship was the crème de la crème of kinky sex. It would take a rare man to turn that down – especially one who seemed already partial to pain.

I recalled Dave's expression in the photograph Chester had stolen. Although Dave had been virtually impaled on a stake in the centre of the yew hedge, he looked quite cheerful.

Topaz squeezed my arm. 'Well? Have you thought of something?'

'I'm working on it.' I needed to be careful. Topaz might well be a mine of information but she was definitely unbalanced. 'Of course, the *Gazette* is very grateful for all your help.'

'That's all right. I love watching people.' She yawned, sinking her head on my shoulder. 'I'm awfully sleepy. If we don't go soon, I'll be absolutely useless.'

'Let's get out of here.'

Fortunately The Copper Kettle was only a five-minute walk away. I helped Topaz to her feet and steered her towards the door.

'Vicky, you're so nice to me,' Topaz mumbled, clinging to my arm. 'Let's be lesbians. Women are so much more *loyal.*'

It was cold outside. Dark clouds scudded across the sky, threatening rain once again. Yellow streetlamps lit our way along the deserted High Street. How wrong I had been about Gipping being a dull town. The place seemed riddled with sex fiends and perverted Satanists.

Lady Trewallyn consumed my thoughts. Surely if she had unlimited access to the dark arts, the appearance of her American friend would not pose a threat. Wouldn't she simply zap him with a handy curse? I didn't believe in all that rubbish about curses, but many people did – especially in the country. Yet, the way she physically attacked Chester that morning in the churchyard was emblazoned on my memory. Perhaps they were lovers from the past and *Kandi* was her bedroom nickname?

I shivered, partly from cold, partly from excitement at my excellent speculation.

'Vicky, you're trembling,' said Topaz. 'Don't worry. I'm nervous, too.'

The fresh air had sobered her up. With a sinking heart, I remembered her earlier suggestion that we should have a lesbian trial run.

We had reached The Copper Kettle. I'd have to think quickly if I wanted to avoid a Topaz temper tantrum. 'I think it's best that we keep our relationship on a professional level for now.'

'I don't agree,' she said stubbornly. 'You said you'd help me win Dave back.'

'Of course I will. But this is dangerous work. Besides, company policy says that employees can't mix business with pleasure.'

Topaz sighed. 'I suppose it's a necessary sacrifice.'

'Have you got your key?'

She pulled it from her pocket and looked furtively around before lowering her voice to a whisper. 'When do I get my next instructions?'

The last thing I wanted was her showing up willy-nilly at the office. 'I'll come by tomorrow after work. Remember, you are a *secret* informer. Mum's the word!'

'So who is my target? The American or Lady Trewallyn?'

I wasn't quite sure and needed to buy some time. 'I'll let you know. It's all hush-hush at the moment.'

Topaz frowned. 'What about Barbara? Won't she say something? She was there when you hired me.'

'I'll handle her.' The whole thing was spiralling out of control. Judging from Topaz's handling of my scarf, I already knew she was capable of blackmail.

Topaz gave a quick scan of the street – somewhat pointless considering we'd been standing outside, exposed, for several minutes.

'Tomorrow,' she mouthed, silently. And, with a brief tap on my shoulder, she disappeared inside the cafe.

I set off for home, horribly aware that I had just made my life one thousand times more complicated. Not only had I impulsively offered Topaz a non-existent job, I had embroiled myself in some bizarre love triangle that involved the prime suspect in a murder case. If that weren't bad enough, I'd stumbled upon a band of devil worshippers.

It was time to do some research of my own. Where did Sir Hugh meet Lady Trewallyn? Hadn't Sir Hugh's first wife died of a heart attack, too? The *Gazette* was proud of its long history of wedding and funeral reports – and, thanks to Barbara's meticulous record keeping, it shouldn't be too difficult to find out. Barbara was old – she might even remember it first-hand.

Suddenly my landlady's face popped into my head. Why hadn't I thought of her before? As owner of Cradle to Coffin Catering, she'd know the scoop on everyone from Gipping, literally from birth to death!

As I spent half an hour a day with my landlady between the allotted breakfast time of 7.45 a.m. and 8.15 a.m., it would be a perfect opportunity to ask a few friendly questions over tea and toast.

But wait! How could I have been so insensitive! I'd always assumed Mrs Poultry's sour demeanour was a personality flaw despite Ronnie's romantic ravings.

Well, I'd soon remedy that. I'd offer her the job as my informer first thing in the morning. And what's more, I bet she'd be delighted.

18

'Gipping is such a lovely town,' I said, stirring my breakfast cup of tea.

As was her usual habit, Mrs Poultry hovered out of my line of sight just behind my shoulder sucking one of her ghastly cough drops. A friendly morning cuppa seated together at the kitchen table was not our routine. Her modus operandi was to wait until I had downed the last sip of tea and swallowed the final crumb of toast. Then she'd pounce, whisking away my plate and mug to declare the kitchen closed.

'I expect you were born here?' I said with a pleasant smile.

'Why?'

'Just curious.'

'Have you finished your toast?'

'Not yet.' Honestly! I still had half a slice left on my plate. I reached for the strawberry jam.

'Only a teaspoon, mind,' grumbled Mrs Poultry. 'It's expensive.'

My landlady was proving to be annoyingly uncooperative. Recruiting an informer was always a delicate situation – unless it was someone like Topaz who had actually volunteered to be my High Street spy.

As a rule, no one liked to think others viewed him or her capable of telling tales. Dad found a mixture of flattery, as in *'we couldn't do this without you'* along with the gentle reminder that *'if you don't help us, we will be forced to'*, was generally most effective.

Unfortunately, Dad's tactics failed with Mrs Poultry. Having hoped to soften her up, I'd praised her catering service to the heavens. I'd raved about her cold cuts and gone into raptures over her moist fruitcake, but to no avail. My landlady's response had been a cold, hard stare.

'Your job must be fascinating. Christenings, weddings, funerals!' I went on gaily. 'And the name – Cradle to Coffin Catering – sheer genius!'

Still silence. But I was undeterred. 'How wonderful to be present at the beginning of life and then at the very end. Imagine what you must see.' I chuckled indulgently. 'Gosh. I'm sure you know everything there is to know about the citizens of Gipping and that is why—'

'Are you asking me to spy on my customers?' Mrs Poultry snapped.

'Of course not,' I said, feeling the colour rise in my cheeks. 'Being new to Gipping, I sometimes need help on family backgrounds: little details that might add a bit of local colour to the odd obituary or—'

'Most certainly not!' Mrs Poultry was indignant. 'Cradle to Coffin Catering has a reputation for privacy. Why else would our motto be "Delicious, Dependable, and Discreet"?'

'No, I was—'

'You journalists are all the same!' She snatched my plate away – I still had one crust left – and stomped over to the kitchen sink.

Blast! I'd better try something else. I racked my brain and suddenly remembered Ronnie Binns. Every woman likes to feel

122

she's adored. Why not Mrs Poultry? Assuming she'd been a widow for many years, she had to be desperate for manly attention.

'Oh! I almost forgot to tell you, I ran into Ronnie Binns at Gipping Dump,' I said, watching my landlady struggle to drag on a pair of Marigold gloves. Her arthritis was playing up. 'He seems rather enamoured with you. He might even be available.'

Mrs Poultry spun towards me, her eyes flashing with rage. 'How *dare* you discuss me in that *disgusting* manner with that smelly little man!'

'He thought you had nice dustbins.' I faltered, unprepared for such fury. 'Your name only came up because he was telling me about the mutilated chickens he'd found at The Grange.'

Mrs Poultry – Marigolds on at last – folded her arms across her ample bosom. 'And why should that interest me?'

'Are you familiar with the steamy bestseller *Voodoo Vixens*?'

'Utter filth. I don't read penny dreadfuls and neither should you,' Mrs Poultry exclaimed. 'Why?'

'In the book, there's a sacrificial scene, which I think is . . .' Abruptly, I fell silent. A peculiar prickling feeling ran up and down my spine. Dad would call it my inner-warning system. Why would Mrs Poultry – she, who never gossips – be interested? Unless? I was struck by an alarming thought. Adopting as casual tone as I could muster, I asked, 'Do you know Annabel Lake?'

'No. Should I?'

Of course, she would deny it! What a fool I was. Hadn't Annabel boasted of having other informers? Mrs Poultry was practically the eyes and ears of Gipping! Even though my landlady had not attended Sir Hugh's actual funeral service, she *still* went to spy on the proceedings. I saw her with my own eyes hiding under that hawthorn bush in the cemetery. And who would have paid her to do that? Annabel! Thank God I hadn't told Mrs Poultry about the poison and chicken feathers. It would have got right back to Annabel!

I looked at the kitchen clock and scrambled to my feet. 'Goodness! It's eight fifteen. Thanks for breakfast. Must go.'

At least one part of the mystery would be solved today. Being Friday, the newspaper was going to press. If Annabel were lying, Trewallyn's death in mysterious circumstances would be plastered over the front page. If she were telling the truth, then there were three people who knew what had really happened to Sir Hugh – Coroner Sharpe, myself, and the killer.

I'd had no luck questioning Mrs Poultry but I knew Coroner Sharpe liked me. We had a lot in common – funerals, for starters. Perhaps, during my lunch hour, I would pick up egg-and-cress sandwiches for two and pop into the morgue for a quick chat.

Call it inheriting my father's genes, but instinct told me that whatever appeared on the front page today was just the tip of the iceberg.

19

The reporters' room was a den of frenzied activity. Unfortunately, it was all focused around my desk. I watched, with a growing sense of unease, as Pete rifled through my drawers and sifted through files.

'Vicky! Where the hell are they?' Pete's cigarette was stuck to his lower lip and bobbed up and down as he spoke.

A ghastly feeling of premonition washed over me. 'What are you looking for?'

Annabel emerged from under my desk. 'They're certainly not down there.'

'Randall's photographs,' said Pete. 'Trewallyn's death is back-page news. Hedge-jumping is a page-one *go*!'

'Page one? You're giving me a page one?' Annabel had *not* been lying! Yet, how could the heart attack story be true? I'd have to think about that later. Right now, I was faced with the chance of a lifetime and couldn't even follow through. It just wasn't fair.

'It's no good without photos,' said Annabel, thrusting her boobs in Pete's direction. 'My tractor story is perfect. I've got a super snap of the new Massey-Ferguson.'

'Who cares about tractors? Hedge-jumping spells danger. Man against nature. Right, Vicky?'

I smiled weakly. 'Right.'

'So come on, *think*! Without Randall's photos, we're dead.'

'I thought you Girl Guides were always prepared,' Annabel sniggered, adding, 'I bet she's lost them.'

'I heard that!' I said defensively. 'I know exactly where they are.'

No sooner had the words tumbled out of my mouth, I knew I'd made a mistake. Chester had stolen Dave's photographs. They had gone for good.

'Well, what are you waiting for? Go and get them,' Pete said.

'They're at home.' This could give me some time to find a solution.

Pete glared. 'You'd better be quick. We're leaving for Plymouth in twenty minutes.'

'I'll go right now. In fact, I'll deliver them later to the printers myself.'

'You don't have a car,' Annabel said with a hint of malice.

'I'll catch a bus.'

'Annabel's got a bloody car,' Pete said sharply. 'She'll drive you home. Make sure you're both in Plymouth by four.'

'Plymouth!' Annabel's face lit up with delight. 'Wow!'

'Vicky, we'll set your stuff last.' He stalked back into his office, shouting, 'And don't screw up.'

I felt the colour drain out of my face. 'It's okay, Annabel. I don't want to be any trouble.'

Annabel grinned. 'Oh my God. We're going to *Plymouth*!'

As well as housing our newspaper's printing press, Plymouth's main claim to fame was the presence of HMS *Dauntless*, home to several hundred sailors and every single woman's fantasy.

'If we get there early enough, we might be able to drive by the docks,' Annabel enthused. 'We might even see *sailors*!'

It was amazing that the prospect of lithe men in uniforms

suddenly became more important than Annabel's farm machinery on page one. However, I was far too distracted with the knowledge that this week's publication rested entirely on my shoulders. The newspaper had never missed an edition – even during World War II when bombs were dropping on Plymouth itself.

The BMW was parked outside the office. Topaz was sitting in the cafe window, clearly taking her job as High Street spy extremely seriously. The moment she saw us she ducked out of sight.

'How many times have you been to Plymouth?' Annabel started the engine and we eased into the morning traffic. 'Don't you just *love* that town?'

'Too many times to count,' I said curtly. The truth was, I had never been to Plymouth and, perhaps on any day other than today, and with anyone other than Annabel, I would have relished an opportunity of spending a day in such a nautical metropolis.

Annabel pulled up outside 10 Rumble Lane. I was relieved to see Mrs Poultry's ancient Morris Traveller gone. My landlady was out.

'Hurry. We're on a deadline,' said Annabel.

Scrambling from the car, I ran up the path and hurried around the side of the house to the downstairs loo window. Pulling my Swiss Army knife out of my pocket, I slipped the window latch and clambered in. Why should I pay extra money for the privilege of having a key?

Minutes later, I returned to the car brandishing a sealed white envelope containing a coupon for washing powder. Hopefully it would give the illusion that the envelope contained *something*. When I handed it to Pete and he discovered the contents, I would simply accuse Mrs Poultry of accidentally picking up the wrong one on her way to the supermarket. It would be a genuine mistake and surely no one got fired for those? They'd have no choice other than to run the story minus the photograph.

'To Plymouth!' I said, with forced gaiety.

Annabel executed a perfect three-point turn. As she floored the engine, Topaz's remark about the BMW's ownership came back to me.

'This is such a lovely car. Is it yours?'

'Of course it is.' Annabel bristled. 'Just what are you trying to say?'

'I wondered why you keep the plastic on the back seat and the dealer paper on the floor.'

'What's it to do with you?'

'Just making conversation,' I said quickly. 'It's nothing like Pete's. That van of his is filthy.'

Annabel smiled, seemingly relieved to change the subject. 'God! Isn't it awful? He's such a pig.'

We laughed, and for the first time, I felt a pang of longing. I had so hoped we'd become friends. This adventure to Plymouth would have been fun. Instead, I had to pray for a miracle of biblical proportions to magic Dave's photographs into the envelope on my lap.

The BMW roared past a signpost to the Cricket Pavilion. 'Stop the car!' I shouted.

Annabel hit the brakes, fishtailing on the wet road. 'Good grief! What's wrong?'

Dave Randall lived at Cricket Lodge, which had to be close to the abandoned Cricket Pavilion. He might even be home and was bound to have some extra photographs lying around.

'I need to check the spelling of one of Trewallyn's mourners,' I said eagerly. 'She lives down that lane.'

Annabel was not thrilled. 'Vicky, you are the absolute *limit*. Couldn't you have telephoned?'

'She doesn't have a landline,' I declared. 'Remember? There aren't any mobile phone signals until—'

'I'm perfectly aware of what happened to the belfry at St Andrew's and more besides. As a matter of fact . . . never mind,' Annabel said. 'Wait a moment. This is about Salome Steel, isn't it?' Her face contorted with envy. 'Ha! I knew it! I knew you were up to something!'

'No, it isn't. Honestly.' *Blast!* In all the excitement, I'd forgotten all about *Paparazzi Razzle*! The tacky London tabloid had offered a substantial sum of money in exchange for exposing the identity of the author of *Voodoo Vixens* who was rumoured to be hiding out in Devon.

'And you thought I wouldn't guess?' Annabel was triumphant. 'Everybody wants to know who she is.'

'Well, I don't.' Frankly, I thought it was appalling. I knew how important it was to keep one's anonymity. My parents wouldn't be in Spain if it hadn't been for A HANDSOME REWARD FOR ANYONE WHO COULD REVEAL THE WHEREABOUTS OF NOTORIOUS JEWEL THIEF, THE FOG. It made my blood boil.

'Okay. We'll *share* the money,' Annabel went on. 'Can't be more fair than that.'

No! If Annabel accompanied me to Dave's house, the cat would be out of the bag.

'Wait!' I said desperately, trying to think of a plan. 'Annabel, I swear on my mother's grave that I have absolutely no idea who Salome Steel is.'

'Oh my God, Vicky. I didn't think!' Annabel's expression unexpectedly softened to one of compassion. 'How utterly tactless of me.' She patted my arm. 'You poor thing. Pete told me you were an orphan.'

'It's all right,' I muttered, squirming with the lie. 'Life goes on.'

'But I forced you to think about . . .' Annabel hesitated. 'Your mother's *grave*.'

'Don't worry about it. I don't,' I said, adding quickly, 'What I mean is, I throw myself into my work. It keeps my mind occupied. That's why I'm so particular when it comes to accurate reporting.'

'You're right. You can't bring back the dead.' Annabel nodded. 'Let's check that mourner's spelling. The reputation of the newspaper is at stake.'

She swung the BMW off the main road and into a lane flanked by ten-foot-high hedges. Moments later, Annabel was forced to slow the car down to a snail's pace as the lane became narrower and narrower. It was like driving into a leafy funnel.

Hedges that were neatly clipped at the entrance became denser and more unruly. Razor-sharp branches fell in swaths across the BMW's roof and bonnet, scraping the sparkling paintwork.

Annabel began to panic. 'Oh my God,' she said, wincing, as yet another branch whipped across the windscreen, splattering it liberally with sap and flies. 'This is *ridiculous*!'

'We must be nearly there.' I gripped my notebook tightly. I'd seen horror films that started out like this: two girls on a deserted road leading to terror and a grisly death.

Suddenly, what little road surface there was fizzled out altogether and became a mud-rutted cart track flooded with such an expanse of water it resembled the English Channel.

'Right,' Annabel said. 'That's it! This is *stupid*!' She cut the engine and folded her arms petulantly across her magnificent bosom. 'I'm not driving any farther.'

'Oh dear.' I was relieved. 'We can't exactly turn around.' The hedge on either side was a snug half inch away – even opening a car door would be impossible. Perhaps we'd get stuck! We'd be trapped in this wilderness for weeks, or at least until the paper went to print. My job would remain secure at the *Gazette* because everyone would be so relieved we had not been murdered.

Annabel restarted the car. Her face had flushed an ugly red that clashed with her auburn hair. I'd never seen her so angry and was even a little afraid.

We edged towards the water. Surely she wasn't planning on driving through it! I grabbed her arm. 'Annabel, it could be really deep.'

'Hold tight.' She revved the engine several times as if waiting for the starter's gun at Le Mans. All of a sudden, the BMW took off. Its tyres kicked up fountains of muddy water as we ploughed on through the giant puddle, which, mercifully, turned out to be quite shallow. Annabel whimpered as clods of thick sludge spattered onto the roof, windows and bonnet. Then, the BMW, suddenly freed from the constraints of its watery trap, catapulted onto dry ground with a loud *whoosh.*

I couldn't help but be impressed at Annabel's expertise and once again felt that familiar sense of inferiority at yet another of my rival's talents – rally driving.

'There's the Cricket Pavilion,' I said as the fuzzy outline of a building appeared through the mud-coated windows. It was a typical end-of-war prefabricated one-storey rectangle with a high-pitched corrugated iron roof. A rotting veranda, covered in graffiti, bordered one outside wall overlooking what used to be a perfectly groomed cricket ground. It now lay knee-deep in nettles and rusty bicycle parts, inexplicably standard fare for abandoned buildings wherever the location. A large sign said DANGER, KEEP OUT!

'No one can possibly live here,' moaned Annabel. 'This is so *unprofessional* of you, Vicky.'

I saw a wooden sign pointing to a path through the pine forest.

'Cricket Lodge is through there.'

Annabel scowled. 'How do you know she's home?'

'She's an invalid,' I said, and flung open the passenger door before Annabel could stop me. 'Won't be long.'

Leaving Annabel staring at her beloved BMW, now slathered in thick, sticky muck, I set off at a trot and took the path through the woods. All noise was cushioned from the thick pine needles that lay strewn on the path. There was a small clearing up ahead where I could make out a chimney.

Cricket Lodge was creepy. The former hunting lodge was a miniature replica of The Grange. It even had a pair of ugly gargoyles peering from beneath the gabled roof. I was surprised that Dave Randall actually *lived* on Trewallyn's property.

Perhaps he even worked for the family? Suddenly, I recalled his words that day in the nook when he had said he 'had to return for the pheasants'. Could Dave be Trewallyn's resident gamekeeper?

'Hello! Anyone home?' I rapped smartly on the front door. There was no reply. 'Dave? Mr Randall?' My voice sounded stifled, swallowed up by the dense thicket that surrounded the lodge. Perhaps Dave was outside logging or indulged in some other manly occupation? Perhaps he would be stripped to the waist, washing himself from a wooden barrel filled with rainwater like the gamekeeper in *Lady Chatterley's Lover*? I'd often been sceptical of life mirroring art, but here was a perfect example. If Topaz was right, Dave Randall was a modern-day Mellors complete with his very own Lady Chatterley. I might even surprise them going at it right now!

At the rear of the house, the silence was even more oppressive, filling me with unease. A second grassy track ran east towards the pine forest beyond. Hugh's Folly could just be seen peeping above the treetops. Trewallyn's estate was vast. Annabel and I must have taken the old, disused trade entrance.

Suddenly, the hairs on the nape of my neck stood on end. The back door lay wide open. I'd always pooh-poohed the saying as a cliché used by fraudulent mediums, but now I was experiencing it for myself: something evil was lurking inside Cricket Lodge.

A chilling thought struck me. I had seen Chester write down Dave's address when he stole the photographs. He knew where Dave lived. Dave could already be dead. Chester had shown a violent side in the churchyard. The way he had tossed Lady Trewallyn over his shoulder indicated a man with a temper. Poor Dave could have been strangled, stabbed, or even shot – Chester was American and was sure to have a gun.

Annabel's car horn broke the silence, snapping me back to reality. I shrank against the lodge wall. The killer could still be inside cleaning up.

I longed to flee but I was a professional reporter. If it turned out that Dave was, indeed, dead, I'd be first on the scene, which would make a terrific page-one scoop. Life was so ironic. Although Dave's photographs had been stolen, he was still fated for front-page fame.

Annabel's horn tooted with three insistent beeps. There was no time to lose. I braced myself for the inevitable bloodbath within and stepped inside.

20

Inside, Cricket Lodge was gloomy. A low ceiling and two tiny, leaded windows, thick with dust and cobwebs, flanked a decorative Victorian fireplace. What natural light there was came through the open door.

My heart was pounding as I scanned the main living area for any sign of blood. The place was dank and smelled of old socks. Newspapers and a few empty beer bottles littered the floor. A broken carriage clock sat on the mantelpiece alongside several hedge-jumping trophies.

A worn brown sofa not exactly conducive to romantic athletics was pushed against one wall. A coffee table acted as the dining area, still holding the remnants of what, I guessed, could be breakfast.

The place seemed deserted but I had to make sure. Two closed doors led off the tiny living room. Presumably one was the bedroom.

If Dave were dead, he'd most probably be in the bathroom, a favourite location for killers, due to the convenience of post-death clean up. No doubt, Dave would be naked, his toned and muscled legs – an athlete's perk – draped over the lip of a bathtub filled with bloodied water.

I stared at the door with trepidation. Frankly, I felt a bit frustrated. If Dave were alive, I'd be trespassing, and therefore, it would be an offence to rifle through his stuff. If he were dead, I'd be tampering with evidence.

The BMW horn blared imperiously again, galvanizing me into action. I marched to one of the two doors and threw it open.

It was Dave's bedroom and even more dingy than the main living room. As my eyes slowly adjusted to the gloom, a disturbing sight awaited me on Dave's pillow.

Steeling myself to approach Dave's bed, I was confronted with a legless chicken corpse with a hideous orange-speckled head. Some kind of note was pierced with a hatpin and secured to the poor bird's breast. With a gasp, I realized it was the very same chicken I'd seen lying in the dustbin at The Grange. I'd tossed the Chinese carton on top of it with the sweet-and-sour sauce leaking out of the bottom. There was no doubt now. Chester and Lady Trewallyn were in cahoots.

The note would confirm my suspicions. With trembling fingers, I eased it aside with my pencil, astonished to find it wasn't a note – it was a photograph.

In fact, it was one of the two photographs that Chester had stolen from my desk two nights ago. The hatpin, holding the photograph in place, was stuck exactly through Dave's trophy, which he clutched so triumphantly to his heart.

This was the proof I needed. Topaz was right. Witchcraft was rampant in Gipping. Lady Trewallyn must be the High Priestess and Chester the Horned God. They'd murdered Sir Hugh and now Dave was the next victim. The fact that the chicken legs were missing must be part of the ritual. I'd watched enough horror films to know that the warning came first – then the killing.

I was in a dilemma. I could take Dave's photograph, clean it up, and present it to Pete. No one would be any the wiser and I'd get my page one. Or, I could hold out for the bigger scoop and catch the coven of witches red-handed.

I was no longer satisfied with getting a front-page story. I was determined to reach for the stars. My story was going to go national.

21

Having decided to leave the crime scene intact, I jogged back to the waiting BMW with quite a spring in my step. I had a secret – one that gave me a peculiar sense of power over Annabel. Pete's anger at my failure to produce Dave's photographs would soon be forgotten once I told him I suspected devil worship was rife, right here in Gipping.

Meanwhile, I still had to face the journey to Plymouth and Annabel's pubescent ramblings on the merits of mariners. I couldn't afford to make her suspicious – after all, I was, for all intents and purposes, facing the sack. It might be prudent to switch tactics and throw myself at her mercy. With fame and fortune heading my way I could afford to be generous now. Let her have her glory. Let her dreary tractor story have its day.

As I reached the clearing, Annabel was waiting. In one hand was my white envelope, in the other, the washing powder coupon. What appalling nerve to open an envelope that was not addressed to her!

'You're such an idiot!' she yelled. 'Pete will be furious!'

Bracing myself for more insults, I took a deep breath and

assumed an expression of utter anguish. 'Annabel! Whatever's wrong?'

'Just as well I checked,' she said. 'You picked up the wrong envelope!'

'Oh *no*!' I cried, clasping my hands to my chest and sinking to my knees. I'd seen black-veiled women in Jerusalem adopt such a stance at the Wailing Wall and thought it a brilliant technique to generate compassion.

Annabel's mouth dropped open in surprise. 'Steady on,' she said, helping me to my feet. 'If you go on like that you'll have a heart attack.'

'What am I going to do? Oh God!' I turned away, feigning deep distress, and staggered towards her muddy car.

Annabel hurried after me. 'Look, calm down. It's not the end of the world.' So proving the curious theory that when one person is hysterical, the other automatically affects an air of supreme calmness, no matter what the circumstances.

'Let's get in the car and we'll sort it out.' Annabel opened the passenger door and guided me in – even putting her hand on my head to prevent an accidental bump on the doorframe. 'Hush now. Hush,' she crooned.

I was stunned at just how effective my mock breakdown had been. Annabel's concern seemed genuine. Frankly, it was embarrassing.

Annabel started the car and we headed back down the lane. I stole a quick glance, expecting to see her deep in concentration, formulating a plan to save my job. Instead, she wore a smug smile. It was only when we smoothly negotiated the muddy water hazard, and Annabel did not even wince, that I became suspicious.

'What should I do?' I said, inserting a note of fear into my question.

'I have a plan. I'll deal with Pete. He'll believe anything I tell him.'

'Oh, Annabel, you are so clever!' I gushed. 'How I *wish* I was like you.'

'Lots of people want to be me, Vicky.' Annabel checked her reflection in the rear view mirror and smiled at herself. 'Let me give you a tip on dealing with men. It's simple.' She paused dramatically. 'Lather them with compliments, make them feel important, and they'll be like putty in your hands. Look at Pete!'

'He's *so* in love with you.'

'I know,' she said with a sigh. 'And he's not the only one.'

'It must be lovely to be you.'

'Let me tell you something,' said Annabel in a confidential tone. 'I used to be just like you. Awkward, naive—'

'Actually, I'm just—'

'No! Let me finish,' she commanded. 'Then, something awful happened – I don't want to talk about it – but it made me realize that life is all about looking after number one. If you don't look after yourself, no one else will.'

Annabel's philosophy surprised me. Beneath her brash exterior, could there be some childhood hurt? I'd always assumed she'd been born with a silver spoon in her mouth – everyone knows it's hard to feel sympathy for someone with a new car. Yet whatever had happened in Annabel's past was surely small fry compared to the burden of having a criminal for a father.

At the main road, she stopped the car and turned off the engine. To the left led the road to Plymouth, to the right, Gipping.

'I've decided. I'm taking you back to the office,' she said crisply.

'What about Plymouth?'

'Stop worrying.' Annabel reached over to the back seat, retrieved a manila folder, and tossed it into my lap. 'Take a look at that.'

It was a glossy photograph of a Massey-Ferguson tractor. A strapping man, dressed in dungarees and cap, leaned out of the cab holding aloft – inexplicably – a duck.

'Fortunately I came prepared,' said Annabel with a smirk. 'Pete will *have* to use this on page one now.'

This time my paranoia was real. 'What are you *really* going to tell Pete?'

Annabel thought hard for a moment. 'How about your stupid landlady picked up the wrong envelope? No one gets fired for a genuine mistake.'

An hour ago, we would have been in complete agreement. But now I knew I just couldn't trust her. 'I'd rather explain it to Pete myself, in person.'

'It's up to you, of course.' Annabel paused, adding darkly, 'If you can handle him, please, go ahead.'

'You said all I had to do was flatter him.'

'You know how he expects to be flattered, don't you?' Annabel said, readjusting her bra and giving each magnificent breast a reassuring pat.

I had a good idea of how Annabel *flattered* Pete. I wasn't born yesterday.

'Yes, of course,' I said with a confidence I did not feel, and looked down at my pathetic double-A cups. 'He's just a man, isn't he?'

Annabel simply raised her eyebrows at me, started the car again, and turned towards Plymouth. Barely half a mile later, we joined the rear of a long crocodile of cars stuck behind a huge tractor, which was travelling at a mind-numbingly slow pace.

'This is all we need,' grumbled Annabel, checking her watch. 'Five miles an hour!'

'How lucky that you had your tractor piece with you,' I said, pointedly.

'Luck had nothing to do with it. As I said, you've got to look after number one. Watch out for any opportunity and go for it. The world is not for the weak, you know!'

As I suffered another pang of inferiority, I couldn't help feeling she would get on well with Dad. I wondered what he would make of my smug rival. He'd never feel undermined by her patronizing attitude. In fact, Dad would use it to his advantage.

'Gosh. You're so right!' I said, adding slyly, 'You must have some terrific informers.'

'Oh! Anyone can have informers, Vicky.' Annabel sneered. 'No, it's *instinct* that gets a story. Either you've got it or you haven't.'

'Which is why you dismissed Ronnie's *devil* chickens at the dump as ridiculous,' I said, hoping with all my heart that was true.

'Exactly.'

'Wow.' This was good news. Annabel really hadn't seen the connection between Trewallyn's dustbins and the dump, after all. 'What other qualities make a good journalist?'

'I'm glad you feel you can ask me,' Annabel said. 'A lot of people don't because they're threatened by my expertise.'

'Not me,' I said through gritted teeth. 'I just want to learn.'

'Let me see . . .' Annabel mused for a moment. 'Persistence.'

'Persistence? Can you give me an example?'

'Well . . .' Annabel considered. 'Ah yes! When Brian the messenger didn't show up as planned, I didn't just sit around and cry. I drove to The Marshes and waited outside his flat until he came home.'

I swear my heart missed a beat. 'You *saw* Brian?'

Annabel smiled at the memory and went on. 'A few choice words of flattery and a twenty pound note bought me a copy of the report.'

'A copy?' I was stunned. 'With no questions asked?'

'Really, Vicky, don't be dense.' Annabel sighed. 'Of course, I flashed my press card. Brian accessed Sharpe's files from his home computer.' She chuckled. 'In fact, he seemed very relieved to see me.'

'I bet he was!' I joined in with a laugh that was a little too hearty. 'I suppose he made some excuse about not showing up at the *Gazette*?' It was a gamble but I had to know.

'Who cares? It's the results that count.'

But I cared. Why hadn't he told Annabel he'd already given

141

the report to me? Brian's behaviour made no sense. Perhaps he was smitten by my *cool* eyes and was hoping I'd come and demand an explanation in person. Or, was he trying to cover up Sir Hugh's murder by replacing the original report with a fake?

I knew then exactly what I had to do.

'What's the matter, Vicky? You've got a funny look on your face.'

'You're right,' I said with an exaggerated sigh. 'I don't think I'm up to handling Pete, after all.'

Annabel looked smug as if to say I told you so.

This time, her snotty attitude didn't bother me. I'd phone Pete at the printers and tell him I was pulling my hedge-jumping story. The reason? Dave was implicated in a far bigger scandal. When asked for details, I'd imply it had something to do with sex but that I couldn't say more until I'd double-checked the facts.

It was time to pay Brian a friendly, but discreet, visit at the morgue. But first, I'd have to deal with Pete's wrath.

22

Pete's reaction to my revelation was mixed. After ranting for a full five minutes about what I expected him to do with an empty front page, he'd become enthusiastic about the forthcoming scandal. Of course, I'd sprinkled the word *tits* liberally into my findings as well as alluding to sexual deviations that involved at least two naked participants brandishing whips. I'd also made Pete promise to let the story belong exclusively to me – otherwise I might leak it to the *Bugle*.

Barbara's disappointment on learning there would be no first-hand accounts of sexy-sailor sightings in Plymouth today was not as acute as I feared. She had the two wooden doors open, which separated reception from the window display recess fronting the High Street.

'It's about time the window was changed,' I said, joining her as she stood, hands on hips, surveying a rather sad collection of *Gazette* artefacts – an ancient, cracked carthorse collar, a threadbare scarf with GIPPING GROWLERS, the local football team, written in faded black on yellow, and a photograph of the Gipping carnival queen being crowned in the pouring rain.

'Can you believe it, Vicky?' Barbara's eyes shone with

excitement. 'Pete actually agreed!' She fanned her face dramatically and chattered on, 'I was so nervous I didn't sleep all night.'

'What happened?' I had no idea what she was talking about and stole a quick glance at my watch. If this turned out to be one of Barbara's lengthy he-said-she-said stories, I'd miss Brian at the morgue. It closed at five.

'As you know, *Paparazzi Razzle* is launching its Find Salome Steel celebrity search competition,' Barbara cried. 'So, I thought, if Salome Steel lives in Devon, it was only right that the *Gazette* should have a contest, too!'

'What a clever idea, Barbara,' I said, though to be honest, I felt sorry for Salome Steel – yet another victim of our society in which cherished anonymity counted for nothing. Dad was right when he said the country was going to the dogs.

'What's the prize?'

'A day trip for two to Land's End . . . frankly, Vicky dear, I know how much you love to chat but . . .' She pointed to the window. 'I must get on. What do you think about a black banner with *Voodoo Vixens* written in red?' She cocked her head to one side. 'Perhaps a skull?'

'Sounds lovely.'

'Be a dear and give me a leg up.' Barbara grasped the three-foot ledge with both hands and raised one knee, giving me a good view of scarlet bloomers edged with black lace. Recoiling from the sight, I hoisted her inside and made my escape.

23

The morgue was conveniently located at the rear of Gipping Hospital behind a walled courtyard. It was a plain one-storey, redbrick building with a flat roof and no windows, presumably to deter morbid members of the public from taking a peek inside.

Leaving the bustling High Street behind me, I turned into Scalpel Avenue, a quiet residential area lined with dreary Edwardian semidetached houses with bay windows and pebbledash.

One of these belonged to Messrs Ripley and Ravish, Gipping's popular funeral directors – Dust to Dust with Dignity. Both hearses were parked on the street – a rare sight during these cold, winter months when hypothermia was one of the main causes of death in the elderly.

It had only just turned 4.30 p.m. With any luck, I'd catch Brian before he went home.

Before I could give this more thought, a horrible sound of grinding gears broke the afternoon silence. A familiar Morris Traveller crawled into view. I was surprised to see Mrs Poultry, who generally only drove into town on market day. If she'd been visiting someone at the hospital – unlikely, as she had no friends that I was aware of – the car park entrance was off the High Street. Then, it occurred to me that Scalpel Avenue eventually became Tripp Lane, which offered a shortcut to Refuse Dump Drive, Gipping County Council Rubbish Tip – and Ronnie Binns! Even though Mrs Poultry had appeared repulsed by my message that Ronnie praised her dustbins, she must have changed her mind.

I gave a friendly wave as my landlady slowly drove past me at her usual snail's pace but she pretended not to notice. Her eyes were focused on the road ahead, and her hands tightly gripped the steering wheel. Obviously she was embarrassed that I'd guessed what she was up to. I wasn't offended. The thought that I could be responsible for bringing two lonely senior citizens together in such a cruel world brought a warm glow to my heart.

I strolled through the morgue gates and was greeted by the sight of Coroner Sharpe's black Mercedes Coupé parked alongside a sky blue Vespa LX 50. Recalling Brian's sky blue scooter helmet, I assumed the bike was his. With half an hour to go, I looked around for somewhere to wait unseen.

A few yards away, tucked against the wall bordering the road, stood a large black and red striped bin marked HOSPITAL WASTE. Ignoring the stench, I settled behind it to wait.

I didn't have to wait long. Moments later, the tinkling sound of female laughter caught my attention. I dropped to my knees and peeked around the side of the Dumpster.

Coroner Sharpe was helping a woman wearing a stylish Burberry raincoat and matching bucket hat into the passenger's seat of his car. She had her back to me but from the way she squeezed his arm and whispered something into his ear, I could tell there was a sexual je ne sais quoi between them, especially when Sharpe pinched her bottom.

Sharpe climbed into the driver's seat, started the engine, and turned the Mercedes around. As he passed my hiding place, I practically fainted. The passenger in the front seat wore a slash of red lipstick. It was Lady Trewallyn!

So much for the grieving widow! I thought back to the graveyard scrap at Sir Hugh's funeral when Chester tossed Her Ladyship into the mud. Even then I'd thought Sharpe had rubbed Lady Trewallyn's dirty knees with just a little too much enthusiasm. Tragedy must have thrown them together.

Annabel had said it was instinct that made a good journalist. My instinct told me that Lady Trewallyn had bewitched the old man just like she had bewitched Dave Randall – enough to get Sharpe to change the coroner's report.

I found Brian, wearing pale green overalls, washing down the floor in the morgue lobby. He took one look at me, threw down the mop, kicked the bucket of soapy water in my direction, and tore off down the corridor, vanishing through a door marked EXIT.

I ran after him – narrowly avoiding breaking my ankle on the slippery floor – and burst out of the building. I raced to the front but was only in time to hear the sound of the tinny Vespa motor erupt into life. Brian had fled. *Blast!*

I felt excited knowing Brian had something to hide! Far from discouraged, all I needed to do was go back to the *Gazette,* find his address, and go and wait – just like Annabel had done.

As I turned into the High Street, a police car tore past with its lights flashing and siren screaming. A growing stream of pedestrians hurried after the disappearing vehicle, chattering with speculation.

'What's happened?' I said, catching up to an elderly man with a limp.

'There's been a traffic accident down at the bridge,' he shouted, breaking into a lopsided trot. 'Hurry, or you'll miss it.'

For a moment, I hesitated. With Pete and Annabel in Plymouth, there was only a small window of time to find Brian's address. However, being first on the scene of a scoop had to take priority.

I took the shortcut through the market square, over the wooden stile, and along the footpath that bordered the River Plym. Ten minutes later, I reached the front line.

The situation on the bridge looked dire. A mangled sky blue Vespa protruded from beneath the front of a bright yellow combine harvester. My stomach turned over. *Brian!*

What rotten luck! I hoped he wasn't hurt – my front page splash depended on his evidence.

I pushed my way through the surging crowd as a policeman was trying to cordon off the bridge with two orange cones. 'Back! Back, I say!'

To my dismay, I saw it was DC Probes. The moment he noticed me, his face lit up. 'Help! Over here.'

At last I had a chance to flash my press card, and the crowd parted like the Red Sea. The combine harvester spanned the ancient narrow bridge. Brian must have attempted to squeeze through the small gap, overbalanced, and tumbled under the giant wheels.

'I can't hold them,' Probes said exasperated, as a particularly aggressive woman in a red-checked headscarf stamped on his foot and told him that Plym Bridge was a notorious accident black spot and should have been closed to traffic years ago.

'Has anyone seen the motorcyclist?' I said anxiously, scanning the curious faces.

'Yeah. That's him, I reckon,' said a thin youth sporting a nose stud. 'Right there.' He pointed to what seemed like a pile of green rags lying under the chassis.

'Oh God, *Brian!*' I felt sick, having never been this close to a broken body before – especially one that had been very much alive a few minutes ago.

Moments later, a wailing siren and flashing blue lights broadcast an ambulance approaching. It sped towards the bridge at high speed, scattering the crowd and flattening the traffic cones. Two ambulance drivers – one fat, the other thin – leapt out. They hurried to the rear of the vehicle, opened the doors, and pulled out a stretcher.

A second panda car screamed to a halt alongside the ambulance and disgorged its occupants, one of which was the obnoxious Detective Inspector Stalk. He strutted over to the nosy bystanders, brandishing his truncheon and looking dangerous.

'Move along, move along! There's nothing to see here.' His commanding tone had the desired effect. The crowd meekly obeyed and moved away, apart from the woman with the red-checked headscarf, who stopped to pick up Brian's sky blue helmet. 'Souvenir,' she said proudly, to anyone who would listen.

'Now, madam, put that down!' ordered Stalk. 'It's evidence.' The woman flung the helmet to the ground in a huff and stomped off.

The paramedics dragged the rags out from under the vehicle. Brian's face was a bloodied mess, his left leg skewed at a weird angle.

Stalk peered at the body. 'He looks dead to me.'

I turned away in anguish. Even though I was deeply distressed, a fabulous headline popped into my head: RIDE WITH THE WIND, DIE WITH THE WIND – A BIKER'S FINAL JOURNEY! A VICKY HILL EXCLUSIVE!

The fat paramedic solemnly handed Stalk a blood-stained leather wallet. Stalk examined the contents and gestured for me to come over. 'You're from the paper, aren't you?'

'Yes, that's right. Vicky Hill.' My heart started to pound. What if Stalk found out I was the last person to see Brian alive? Hadn't I stolen the coroner's report? What about impersonating Annabel? Oh God! What if they found out about my parents? *Get a grip, Vicky.* I pinched my arm, whisked out my reporter notebook, and forced myself to sound professional. 'Do we have an identity yet?'

'These kids don't fasten their helmets. Think they're immortal,' grumbled Stalk, thumbing through the wallet. 'Name's Dickson, Brian Dickson.'

'With a *K* I presume?'

Stalk ignored me and turned to face Probes who was walking towards us, his face ashen. 'Probes! You'd better track down the parents and all that crap.'

'Yes, sir,' Probes said, adding with a sob, 'He was an orphan – just like Ms Hill here.'

I turned red, having already forgotten that particular lie of mine.

'Was Brian Dickson a friend of yours?' said Stalk.

'No,' I said quickly. 'I've never seen him before in my life.' I bit my lip and looked away. How could I have used that old line? It had guilt written all over it!

'I was talking to Probes.' Stalk regarded me with suspicion.

Probes made a peculiar gulping sound, and whispered, 'Looks like he's not going to make it, sir.'

To my surprise, my eyes welled up with tears.

'Are you all right?' Probes touched my arm, his voice heavy with concern.

'I'm fine, thank you. I've never seen . . .' My voice cracked. Was it possible I was in some way responsible?

Brian's body was gently loaded onto the stretcher. Probes took the white sheet from one of the paramedics. 'May I do the honours?'

Without warning, Brian sat bolt upright. His eyes snapped wide open. We all leapt back in surprise. I actually screamed.

Manically, Brian pointed his finger straight at me. 'You! Annabel! You must . . .'

I shrank back, mortified.

'Steady, lad,' said the thin paramedic, trying to push Brian back down and force an oxygen mask over his face. Brian knocked it to the ground.

'Let him speak,' Probes cried. 'Oh God, Brian. Talk to me.'

'She knows about us,' Brian raged on. 'She knows!'

'What's he talking about?' Probes turned to me. 'Who knows?'

'He's delirious,' I said desperately.

'Annabel!' Brian gasped, struggling for breath. 'You've got to—'

And with that, he immediately slumped backwards onto the stretcher.

150

'He's gone,' observed the fat paramedic dispassionately.

Probes elbowed him aside and began to administer CPR. 'Come on,' he shouted. 'Come on, *Brian!*'

'He's a goner, I tell you. Internal bleeding.' The paramedic turned to me with a shy smile. 'Name's Steve, by the way.'

'Hello. Nice to meet you,' I said, glad to add another new contact, yet too traumatized by Brian's deathbed revelation to want to chat. 'Is he really dead?'

'Those combine harvesters are built like tanks,' said Steve as we watched Probes valiantly pound Brian's chest and breathe into his bloodied mouth. 'I've seen a lot of farmers come to grief under those wheels.'

Out of the corner of my eye I watched the young policeman's frantic efforts. He'd appeared so nerdy when we first met at the *Gazette,* yet seeing him in action I felt an unexpected frisson of desire even more shameful, given the circumstances.

Finally, Steve dragged Probes away and covered Brian's face with the white sheet. It was hard to believe he really *was* dead.

'Hope we meet again,' Steve said with a wink. 'What was your name? I'll give you a jingle.'

'Vicky Hill.' It felt wrong to be chatted up, somehow.

The paramedics completed their duties, slammed the doors shut, and sped off with the siren blaring once more.

Probes sank onto the edge of the pavement with his feet in the gutter. He shook his head in despair. 'Too late. It's all my fault.'

I was surprised at his obvious distress. Had he been *that* friendly with Brian? Or perhaps he was an exception to the rule – a copper with a heart?

Other than what remained of Brian's Vespa and the abandoned combine harvester, we were alone on the bridge. Stalk must have closed down all access to this side of town until the tow truck arrived to remove the wreckage.

Probes removed his helmet, slowly scratched his head, and frowned. 'Brian *knew* you.'

'Everyone knows me,' I said gaily. 'It's the nature of my job.'

'No, he was specific.' Probes looked at me, his expression hard. 'And he called you *Annabel*.'

'He didn't *call* me *Annabel*. He just shouted, "*Annabel*"!' I looked at my watch. 'Good Lord. Must go. Barbara will wonder where I am.'

'Ms Hill!' Probes scrambled to his feet. 'I know the press and the police don't often see eye to eye but . . . Brian was my friend.' He paused. 'If you know of anything strange, any tiny detail, however insignificant—'

'Sorry. I don't.' Was he deranged? I would never tell a copper about Pete's arrangement with the dead youth. That would make me a snitch. Dad said that those that snitched to the cops were the scum of the earth. But wait! Wasn't Brian's demise just a tragic accident?

'Surely you don't suspect foul play, officer?' I had to admit the possibility took away some of my own guilt. Hadn't I simply startled him? Maybe he thought I wanted my money back – after all, he had been paid twice for information.

Probes stepped towards me. I caught a whiff of his manly scent. All that hard work attempting to resuscitate Brian had given him a musky odour. He lowered his voice. 'Can we speak off the record?'

Here we go, I thought, and braced myself for the inevitable Columbo moment.

'Ms Hill, I want us to work together. Share information. Help the community.'

'Sounds lovely,' I said, glad that Dad wasn't here. 'You go first.'

Probes took a deep breath. 'I think we're looking at another murder.'

'*Another* murder?' *Blast!* Brian must have revealed the contents of the original report to his friend Probes, after all. Probes must have known all the time about my part in the tragedy. *Tread carefully, Vicky.*

'Are you saying someone else is dead?' I pretended to look shocked. 'Good grief! Who?'

Probes scowled. 'I think it's best if we continue this conversation down at the station.'

They were the words every man, woman, and child feared most of all. Imminent arrest. I'd be the proverbial 'helping police with their inquiries', the classic, good-as-guilty, cheap one-liner, fed to the media.

Probes couldn't prove a thing. The coroner's report was safely hidden in the water tank in my attic bedroom. Brian hadn't asked for a signature when he gave it to me, either. It was his word against mine – and let's face it, dead men tell no tales. I was sitting pretty. In fact, maybe it wasn't so bad, after all. Just how well had the redheaded copper known Brian, and why had Probes said it was all *his* fault? I was sure I could wheedle the truth out of him with a few cunning questions.

Rewarding Probes with a dazzling smile, I adopted a tone of supreme confidence. 'I'd *love* to come to the station! Shall we meet there at four?'

24

I was no stranger to police stations. Many a time I'd sat with Mum in the waiting room when Dad was helping the coppers with their inquiries. We'd pass the time reading magazines like *Prison Widow* and *Inside – Outside: Surviving Without Your Man.*

As Probes escorted me along the bustling corridors, I smiled cheerily at everyone I passed for fear they'd believe I'd been arrested.

'In here,' Probes said, ushering me into a cramped corner office filled with traffic cones – I counted eleven and hadn't even peered into tucked-away nooks and crannies.

'Kids steal them,' Probes said, kicking one out of the way. He gestured for me to take a plastic chair in front of a desk stacked with files. 'Please sit down. I'll go and make some tea.'

'Lovely. Milk and one spoonful of sugar.'

Probes left the room. I leapt to my feet, not wanting to miss this marvellous opportunity to inspect a policeman's office.

One wall was devoted to photographs of stolen silver ranging from silver tea services and tankards to candelabras. I couldn't help thinking that Dad would have been tempted by the silver

George III footed tea urn. He always had a weakness for a nicely turned spigot.

Alongside the photographs was a detailed street map of Upper and Middle Gipping. Red flags indicated those homes that had been burgled. Blue flags showed which homes had burglar alarms. Dad colour-coded his maps, too, only he included yellow flags for homes with guard dogs. I made a note to tell Dad that whomever masterminded this operation was a genius at disabling burglar alarms. To my practised eye, I calculated the stolen loot must be worth at least seventy-five thousand pounds on the black market.

Stepping carefully over the traffic cones, I headed for the far wall next to the window. Written in black marker and underlined were the words, SUSPECTED ECO-WARRIORS. A photograph of a group of nine men and women standing outside Tesco Superstore looking tough was accompanied by the question *Do You Know These People?* Apart from the sullen faces of the Barker brothers – no surprises there – the others were not local. Only one looked really dangerous – a heavyset man in his early twenties, with a shaved head and handlebar moustache: WANTED FOR FAILURE TO APPEAR IN COURT, DRIVING WITHOUT A LICENCE AND DISTURBING THE PEACE.

'Vicky! Can you open the door?'

Probes had returned with two mugs of steaming hot tea balanced on a cardboard shoe box. Carefully, he set them down on the desk. 'Before we continue, there is something I have to tell you.' Probes placed his hands firmly on top of the lid, his expression grave.

I hated that awful phrase because it always accompanied bad news: Grandma has died; the cat got run over; Dad has gone to prison.

'We have reason to believe there were two coroner's reports,' Probes said. The shock caused me to violently inhale, sending me into a ghastly coughing fit. Probes hurried to my side,

155

thumping my back with the same abandon he had used to pummel the dying Brian's chest.

'Stop!' I gasped, pushing him away. 'I just need a minute.' I put my head in my hands to compose myself. *Blast!* Taking a deep breath, I went on, 'I thought Sir Hugh had a heart attack.'

'Brian had mentioned something unspeakable about . . . chickens.'

'Chickens?'

Probes leaned towards me and said in a low voice, 'Under our new arrangement, what I'm about to show you is strictly off the record.'

'Arrangement. Of course.' I made a silent prayer for Dad's forgiveness.

Probes took a deep breath, his expression grave. 'Do you believe in witchcraft?

'Like *Buffy the Vampire Slayer*?' I suggested.

'No, not vampires!' Probes answered vehemently, and stared at me hard. 'I must know, Vicky. *Do* you believe?'

I hesitated, unsure how to answer. *Was* I a believer? Suddenly, I was aged eight, back in Sunday school learning about Christian miracles. The vicar was enthusing about Jesus's feeding of the five thousand with a mere five loaves and five fish. I had scornfully pooh-poohed the idea and told the vicar he was dreaming. He had been predictably furious and promptly banished me from the group for heresy.

'Of course I do,' I said.

'I found this in Brian's motorcycle pannier.' Probes slowly opened the lid and lifted out a miniature toy Vespa. A tiny wax figure was tied to the bike with black thread. Its face was stuck with pins. The front of the scooter was mangled.

I shivered. 'That's horrible.'

'And this, too.' He tipped the box towards me.

I felt the colour drain out of my face. Two chicken legs complete with gnarled claws, also bound with black thread, nestled on a bed of straw. My first thought was they must belong to the same bird languishing on Dave Randall's bed.

It was hard to tell. When you've seen one chicken leg, you've seen them all.

'Of course, I've seen this sort of thing before.' Probes's voice was tinged with excitement. 'But not in Gipping.'

Probes picked up a magnifying glass and stepped around the desk beside me. I caught a whiff of his musky masculine scent as he stood close to my shoulder. 'The wax figure is called a *poppet*.'

He handed me the glass. 'Incredible attention to details.' The front wheel of the miniature motorbike lay twisted under its crossbar. A piece of paper the size of a postage stamp was glued to the back of the rear wheel.

'Is that a licence plate?' I was fascinated. The tiny figure wore painted-on black simulated leathers. The doll even sported a sky blue paper helmet.

'It's Brian, isn't it?' My skin prickled. 'What's written on his jacket?'

'Black Sabbath.' Probes had a feverish glint in his eye as he leaned forward to whisper in my ear. 'I believe there are *Satanists* in our midst.'

'Wow. Black Sabbath!' I said. 'So, Brian was a Satanist?'

'Black Sabbath is a band from the seventies, you fool,' Probes said exasperated.

'There's no need to be rude.' I was indignant. 'I didn't have to come here and help you out.'

'Forget it. This is a waste of time.' Probes turned on his heel and went to stare out of the window.

'I'll be off, then.' I couldn't leave his office quick enough. 'Bye.'

Yet, the moment I closed the door, I realized I'd let my hot temper get the better of me. Wasn't the whole purpose of going willingly to the police station to find out why Probes was so upset about Brian's death and why he'd said, 'Too late! It's all my fault!'

It was no good. I'd have to go back. Perhaps even I would try Columbo's just-one-more-thing tactic and see how Probes liked it.

Quietly, and without knocking, I pushed open the door and froze in my tracks.

Probes stood motionless in front of the desk facing me. He had a curious glazed expression in his eyes as he held the model of Brian and his motorcycle up high, as if offering them to the stars. Solemnly, he placed the gruesome poppet back into the shoe box.

I lurked in the doorway and watched in astonishment as the copper began to wave his hands in a clockwise, then counter clockwise direction. He mumbled some kind of incantation before finishing the ritual off with a spectacular double-arm wheel, knocking over a plant and pot of pencils. He seemed in a trance.

Probes picked up a glass jam jar that held something that looked remarkably like rabbit droppings. Tipping a few into his hand, he sprinkled them over Brian's 'remains' in the shoe box, and shouted, '*Exitus acta probat!*'

Good grief! I couldn't believe it! Probes was one of them! I'd caught a member of Gipping Constabulary right in the act of a Satanic ritual!

With a mixture of horror and elation, I backed out of the door, turned, and walked away as quickly as I could without attracting attention. The policeman's nerve was astounding. He was practising witchcraft in broad daylight. And in a police station!

Outside, I took in great gulps of fresh air and replayed the events over and over again. But my elation turned to gloom when I realized that without a camera to record this sensational discovery, the story was worthless. It would be the copper's word against mine. I swore at that moment *never* to be without a camera again.

As I walked home, I started to put the pieces of the puzzle together. Was Probes a witch or a warlock? I'd better check the correct terminology. Perhaps Probes *and* Chester had left the billet-doux on Dave Randall's bed as some kind of warning? Good grief! Could I be next?

When I made the decision to become a top investigative reporter, I knew that exposing the truth was not supposed to be a walk in the park, but I never expected to face such peril in *Gipping*.

As I turned into Rumble Lane and saw Mrs Poultry's Morris Traveller parked in the drive, I was unexpectedly glad that she wasn't the kind of nosy landlady who would bombard me with meaningless questions. I knew Topaz was expecting her next set of instructions but I couldn't face a post-mortem on our intimate drink last night. I was tired and wanted to soak in a long, hot bath. I'd run it shoulder deep – to hell with Mrs Poultry's no-more-than-three-inches-of-water rule.

Later that night, I lay in bed unable to sleep. I kept remembering Brian's warning, 'She knows about us!' and 'You've got to—' Got to *what*? I wished I could ask Mum and Dad for their advice.

It had been over a month since I got the second postcard from Costa Brava. It simply said *Business is good.* Sometimes, I wondered if they actually received the letters I sent, care of Ye Olde Matador Pub. No doubt it was too risky for them to write. Thanks to the stringent antiterrorist laws now in force, even Her Majesty's mail is no longer secure.

I was surprised to feel a tear crawl down my cheek and drip into my right ear. *Buck up, Vicky.* It was vital I get a good night's sleep. Tomorrow being Saturday, the *Gazette* hit the newsstands. If Annabel managed to snag her front page scoop, after all, she would be utterly unbearable.

I must be ready.

25

'Congratulations on making the front page,' I said to Annabel, who seemed far from happy about her tractor exclusive. She sat hunched over her desk, gloom seeping from every pore.

'I didn't even get a by-line,' Annabel moaned, flapping the newspaper at me. 'I've also been obliterated by a giant advertisement for fertilizer. Look!'

It was true. Apart from the small paragraph advertising the merits of purchasing a Massey-Ferguson, half the page was devoted to a revolutionary new fertilizer, said to be *the* dung of the twenty-first century.

'No offence, Annabel,' I said, pointing to the – what I considered, lame – lead headline, GIPPING CAT BURGLAR STRIKES AGAIN: A PETE CHAMBERS EXCLUSIVE! 'If I had to choose between reading about burglary or dung, I'd pick burglary every time.'

Annabel scowled. I gave a reassuring pat on her shoulder. When one's rival seems crushed, it's only sporting to show a little sympathy. 'Disappointment comes with the job – it's the nature of the beast.'

'You've got some nerve!' Annabel shook me off.

'What do you mean?'

Annabel thrust out her chin. 'Pete told me you phoned and promised him some fantastic and far-fetched scoop.' She gave a nasty snicker. 'You said you'd discovered – I quote – "Randall is part of a depraved sex ring run by perverts and the local council."' Annabel rolled her eyes in mock despair. 'Honestly, Vicky! How desperate can you get?'

I'd discounted pillow talk. Of course, Pete would have told her, verbatim. 'I'm not desperate at all. It's true.'

'What's more' – Annabel tossed her head, nostrils flaring – 'you told Pete . . .' She paused to draw in an indignant breath. '"Annabel has a *little* tractor story that I suppose might do."'

'But we agreed—'

'I wanted to tell him myself.' Annabel seethed. 'It was my idea. I *saved* your hide. You owe me.'

Was she that insecure? 'For God's sake, it's not the end of the world.'

'It may well be. For *you*,' she declared in a threatening voice. 'Well, all I can say is you'd better not be making all this up. Pete phoned the nationals yesterday: the *Mirror,* the *Sun* – even *The Times.*'

'The Sunday papers?' I was stunned. Sunday papers were the crème de la crème of journalistic aspirations.

'Pete expects your *sensational* story by Friday, a mere six days away,' Annabel declared. 'By *noon.*'

'Trust me, it won't be a problem,' I said, confident of my recent discoveries. All I needed was proof. I already had a couple of catchy headlines: GIPPING'S LADY CHATTERLEY LOVE TRYST AS HUSBAND LIES DEAD: A VICKY HILL EXCLUSIVE! Or if I could get proof: LOCAL BOBBY TURNS BLIND EYE AS YANKEE WIDOW DABBLES WITH DEVIL. A corrupt copper would be the icing on the cake. Plus, nailing a policeman would make my dad proud.

'Well, don't get too complacent.' Annabel sneered. 'I've been secretly working on a *shocking* front-page exclusive for ages

161

now. Even Pete doesn't know what's it about,' she went on. 'But the moment he does, he'll lose all interest in your little story anyway because mine has money, sex, power, and *photographs*!'

'May the best scoop win,' I said, conscious of a peculiar leaden sensation in my stomach.

Pete strolled in. 'Morning, girls.' He seemed in a rare good mood. 'Vicky! How is my young star this fine morn?'

'Excellent, thank you,' I said, smiling broadly and shooting Annabel a triumphant look. Usually he focused on her, but today I was queen. I had to admit it was quite lovely.

'Any news yet?' he said with a leer. 'Got any titillating scraps to keep us going?'

His question caught me off guard. 'There was a fatal motorcycle accident yesterday.'

Pete guffawed. 'Very funny. That's what I like about you – your sense of humour.'

'No, there really was. Brian Dickson, the messenger from the coroner's office.'

'Our Brian? Bugger!'

'Was he a friend of yours?' I asked, all innocence, delighted to take the heat off me.

'You could say that.' Pete glanced over at Annabel. 'Did you hear that? Brian's kicked the bucket.'

I followed his gaze to see Annabel's features undergoing extraordinary contortions. She was in the process of mouthing at me, 'Don't say anything about me. Pleeease.'

Pete scowled. 'What the hell is wrong with your face?' Annabel looked mortified.

Pulling one of the two cigarettes lodged above his ear, Pete stuck it between his lips and lit up. Inhaling deeply, he turned to me and said, 'Give me the facts.'

'Brian collided with a combine harvester on the Plym Bridge,' I said bluntly. 'The cops have the details.'

'Annabel,' Pete growled, 'I want *you* dealing with the police on this one. Just you.'

162

Annabel, all business, got to her feet and picked up her shoulder bag. 'I'll get to the station right away.'

I panicked. 'No! It's too soon.'

'Why?' Pete and Annabel chorused.

'The cops have to tell Brian's parents first.' I knew he was an orphan, but they didn't. 'Police procedure.'

'You're right. Bugger.' Pete thought a moment. 'Vicky, into my office.'

My heart skipped a beat. All newfound smugness evaporated in a flash. It had always been Annabel who had been cloistered for hours in Pete's office. Had I replaced Annabel in every way imaginable?

Pete paused in the doorway. 'Let's have a cuppa?'

'I'll make it,' I gushed.

'No, Annabel will do it. Annabel!' he barked, ushering me in front of him. 'Tea!'

Annabel's mouth dropped open, appalled. 'I don't do tea.'

'Milk and one sugar, please,' I said.

'Come on, Vicky.' Pete gave my behind a playful tap, pushed me into his office, and shut the door.

'Over there.' Pete pointed to a tartan two-seater sofa pushed against the wall. It made the cluttered room even more cramped. Framed family photographs were on his desk.

Oh God. This is it. My knees began to tremble violently. Surely, he wasn't really expecting some form of sexual gratification this early on a Saturday morning? It was only nine thirty.

'Don't be shy.' Pete started to rifle through his top drawer, clearly oblivious to my confusion. 'I know it's your first time in here, but it won't be the last.'

My hands felt clammy, and my mouth went dry. What could he mean, *first time*? Resigned to my fate, I slipped off my shoes and lay back on the sofa. We'd have to be awfully quick. Annabel could appear at any moment with the tea. My mother's words echoed in my ears: 'Be careful what you wish for.' I'd

163

wanted to lose my virginity. I only had myself to blame. Pete was going to be the lucky man, and in an odd way, I was doing this for the greater good of journalism.

'What are you doing?' he said, horrified at my prone state. A sheet of paper was in his hand. 'Are you tired?'

Startled at his tone, I sat bolt upright.

'This is no time for *naps*,' he admonished. 'There's work to do, young lady. I've got a lot riding on your scoop.'

'Sorry,' I mumbled, surreptitiously slipping my shoes back on. 'Didn't sleep well last night.'

'This is a list of town officials.' Pete handed me the paper. 'It would be bloody brilliant if we could nail old Rawlings.'

'The mayor?'

'Serve him right. He's always a right bastard to the press.'

I took the list and, with a sinking feeling, realized my life was becoming more complicated by the second.

'And that stuck-up magistrate. What's her name?'

'Margaret Pierce?' I said.

'Yeah. See if you can catch them both at it.'

'What if they're innocent and—'

'Pierce is trying to win the Conservative seat in the next election,' Pete said. 'This will put the kibosh on her chances.'

I felt uncomfortable. 'Doesn't she do a lot of charity work for the blind?'

'Who the hell cares?' Pete said cheerfully. 'Charity work doesn't sell newspapers. Sex does.' A light seemed to go on in his head. 'Do you think they're into bondage?'

Thankfully, a tap at the door saved me from replying. 'Enter!' Pete shouted.

Annabel came in, labouring under a tray with three mugs of tea. 'I thought I could join you,' she said with a grimace, putting the tray down on the desk with a thump. It wasn't *that* heavy!

'I've added milk and sugar,' Annabel said, handing Pete a mug emblazoned WORLD'S GREATEST DAD! She pointed to the remaining mug. 'Yours.'

164

I noted mine was black and oversteeped. 'It looks perfect.'

Clearly, she was determined to join us. Annabel took her mug and sat down beside me on the sofa.

Pete's phone rang. 'Yep?' he said, pausing to listen to Barbara chirping on the other end of the line. 'Well, tell him it's too damn bad.' He slammed the phone into the receiver. 'That Randall bloke is in reception, pissed off that he wasn't in the paper this week.'

In all the excitement, I'd forgotten my promise to Dave. I jumped up. 'I'll just pop downstairs—'

'I wonder what happened to his *photographs,* Vicky?' said Annabel spitefully.

'Wait a minute,' Pete said, 'isn't Randall your informer, Vicky?'

'Sort of.' I refused to look at Annabel.

Pete thought long and hard. 'Tell him we'll run his story next Saturday instead. The nationals will carry your scoop on Sunday.' He rubbed his hands together with glee. 'We'll be the *preview.* "You read it here first." Brilliant!'

'Good idea, Pete,' said Annabel, making a supreme effort to draw attention to her cleavage by adjusting her bra. 'Unless a more *sensational* story comes in, right, Vicky?'

'Take Randall to lunch,' Pete enthused, ignoring Annabel's last remark. 'All expenses paid. Keep the receipts.'

'Great,' I smiled, edging towards the door. As Pete took a hefty swig of tea, I caught Annabel's attention with a gentle cough and crossed my fingers, mouthing, '*Pax*?'

Grudgingly, she raised her fingers in response and muttered, '*Pax*.' It may be a childish playground agreement, but considering we both had secrets to trade, it would seal the deal.

Walking downstairs, I felt giddy with relief. Dave's unexpected appearance had been my saving grace. Not just from the clutches of my lecherous boss, but Dave's very presence had substantiated my story and made me look *really* professional. I'd also learned a vital lesson. Annabel believed it was feminine wiles that clinched the hot assignments. Yet here was I, a whisker away from the scoop of the century, and still a virgin!

Of course, I needed proof, but now with the go-ahead to take Dave to lunch, there was nothing like alcohol to loosen the lips and reveal sordid secrets. I pushed open the door to reception to greet my informer.

Life was good.

26

'I'm not in it, am I?' Dave fumed, flapping Saturday's edition of the *Gazette* in my face. 'You promised me a full-page feature!'

Dave's outburst left me speechless. Where was the mild-mannered man of three days ago when I had had to practically *beg* for his hedge-jumping exclusive? How typical of the general public who claim to shun fame, yet once they get a taste of it, become prima donnas.

'Can I get you a cup of tea, Mr Randall?' asked Barbara sweetly, popping up from behind the counter.

I stifled a yelp of surprise. Barbara was wearing an African tribal headdress made of scarlet feathers and colourful beads. Around her neck was a necklace dangling with plastic skulls.

Dave shot me a nervous look. 'No, thanks.'

'Barbara's organizing a—'

'Competition. Whoever guesses the real author of *Voodoo Vixens* wins a coach trip for two to Land's End,' Barbara enthused, adjusting her headdress that had begun to slip rakishly over one ear. 'Every week the *Gazette* will provide a vital clue.'

'That's right,' I said, glad that Barbara's astonishing getup had thrown Dave off his stride.

Barbara whipped out a makeshift entry form. 'Just jot the name down on here and pop it into this box.' She tapped a padlocked, wooden letterbox on the counter. 'If you need privacy, you can use the nook.'

'Thanks, Barbara. Mr Randall, shall we?' I turned to face the nook and was startled by another transformation.

Plastic green palm fronds were pinned to the star-spangled curtain. A pair of maracas sat on top of a large drum on the floor to the right of the entrance. I guessed that Barbara had borrowed the props from the Gipping Bards, our local amateur dramatic society who had just put on a highly ambitious production of *The African Queen*.

As I feared, the interior of the cramped nook supposedly resembled the inside of an African hut. A black and white striped fake-fur rug was nailed to the back wall. The green plastic chairs were covered in old sacking. But the *pièce de résistance* was the pale brown giant stuffed gorilla sitting on top of the small table.

'I want an explanation.' Dave's bewilderment returned to annoyance. 'And it had better be good.'

Mustering one of my warmest smiles, I said, 'The truth is, Dave – can I call you Dave? My editor wants to do a rather *special* story on you. A front page.'

'He does?'

'In fact, he's asked me to take you to lunch tomorrow,' I said. 'All expenses paid.'

'You're on,' Dave said. 'But I want the photographs back.'

'Absolutely.' I was perplexed. Chester had them – apart from the one on Dave's bed that was pinned to the chicken legs. Did this mean Dave had not seen them at all? Could someone have removed them secretly? And if so, why?

'Shall I go and fetch Mr Randall's pictures?' Barbara whisked the curtain aside. I should have known she'd been eavesdropping. 'Are they upstairs?'

'Actually, those photographs were great but we need more

action shots,' I said quickly. 'Limbering up; on the launch pad; maybe one at Cricket Lodge – "A champion relaxes at home." That kind of thing.'

'Oh, yes, *yes!*' Barbara clapped her hands in raptures. 'Our readers will love it.'

Dave grunted something unintelligible but looked pleased. 'Come to Riley Lane on Wednesday afternoon. There's a virgin box I'd like to sink my teeth into.'

'I'm sorry?' I blushed scarlet. Barbara clutched at her throat and had to steady herself against the back of my chair.

'Boxwood, or *Buxus handsworthii* to the layman,' Dave said wistfully. 'Wide, thick, and untouched. Six glorious feet of splendour.'

'Sounds perfect,' I said, struggling to suppress the image conjured up by Dave's reference to a virgin. 'I'll still need to discuss details over lunch, of course. How about tomorrow, shall we say—?'

'Noon. The Three Tuns.'

As I watched Dave exit the reception – giving Barbara a wide berth – I thought things had gone rather well. I'd neatly sidestepped the tricky missing photograph situation, got an interview *and* a photo shoot. This reporting lark could be fun especially now I had an expense account.

'I hope he's not expecting a pricy lunch,' Barbara said, automatically throwing a damper on my good spirits. 'You *do* realize that as a trainee reporter, you aren't eligible for reimbursement?'

'Pete said—'

'It's up to Wilf. He's the editor.' She gave me a conspiratorial smile. 'My advice is to eat before you go. If he has any manners, he won't eat if you don't.'

The Three Tuns was renowned for their Sunday lunch special and I'd been looking forward to it. But, sometimes we all have to make sacrifices to get what we want. If I had to pay for Dave's confession myself, it would be money well spent.

27

It was just after noon. The public bar, heavy with cigarette smoke, was packed with Sunday lunchtime drinkers.

'How big is a pitcher of scrumpy?' I asked Arthur, the ruddy-faced barman. A sign behind the bar at The Three Tuns pronounced the local cider as today's house special at the bargain price of five pounds.

The barman produced a huge jug and thumped it down on the counter. 'Bloody good value, if you ask me.'

'I'll take it. Two glasses, please,' I said, certain this would last long enough to get Dave to admit to his affair with Lady Trewallyn and, with luck, discovering Sir Hugh's body.

'You be careful now. That's real Devonshire scrumpy.' Arthur grinned. 'It'll knock your socks off.'

'It's only cider, isn't it?'

'Only cider? Only *cider*?' Arthur laughed, shaking his head.

Dave was sitting at the same corner table I'd shared with Topaz the other night. He was sprawled in a high-backed wooden bench, his eyes closed.

I set the pitcher and glasses onto the table with a thump. 'Scrumpy,' I announced. 'Wake up!'

Dave's eyes popped open. 'Bloody hell. A whole jug!'

Carefully, I poured out two glasses, noting the liquid was the same colour as urine, and sat down beside him.

'What are you having?' Dave said.

'I had a huge breakfast.' I hoped he didn't hear my tummy grumble. 'But, please, have what you like.'

'Roast beef and all the trimmings. Yum.'

Barbara was wrong about Dave's manners.

'Whoa!' Dave exclaimed, taking a sip of scrumpy. 'This is the real local stuff.'

'Cheers!' I had a lot riding on this good local stuff.

'Bottoms up,' said Dave as he put away another glass.

Gingerly, I took a sip. It tasted of apple juice. Frankly, I couldn't understand what the barman was fussing about. Scrumpy seemed perfectly harmless to me.

'So come on, Vicks, what's new at the *Gazzzzzette*?' Dave's elbow nudged me hard in the ribs. 'You know everyone and everything. Right?'

'Yes I do,' I giggled. 'I *really* do.'

Three empty pitchers stood on the table. Lunchtime drinkers had morphed into early evening revellers. I never realized what a lovely pub The Three Tuns was, filled with lovely people.

After the second pitcher of scrumpy, I had decided to abandon the interview. Dave had pointedly ignored all my attempts at casually dropping his employers into the conversation. Instead, I'd had to listen to him droning on about hedge-jumping and the merits of the Fosbury Flop versus the traditional Straddle. He was quite sweet, really. I felt flattered that he shared his dreams with me – including the wild hope that Plym Valley Farmers would sponsor his lifelong ambition to introduce hedge-jumping as an Olympic sport. Even when I pointed out that some countries – Africa or parts of the Middle East – did not have hedges to practise on, he took it well. I could

171

see why Topaz was so enamoured. He really was one of the most attractive and wittiest men I had ever met.

'I've done all the talking,' Dave announced suddenly, slapping his hand on my knee. 'Enough of me. Tell me about you. Tell me everything.'

'I make a lot of tea,' I said, conscious of his hand resting on my knee and rather liking it.

'You cover funerals, don't you?' Dave said casually.

I felt flattered. He *knew* who I was! He must have been asking about me. He must fancy me.

'All of them,' I said, taking another sip of scrumpy. 'Yep. That's me. I haven't missed one since I moved to Gipping.' I raised my glass. 'I am the funeral *queen*.'

Dave's glass clinked mine. 'To the funeral queen!'

'Hurrah!' I cheered. We drank and slammed the glasses down on the table.

'So why did Annabel Lake cover Sir Hugh's obituary?' Dave said suddenly.

It was as if an ice-cold bucket of water had been thrown over my head. Dave wanted to talk about Annabel. How typical! Every man on the planet wanted to talk about *her*.

'She's my junior, you know,' I said haughtily. 'She went to The Grange with our chief reporter – still training, obviously. Actually, it's taking the names at the church that needs *skill*. I remember everyone who goes to my funerals – and even those who don't.'

'Wow.'

'Like you.' I wagged my finger at him. 'Naughty Dave. You should have gone to poor Sir Hugh's.'

'I had my reasons.' A shadow crossed his face. 'The fact is—'

'Another scrumpy on the tab, Vicky?' said Arthur, looming over us with a fresh pitcher in hand.

'Yes, yes. On the tab. Bye.' What rotten timing! Somewhere through my alcoholic haze, I sensed Dave's confession brewing.

'You'd better watch out for her, Dave,' said Arthur with a wink. 'She's a bit of a goer.'

Dave leered. 'Really?'

'Ask her about her lady friend – the girl from The Copper Kettle. Nudge, nudge, wink, wink. Know what I mean?' With a chuckle, Arthur bore off the empty pitchers, pushing his way back through the punters to the bar.

Dave turned to me, intrigued. 'What's he on about?'

'Let's talk about the funeral.'

'I'd rather talk about you.'

Blast! The barman had ruined everything by his stupid remark. Dave tucked a strand of hair behind my ear. His touch felt electric. What if I reverted to Topaz's original plan of suggesting a threesome, after all? If it got me closer to Lady Trewallyn, then so be it.

'Topaz and I aren't serious,' I said, putting my hand on Dave's thigh. 'It's just some harmless fun.'

Dave looked puzzled. 'Topaz who?'

'You are hilarious!' I laughed. Men were so transparent. Now he was interested in me, he wanted to conveniently forget she existed. 'Topaz Potter. Your *ex-girlfriend*?'

Dave's expression remained blank. I lowered my voice. 'We thought you'd fancy a *ménage à trois*?'

'A what?'

'Threesome.'

Dave's eyes widened with disbelief. He leapt up, waved at Arthur, and gave him the triumphant double thumbs-up.

Sitting back down he threw his arm around my shoulders. 'Listen, luv, I don't know who the hell she is, but I'm game.'

'Wait a minute!' This was a turn up for the books. 'You swear you *really* don't know her?'

'Cross my heart and hope to die.' He stuck his finger in my ear. 'Do you like that?'

I jumped, feeling all atwitter. If only I hadn't drunk so much scrumpy. Why would Topaz lie about Dave? I must sober up. 'Do you know a man called Chester Forbes?'

For an answer, Dave belched and yanked me to my feet. 'I'm

ready!' Mum always said that when a man's passions were aroused, all the blood ran out of his brains. Dave was living proof.

'Mr Forbes came into the *Gazette* and specifically asked for you.' I pressed on, determined. 'He didn't seem to think hedge-jumping was environmentally friendly.'

'Yeah, well, can't please everyone.' Dave grabbed my bottom. Hard. 'But I think I know how to please you.'

A quiver of lust unexpectedly swept through my loins. Any further questions I may have had for Dave vanished. He was available. He was free – and he wanted to please *me*.

'Your place or mine?' Dave wiggled his eyebrows seductively.

'Yours.' I didn't fancy losing my virginity in my attic room with Mrs Poultry overhearing my cries of delight. It would also give me a chance to give Cricket Lodge the once-over.

I linked my arm in Dave's and we weaved towards the door.

'Goodnight, Vicky,' Arthur called out. 'Hey! You're *in* there, lad.' A cheer erupted from the bar. A few men slapped Dave on the back. I'd never felt so popular.

The fresh air hit me the moment we left the pub. I was pleasantly tipsy but a bit worried about Dave's capacity to drive. I looked at him narrowly to see if he were unsteady on his feet. Before I could assess the situation, he'd grabbed my arm and steered me towards an old green Land Rover.

'In you go.' Dave opened the passenger door and hoisted me inside as if I were a bag of grain.

Inside, the Land Rover was spotless and, as expected, filled with hedge-jumping paraphernalia. In the rear, green Wellington boots were secured neatly alongside the bench together with a pair of moleskin trousers and heavy jacket. Hedge clippers, a vicious looking scythe, rolls of barbed wire, and binder twine were tucked in a purpose-built grid along the side. I supposed he always kept these things with him in case he came across a pristine hedge, ripe for leaping, and couldn't stop himself from taking the plunge.

'You okay?' His voice sounded slurred, unless my hearing was impaired.

'Great, thank you.' I felt a rush of anxiety. My knees began to tremble. Although in the pub I'd made the momentous decision to let Dave be the one to take my virginity, now we were actually on our way to do the deed, I was having second thoughts. Yet, surely it was natural to feel what my mum called 'wedding-night jitters'?

'You all right?' Dave asked again, this time with a meaningful wink. He fumbled around with the ignition key.

'Fine. Truly.' He really was plastered. Perhaps he wouldn't even be able to perform. I'd read that 80 per cent of men who drank too much alcohol had sexual problems. I certainly wasn't ready to cope with that. I hardly knew what to do as it was.

Dave finally started the engine. Diesel sounded so different from the sexy roar of the black Porsche. I felt a pang of regret that I was being driven to the scene of such an important once-in-a-lifetime moment in such an inferior vehicle.

We tore out of the car park and skidded right, narrowly missing a stone pillar. Fortunately, there were no police cars lurking in the shadows. The Land Rover sped along the narrow lane, back towards the town centre.

'Aren't we going to your place?'

'We're picking up Teresa.' Dave gripped the steering wheel tightly, focusing hard on the narrow road. 'Where does she live?'

'You mean Topaz.'

'Or Annabel?' Dave said suddenly. 'Do you think she'd be up for it?'

The mention of Annabel abruptly put an end to my ardour. I wanted to lose my virginity, but not with a drunk who was happy to sleep with anyone – especially *her*.

I wanted to go home now. Somehow I had to extricate myself from this situation without jeopardizing my cover. Rumble Lane was just around the corner. Mrs Poultry strictly forbade male visitors. I'd get him to walk me to the door and then act all disappointed when she turned him away. Mum says men are even keener when they get rejected.

Reaching over, I stroked Dave's thigh. 'I can't wait another minute longer,' I said, trying out one of Annabel's low, throaty laughs. 'I only live a minute from here. Let's go to my place.'

'Won't Teresa be disappointed?'

'Devastated,' I said. 'But don't worry. You'll have your work cut out just satisfying me.'

'Bloody hell.' He gave me a delighted grin.

'Turn left here and stop by the third streetlamp,' I went on. 'I live at number ten.'

Mrs Poultry's Morris Traveller was parked in the drive. The house was in darkness. Surely, she couldn't be in bed already? It was only just after eleven!

'What a shame!' I exclaimed. 'I thought my landlady would have been out, but she's at home.' I didn't relish the thought of waking her up. 'You'd better drop me off here.'

Dave didn't seem to hear. We swung into the narrow drive, clipped the wooden gatepost, and stopped only inches away from the Morris Traveller's bumper.

The Land Rover's headlamps were on full beam, illuminating the entire front of the house. 'For God's sake! Turn them off!' I shrieked. A light went on upstairs.

Dave cut the headlights and turned towards me. 'Let's do it on the front lawn.'

Lady Trewallyn might be happy frolicking naked under the moonlight, but even if I had decided to go through with it, this would have been my first time. Losing one's virginity was supposed to be special.

'The grass will be wet,' I pointed out. 'We don't want to catch a chill.'

'I've got some plastic sheeting in the back. We can lie on that. Come on!' Dave scrambled out of the Land Rover but missed his footing and disappeared from sight. Reluctantly, I followed. Whatever romantic feelings I may have left for him

176

were fast evaporating. He was a drunken idiot. If he thought I was going to sacrifice myself to his loutish fumbling, he was wrong.

Dave staggered to his feet and pulled me towards him. We fell against the Land Rover. Grinding his hips against my body, he clamped his mouth onto mine. His tongue felt as if it were drilling for oil. All I could think about was Mrs Poultry's horror should she see us. She may not attend the services in the church itself, but I could tell she had Victorian values.

'Remmmaxxx,' Dave muttered, not even pausing to speak. 'Ymm gomm to like mmm.'

I felt absolutely nothing. No desire, not even a tiny quiver of delight, which was more than I could say for Dave. Something hot and hard was pressed into my thigh.

Finally, I managed to push him away. He was out of breath. I remembered Mum's warning that, once a man got aroused, it was very cruel to stop them – something to do with their anatomy overheating. I was in a dilemma. I had the action-shot photo shoot on Wednesday. I couldn't afford to annoy him.

'Dave! Wait!' I pressed my fingers to his lips, whispering seductively. 'I'm a noisy lover. I can't truly let myself go out here. What if someone were out walking their dog?'

'I don't care.'

'Let's do it Wednesday at your place.' I crossed my fingers. 'I can't resist a man in moleskins.'

'I can't stop now, baby.' Dave grabbed my breasts and began massaging them furiously. 'Come on, give it to me—'

'Get off!' I stamped on his foot, hard. Dave yelped.

'Listen. Tonight is not going to work,' I said firmly. 'Wednesday is much better. I'll even bring Topaz.'

'Okay.' Dave swayed a little, seemingly disorientated. 'I feel a bit dizzy.' Mum was right.

'Good, that's settled.' I began walking up the path. 'Bye.'

'Don't I get a proper goodnight kiss?' Dave tripped, then hurried after me. I broke into a trot.

He caught up with me at the front door. We tumbled into the porch. There was an explosion of light and Mrs Poultry stood framed in the doorway, dressed in a long, high-necked red tartan dressing gown. Her hair was in curlers, her expression stony.

'Hello, Mrs Poultry,' I said, trying to sound normal. 'I hope we didn't wake you?'

Mrs Poultry didn't acknowledge me, having turned her hostile stare on Dave.

'This is my friend, Dave—'

'Yes, I know Mr Randall.'

I was impressed. Dave's fame as champion hedge-jumper had even reached Mrs Poultry's ears. Considering she was someone who claimed she didn't read newspapers or indulge in idle gossip, Dave should be proud of himself. I basked in his fame. It's always nice to be with a man who attracts admiration wherever he may roam.

I turned to Dave, half expecting him to offer her his autograph, but was astonished to see his face drained of all colour. Without another word, he spun on his heel and darted back to the Land Rover. The engine roared into life. Dave threw the vehicle into reverse, clipped the gatepost again, and vanished into the night.

'Well, fancy that!' I exclaimed. 'I had no idea he was so shy.'

'He'd better pay for the damage.' Mrs Poultry glowered. 'Come with me. *Now*!'

Inside the house, I steeled myself for an extended reprimand on the no-men-allowed rules.

We entered the kitchen. For a fleeting moment, I wondered if she was going to offer a hot cup of cocoa. Instead, she gestured for me to sit down at the kitchen table. I noted it was already laid up for morning breakfast.

'I'm afraid I am going to have to ask you to leave at the end of the week,' Mrs Poultry declared. 'This is a boarding-house, not a brothel.'

'Leave?' I was sure I had misheard. It wasn't as if she had caught me in bed with Dave.

'And you've been drinking.'

'I was interviewing Dave for the newspaper. It was a business lunch that ran longer than I thought,' I said defensively. 'I know the house rules. He was just being a gentleman and escorting me to the door.'

Mrs Poultry's expression remained cold.

'Please let me stay,' I pleaded. 'I like it here and you are the best landlady I have ever had.' Actually, she was the *only* one I'd ever had.

The truth was, I didn't have anywhere else to go. In the whole of Gipping, Mrs Poultry had been the only boarding-house to accept cash and not bother with references. Dad had insisted bank accounts and paper trails could lead back to him in Spain.

'What's more, I'm fed up with the excessive bathwater you've been using,' she continued, 'to say nothing of the extra jam.'

'I'll pay for them.' I had no money left in my purse and owed The Three Tuns a fortune. 'Tomorrow.'

'What would your mother say?' Mrs Poultry scolded. 'The youth of today have no sense of gratitude. No morals. No decency.'

'The problem is, I've never had any parental guidance.' I took a deep breath, adding mournfully, 'I'm an orphan.'

'The world is full of orphans, Victoria.' Mrs Poultry was relentless. 'But do you see them acting like trollops? You are well on the way to leading a life of filth and depravity.'

'Please give me one more chance.'

Mrs Poultry sat down at the table and unwrapped a cough drop. As she sucked it slowly, she began smoothing out the purple wrapper whilst she pondered on my fate. The scrumpy had worn off. I was tired.

Having folded the paper into a perfect square, Mrs Poultry stood up, and said, 'I'm a fair, charitable woman. I wouldn't want it said that I turned an orphan out into the cold,' she declared. 'You can stay – on the one condition that you never speak to Dave Randall again.'

'Thank you,' I said, having no intention of doing as she asked. I had to consider Wednesday's action-shot photo shoot. 'I'd best get to bed.'

As I climbed the stairs to my attic bedroom, I reflected that I'd got out of that awkward situation pretty well. I was not going to be evicted, I was still getting the photos of Dave on Wednesday, and – more important – I hadn't lost my virginity to a drunkard.

I lay awake for a long time. I decided not to tell Topaz that Dave couldn't remember her real name. She seemed the fragile type. If only I could think of something to keep her occupied.

Surely, Topaz must be privy to all sorts of tittle-tattle in the cafe? Perhaps she could make some discreet inquiries about Probes and his witchcraft interests?

Tomorrow was my official day off. I'd already planned to pop into the office and see if I could get my hands on the fake coroner's report. With only a skeleton staff operating on a Monday – Tony writing up the weekend sports results, and Barbara manning the phones – it should be a piece of cake.

28

It was almost noon when I stood outside the *Gazette*. Once again, The Copper Kettle was closed. I was struck by a horrible thought. What if something had happened to Topaz? What if I had inadvertently put her in danger? What if she were lying there, strangled?

Rapping smartly on the front door, I pressed my nose against the glass. The place was deserted. Even the chairs were upside down on the tables.

I stooped down to open the letterbox. 'Yoo-hoo, Topaz!' I called out. 'It's Vicky!'

There was no reply. I ducked down the narrow footpath that ran alongside the building to the rear. Glancing up at the stone facade I noticed curtains drawn in the upstairs flat. I tried the back door. It was locked. Glancing around, I picked up some small stones and hurled them at the windows. 'Topaz! It's me, Vicky!'

After several agonizing moments when my mind went through every conceivable mode of murder imaginable, Topaz pulled open the curtains, opened an upstairs window, and leaned out – minus her wig. Her hair was dark brown and cropped short.

'What do you want?' she cried.

'I came to say hello.'

'I was asleep.'

'It's nearly lunchtime!' I was appalled. How lazy! 'Can I come in?'

'All right,' she said grudgingly, and closed the window. A few moments later, she unbolted the back door.

Topaz looked distinctly dishevelled in a pink tie-dyed kaftan, clasping a violet knitted shawl around her shoulders. She wore no makeup.

'Good grief! Are you ill?' I said, staring at her wig, which was slightly off centre and had obviously been donned in haste.

'Why?' Topaz stepped aside to let me pass, then bolted the door behind us. Without a word, she padded along the hall and into the kitchen – if you could call it such.

Basic was the only word I'd use to describe it. It was hard to imagine anyone could cook in such shoddy surroundings. A two-ring hot plate sat on top of the draining board. There was no stove, only a microwave. A waist-high refrigerator stood in one corner with a toaster on top. I counted two saucepans, one frying pan, a kettle, and a spatula. A pile of unwashed dishes sat in the sink. The whole place needed a good clean and smelled similar to our basement across the street.

In a basket in the corner slept a very old black Labrador with grey whiskers.

'I didn't know you had a dog,' I said. 'What's her name?'

'Slipper,' Topaz said. 'She's deaf.'

'Not much of a guard dog, is she?' I said, trying to make a joke.

Topaz glowered and flopped into one of the two shabby armchairs that flanked the small Victorian fireplace filled with litter. 'Actually, she used to be a guide dog for the blind.'

'Why is the cafe closed?'

Topaz sighed. 'I don't feel like working at the moment.'

Not *work*? I had been brought up to work hard. Only the rich could afford to be idle.

'You can't just please yourself! You're running a business. People expect you to be open.' It certainly explained her lack of customers. Why walk all the way to the top of the High Street for a cuppa only to find it closed?

Topaz shrugged. 'Why should you care?'

I felt guilty. Someone must have told her that Dave and I were out together yesterday. Clearly, she was jealous. Coupled with my rejection of her on Friday, it had proved too much for her to handle. 'Did I tell you the newspaper has asked me to do a hedge-jumping feature on the Randall chap?' I asked casually.

Topaz's expression hardened. 'No, you didn't.'

'I had a meeting with him last night.'

'You didn't say anything about me, did you?' she said, turning red.

'It was purely business.' I remembered how Dave had slammed me against the Land Rover and stuck his tongue in my mouth. Having had time to think about it overnight, I decided I had liked his suggestion of love on the lawn, after all. He seemed spontaneous, passionate – probably an exciting and inventive lover. No doubt Lady Trewallyn had taught him a thing or two. I'd only chickened out through nerves.

'Vicky, this is embarrassing,' Topaz said sheepishly, bringing me back to reality with a jolt. 'You know the other night in the pub?'

'Yes . . .'

'When I've had a lot to drink, I tend to say silly things.' She began to laugh. 'You see, I've never ever met Dave Randall.'

'Goodness! You had me fooled!' I hoped my face did not betray my annoyance. Did Topaz think I was born yesterday? I recalled her hatred of Lady Trewallyn, her tears and histrionics. *Blimey!* She had even tried to persuade me to be a lesbian and been flirting with me well before her first Babycham.

'Don't be angry, Vicky.' Topaz played with the silver locket around her neck. Her eyes filled with tears.

This time I wasn't deceived. People lie to hide something.

I'd get it out of her soon enough. 'I'm not angry,' I said smoothly. 'That's what friends are for. Sharing secrets. Sharing fears.'

Topaz shot me a grateful smile. 'I knew you'd understand.'

We lapsed into an uncomfortable silence. Topaz was so unpredictable. If only I didn't need her spying services.

'Guess what? I've got an undercover job for you.' I braced myself for her squeal of joy.

Topaz frowned. 'Does it have to be today?'

Her apathy was seriously beginning to irk me. I gestured to the mess in the kitchen. 'You can't just sit around moping. I thought you wanted to work for the *Gazette*?'

Topaz shrugged. 'It depends what it is.'

There was a long pause while I counted to ten. 'I want you to find out about that new copper, DC Probes.'

'He's a policeman.'

'Yes, I know that.' What was wrong with her? Was she being deliberately obtuse? 'I just need some background information: where did he live before he moved here? Are his parents alive? Does he have brothers and sisters? That sort of thing.'

Topaz slowly shook her head. 'I'd rather not.'

'For heaven's sake, it's not difficult.' I was exasperated. 'When he comes into the cafe, you just ask a few friendly questions.'

'I haven't been open very long,' she said in a sulky voice. 'I just don't want to attract attention, that's all.'

With my upbringing, one thing I know is that when someone does not want to attract attention, it's because they are doing something illegal.

'What about Coroner Sharpe? Does he ever come in for a cuppa?'

'I don't know who he is,' she said stubbornly. 'Isn't there something else I can do that doesn't take up so much time?'

It suddenly dawned on me that I was definitely wasting mine. As an informer, Topaz was less than useless.

'Tell you what,' I said. 'Why don't we hold off on you working for the *Gazette* until you're not so busy?'

'Do you mind? I *am* utterly frantic, at the moment.' Topaz got to her feet and stretched, thrusting her breasts in my direction.

Still trying that on, I thought with scorn. 'Well, I don't know about you, but I have a lot to do.'

I left The Copper Kettle deeply perplexed. It was of little consolation that Pete need never find out the *Gazette* had nearly hired a psychopath. Something was niggling me. Who was Topaz Potter? And why did she feel the need to wear that wig? She was new to the area and clearly had absolutely no business sense. Only a few days ago, she had been obsessed with Lady Trewallyn and Chester Forbes, to say nothing of her broken-hearted grief over Dave Randall. It was obvious Topaz was hiding something and I was determined to find out what it was.

29

As I crossed the street, I saw Barbara standing in the *Gazette* window, putting the finishing touches to her banner – VOODOO VIXENS: WHO IS SALOME STEEL?

'I thought you were off today,' Barbara said, as I helped her down from the recess. 'I need someone to help with the heavy lifting.' She pointed to an iron, waist-high cauldron that I hadn't noticed. 'It's for the window display.'

'I'm in a bit of a rush. Can't Tony give you a hand?'

'Tony?' Barbara scoffed. 'He's far too weak. We need a real man – someone with a nice set of biceps like Jimmy Kitchen.'

Not Jimmy Kitchen *again*. 'Where on earth did you find such an enormous pot?'

'Down at the abandoned wool and textile factory.' Barbara beamed.

'But it's heavy. How did you get it all the way up here?' I was puzzled.

Barbara's face reddened. 'A . . . *friend* dropped it off.' She coughed and looked away. This was a turn up for the books. I thought all Barbara's romantic adventures were lodged deep in her past.

'Everyone will be here tomorrow,' I said. 'Let's try to roll the thing into the corner until then.'

Given that Barbara's bad toe was playing up, it took us a full fifteen minutes to manoeuvre the cauldron next to the drum outside the nook. Try as I might to extract information on Barbara's mystery friend, she remained stubbornly silent. I made a mental note to ask Topaz if she'd seen anyone delivering a pot though didn't hold out much hope. Topaz had seemed particularly dense this morning. 'Do you know where Tony went for lunch?'

'He left for The Warming Pan about forty-five minutes ago.'

Good. It was a long walk to the other end of the High Street plus service there was notoriously slow. 'He should try The Copper Kettle,' I said. 'It's closer, and Topaz needs some regulars.'

'She needs to offer free cups of tea and perhaps a nice Victoria sponge cake,' Barbara declared. 'She won't find it easy attracting new customers. They remember The Kettle as a junk shop. People don't like change.'

'*A junk* shop?'

'Sold odd bits of furniture, cheap prints, old pots and pans,' Barbara said. 'All proceeds went to Guide Dogs for the Blind. Very worthy cause.'

This was interesting. Topaz had probably bought the junk shop and its contents, dirt cheap. She'd merely rearranged the furniture and stuck a sign on the front door. Still, I couldn't criticize her. Didn't we all have dreams?

Fortunately all further conversation stopped when Barbara had to answer the phone. I dashed upstairs to sneak into Pete's office before Tony returned.

To my alarm, Wilf, puffing away furiously on his pipe, was standing in the reporters' room holding a manila folder. I'd forgotten our elusive editor practically lived at the office.

I always found Wilf disconcerting. He had a bright blue glass eye that didn't quite fit right. I was never sure if he was looking at me or not. 'Morning, sir,' I said, stealing a look at the title on the folder. I'd always been able to read upside down – another birthday party game invented by Dad. To my astonishment, it was the fake coroner's report.

Wilf took the pipe out of his mouth. 'Annabel, is it?'

I bristled. 'Vicky Hill, actually, sir.'

'Ah! The young gel getting our front-page scoop.'.

'That's right.' I beamed. Obviously Wilf's eyesight had initially been to blame for mistaking me for Annabel, but once he heard my name, he knew exactly who I was.

'I thought we could have a little chat in my office,' he said. 'Care for a cuppa?'

'I'd love to!' I was having tea with the editor of the *Gipping Gazette*! Although Pete had power, Wilf was the king.

Wilf's office was cluttered, to say the least. Bulletin boards stuck with photographs and newspaper clippings from the nationals littered every surface. Piles of old editions were stacked in towers on the floor, necessitating skilful navigation to cross from one side of the room to the other.

'Tea might be a bit strong,' said Wilf as he poured thick liquid from a brown teapot into a cracked mug, adding powdered milk and four teaspoons of sugar. 'I made it this morning.'

I glanced at the clock. It must have been steeping for at least four hours. I took a sip and practically gagged. 'It's delicious.'

I perched on the edge of a plastic chair in front of Wilf's desk. The coroner's report was tantalizingly inches from my grasp. I fought the urge to distract him in some way and steal it from under his nose.

I watched Wilf take great pains to line up his pipe-cleaning utensils on a small mackintosh square, placed neatly on a sheet of newspaper. A tin of Sir Walter Raleigh tobacco – IT SMOKES AS SWEET AS IT SMELLS – lay open, alongside a pipe rack holding three Dunhill pipes.

The silence between us lengthened as Wilf began to scrape the bowl out with a small penknife. 'Why don't you tell me a little about your scoop,' he said eventually. 'Pete is very secretive about it. Claims it will change the history of our newspaper.'

I hesitated. First of all, I had nothing concrete to tell; and secondly, Pete must have his reasons *not* to have told Wilf. 'Oh! You know how Pete is!' I said cheerfully. 'I think he'd rather tell you himself.'

'Is that so?' Wilf carefully filled the bowl with tobacco and tamped it down. 'I've worked here for over forty years, you know. The *Gazette*'s never run a story we were ashamed of.'

I nodded a hearty agreement. 'That's why I'm proud to be working for you, sir.'

'I've known Pete since he was a nipper.' Wilf struck a match and lit his pipe. The tobacco caught; he sucked in deeply. True to Sir Walter's promise, the smoke *did* smell sweet.

'From time to time, Pete gets carried away with new-fangled ideas,' Wilf went on. 'Sometimes, he doesn't understand our readers. They want things to remain the same. They know if they open to page two, they'll get Gipping Gossip. They know if they turn to pages eleven and twelve, there's an obituary spread.'

'That's my section, sir,' I enthused.

'Gipping prides itself on tradition. We're a happy paper.' Wilf drew on his pipe. 'We want happy stories.'

I reflected on the dozens of funerals I attended weekly. Although they weren't exactly happy, the post-service parties were often a lot of fun.

Wilf's active eye blinked at me intensely. 'Has someone won the football pools?'

A sinking feeling was beginning to form in my stomach. Could Wilf, or Gipping for that matter, handle murders, sex fiends, and Satanists? 'My story is still in the early stages.'

'It can't be too early. We go to press on Friday. I've reserved the front page for you,' he said. 'When old Reggie won half a million pounds, we gave him six whole pages. The public loved it. That's why, what's her name, in reception—?'

'Barbara Meadows.'

'That's it. Her Salome Steel competition is a good idea.' Wilf drew on his pipe. 'We want something along those lines.'

I took a deep breath, adding tentatively, 'I was thinking a nice little ritual murder might make a change.'

'A what?' Wilf's pipe dropped onto the desk. Even his glass eye seemed to show alarm. 'Murder? Good heavens, Vicky! Can you imagine the shadow of despair that would fall upon us if we believed there was a murderer in our midst? Mistrust would be rampant. Families could be torn apart by suspicion.'

'It was just an idea,' I said weakly.

'Stick to tradition and you'll make staff writer. You might even get a laptop.' Wilf scooped up a pile of files from his desk. 'Here, give this lot to Betty in reception.'

I couldn't believe my luck. One of them was the fake report.

Even though I finally had it in my grasp, I left Wilf's office with a heavy heart. It had never occurred to me that the editor would reject my front-page story. Pete was right. Wilf really did live in the dark ages.

Thoroughly discouraged, I sat down at my desk and flipped through the report. It was exactly as Annabel had claimed. Sir Hugh had died of a heart attack and was discovered in the library by Lady Trewallyn at five minutes to midnight. There was no mention of a yew hedge, poison, or chickens. The only thing the two conflicting reports had in common was Coroner Sharpe's signature. I decided to sneak it home to compare the two to make sure. Although, seeing Lady Trewallyn canoodling with old man Sharpe outside the morgue was proof enough to me of a cover-up.

Tucking the report inside my safari jacket, I went downstairs and was about to dump the files on the counter for Barbara when I had an idea: why not offer to file them myself? It would be a good excuse to gain access to Barbara's archive cupboard.

Since Gripping boasted an accurate record of births, deaths, and marriages, it might be prudent to do a little background check on Lady Trewallyn. Instinct told me she was guilty and it was my duty as an investigative reporter to give the town the truth, whatever Wilf might say.

30

At first, Barbara was reluctant to accept my offer of help, insisting it was my day off.

'Actually, Wilf suggested I give you a hand.' I crossed my fingers and prayed Barbara wouldn't check. 'He's worried about the amount of work you're doing.' This was a bald-faced lie. Barbara seemed to spend most of the day on the phone gossiping to her friends.

'Wilf said that?' Barbara looked pleased. 'Goodness. I didn't think he noticed me at all.'

'He thought the competition was a good idea.' I didn't want to add that he didn't remember her name. 'I insist on helping you with the filing.'

'I *would* like to finish my display,' Barbara said, adding, 'I can't believe Wilf was worried about little old me.'

Barbara lifted up the countertop for me to duck through from reception into her kingdom beyond. Other than a box of tissues, her favourite tortoiseshell mirror and comb, and a hand-knitted purple cardigan in a cubbyhole under the counter, the area was scrupulously tidy.

Since Barbara called herself *Miss*, I assumed she had never married. She appeared to be the quintessential career receptionist. Her job was probably her life.

The archive room was in the left-hand corner next to a bank of olive green filing cabinets. We stepped inside. I felt let down. Somehow, I assumed it would resemble the public records department in the library – miles of narrow paths dividing endless shelves of boxes and books. This room was nothing more than a large storage cupboard.

Barbara gestured to a narrow wooden table in the centre, where a large stack of various-size newspaper clippings and sheets of paper spilled over the TO FILE tray.

She pulled out a low stool-cum-stepladder from underneath the table. 'I spread all the articles onto the table and put them into categories.' Gesturing for me to sit down, she went on, 'It's a little cramped but I rather like to eat my lunch in here. It's important to take a breather from the turmoil of reception.'

'It's certainly snug.' Lit by a solitary naked light bulb and with no windows, it was stuffy and horribly claustrophobic.

'If you have any questions, let me know.'

Floor-to-ceiling wooden shelves stood on three sides, packed with dozens of labelled cardboard boxes sorted by subject and year. Funerals took up one entire wall, weddings and births, the second. The third was shared equally between social events including the Women's Institute, flower shows, jumble sales, and court transcripts. One of the boxes was bright yellow and labelled: WINNER FOOTBALL POOLS 1990 – R. SHARPE.

'I didn't realize it was the *coroner* who won the pools,' I said, pointing to the box. I'd forgotten Coroner Sharpe's first name was Reginald. 'Wilf said he got half a million.'

'He never married, you know. Didn't want to be tied down,' Barbara declared. 'Quite the ladies' man. Women can't get enough of him. He's—'

'I'd better make a start.' I knew what was coming – another of her trips down memory lane. In the beginning, I had been genuinely interested – you can learn a lot about life from the elderly – but after hearing the same story a dozen times, tedium sets in.

Barbara seemed disappointed. 'I'll leave the door ajar. If you need anything, just shout.'

To Barbara's credit, her archaic filing system was highly organized. In twenty minutes I'd put away Barbara and Wilf's papers and could now turn my attention to the Trewallyn nuptials.

Working backwards, it didn't take long to locate the wedding feature. To my surprise, Sir Hugh had remarried a mere two months before I had moved to Gipping myself. Apparently he and Lady Trewallyn had met on board *The Golden Dawn,* a luxury cruise ship specializing in the recently bereaved, whose slogan was THE LOVING DOESN'T HAVE TO STOP.

A black-and-white photograph with the caption SIR HUGH REMARRIES ON THE OCEAN WAVES showed the new Lady Trewallyn wearing a minuscule bikini top that barely contained her bosoms and a sarong. Her hair was pulled back tightly off her face and decorated with a large hibiscus flower. Sir Hugh stood by her side, clad in traditional English tweeds and deerstalker hat. They made a strange couple. Apparently, Sir Hugh was 'thrilled to find love again at seventy-five' and Katherine Vanderkamp said he was as 'cute as a button' and that 'true love only sees the soul within'.

The article went on to say how Sir Hugh, grief-stricken following the tragic death of his first wife three months prior, had taken a Caribbean cruise and met American socialite Katherine Vanderkamp on board ship. Mrs Vanderkamp had recently lost her husband, famed anthropologist and expert on African tribal rituals, in a car accident.

Eureka! Here was further confirmation of Lady Trewallyn's guilt – right down to the African connection – except for one thing. If she were a wealthy widow already, why would she poison the penniless Sir Hugh?

Think, Vicky, think! Of course, it was obvious. Lady Trewallyn had dabbled in the dark arts with her first husband and got a taste for it – orgies, in particular. Mum says once married couples deviate from normal sex there is no turning back. Maybe that's where Dave Randall, and others of his ilk, fitted in? Lady Trewallyn was insatiable. Sir Hugh had been an old-fashioned gentleman. Perhaps he discovered her sordid secret and wanted to expose her. Lady Trewallyn had to get rid of him to avoid a scandal. Chester Forbes was a ghost from her past and threatened to tell all unless she paid for his silence. It certainly explained her horrified reaction at the graveside. All I needed now was proof.

Satisfied with my findings, I turned to the funeral files. Within minutes, I had found Lady Clarissa's obituary and was almost overcome with pride at being associated with a newspaper that kept such scrupulous records. It seemed I hadn't understood the fundamental philosophy behind the *Gazette* at all. I had regarded being a funeral reporter as a chore and a curse instead of what it really was – preserving history for all mankind.

I unfolded the newspaper and turned to the obituaries on pages eleven and twelve.

In the bottom right-hand corner was a grainy, full-length snapshot of an elderly woman with a perm and twinset with a Labrador sitting at her feet. A short article followed saying that Clarissa Turberville-Spat had been born in Kenya where her father, Colonel Turberville-Spat, owned a coffee plantation. Lady Clarissa had met Sir Hugh during her annual visit home to England for the Cheltenham Gold Cup in 1963.

After placing the winning bet on Mill House, Sir Hugh proposed. They spent forty-five happy years together. Her ladyship liked collecting stamps and was an avid supporter of Guide Dogs for the Blind. Ethel Turberville-Spat, her niece and sole heir, was included in the list of mourners.

Apart from the niece, I was familiar with all the names though, personally, I thought the article dull and wondered who wrote it. There was none of the human insight I liked to include in my obituary writing.

'I was there when she died, you know.' Barbara's voice made me jump. I hadn't heard her come in. 'Everyone said she had a weak heart, but frankly, it was absinthe that did her in.'

'Goodness! Do people still drink that stuff?'

'It's supposed to heighten the sexual experience, though it didn't do much for me.' Barbara's eyes assumed a glazed expression. 'Apart from—'

'You say you were actually *present* when Lady Clarissa died?'

'What, dear?' Barbara dragged herself away from whatever torrid memory she was reliving. 'Oh yes. Clarissa keeled over at Maurice Wheeler's funeral wake – *right* in front of me. One moment she was laughing at some joke and the next . . . well . . .'

'Sir Hugh runs off and marries an American heiress on the rebound,' I said flatly. 'That must have come as quite a surprise.'

'It certainly did to Henrietta.' Barbara nodded and took a deep breath, clearly getting ready for the next round of revelations. 'Of course, *Henrietta*—'

'Is that the time?' I looked at my watch. I'd had my fill of Barbara's gossip today and had no interest in listening to one of Barbara's friend's sob stories. 'I really must dash. I must say your filing system is excellent.'

'It's what I do best.' Barbara beamed with pride.

I left Barbara locking up the cupboard, and slipped out. I couldn't get home quick enough. I had a busy night ahead. As an investigative reporter, it was all about gathering facts. Although concrete proof that Katherine Vanderkamp had killed her husband through sorcery still eluded me, I knew I was on to something.

As for the coroner's reports, I needed to compare the two signatures. If they matched, it confirmed my hunch that Coroner Sharpe was part of the coven, too. How convenient! Lady Trewallyn could murder whom she pleased and have her crime covered up by the coroner, who, in turn, was protected by the police. It made me wonder about the countless funerals I had

196

attended over the past few months. Could it be that half of them were human sacrifices?

With that horrible thought in mind, I hurried back to Rumble Lane to change into my blue flannel pyjamas and do some serious bedtime reading.

31

In the privacy of my attic bedroom, I extracted the original coroner's report from the plastic Tupperware in the water tank.

From my underwear drawer, hidden beneath my woollen socks, I retrieved a jeweller's loupe – a useful gift from Dad on my sixteenth birthday – and vital for studying forged signatures.

I turned to compare the back page of both reports. My suspicions were correct. The two signatures were not only identical, but signed with the same fountain pen.

As a member of the medical profession, Coroner Sharpe wrote in an illegible doctor's scrawl, which even a seasoned forger could not duplicate. The initiating S had matching intricate swirls; the H and P had unusual loops and hooks. One of the reasons Dad stopped dealing in art was because good forgers were too expensive.

This was all well and good, but what was my next step? I could hardly expect Sharpe to confess to being part of the coven. With Brian six feet under, it looked like I'd reached a dead end – no pun intended. Getting hold of Brian's poppet could have been used for evidence but, of course, Probes had that safely tucked away in a shoe box. Maybe Annabel was right: I wouldn't be able to pull it off, after all.

Depressed, I put the coroner's reports under my pillow and climbed into bed, hoping for a flash of inspiration.

I was just about to nod off when a loud knock on the door startled me. I sprang out of bed.

'Victoria?' Mrs Poultry said, rattling the handle. 'Open the door at once!' Thank God I had had the foresight to lock it. 'There's someone to see you.'

Someone to see *me*? My stomach turned over. The only night visitors the Hill family had wore dark blue uniforms and carried handcuffs. Topaz must have betrayed me to the cops. *Oh God!* I was going to be arrested.

'Be right there!' I gave the room a once-over, straightened the bedclothes, and went to let Mrs Poultry in.

'Oh my God, Vicky!' To my astonishment, Annabel pushed past my landlady and threw herself onto my bed.

'What are you doing here?' I said, instantly wary. Annabel's face was pale, her hair in disarray – although I noted freshly applied lipstick.

Mrs Poultry stood in the doorway, arms akimbo, sucking a Coff-Off. 'I'm afraid your friend can't stay here. No visitors after nine o' clock.'

'Mrs Poultry, this is Annabel Lake,' I said, trying to collect my thoughts. 'Annabel, this is my landlady, Mrs.—'

'Yes, I know who she is,' Mrs Poultry snapped. Of course! Why was I surprised? Everyone knew Annabel.

I pulled my rival to her feet and tried to bundle her towards the door. 'She's just leaving.' Annabel's feet seemed glued to the floor. She wouldn't budge.

'I'm not leaving without Vicky.' Annabel was defiant. 'She's the only person I can trust.'

Although severely disturbed by her arrival, my heart swelled with happiness. How odd life is. I had always assumed Annabel had tons of friends. Knowing that she rated *me* as her number one chum changed everything.

Annabel grabbed my shoulders and stared intensely into my eyes. 'Something has happened, Vicky. You must come. This is what we journalists do. This is our calling!'

'Can't it wait until the morning?' I said acutely aware of Mrs Poultry's disapproval.

Annabel shook her head. 'No. It's a matter of life or death. We must go *now.*'

'Don't say I didn't warn you.' Mrs Poultry's face was grim.

If I risked eviction, so be it. Annabel needed me. 'Let me change into my clothes.' I was wearing my pyjamas.

'There's no time. They might still be there,' she said, grabbing my hand and dragging me past Mrs Poultry.

We thundered down the stairs. 'At least let me change my slippers,' I yelled, but Annabel had already dashed out of the front door.

Grabbing my safari jacket from the hall coatrack, I threw it on over my pyjamas and kicked off my slippers. *Blast!* I'd left my shoes in the bedroom. Unwilling to meet Mrs Poultry on the stairs, I slipped on her wellington boots. Annabel was already revving up the engine outside. She sounded the horn three times, loud and hard.

'Come on!' Annabel's BMW began to move off before I'd even closed the passenger door. She gunned the engine. I put on my seat belt. We peeled out of Rumble Lane and tore onto the main road heading away from the town.

'For God's sake, tell me what's going on,' I said, holding on to the edge of my seat as she took a particularly sharp corner, almost throwing the BMW up on two wheels.

Annabel didn't answer, being too focused on her driving. One hand tightly gripped the steering wheel whilst the other manipulated the gear stick with great skill.

As we drove on, I began to curse my lack of foresight. First of all, I was dressed in my pyjamas; secondly, I had stolen Mrs Poultry's boots; and third, she might even at this moment be collecting my things and tossing them out of the window.

Abruptly, Annabel turned down a gravel lane signposted GIPPING CANAL – TRESPASSERS WILL BE PROSECUTED.

'Where are we going?' Pebbles spun off the tyres, no doubt chipping away at the paintwork but Annabel only slowed down when the lane turned into a bridleway, barely wide enough for one car. A thick and ghostly mist drifted across the windscreen in waves, casting an eerie sheen. Visibility was down to no more than five feet. On the driver's side, I could just make out a thick hedge and on mine, the flat blackness of deep water.

'We're not allowed down here. We're trespassing.' I felt scared. We were also too close to the bank for my liking. The day had been filled with lunatics. Why shouldn't Annabel be one, too? I recalled her fury at having to make the tea. What if she believed I'd usurped her position as Pete's mistress? How easy for Annabel to push me into the canal! Everyone knew I was an orphan. She'd just announce I'd run away. Even Mrs Poultry wouldn't care because I'd paid up until the end of the week and it would save her the bother.

Stifling a sob, I pinched the inside of my thigh, hard. I had to get a grip. Who knew what Annabel had discovered? Although we were now bosom buddies, it didn't change our professional relationship. We were still rivals and still in a race for that front-page scoop.

The mist cleared to reveal a quaint one-storey cottage next to a huge gated lock. Annabel pulled up outside and cut the engine. The place was in complete darkness and very creepy.

'What are we doing here? We'll be in trouble,' I whispered. 'Isn't this—?'

'Beaver Lock Lodge, yes,' Annabel said in a low voice. 'I live here.'

'You live *here*?' All curiosity was replaced by pure envy. 'All by yourself?'

Annabel must be loaded. Beaver Lock Lodge was one of five identical cottages dotted along the twelve-mile length of Gipping

Canal. Only two weeks ago one had been for sale in the paper for over two hundred and seventy-five thousand pounds. How on earth could she afford it?

'Sssh!' she hissed. 'Can you see anything?'

'What am I supposed to be looking for?' I said irritably.

'I came home and saw someone moving around inside with a flashlight.'

'Well, there's no one here now.' If there was one thing I knew for certain, it was how burglars operated. They move in, do their business, and move back out. If startled, they don't hang around to see who it is.

'Are you sure?' Annabel made no move to get out of the car. We sat there in darkness. It was cold.

'Maybe it was that cat burglar,' I suggested. 'Why didn't you just go to the police?'

'Not yet,' Annabel said. 'You see, I think I'm on to something.'

I detected a tinge of excitement in her voice, which I didn't like one bit. 'Your shocking exclusive, I suppose,' I said lightly. *Please God, don't let her story be better than mine.*

'Perhaps.'

'In that case, why ask me?

'I'm not as brave as you—'

'Of course you are,' I said, steeling myself for the inevitable insult that usually followed one of Annabel's compliments.

Annabel gave a wry laugh. 'I mean, you're really one of the boys out in the field, risking life and limb.'

'That's true—'

'I mean, you have to admit, you don't even care what you *wear*.' Annabel pinched the material of my safari jacket and pulled a face.

'I'm freezing.' I opened the car door. 'Let's go. Come on.'

'I don't want to,' wailed Annabel, in a childish voice, but followed me all the same.

My heels already had blisters thanks to Mrs Poultry's

202

ill-fitting wellingtons. I trudged up the path and tried the front door. It opened at my touch. 'Someone's definitely been in.'

'I don't usually lock it.'

'Do you know that ninety per cent of burglars are opportunists?' I said sternly. 'They've probably been casing the joint for weeks.' I snapped on the lights.

'Oh!' Annabel screamed, and rushed into the centre of the room, twirling in circles like a dervish. 'My things! My lovely things!'

There was no doubt about it. The room had been ransacked. Cupboards and drawers lay open with all their contents heaped in the centre of the floor. Pictures had been removed from the walls and propped against the furniture. Sofa cushions were tossed to the side. But there were no upturned plants on the floor; no tomato ketchup squirted over the sofa. Even the glass drinks cabinet was untouched.

'Annabel! Calm down. Let's take a deep breath and find out what has been taken.'

As a former lockkeeper's home, it was small with a living room, galley kitchen, and two doors leading off the tiny entrance hall. It looked expensively furnished with all the fittings and fixtures made from the highest quality. Lace was everywhere – draped over the backs of chairs and on every conceivable surface. The living room seemed more of a prostitute's boudoir, rather than the Flemish look – presumably – that Annabel had hoped to achieve.

'Why me?' Annabel perched on the edge of the sofa frame, looking bewildered.

'Where do you keep your jewellery?'

'In the bedroom.' Annabel pointed to a door where her name was emblazoned with angel stickers. She clutched at her throat. 'I can't go in there. What if they've . . . you know . . . done a number two, on my things.'

'A what?' I was exasperated. 'Oh really, Annabel. Don't be so silly.' It was true that sometimes burglars – particularly troubled teenagers – thought it hilarious to leave a personal calling card.

'I think I'll stay here.'

Annabel's bedroom was painted dusty pink and gold. Pushed against the far wall was a flamboyant four-poster bed adorned with what looked like Belgium's entire lace supply. A gigantic red velvet heart-shaped cushion complete with huggable arms was the *pièce de résistance*.

I was seized by an astonishing epiphany. Why hadn't I realized it before? Annabel must be some kind of escort girl. That was why she kept the door unlocked for late-night callers. It certainly explained why she had money to burn – and a brand-new car.

'Is everything all right?' whispered Annabel, who had sneaked up behind me. 'Oh! Oh! What's that?' she squealed in my ear. 'The pillow! The pillow!'

Something was visible above the heart-shaped cushion. I approached the bed. Instinctively, I already knew what it was. A poppet.

'Don't look!' I had to think. This poppet was distinctly different from Brian's. Whereas Brian's was beautifully detailed, this was an ugly doll made of papier-mâché. It wore crudely painted-on black trousers and a yellow top. Strands of orange wool were glued to its head. A hatpin was pushed through one pencilled-on eye.

Annabel peered over my shoulder and screamed again. 'It's a doll!'

Her fright seemed genuine. Suddenly, Brian's words – 'You've got to—' came back with startling clarity. Brian knew I wasn't Annabel Lake but had kept my secret. He knew I had the original coroner's report – perhaps its existence had leaked out, and someone had believed Annabel had kept the damning evidence. *That's* what this was all about. The poppet was a warning.

'Don't worry. It's nothing but a childish prank.'

'I don't know any children.' Annabel headed for her wardrobe and started rifling through her shoes. 'My jewellery's still in here.' She paused quizzically, hands on hips. 'Let me see . . . if it's not jewellery, it must be—'

'That *big* story you're working on?'

'Wait a minute,' exclaimed Annabel. 'Maybe it's to do with Salome Steel? I don't read her books but aren't those doll things in them?' Annabel frowned. 'Or perhaps someone got the idea from *reading* her books?'

Blast! Annabel was getting warm. But wait – hadn't Topaz made some comment about Annabel's bigwig lover? It was worth a try. 'You could be right,' I said. 'Maybe it's a warning from an angry wife?'

Annabel turned pale. 'You don't know what you're talking about.'

'It's all right, your secret is safe with me,' I said. 'We're friends, remember?'

'I swore I wouldn't tell a soul.' Annabel sat on the edge of the bed, and began quietly, 'It was when I started to research this *huge* story. I interviewed Walter and one thing led to another. We just fell in love.'

'Walter? Walter *Rawlings*?' I was incredulous. 'The town *mayor*?'

Mayor Rawlings was also head of the town planning department and had fingers in all sorts of West Country pies from car dealerships to being on the board of Devon Satellite Bell.

Annabel looked wistful. 'Walter says his wife doesn't understand him. He says sex is mechanical with her and . . .' She blushed. 'We're even talking marriage.'

The penny dropped. 'This cottage is his, isn't it? And the BMW?'

'The car was a gift,' she said defensively.

Annabel was a fool. I even felt a tiny bit sorry for her. Everyone knows a man never marries his mistress!

'Is that why you didn't call the police?'

'I couldn't. Walter's wife is Detective Inspector Stalk's cousin.'

'I'm right. She sent that poppet as a warning,' I said.

Annabel's face fell. 'It's no wonder that Walter doesn't love her. What a wicked thing to do.' Annabel frowned. 'But why would she mess up the living room?'

'To find out what jewellery he's been buying you.'

'Why look behind the picture frames? She didn't even go in my bedroom.' Annabel stood up and began to pace around the room. 'No! I think I'm going to tell Walter,' Annabel exclaimed. 'He should know what she's capable of.'

'You can't tell *him*!' I was alarmed. 'What if he ends the affair?'

Annabel looked worried. 'Don't say that.'

'Look,' I said in a soothing tone, 'why don't you jump into bed and have a good night's sleep? You'll have a clear head in the morning. It's already – *bugger* – *midnight*!'

It was, indeed, midnight. I felt the colour drain out of my face. I was already on borrowed time as far as my landlady was concerned. Even though I could sneak in the downstairs loo window, she'd probably be waiting up. I suddenly felt incredibly tired. The thought of slinking back to Rumble Lane to face Mrs Poultry's wrath was more than I could bear.

'Would you like me to stay the night?' I ventured. 'Unless, of course, you are expecting anyone?'

'I only see Walter twice a week.' Annabel hesitated. 'I must admit feeling weird with that thing on my bed. Would you . . . would you mind getting rid of it?'

I perked up. What a stroke of luck. God was smiling on me, after all. I needed a poppet as evidence! 'Of course. Can you get me a plastic bag?'

Annabel needed no further encouragement. She darted out of the bedroom to return moments later with a Tesco plastic shopping bag. Carefully, I slipped the fragile doll inside.

'You *are* going to throw it right away, aren't you?' Annabel said. 'It gives me the creeps.'

'I'll chuck it into the canal in the morning.' Naturally, I had no intention of doing such a thing.

'Oh, Vicky,' Annabel said. 'Do you think they might come back?'

'I doubt it. But promise me you'll always bolt the door.'

I returned to the bedroom. 'Do you have a blanket and pillow? I'll sleep on the sofa.'

Annabel turned red. 'Look, I still feel a little nervous. You can share my bed . . . but don't get any *funny ideas.*'

'What do you mean?' I said hotly.

'It's something that Barbara said, that's all. Don't get defensive. Live and let live is what I say. Come on, you can help me build a barrier.'

Annabel started banking up pillows and cushions down the centre of the four-poster bed as if she were building the Great Wall of China.

'You take the left side.' Annabel stood back to admire her handiwork. 'I'm going to change in private.'

I removed my safari jacket, kicked off the Wellington boots, and climbed into bed. There wasn't a great deal of room. It was no surprise that Annabel had deliberately divided the bed in her favour.

Minutes later, she sauntered in, wearing a flimsy, pink, transparent baby doll negligee. I felt a pang of envy. Annabel's breasts were enormous. No wonder she couldn't help thrusting them in men's faces. They practically had a life of their own.

Annabel folded her arms across her chest. 'What are you staring at?'

'Nothing,' I said, turning away from her and pulling the fluffy pink comforter up to my chin. 'Gosh, I'm tired.'

Annabel fidgeted for ages. Although I was exhausted, I couldn't sleep, either, and wished she would say something. As we lay in the dark, I couldn't help remembering Brownie camp.

Long summer nights sleeping out under the stars, sharing secrets, having midnight feasts, and eating chocolate until we were sick. How simple life had been back then.

Once again, I wished Annabel and I were real friends. Tonight, I had seen a different side of my rival. She had seemed vulnerable, even appealing to me for help. Perhaps I had misjudged her. After all, it can't be nice to have a hate doll and geriatric lover, even if she did score an expensive house and car. Before I had a chance to offer some words of friendly comfort, gentle snores and even breathing signalled that Annabel had finally fallen asleep.

I lay awake thinking about the poppet for hours. Of course, it was a warning but from whom? Chester, Probes, or Lady Trewallyn? The significance of the two coroner's reports was growing larger by the minute. If it hadn't been for my quick thinking, Annabel might have worked out how she was connected. It was sheer genius to blame the poppet planting on Walter's wife. Much as I disapproved of Dad's infidelities, they gave me an invaluable insight on the way hoodwinked wives took their revenge.

I was not looking forward to tomorrow. I expected to be evicted. Perhaps Annabel would let me stay here? I could make myself scarce when she was entertaining. I'd even get a lift to work every morning. Best of all, I could keep an eye on her.

Satisfied with my plan, I finally drifted to sleep, imagining how wonderful it would be to live at Beaver Lock Lodge.

32

It was the distant drone of a Hoover that eventually woke me up from a deep slumber. For a moment, I wasn't sure where I was. Mrs Poultry never vacuumed this early. Then, I remembered this wasn't Rumble Lane.

Opening my eyes, I came face-to-face with a wall of pillows. I was in Annabel's luxurious four-poster bed at Beaver Lock Lodge.

As I lay there languishing in her pink satin sheets, I thought how considerate of my new best friend to let me sleep in. No doubt she was clearing up the mess left by the intruder in the living room. With any luck, she would have put the kettle on so we could enjoy a leisurely breakfast before leaving for work together.

My morning stretch ended abruptly as the bedroom door flew open and an elderly woman with light brown frizzy hair and dressed in a pink floral housecoat roared in with the Hoover.

Startled, I leapt out of bed. Annabel's business on the side must be doing very well to afford a daily help.

'Oh!' the daily exclaimed as she turned off the machine. 'I didn't know Annabel had company.'

I recognized the woman instantly – she was one of my mourner regulars.

'Mrs Millicent P. Evans, wife of Mr Leonard R. Evans? We've met before,' I said, offering my hand. 'Vicky Hill, *Gipping Gazette.*'

Mrs Evans stared at my chest and began to back away. I realized the top three buttons of my pyjama top had come unfastened. Her eyes darted towards the unmade bed.

'This isn't what you think it is,' I said, deftly doing the buttons back up. Annabel might not care about her reputation, but I certainly did. I pointed to the wall of pillows that divided the bed and laughed. 'Annabel and I work together. We're just friends.'

'Well, you never know these days.' Mrs Evans looked relieved. 'Annabel needs a good *friend.* That's what I keep telling her. Annabel, I say, you need—'

'I expect my friend is in the kitchen making some tea,' I said hopefully.

'Oh no.' Mrs Evans shook her head. 'She's already gone.'

Gone? A horrible feeling started to form in my stomach. I began to cast around for my wristwatch. I could have sworn I left it on the bedside table. 'You wouldn't have the time, would you?'

'I start at nine—'

'*Nine!*' I shrieked. 'Excuse me.' I charged past her and into the living room – now spotlessly tidy – having distinctly remembered seeing an ornate grandfather clock standing in the corner.

To my horror, it was nearly ten thirty! *Blast!* How could I have slept so late? Surely, there must be a misunderstanding. Annabel knew I had no clothes or means of transportation. Perhaps she'd forgotten I was staying? I was a quiet sleeper and the feather barrier between us was so high, she can't have noticed I was there. I was determined not to take it personally. Once she realized her mistake, I was certain she'd be full of heartfelt apologies.

That aside, I had to get to work quickly. Although I didn't relish going home to Rumble Lane to face the music, I needed a change of clothes. There was no question of me squeezing into Annabel's stuff. She was half my size.

I headed for the front door where Mrs Poultry's Wellington boots were standing on a fresh sheet of newspaper along with the Tesco shopping bag. I retrieved my safari jacket that was draped around the back of the chair and was about to put it on when Mrs Evans emerged from the bedroom brandishing her duster and carrying a can of Pledge furniture polish.

'They've forecast rain,' she cried. 'Oh! You'll catch your death dressed like that.' She whipped off her housecoat to reveal a faded Gipping Growlers football shirt and grey leggings clinging to robust thighs. 'Why don't we pop this over the top of your pyjamas? We need to keep that bottom of yours warm.'

Another comment about my bottom, I thought. 'My jacket's just fine,' I said, pulling it on and thrusting my bare feet into the Wellington boots. Catching a glimpse of my reflection in Annabel's full-length mirror next to the front door, I shuddered. Could that really be me? I looked a fright with my unbrushed hair sticking up in spikes and crumpled pyjamas.

Mrs Evans grasped the front of my safari jacket and began doing the buttons up, yanking the fabric tightly as if I were a small child. 'There we are. Let's keep out the draught. Have you got gloves, dear?'

'I'm not cold. Thanks. Must go.'

Picking up the plastic carrier bag, I stopped dead. A note was stuck to it with tape – *For Vicky*.

I stared at it for several moments. Why would Annabel put my name on it if she expected to see me in the morning? The cold truth hit me hard. Annabel had deliberately let me sleep in. She must have hidden my wristwatch, too. What a rotten trick to play. Well, two can play at that game.

I opened the plastic bag and peered at the poppet inside. 'Oh no!'

'What's the matter, dear?'

'I expect Annabel just forgot.' I adopted a worried frown and pointed at the note *For Vicky*. 'She was supposed to have left some papers in this bag.'

Mrs Evans's face was etched with concern. 'Were they important?'

'Yes. Very. It's that story she's working on with Mayor Rawlings.'

Mrs Evans made a strange clicking sound of disapproval that I realized came from her ill-fitting dentures. 'No good will come of that, you mark my words.'

'You're absolutely right.' I wasn't sure if Mrs Evans was talking about Annabel's affair or the story but to my delight, sensed the daily was eager to chat. What would it matter being another five minutes late in the great scheme of life?

'I said to her, Annabel, I said,' Mrs Evans went on, 'be careful of men who promise to make you a star.'

'He said that?' I felt a twinge of envy. Mayor Rawlings was a powerful man in Devon with a lot of influence. He'd even been on *Westward Television Celebrity Squares*.

'Oh yes. It all starts with the promises.' Mrs Evans sat down on the hall chair, clearly ready for a long gossip about her employer. 'That's what happened to my daughter, Sadie.'

'Sadie Evans is *your* daughter?' Everyone at the *Gazette* had heard of Sadie Evans's performance at The Banana Club on Plymouth Hoe. According to Pete, Sadie's pole-dancing skills made grown men cry.

'It's the lure of the older man, you see. They've got money and a nice car, thank you very much, but they never leave their wives.'

'Men never marry their mistresses,' I said firmly.

'Oh, I *know*. I kept telling—'

'I'm worried that this story they're working on together could be dangerous,' I said. 'I wonder what it could be . . .'

Mrs Evans's brow furrowed in concentration. Her teeth

clicked three times. 'It might be something to do with that Folly up at The Grange.'

'Hugh's Folly in Trewallyn Woods?' *Blast!* So Annabel really *was* working on a story with Rawlings.

Mrs Evans nodded. 'I overheard her on the phone. Something about comings and goings in the middle of the night.'

My God! Was it possible Annabel was pursuing the very same story as myself? 'Naturally, Lady Trewallyn is involved.'

'Oh yes,' Mrs Evans declared. 'I believe it was her idea. I clean at The Grange. Fridays. The mayor was up there one morning when I was cleaning the windows.'

'The mayor *met* with Lady Trewallyn?' This was a severe blow to my plan.

'Very chummy, they were. Yes, I remember now. I thought to myself, I thought. That man's going to break Annabel's heart but who can blame him. Lady Katherine is such a lovely woman.'

'Men certainly do seem to fall in love with her.' My glee at knowing Annabel's heart could be broken by a very real rival was suppressed by the very real knowledge that Lady Trewallyn must be recruiting all the available men in Gipping to frolic in her coven.

'Her ladyship knew all about Sadie's profession,' Mrs Evans said. 'We had a lovely chat. They call them exotic dancers now, you know.'

'It must have been a terrible shock to her when Sir Hugh died,' I declared.

'Oh yes. Devastated, she was. They were devoted, you know.'

'Apparently, Dave Randall found the body in a hedge,' I said innocently.

'What rubbish.' Mrs Evans snorted. 'Her ladyship told me *she* found Sir Hugh in the library.'

She would say that.

'Randall was always hanging around all loved up, but then

213

again, she had that effect on men.' Mrs Evans got to her feet. 'Well, I must get on.'

'You've really been a great help.'

'Anything for our Annabel,' Mrs Evans said with a click of her dentures.

Suddenly, an odd expression flooded her face as if a light went on upstairs. 'Don't you lodge with Mrs Poultry?'

'Yes. Why?'

Mrs Evans grabbed my arm. 'It's the Salome Steel competition,' she said in a furtive whisper. 'I've heard on the grapevine that she knows who the real author is.'

'Really?' I was surprised Mrs Poultry would even care, considering she'd declared *Voodoo Vixens* as utter filth.

An awkward silence fell between us until it occurred to me that Mrs Evans wanted me to ask Mrs Poultry who the author was. There was no way I would ask my landlady.

'The *Gazette* is giving out clues every week,' I said. 'Perhaps I can slip them to you ahead of time?'

'And in return, I'll keep an eye on our Annabel.' Mrs Evans sighed. 'I'm not asking for myself. It's for Sadie.' She pulled a scrap of paper towel out of her apron and dabbed at each eye. 'Ever since she went on the stage, Mr Evans has banned her from the house. I haven't seen her for months. Have you any idea how it feels not being able to see your own kin?'

'Yes, I do.' I did, actually, and it was dreadful.

'Not being able to share Saturday morning shopping?' Mrs Evans cried. 'No evening Bingo on a Thursday at the social club.' Mrs Evans swallowed hard. 'Land's End would be such a *special* day out for us.'

'And Mr Evans need never know.'

Mrs Evans brightened up. 'I'm told on a clear day you can even see France!'

I didn't have the heart to tell her seeing France from Land's End was a geographical impossibility. 'I'll see what I can do. Must go. Bye.'

Outside, the spatter of rain had turned into a steady drizzle. It was so murky that I couldn't even see the canal, only yards from the front door.

In no time at all, my safari jacket clung damply to my chest. My hair stuck to my head; water dripped off the tip of my nose. I felt utterly depressed and wanted to cry. Far from being thrilled at discovering Annabel's secret scoop, I realized not only was she working on the same exclusive as me, she practically had her story in the bag.

True, I had recruited an excellent informer. Mrs Evans seemed a good sort of person genuinely concerned for Annabel's welfare. Even her desire to cheat in the Salome Steel competition was endearing. It was for her daughter, after all.

Mrs Evans was warm, kind, and caring – nothing like my mother who was never one for mollycoddling. *Good grief!* Surely you're not jealous of Annabel's daily help!

Annabel, Annabel, *Annabel.* What had I ever done to deserve such an enemy? My mild dislike for her morphed into cold loathing. My eyes began to sting with unshed tears. Then, I thought, why not shed them? It wasn't as if anyone cared.

The crunch of car tyres brought me up short. Ahead, a dark shape emerged through the morning gloom. My heart lifted. Perhaps Annabel had suffered an attack of conscience and had come back to pick me up? My stomach went over as the car drew closer. It wasn't Annabel's BMW, it was the black Porsche.

Blast! My first thought was to turn round and hobble back to the relative safety of Beaver Lock Lodge until it occurred to me that must be exactly where the Porsche was heading. *Good God!* Was it possible that *Chester* had planted the poppet as a warning to Annabel and he was now on his way to finish the job? What about kindly Mrs Evans? Would he kill her, too?

I stopped. Paralysed. The car would be upon me in seconds. With the canal on one side and the hedge on the other, I was done for.

33

'Is this the way to Beaver Lock Lodge?' called out a familiar voice as the Porsche stopped alongside me. 'I'm looking for the reporter, Annabel Lake.'

What nerve! The killer was even asking for directions! 'Good morning. Horrible weather we're having.'

'*Shit!*' Chester removed his sunglasses and leaned out of the window. 'Vicky? Is that *you*?'

'Hullo.' I gave a weak wave. 'Didn't recognize you for a moment.'

'What the hell are you doing here? No! Don't tell me.' Chester's voice was laced with sarcasm. 'Out for an early morning hedge-jump practice in the rain – *and*, in your pyjamas?'

'That's right.' I forced a hearty smile. 'There's an excellent privet down there.'

'Is that so?' Chester regarded me with great amusement. 'Then you must know Annabel Lake.'

I hesitated for a fraction. *Careful, Vicky.* If I admitted to knowing her, he'd soon figure out we worked at the *Gazette* together and my cover would be blown. There was also poor

Mrs Evans. I didn't think she'd need much torture to reveal all she knew.

I had to stop Chester from going to Beaver Lock Lodge. Even if it meant putting my own life in danger. 'Does Annabel Lake drive a silver BMW?' I asked innocently.

Chester nodded.

'She passed me at least an hour ago,' I said, pretending to shiver with cold. 'Goodness, I shouldn't have stopped to chat. It's freezing and I have a *very* long walk home.'

'Let me give you a ride,' he said, switching off the engine.

'Are you *sure*?'

'Oh, I'm sure.' Chester got out and slid into the narrow space between the hedge and the car. 'You'll have to clamber over the driver's seat.'

He closed the door and pulled me close to him where we did a clumsy do-si-do so I could get in his side.

'Allow me to take your bag.'

'No! I can manage!' I snapped. If he looked inside, he'd know I'd found the poppet! He'd know I'd guessed his game. I hurled myself over the bucket seat, promptly getting my pyjama leg hooked over the gear stick.

'Careful now.' Chester sounded amused. 'Do you want a hand?'

I felt mortified. No doubt he was getting a good thrill looking at my bottom – just like all men do. 'No, thanks.' I yanked at the fabric. The leg tore. I fell and hit the side of my face on the dashboard and rolled onto the plastic bag. There was a nasty crackle and snap. *Blast!*

Could my day get any worse? I then thought, of course it could! I was getting into a car with a *murderer*!

Chester slipped into the driver's seat, pulled on his seat belt – I swiftly fastened mine – started the engine, and eased the car forward.

'Wait!' I cried, suddenly realizing that the only turning space was at Beaver Lock Lodge. We'd have to drive to there after all and, knowing my luck, Mrs Evans was bound to spot us. 'You'll have to reverse back to the main road, I'm afraid.'

'Why?'

'A few minutes before you arrived, the Gipping County Council dustcart drove down there to empty the bins,' I said wildly. 'It's Tuesday. We're bound to meet it coming back.'

'No problem.' Chester deftly thrust the gear stick into reverse and we flew backwards at high speed in a dead-straight line. It was the mark of a professional getaway driver. I couldn't help but feel impressed.

PAAARRRP! PAAARRRP!

'Goddamit!' Chester slammed his foot on the brakes.

Ronnie Binns and his dustcart – marked clearly GIPPING COUNTY COUNCIL – had just entered the gravel lane leading to Beaver Lock Lodge and was blocking our exit.

'I could have sworn it had gone past me,' I muttered, wondering if Gipping County Council really *did* empty Annabel's bins on Tuesdays or was it just an excuse for Ronnie's visit?

Ronnie reversed a few measly yards, enough to wave Chester through with a fanfare of flashing lights and another long *PAAARRRP* on his horn. We bumped over the corner of a grass verge and turned into the main road.

'I suppose I'd better tell you where I live,' I said lightly, stealing a glimpse at my chauffeur. Chester's face looked like thunder. 'I live in Rumble Lane. It's not too far,' I chattered on. 'It's really kind of you to give me a lift.'

Chester still did not answer. Then, without warning, he slammed his foot down hard on the accelerator! The force pinned me to the back of my seat. I glanced at the speedometer. We had already hit seventy miles an hour! To my horror, Chester took a hairpin bend without slowing down, overtaking three cars in quick succession, and ignoring the blaring horns of enraged motorists.

I clung to the side of my seat as Chester drove faster. We reached a T-junction. He barely paused, cutting across oncoming traffic with only a whisker to spare, narrowly missing a cyclist. 'Gipping is that way!' I cried as we sped away from the town.

Chester merely increased his speed. 'Please slow down,' I begged, but my pleas fell on deaf ears. To my dismay, we flew past a sign saying GIPPING – COME AGAIN SOON and headed out towards the open moors.

Stunned, I stared out of the window at the passing countryside, feeling a pang of longing in the knowledge that I would never live to experience sexual ecstasy, let alone have a husband and children.

Suddenly, Chester turned left into an empty car park. Except for three wooden picnic tables and a vandalized concrete hut marked TOILETS, the place was deserted.

This is it, Vicky.

The Porsche came to a bumpy stop. Chester switched off the engine and turned to face me. 'It's time you and I had a little chat.'

I nodded meekly, clutching the plastic bag to my chest.

'You're an interesting young woman,' Chester said. 'Someone who lies as much as you do must have something to hide.'

With a sinking heart, I knew what I was up against. Interrogation. I recalled Dad's advice:

1. *Stick as close to the truth as possible.*
2. *Do not admit to anything without a lawyer present.*
3. *Be polite and never engage.*

Chester stroked his chin thoughtfully. 'Let's start with that louse, Randall. You told me you hardly knew him but I hear you and he were hot and heavy on Sunday night.'

Seeing my shocked expression, he added, 'It's a small town. Word gets around.'

'We hadn't met last week,' I said hotly. 'We only really met *this* week and what's it to you? Dave and I are both single.'

Steady, Vicky.

'Dave's small fry,' Chester went on. 'You are far more interesting. What exactly were you doing skulking around pigsties at The Grange?'

'I told you, I was practising my hedge-jumping skills.'

'After a Chinese takeout?' Chester sneered. 'You thought I wouldn't check what you were up to?' He leaned over towards me, his voice heavy with menace. 'It's you, isn't it? You're the one planting those chicken corpses all over Gipping!'

Affronted, I cried, 'It most certainly is not!'

'You think I don't know what's happening in the woods?'

The woods again! I was intrigued by Chester's accusation. If he thought I was involved in Lady Trewallyn's coven, it meant he was no longer soup du jour in her bed. It certainly explained why he was so furious with his ex-lover at the graveside; why he was lurking at The Grange; and why he broke into the *Gazette* to steal Dave's photographs. He'd found out she was sleeping with Dave and was mad with jealousy. I bet he didn't know about Sharpe yet, either!

Instead of getting rattled, I knew this was the perfect time to strike a deal. He was bound to have vital information to back up my scoop. What's more, if my hunch was right, and he had been tossed out of the coven, he'd be willing to talk.

'The good news is that Dave and Lady Trewallyn are no longer an item,' I said. 'The bad news is that she's met someone else.'

Chester turned pale. 'Who?'

'Coroner Sharpe. I saw them on the day of the funeral actually. Just after you left. There was instant chemistry. Then, I saw them canoodling at the morgue,' I added. 'He's very wealthy. Won half a million on the football pools.'

Chester's shoulders slumped. He fell silent and looked morosely out of the window, no doubt crushed by my revelation. Perhaps he really loved her, after all.

I reached out and gave his arm a compassionate squeeze. 'I'm sorry. Do you want to tell me about it?'

'Sure, I'll tell you.' Chester turned back to me, his expression hard. 'For ten thousand pounds.'

Was he insane? The most the *Gazette* ever paid for information was fifty quid and that was in three instalments. 'Why would I pay *you* ten thousand pounds?'

'Because you're a newspaper reporter.' Chester gave a harsh laugh. 'As a matter of fact, I was on my way to see Annabel Lake when I conveniently ran into you.'

For once, I was stumped for a reply. So he *had* known all along.

'Did you really think I didn't see you hiding at the *Gazette* the other night?' Chester demanded.

I felt my face redden but brazened it out. 'I was working late and you startled me,' I said.

Anxious to avoid the alarm snafu, I changed the subject. 'Goodness! You *must* have quite a sensational story to warrant that kind of sum.'

'It's time everyone knew the truth behind Katherine Vanderkamp,' Chester said. 'And I've got proof! If you're not interested, I'm sure Annabel—'

'She's just a trainee.' I hoped my face wouldn't betray my excitement. Proof meant photographs! He might even have one of Lady Trewallyn prancing around naked! But how could I persuade Chester to give me the prize without paying the money?

'Naturally, we've known about the goings-on in the woods for some time,' I declared. 'Plus, Lady Trewallyn isn't a local, so that would lower the price.' I pretended to consider his proposition. 'Obviously, I'll have to see the evidence first, but I'm sure my editor will negotiate—'

'I don't negotiate. Deal or no deal,' Chester said.

Blast! 'Give me twenty-four hours.'

'All right,' Chester said grudgingly. 'After that, I'll go elsewhere.'

He reached into his pocket and took out a scrap of paper and scribbled a number down. 'That's my mobile. Call me.'

I put it in my pocket. Chester started the engine. The Porsche roared into life.

As we headed back to the safety of Gipping, I considered Chester's accusation that I'd been guilty of planting the chicken corpses 'all over Gipping'.

'Just one more thing,' I said à la Columbo. 'Those chickens. For the record, I'm a vegetarian and would never do anything to hurt one of God's creatures.'

'Nor would Kandi,' Chester said. 'She's an animal activist. Anti-fur, campaigns for battery chickens, that kind of thing.'

Lady Trewallyn must be an eco-witch.

'Someone was trying to frame her.' Chester's voice hardened. 'But I don't care any more. She and I are finished.'

All thoughts of Chester's revelations vanished as the Porsche turned into Rumble Lane. I couldn't believe it. A police car was parked outside number 10. For some horrible reason, Mrs Poultry had called the cops.

34

'You did say number ten, didn't you?' Chester pulled up behind the police car and let me out. 'Goddamit, I hate those sons of bitches.'

'Me too,' I said, unable to shake the fear that Mrs Poultry had found the coroner's reports.

It was only when he drove off that I realized I couldn't ring his mobile. *You idiot, Vicky!* He could be staying anywhere in Gipping – or Devon for that matter. *Damn and blast it!*

I hobbled the short distance up the drive wincing with pain at every step. My blisters had been rubbed raw. To my dismay, Mrs Poultry was waiting for me at the front door. Her arms were folded across her bosom, her face stern.

'Where have you been all night?' she demanded. 'What happened to your face?'

'I walked into a door,' I said. 'I was with Annabel, remember?'

'Lying is the tongue of the devil!' she scolded. I wondered if she had seen me getting out of Chester's car. Before I could defend myself, Mrs Poultry stared at my feet and declared, 'My wellingtons, I believe.'

Turning on her heel and stomping inside, she said over her shoulder, 'Detective Constable Probes is waiting in the kitchen.'

I kicked off the boots and hung my wet safari jacket on the hall coat stand.

'And don't go sneaking upstairs,' Mrs Poultry shouted from the kitchen. 'Come in here, *now!*'

Gritting my teeth, I braced myself for the inevitable interrogation. I was still baffled by what I was supposed to have done.

Probes leapt to his feet as I walked in. His eyes widened as he took in my blue flannel pyjamas – rather the worse for wear – and bare blistered feet. I looked at him, defiant. 'Morning, officer. To what do I owe this pleasure?'

Probes cleared his throat and retrieved a small notepad and pencil from his top pocket. 'Mrs Poultry informs me that your friend Annabel Lake seemed very upset last night. When you didn't return home, your landlady became worried. Would you like to tell me what happened?'

'Nothing happened,' I said, wondering if it had been Probes who'd broken into Beaver Lock Lodge and left that poppet on Annabel's bed.

'That's not what I heard or saw, Victoria,' Mrs Poultry said coldly. Turning to Probes she added, 'I wouldn't have wasted police time if I hadn't been deeply concerned.'

I was astonished. What business was it of hers? For the past few months she hadn't cared if I'd lived or died. Now, all of a sudden, she cared.

'It's personal, actually,' I announced.

'And the bruise?' Probes pointed to my face.

'Annabel,' I said solemnly. I could virtually feel waves of disbelief emanating from Mrs Poultry. I didn't dare to even look at Probes. 'I know I should have telephoned Mrs Poultry and told her not to worry, but . . .' I trailed off. 'You know how one gets swept up in the heat of the moment.'

'Quite.' Probes coughed and looked down at his shoes. 'Well,

I think that explains everything,' he said, closing his notebook and carefully putting it back in his top pocket with his pencil. 'Can I drop you off anywhere, Ms Hill? After you've got *dressed,* of course!'

'There is no need, officer. I'll take Victoria to work. It's on my way to market.' Mrs Poultry gave him a dazzling smile – a rather terrifying sight given that I'd never seen her upper and lower teeth exposed at the same time. 'I'll see you out.'

The second they left the kitchen I grabbed the plastic bag and ran up to my room. My mouth felt dry as I threw open the bedroom door, prepared for the worst. To my relief, it was exactly as I'd left it – the coroner's reports were still beneath my pillow untouched, and the plastic-covered postcards still in the water tank.

A tap on the door startled me. I darted over and opened it a crack. 'Yes?'

Mrs Poultry was standing on the landing with a mug of tea in one hand. For a moment, I thought it was for me, until she took a sip. 'We're leaving in five minutes.'

'Thanks.' My mouth watered. I could have done with a cuppa.

Turning back to the incriminating evidence, I decided it would be wise to hide both coroner's reports in the water tank inside the plastic bag with Annabel's poppet. But when I opened it, my worst fears were confirmed. The papier-mâché doll was completely crushed. *Blast!* I'd even had a good headline: HERALD OF DEATH, DOLL OF HATE.

'Are you ready?' Mrs Poultry called up from downstairs.

'Be there in a minute,' I shouted. I shoved the reports into the bag, opened the wooden panel, lifted the lid off the water tank, and carefully wedged the package behind the ball cock, just below the waterline. Quickly, I dragged my pyjamas off, pulled on a pair of jeans and navy blue sweater. Unfortunately, the dampness of my safari jacket meant I had to resort to my emergency fluorescent yellow cagoule.

Mrs Poultry, dressed in tweed coat and cloche hat, gave the Morris Traveller plenty of choke. It coughed to life on the fourth try. Plumes of exhaust smoke surrounded us like a blue cloud. The Morris made a grating, clanging whine, as Mrs Poultry carefully reversed out of the drive.

'This is very nice of you,' I said.

Mrs Poultry didn't answer. We set off at such an excruciatingly slow speed we were even passed by an elderly man walking his dog. Driving the two miles to work was going to take ages.

Finally, Mrs Poultry spoke. 'I'm disappointed in you, Victoria,' she began. *Here we go.* 'Haven't I told you before about gentleman callers?'

'The man in the Porsche was simply giving me a lift home in the rain.'

Mrs Poultry gasped. 'You must *never* accept lifts from strangers. *Never*!'

'Oh no, he was—'

'There! You see! Already you think he is a nice man,' she declared, taking her foot completely off the accelerator. The Morris shuddered as the engine ground to a halt and promptly stalled. 'Given your unsuitable attire, I pray he did not compromise your purity?'

Compromise my purity? I stifled the urge to giggle.

Mrs Poultry tried to start the engine again. The nauseous smell of petrol wafted through the air vents.

'I think you've flooded the engine,' I said even more consumed by the urge to laugh. 'Actually, Chester—'

'Chester! *Chester*?' Mrs Poultry sneered.

'That's his name. Chester Forbes. He's an American. In fact, he's an old lover of Lady Trewallyn's.' I realized this could be the perfect opportunity to bring up the subject of my landlady's presence at St Peter's. 'He turned up at Sir Hugh's funeral and created quite a scandal at the graveside. Didn't you see what happened?'

'Cradle to Coffin Catering was not asked to provide

refreshments at the house after the service,' Mrs Poultry declared, neatly sidestepping the question.

'What do you think of Lady Trewallyn?' I said. 'She's very beautiful.'

For an answer, Mrs Poultry turned the key in the ignition, and with a jolt, we were off once again.

'She's nothing like his first wife, Lady Clarissa, is she?' I pressed on. 'Apparently, Sir Hugh was devastated when she dropped dead at Maurice Wheeler's funeral party. Wasn't that one of your shindigs?'

'If you've been speaking with Barbara Meadows, she's a notorious gossip and never gets her facts straight. Lady Clarissa was a drunk. The marriage was a sham.'

Mrs Poultry's outburst surprised me but I'd have to grill her later. An ambulance was parked outside The Copper Kettle. Its blue lights were flashing, rear doors open. A small crowd had already begun to gather on the pavement.

'Oh no,' I whispered. 'Topaz!' Something awful must have happened to her. My first thoughts were she'd been murdered. Or committed suicide? Topaz had seemed depressed. I knew she had not seemed her usual self, but instead of showing sympathy, I had callously disregarded the signs. If something had happened to Topaz, it was my fault.

'I'll drop you here,' Mrs Poultry declared, disinterested in the drama ahead. The Morris mounted the pavement with a violent thud so she could let me out.

As I headed for the cafe, I realized the excitement was centred on the opposite side of the street at the *Gazette,* not The Copper Kettle. What's more, the cafe was actually open for a change – obviously taking advantage of potential new customers. I resisted the temptation to stop and congratulate Topaz for taking my advice and instead pushed my way through the surging throng outside the *Gazette.* I had to brandish my press card to reach Barbara where she stood guard at the glass front entrance waiting for me.

227

'Quickly,' she said, opening the door a crack, as if expecting a saleroom rush from those outside. 'What's happened to your face?'

'Door,' I said, gawping at Barbara's. She'd painted two blue stripes down each cheek. 'What's happened?'

I slid through the gap. Barbara closed the door and flipped over the sign, GONE TO LUNCH, even though it was not quite 11.30 a.m.

'Thank God you're here,' she said, gesturing towards the door that led to the inner hallway. 'Annabel's been asking for you. There's been a terrible accident.'

35

Tony, Edward, and Pete stood in an anguished bunch in the doorway that led down to the basement. Barbara's pink bicycle lay on its side in the hall.

I grabbed Tony's arm. 'What happened?'

'The paramedics are—'

'Tripped over Barbara's bloody bike, that's what happened,' Pete said.

'It's not going outside,' Barbara retorted hotly. 'Someone will steal it.'

'Where the hell have you been?' Pete demanded.

'Helping police with their inquiries,' said Probes, miraculously materializing by my side. 'I'm afraid I had to steal her away.'

Pete cursed under his breath. 'What kind of inquiries, officer? Anything I can help you with?'

'Whilst you two chat, I must go to Annabel,' I said, struck by a sudden thought. Was it possible Annabel's accident was connected to the crushed poppet in my possession?

It was difficult to see much in the gloom below. I could make out two men in white coats. Steve's vast bulk virtually spanned the width of the kitchenette. He was kneeling awkwardly over my fallen colleague. The basement door was open where Tom, framed in the doorway, was preparing to give her oxygen.

Steadying myself, I descended the steep, wobbly stairs carefully avoiding a solitary brown three-inch platform shoe three steps up from the basement floor.

The cramped kitchenette was stifling and stank of body odour. It was coming from Steve, who was perspiring heavily through his white coat. I peered over his shoulder and saw Annabel lying on her back with her head towards the open basement door. She looked awful.

Steve swivelled round. His face lit up. 'Oh hello! Remember me? Steve? We met on the combine-motorbike job? That's a nasty bruise on your face. Do you want—?'

''Annabel!' I said, giving Steve a brief nod. 'It's me, Vicky.'

'I rang the *Gazette*.' Steve carried on cheerfully. 'Didn't the receptionist tell you?'

'Can we talk about this later?' I gestured to Annabel. 'My friend is hurt.'

'My shoe . . . oh, Vicky,' moaned Annabel, raising her hand in a pathetic greeting. Tom promptly shoved it back down and thrust an oxygen mask on her face.

'Lie still,' he snapped, adding sharply, 'Steve, pay attention! We're working here. Take this.' He passed him what resembled a long, deflated balloon.

'Later.' Steve winked at me and, turning back to his patient, deftly wrapped the rubber casing around Annabel's leg. 'Ready to pump!' he shouted.

'Tom?' Probes called out. He must have crept down behind me. 'What's the diagnosis on the young lady's leg?'

'We can't say until she's been X-rayed.'

'I'll inform her family,' said Probes.

'Her father's away at sea in the navy,' Pete said, standing halfway down the stairs. 'Mother ran off with the local vet. She's pretty much alone.'

This news surprised me. Perhaps it was the dark secret that Annabel had alluded to? Annabel began to whimper again, mumbling something incoherent.

'What's she trying to say?' I asked.

'She's been ranting and raving about some Folly in the woods.'

'Oh yes, the Folly.' *Thank you, Mrs Evans.* 'Anything else?'

'And a doll.' Steve rolled Annabel onto the stretcher. 'Some kind of death threat.'

'Doll?' Probes turned to me. Our eyes met. He raised his eyebrows and we shared a mutual nod of understanding. 'Did she describe it?'

Steve shrugged. 'Sounded weird to me. Said the doll had a hatpin stuck in its eye.'

'I'd like us to take a look at that,' Probes said to me in a low voice.

'Good idea,' I said.

'We'll load her out back,' said Tom. 'Steve, bring the ambulance into the alley.'

The stretcher carrying Annabel's limp body was lifted over the wall beyond. With the excitement over, Probes, Pete, and I retraced our steps to reception.

'Do you mind if I steal Vicky for a little longer, sir?' Probes inquired. 'Won't be more than a couple of minutes.'

'I've got a lot to do,' I said, desperately hoping that Pete would come to my rescue. 'Isn't Brian Dickson being buried at St Peter's this afternoon?'

Probes gave an awkward cough. 'Not today. I'm afraid I can't say why.'

Pete turned beetroot. 'Vicky, a word?' he said, dragging me over to the far side of reception. 'Now listen here,' he whispered. 'I don't like this any more than you. That bloody copper is on to us. I think he knows I was paying Brian off. That's why Brian's not being buried yet.'

231

Had bribery inadvertently caused Brian's untimely demise? No wonder Pete was worried. 'Do you think—?'

'Sssh,' Pete hissed, jabbing his finger at Probes, who seemed entranced by one of Gipping's sensational stories – PLYM VALLEY TOWER TRAGEDY – framed on the wall. 'There's something fishy about that copper and I want to find out what it is.'

I agreed wholeheartedly. Much as I thought Pete was a creep, his reporter instincts were spot on.

Pete leaned in closely, giving me a full blast of bad breath, and added, 'As Annabel's not here, it'll have to be you. He's a man for God's sake. Flirt with him. Get him to loosen up a bit. Show him your knickers, know what I mean?'

I knew exactly what he meant – in theory – though putting it into practice was another matter. Pete and I strolled over to Probes, who was still engrossed in the press clipping.

'Vicky, why don't you take the officer across to The Kettle for some privacy?' Pete announced. 'The *Gazette* will pay for the refreshments.'

'Officer?' I said, coyly sidling up to him. 'Let's get away from all this bedlam. I'm so hungry I could faint.'

'Well . . . of course . . . if you insist.' Probes looked uncomfortable.

Lunch at The Copper Kettle would give me a chance to check in on Topaz. I was glad she had not ended up in hospital. I knew I'd been hard on her, but sometimes, tough love is necessary. We all needed friends – particularly those who had access to the general public. You could learn a lot about a town's goings-on from the common man.

As we entered the cafe, my stomach grumbled. I was absolutely starving.

36

The moment Topaz saw Probes and me walk in together, she turned deathly pale. I was glad to see she'd cleaned herself up a bit – her olive serge pinafore, though stained, was pressed, and her lace mob cap, a sparkling white. My pep talk had obviously lifted her out of her slump.

'Hi, Topaz. Table for two?' Topaz immediately spun on her heel and vanished through the plastic fringe into the kitchen. 'She's busy today,' I said, by way of explanation for Topaz's blatant rudeness.

Probes removed his helmet and began fiddling with the brim. 'Perhaps we should go somewhere else?'

Surveying the room, I was encouraged to see three customers sitting at a corner table – Mr and Mrs Errol Fairweather and Miss Mary J. Larch. I gave a smile of recognition, which all pointedly ignored. They were probably three of the most miserable mourners in England. Sometimes, I wondered if people regarded me as an omen of impending doom.

Turning to Probes, I said, 'Let's go and sit down anyway. Topaz always keeps a table vacant for me.'

I led him over to the one by the window. Probes pulled out

my chair to let me sit down first – a nice gesture in this day and age – and took the seat opposite. I picked up my chair and scooted round to sit next to him. 'So we can't be overheard,' I said in response to his look of surprise. He edged a few inches away from me. I reminded myself to go easy on him because this was a public place and he was on duty.

Moments later, Topaz fluttered over. She refused to look at either of us, merely slapping two menus down on the table.

'Hi, Topaz,' I said cheerfully. 'It seems business is looking up. What can you recommend on today's menu?'

'Fruitcake,' she said in a sullen voice. 'I'm having kitchen problems.'

'Lovely,' I beamed. 'Fruitcake and tea it is.'

'What about him?' Topaz spat. I was beginning to regret my concern for her welfare but was determined to be pleasant. Then I remembered Topaz's staunch denials of our steamy lesbian conversation from the other night at The Three Tuns. How utterly thoughtless of me! Of course! She was jealous of my relationship with Probes. She probably thought she didn't care about me until she saw me walk in with someone else. *My God!* How fantastic! I'd never been the centre of a love triangle before.

Gesturing to Probes, I said, 'You remember Detective Constable Probes, don't you?'

'No,' Topaz and Probes chorused. Both turned red. I looked from one to the other with growing suspicion. Probes inspected his fingernails, and Topaz pulled at that same irritating loose strand of hair dangling from her lace mob cap. Recalling the wink between them in reception after the break-in, my mind started to churn.

'Look, I know you've met before because I was there in reception when you did,' I snapped. The one thing I couldn't stand was when amateur liars tried to fool a professional. 'It's nothing to me if you know each other. I was merely being polite.'

'Oh! I remember now. After the break-in?' Topaz said, eyes wide.

'Oh yes, that's when it was.' Probes gave a strange half laugh, half snort. The two of them chuckled and made a meal of 'Well, fancy! I don't remember! Losing my mind! Getting old!'

'Good, now that's clear,' I said coldly. 'Perhaps you could bring us some tea?'

'Of course.' Topaz whirled around and fluttered back to the kitchen.

'She gets jealous when I'm with other men . . . or women for that matter. Relationships are so tricky,' I said. 'Do you have a girlfriend?'

'I'm afraid this isn't a social call,' Probes said abruptly. 'Brian's brakes were deliberately cut. It was murder.'

'Murder?' I was shocked. How could Probes sit there and look me in the eye, pretending he had nothing to do with it!

'Why would anyone want to murder Brian?'

'I was hoping you could tell me.' Probes fixed me with a hard stare. 'We think there is a link between this and Sir Hugh Trewallyn's death.'

'Sir Hugh had a heart attack,' I said, all innocence.

'Ms Hill, I'm not being one hundred per cent straight with you.' Probes looked over his shoulder in the direction of the kitchen. He lowered his voice to a whisper. 'I came to Gipping for another reason.'

'Oh?' I forced a smile but I swear my heart stopped.

'It's part of a much larger investigation that I'm not at liberty to disclose at this time.'

'I don't see how I can help you.' I gripped the table tightly for fear of literally falling off my chair. He knows about my parents! He knows!

'When was the last time you saw Brian alive – apart from when he was lying on the stretcher?'

Blast! I could hardly admit that Brian had visited the *Gazette* or worse, that he had fled the morgue the moment he saw me!

'I've never officially been introduced to Brian.' This was true. We hadn't.

'But he recognized you,' Probes said, exasperated.

I shrugged. 'As I may have mentioned before, I'm pretty well known by the general public.'

Probes took out his notebook and flipped it open. 'We have to piece together Brian's final journey.' Retrieving a pencil from his top pocket he went on, 'The accident happened at 4.45 p.m. Therefore, we know he left the morgue before his shift ended. This was unusual. Where were you?'

'Helping Barbara do the filing.'

'Miss Meadows claimed you left shortly before 4.30 p.m. and were in a hurry.'

Damn and blast Barbara! I felt my face turn red. 'Honestly, officer, surely it's the coroner you should be questioning, not me.'

'Apparently Coroner Sharpe has gone on holiday. He left this morning.'

'Alone?'

'Why do you say that?' said Probes sharply.

'No reason.'

'If you are withholding evidence, Ms Hill, you could be in serious trouble.'

'Here we are,' Topaz said, elbowing me in the face. Probes and I jumped apart as she thumped the tray down on the table between us, liberally spilling tea into both cracked saucers. 'Do you want to pay now?'

'Can I have a receipt?'

'Let me.' Probes had whisked out a five pound note. Topaz snatched it out of his fingers without a word and stalked to the cash till by the door.

'Here's your change.' Topaz thrust her hand between us like a knife. Leaning forward into Probes's ear she hissed, 'How *could* you?' And stormed off again.

'I'll give tea a miss.' Probes seemed flustered and knocked over the salt shaker. He got to his feet. 'I'm sorry. I've just remembered I've got to get back to the station. If you think of anything, you know where to find me.'

Thoroughly unsettled, I watched Probes leave the cafe, then stop to talk to someone outside. Pressing my nose against the glass, I saw Topaz and Probes engaged in animated conversation. I jumped up from the table and strode over to the coat stand to the left of the glass door. It was impossible to hear what they were saying, but I could see Topaz was angry. She was waving her hands about and then, to my astonishment, Probes took both of them in his and pulled her towards him to kiss her on top of her lace mob cap.

I slunk back to my table, absolutely crushed. Even though I had trusted neither, I felt doubly betrayed unless . . . the thought seemed ridiculous. Could Probes be bewitching all the women in Gipping? I was right to be wary of him. But the question remained, what the hell were those two doing? Why the secrecy? Why pretend they were strangers?

I cringed as I recalled all those sexual innuendos I made about Topaz to Probes, to say nothing about my so-called date at The Three Tuns. It was so humiliating. I had thought Topaz smitten with me, not vice versa. How the two lovebirds must have laughed at my expense.

I was determined to have it out with her.

Fortunately, the Fairweather lot had finished eating and had gone over to the cash till to pay. Topaz returned, taking their money without so much as a smile or thank-you. She then promptly disappeared through the plastic fringe into the kitchen.

Furious, I got up and marched over to the door, turning the sign to CLOSED.

Topaz was standing at the kitchen sink with her back to me.

'Topaz, I want a word with you.'

She swung round. To my surprise, her face was blotchy from crying.

'Whatever's wrong?' I said, taking her arm and guiding her over to sit in one of the old armchairs next to the Victorian fireplace. I took the other. Slipper snored on in her basket in the corner.

'Did the copper say something to upset you?' I asked.

Topaz frowned and shook her head. She lifted up her serge pinafore and fumbled around for a moment before pulling out a linen handkerchief from some hidden pocket.

'You know, in my job, I have to deal with the police all the time,' I said. 'They can be heartless bullies. He must have said *something*.'

'Oh, Vicky, you're so nice to me. The problem is . . .' Topaz sniffed. 'I've been told not to talk to the press.'

'But I'm not just *press*. We're friends,' I declared. Honestly, we investigative reporters had a hard enough job as it was. 'Not talk to the press? I've never heard of anything so ridiculous. Do you know what I think?'

She shook her head dolefully.

'I think Probes is in love with you—'

'Oh golly!' Topaz's eyes widened. 'How did you guess?'

'It *was* rather obvious.'

'I just knew Colin would give the game away,' Topaz sighed. 'Please don't be angry, Vicky.'

Colin! How could I not be? I'd been fooled and hadn't even seen it coming. Even though I wasn't sure about the whole girl-on-girl idea, frankly, I felt wronged. 'Why lead me on? Why pretend you wanted Dave Randall back?'

'It's a long story.'

'Start talking.' I fumed. '*Now!*'

Topaz took a deep breath. 'Colin and I are first cousins. We grew up in Kenya together. My aunt was his father's sister.'

'So?'

'It means we can never marry.'

'Don't be stupid,' I exclaimed. 'This is the twenty-first century.'

Topaz shook her head sadly. 'My aunt and Uncle Henry – Colin's father – have a horrid genetic heart disease . . . and, of course, Granny went native and ended up in a lunatic asylum.'

Slipper, sensing the tension between us, clambered out of her basket and waddled over. There was something about the dog that was niggling me but I couldn't put my finger on it. As she pushed her velvety nose into Topaz's hand, the truth suddenly hit me.

'You're the niece! Ethel Turberville-Spat!' I was incredulous.

Topaz nodded miserably.

'But why change your name?' I said. 'And why the awful wig?'

Stroking Slipper, Topaz began, 'I didn't want anyone to recognize me. Especially Dave Randall. We had a fling last April when I was staying at The Grange but it fizzled out. Then I heard Dave was actually sleeping with *her*.'

It certainly explained why Dave had never heard of a Topaz Potter. 'Why the disguise?'

'I was at Maurice Wheeler's funeral when Auntie died,' Topaz said.

'You just told me she had heart disease.'

'Yes, but something else killed her. I feel it here.' Topaz thumped her breast. 'That's why I'm undercover pretending to be a waitress. I mustn't be recognized.'

'And the cafe?'

'Auntie left it to me,' she said. 'It used to be—'

'A charity shop for the blind. I know.' Which went a long way in explaining Topaz's lack of culinary skills.

Topaz grabbed my hands, and said urgently, 'Vicky, I know who murdered my aunt. I just can't prove it.'

'Who?'

'Lady Trewallyn and her followers!'

A week ago, I would have agreed with her.

'Topaz,' I said gently. 'Your Uncle Hugh had not even met Katherine Vanderkamp when your aunt died.'

Topaz looked disappointed. 'Are you *positive*?' she asked. 'But he *always* had some mistress or other on the go. If it wasn't *her*, who was it?'

'Katherine met your uncle on a cruise about a month after your aunt's funeral. I read about it in the *Gazette* archives,' I said. 'If you want to be an investigative reporter, you must double-check your facts before you make wild accusations.'

'I *am* sure of my facts!' Topaz stuck out her chin in defiance. 'My aunt was scared. She told me she was out walking late one night and saw something going on in the woods. There was a light in Hugh's Folly. Hooded figures, even!'

Hooded figures! More sightings in the woods! 'Did she tell your uncle?'

'He told her she was imagining it,' Topaz cried. 'She'd even mentioned this to Uncle Henry. He knows some bigwig at Scotland Yard, so when she died, he managed to get Colin sent down here to make some inquiries.'

No wonder the force complained about lack of funds, if they sent off their men on wild-goose chases.

'There were also some family heirlooms missing.' She touched the Victorian locket around her neck. 'A frightfully valuable Georgian tea urn, pieces of silver that were taken from the walnut display cabinet in the drawing room, that kind of thing.'

'The Gipping Cat Burglar,' I said flatly. 'Didn't your uncle report it?'

'He'd gone off on his wretched cruise by the time anyone noticed.' Topaz's eyes filled with tears. 'Uncle Hugh didn't care. He never really loved her.'

For a fleeting moment I wondered if Topaz were capable of killing Sir Hugh. Perhaps Probes was in on it, too? They'd both grown up in Africa. Wouldn't they be familiar with witchcraft? It certainly explained Probes's odd behaviour with Brian's poppet. It would also give Topaz a motive to try to pin the blame on Katherine. She could easily have stuffed the feathers in Sir Hugh's mouth, left the chicken corpses in The Grange dustbins – and on Dave Randall's bed!

'I still don't understand why you wanted me to sleep with Dave,' I asked.

'For heaven's sake, he *has* to know what's going on! He lives in the *woods*.' Topaz paused for breath. 'If you sleep with him, you can find out.'

She had a point. Everyone knows the power of pillow talk. I got to my feet and headed for the back door.

Topaz slipped in front of me to stop me from leaving. She'd done that before. It made me feel very uneasy. 'We could write the story together!'

'Good idea.' *That will never happen.* 'But for now, I need you as my High Street spy.'

'Okay,' Topaz said, brightening. 'I almost forgot to tell you what I saw the other night.'

'Go ahead.'

'Barbara and a scary-looking bald man delivered a large pot to your office.'

'Thanks, Topaz. Bye.'

'You see! You *need* me, Vicky!'

I wasn't interested in Barbara's romantic adventures or Topaz's family problems. My scoop was due in two days' time and I had absolutely nothing concrete whatsoever.

Despite everything that was said, I still believed Lady Trewallyn was a witch and a genius at covering her tracks. Somehow I needed to get to Trewallyn woods to look for clues.

Suddenly, I was struck by a brilliant idea. Annabel was safely in the hospital. Her car was parked outside the *Gazette*. Why not take it for a night-time spin?

37

Hot-wiring Annabel's car was easy. I broke my own record of two minutes, five seconds. I also found my watch. It was hidden in the BMW glove compartment, which promptly dispelled any qualms I'd been harbouring about taking Annabel's car.

Barbara had been in the loo when I left. No one else asked any questions. I simply said Annabel had asked me to go to Beaver Lock Lodge to pick up a few things for her hospital stay.

Luck appeared to be on my side at Rumble Lane, too. Mrs Poultry had announced at breakfast that she wouldn't be back until late. 'You can have a key,' she'd said, adding darkly, 'but I want it back tomorrow morning, without fail.'

As I let myself into the house, the most delicious smell of shepherd's pie wafted through the air.

My mouth watered. Usually the kitchen door was closed, but this evening it was wide open. For one wonderful moment, I thought my landlady had left me some supper. Instead, on the kitchen table was a note simply saying: DO NOT TOUCH MY PIE.

At least her absence meant I could make some toast. Dad always maintained that it was career suicide to go on a night job with an empty stomach.

Without Mrs Poultry's parsimonious eye on me, I spread thick butter on two slices of bread along with three generous teaspoons of strawberry jam and wolfed it down.

After carefully washing up my plate and making sure there were no stray crumbs, I added a little water to the jam pot and gave it a good shake to bring the level of the contents up to expectation.

As a former Girl Guide I lived by our motto: 'Always Be Prepared.' With that in mind, I picked out my only set of racy underwear from Marks and Spencer's Wild Nights Millennium and snipped off the tags. Dave and I had planned for sex on Wednesday afternoon – tomorrow – but I was quite sure he wouldn't mind me turning up earlier than planned.

Over my undies, I donned a pair of thick black tights followed by black leggings and a thermal vest under a black polo sweater, and slipped on a pair of sneakers. The best part was finally getting a chance to wear my black-knitted balaclava that Dad had bought for me one Christmas.

I popped my Canon Digital Rebel – retrieved this afternoon from Ken's Kamera – into a small nylon rucksack, along with a flashlight and a bar of Kit Kat.

Downstairs, I checked my reflection in the hall mirror and was pleased to see I looked a bit like Catwoman. The sleek outfit accentuated my figure. Unlike Annabel, who had to be a size 34 DD and was top-heavy – poor girl – my hips and breasts seemed perfectly in proportion. Even though I say it myself, I looked quite irresistible. Dave was in for a treat!

Annabel's BMW was a joy to drive. I approached the signpost to the Cricket Pavilion and turned into the narrow road. The beam from the car headlights carved out an eerie tunnel, illuminating broken branches and stray boulders.

On the left, just before the giant puddle Annabel had roared through so rashly, a black Harley Davidson motorbike was propped against a tree. My stomach turned over. Tonight was a full moon. Of course, there would be a coven meeting!

I reversed, left the BMW in the undergrowth, and decided to proceed off the main track on foot.

On reaching the clearing in front of the Cricket Pavilion, I thought I'd expire with excitement. There were three cars parked on the apron – a dented Golf Polo, a black Ford Fiesta, and a white Mazda with a bumper sticker saying PLYM VALLEY FARMERS DO IT IN BARNS.

Mrs Evans must have meant the Pavilion, not the Folly. I tiptoed closer. Sure enough, I could hear the murmur of voices coming from inside.

With a pounding heart, I crept up the wooden steps and onto the rickety veranda. Fortunately the windows were boarded up. I edged my way round to the front entrance and slipped inside undetected.

My investigative reporter's mind spun with possible headlines. WITCHCRAFT RIFE IN SLEEPY MARKET TOWN: A VICKY HILL EXCLUSIVE! Or, if they got round to having sex: ORGY DISCOVERED IN CRICKET PAVILION – GIPPING'S DEADLY SECRET.

The voices were coming from behind two double doors that led to the main hall. Shafts of moonlight illuminated a small kitchen on the left strewn with litter, and to my right, a narrow staircase.

Many of these old village halls had minstrel galleries. If my hunch paid off, it would afford the perfect view. I slithered up the stairs and crouched behind the balustrade, grateful for my all-black ensemble. I was completely invisible.

The room below was lit by dozens of candles. Seven figures in black hooded cloaks sat in a circle on empty orange crates drinking Heineken and passing round a family-size bag of crisps. One of them had a sickle embroidered on the back of his cloak. An eighth stood below me at the double doors smoking a cigarette. There was no sign of Lady Trewallyn and the remaining five sorcerers to make up the magical thirteen, but it wasn't midnight yet.

Against the back wall stood a trestle table covered in a black cloth – the altar obviously. I saw no other occult equipment – cauldron, instruments of torture, or those poor chickens – but suspected they'd be kept under lock and key and brought in for the really serious stuff.

I mentally prepared myself to witness some horrors. No doubt there would be an orgy, though frankly, despite the floor being covered in sawdust, the ground looked a bit hard.

It wasn't quite what I expected, but what is these days? This was modern witchcraft, after all.

Carefully, I retrieved my camera and got it ready for the money shot, then settled down to wait. I knew I'd only get one chance and wondered what would provide the best shock value on the front page – an orgy of Gipping citizens or a naked, blood-sprayed Lady Trewallyn holding a sacrificed chicken aloft?

'It's nearly ten fifteen,' grumbled a female voice with a lisp. 'I say we start without him.'

'I'm freezing my balls off,' said the man below me, jiggling from foot to foot. 'If he can't be here on time, he's out.' Three loud knocks sounded on the door downstairs. 'You're late!' he growled. 'Password?'

'Beacon Zap, whatever.' A stocky figure strode in sporting an impressive handlebar moustache. His shaved head gleamed in the candlelight.

'For God's sake, put your hood up,' Sickle Cloak snapped, and got to his feet. 'This is a top secret meeting.'

'Not so secret,' said the newcomer. 'There's a bloody BMW hidden in the undergrowth.'

'What are you talking about?' said the man with the freezing balls.

'Oh shit! It's that reporter girl,' said Lisp Lady. 'Annabel Lake.'

'The one with the big tits?' piped up another male voice.

'You told me you'd taken care of it.'

245

'I put the doll thing on her bed like you told me to,' said Lisp Lady. 'Barry and I—'

'No first names,' said Sickle Cloak. 'Did you find the plans and—?'

A blinding flash of phosphorescent light illuminated the Pavilion. Someone screamed, 'It's her! She's here!'

Candles were extinguished, plunging the room into darkness amid panicked cries of 'Spread out!' 'Get that camera!' 'Flash came from up there!'

I froze. *Bugger, damn, and blast Ken's Kamera!* I hadn't even pressed the button! It had gone off by itself. Pete was right. The bloke was useless.

As the room emptied, I threw myself over the minstrel railing, dropped the twelve feet to the ground, and did a parachute roll. I darted blindly across the room, collided with the table, and dived under the cloth.

'Nothing up here,' shouted a voice from, presumably, the minstrel gallery. 'I bet she's running to her car!'

I crouched on the dirty floor, listening to the sound of footsteps clattering down the steps outside. Then, complete silence.

I felt gutted. Annabel *was* chasing the same scoop as me but she'd been careless. The witches knew what she was up to, enough to leave a warning poppet on her bed.

After counting to 750, I decided the coast must be clear. It was too dangerous to go back to the BMW tonight. They'd have it staked out. Instead I decided to continue with my original plan and make my way to Dave Randall's place.

I felt high on adrenaline and, even though I was trembling from such a near brush with death, *absolutely* in the mood for sex. Would Dave sweep me into his arms the moment he opened the door? Would he . . . *oh God*! I stopped dead in my tracks.

Leaning against a pine tree stood Barbara's pink bicycle.

I was so shocked I thought I'd faint. Surely if Barbara had been in the Pavilion I would have recognized her voice, the woman never stopped talking. Unless – the idea seemed ludicrous – I was wrong about Lady Trewallyn being the High Priestess. Maybe – just maybe, it was Barbara Meadows.

The implications were so huge I felt sick. Barbara would know Annabel was in the hospital. She'd know that someone must have borrowed her car. What were the chances she'd think it was me?

What I needed was a cast-iron alibi and I knew exactly who that could be.

Dave Randall.

38

To my relief, the lights of Cricket Lodge were still on. Not wanting to startle him, I took off my balaclava, ruffled my hair a little, and tapped quietly on the door.

After some minutes, Dave opened it a crack. His face fell. 'What do you want?'

'It's Wednesday in half an hour.' I pushed out my chest the way I'd seen Annabel do. 'I've thought of nothing else since that kiss on Sunday night. I just want you to—'

'I'm not in the mood tonight,' he said, and abruptly slammed the door.

Not in the mood? How humiliating! Was he throwing a temper tantrum because I'd refused to sleep with him on the front lawn last Sunday? *Blast Dave!* It was miles to walk home, and the witches were already out looking for me. He *had* to let me in.

I was about to knock on the door again when I heard the sound of raised voices – one was female. What a cad!

I tiptoed around the side of the house to the bedroom window. A curtain was drawn across with just a chink to allow minimal view but I couldn't see anything. All I heard were a jumble of words, 'never again', 'one last time', 'our secret'.

Absolutely crushed, I turned away not relishing the long walk home. My blisters hadn't healed. I'd be crippled for life.

As I painfully retraced my steps, I was surprised to find Barbara's pink bicycle was exactly where she'd left it. No doubt her followers had insisted on driving her home.

I stared at it for several moments. I could take the old rear entrance to The Grange past the Folly and zip along the river path back to Rumble Lane. Tomorrow, I'd get up early, cycle to the BMW, and make the switch. Easy.

Once I got used to the high handlebars and sitting bolt upright, the bicycle was surprisingly comfortable. No wonder Barbara was fond of it. I still found it hard to believe dear, friendly Barbara capable of murder – naked orgies, yes – but cold-blooded killing?

Back in Rumble Lane, I left Barbara's bicycle hidden in a bed of wild foxgloves in the copse at the end of the cul-de-sac.

Fortunately, Mrs Poultry was still not home. Minutes later, I was tucked up in bed and fell into an exhausted sleep until a loud crash from downstairs woke me up.

It was three in the morning!

I jumped out of bed, my heart thundering in my chest. Someone was trying to break in.

Quietly, I opened my bedroom door and tiptoed out to the landing. To my relief, I heard my landlady's voice and a man's. *Good grief!* Not only was Mrs Poultry staggering about drunk and breaking things, she had brought someone back with her. What were the chances it was Ronnie Binns?

Mrs Poultry's bedroom was directly under mine. I darted back into my bedroom, grabbed a pair of earmuffs from my chest of drawers, and dived under the covers. The thought of them writhing around naked made me gag. Instead, I turned my thoughts to Barbara.

Somehow I had to infiltrate the coven. Barbara had always liked me. She'd probably be thrilled – especially when I confessed I was still a virgin. The problem was, I liked her, too, and felt a little uncomfortable stabbing her in the back.

I suppose this was the heart-breaking side of investigative reporting and something I was too tired to think about right now. I closed my eyes.

Tomorrow was going to be a big day.

39

I wasn't the only one who overslept. Mrs Poultry was still tucked up in bed when I came downstairs next morning. No doubt she was exhausted from her night of passion with Ronnie Binns.

As I took my safari jacket off the hall coat stand, I noticed a padlock on the door to the basement.

Mrs Poultry told me she stored her catering supplies down there but she'd never had cause to lock it before. Unless – *oh God*! I bet last night the two lovers got ravenous and went to make a postcoital snack. She must have discovered the diluted jam, but frankly, this was the least of my problems today.

As I was already late for work, I couldn't switch the bicycle, after all. I hurried to the *Gazette,* agonizing over how to approach Barbara. I could hardly introduce the coven in a friendly chat and tell her I wanted to apply.

In reception, Tony was perched on Barbara's stool behind the counter, nursing a mug of tea and eating a bacon sandwich.

'Where's Barbara?' I said.

He shrugged and pointed to his mouth that was stuffed with food.

Barbara was never late. She practically lived at the office. What if she had had to walk home last night, after all? It had been colder than usual. In fact, many elderly people succumbed to hypothermia in these conditions. The graveyard was full of winter tragedies.

The phone rang. Tony continued to chew his breakfast, picked up the receiver, and handed it to me.

'*Gipping Gazette*,' I said, glaring at him. 'Can I help you?'

'Vicky?' said a mournful voice on the other end of the line.

My stomach turned over. 'Barbara! Are you ill? We were just getting worried about you.'

'My toe is playing up. It's infected. I can't even wear my slippers, let alone walk.' She sounded despondent. I felt guilty. Obviously Barbara *had* walked home. 'But something terrible has happened . . .' She made a strange gulping noise. 'Someone has stolen my bicycle.'

How very clever! Barbara was going to play dumb.

'Have you reported it?' I said.

'No police!' Barbara's voice held a hint of hysteria. 'What do they care about a missing bicycle?'

Naturally, she wouldn't want the police involved. 'Tell you what,' I said. 'I'll make a few discreet inquiries on the condition that you see a professional about that toe.'

'Doctor Jolly the chiropodist will be here any minute.'

Another stab of guilt hit me afresh. If she had to succumb to the medical skills of Jab-it Jolly, she'd be lucky to have a toe left at all. I decided against telling Barbara about Mrs Reynolds's fatal bunion.

'Must go. I'll be in touch later about your bike,' I said. 'Bye.'

Pete burst in waving a two-way radio. 'Where the hell is Annabel's car? It's not outside.'

I felt myself redden. 'Actually, I left it down at Ted's garage this morning. Thought she'd appreciate a full tank.'

He clicked the button on the two-way radio and yelled into it. 'Car okay. Now turn this bloody thing off and give me a break.'

He slammed the gadget down on the counter. 'No bloody peace for the wicked. Where's Barbara?'

'Out with a bad toe.'

'Christ! We're surrounded by invalids here,' he growled. 'Vicky, come with me.'

I trooped upstairs into Pete's office, knowing full well he was going to ask about my scoop.

'Door!' he shouted, and went and sat behind his desk whilst I closed it and stood awkwardly in front of him. Pete lit a cigarette and inhaled deeply. 'We are screwed.'

I didn't comment. I hated being alone with Pete.

'I've got a mate. A freelancer. He called me at bloody seven o'clock this morning to tell me the bloody *Bugle* was running an exclusive about Gipping in today's paper.' Pete slammed his hand down hard on the desk and jumped to his feet. 'This is the *Gipping Gazette*,' he shouted at me. 'If the *Bugle* has trumped us with a local exclusive, we might as well be dead.'

I was beginning to feel sick. Was everyone following the same story as me? 'Do you know what it's about?' I said gingerly.

'If I knew, I wouldn't be having this bloody conversation with you, would I?' Pete fumed. 'There's a leak in this office.'

'Well, it's not me,' I declared hotly. 'I always work alone. My sources are one hundred per cent reliable.' Even if there were other journalists on the trail, no one knew about Barbara's role. 'I'm positive no one else has my story. It'll be huge.'

Pete looked unconvinced. 'You'd better show me what you've got.'

I shook my head. 'No offence, Pete, but my mum – God rest her soul – said "Tell a secret and you tell the world." It's just the way I work.'

'You drive a hard bargain,' Pete declared. 'All right. Tomorrow. Noon. On this desk or you're fired. Oh! And I want photographs.'

'Can I borrow the Nikon digital again, please?' I said. 'You were right, Ken's Kamera is rubbish. Need to take a few final shots.'

'Okay,' Pete said, then frowned. He put his hand in his pocket and pulled out Annabel's car keys. 'Hang on. How could you drive her BMW without these?'

'I used the spare set in her desk,' I said quickly, and snatched them out of his hand. 'But I'll take those. Thanks. Bye.'

As I left the office, I suddenly knew exactly how I'd endear myself to Barbara.

I was going to *personally* return her bicycle.

40

I jogged back to the copse in Rumble Lane, grabbed Barbara's bike, then cycled the same route I took last night via The Grange rear drive.

As I caught sight of Hugh's Folly peeping over the tree-tops, I remembered Topaz's remarks. Her aunt had seen 'a light in Hugh's Folly. Hooded figures even'. So had Mrs Evans. Whilst I was here, it was worth investigating.

To my surprise the padlock was dangling by its hinge. I stood still, listening for any sound of movement but could only hear the wind rustling through the trees. Satisfied I was alone, I opened the door and stepped inside.

Apart from a wrought-iron spiral staircase, the circular room was empty. Speckled light came from the gun-loop openings in the walls, revealing a spotlessly clean stone floor. A broom leaned against the wall. Someone had cleaned the place up.

I decided to explore upstairs.

At the top, I paused to catch my breath. To my right was a mullioned window with magnificent views of Gipping and Dartmoor and, to my left, a doorway covered by a red velvet curtain.

I pushed the curtain aside and peeped in. *Good grief!* It resembled an Arabian harem.

Deep purple cushions were strewn over the floor. Red, orange, and yellow sheets fell in soft folds from the walls. On the ceiling was an enormous circular mirror. An empty wine bottle and two pewter goblets stood on a low coffee table along with three church candles.

This must be the VIP area! This was where the High Priestess and her ladies got ready and waited until midnight. Perhaps the chickens had been stored downstairs? The equipment, too! Obviously, after last night's interruption, the witches knew this place was no longer safe and had decided to move on.

I got out my camera, took some snaps, and as I zoomed in on the pewter goblets, I thought . . . DNA! Retrieving a clean tissue from my safari jacket pocket, I picked up a goblet and froze.

Tucked inside was a purple Coff-Off wrapper.

Of course, Mrs Poultry wasn't the only one who liked this particular brand of ghastly cough drops – but she was the only one who smoothed out the wrapper and folded it into a neat square.

Surely she wasn't part of the coven? Hadn't Topaz accused her uncle of having several mistresses? Maybe I was too eager to think the worst and this was simply a love nest?

Thoroughly baffled, I wiped the rim of both goblets, put the tissue in a baggie, and left the tower. On reaching the Pavilion I ran off a few more shots and cycled on to the BMW and put the bicycle in the boot.

Back at the *Gazette,* I parked Annabel's car in the alley and set off for The Marshes.

All I could think about was dear, friendly Barbara. Even if she *were* a witch, was she capable of murder?

41

'Oh! Where did you find it, you clever girl?' Barbara cried. I was standing on the front porch outside her end of the terraced Edwardian house. She had pulled the front door closed behind her 'to keep the heat in'.

'The Three Tuns car park,' I said, carefully watching her reaction. 'Perhaps someone borrowed it?'

'And I bet I know who, too,' Barbara muttered to herself. Putting on a bright smile she added, 'Well, I mustn't grumble. It could have been dismantled for parts. These bicycles are rare, you know. I've had this since—'

'I'm puffed out from cycling,' I said, short-circuiting one of Barbara's interminable stories. 'Any chance of a cuppa?'

'Not now, Vicky dear. I was just about to take a nap.'

This was a first. Since when had she passed up an opportunity for gossip?

I noticed Barbara's right foot was heavily bandaged. 'Oh, how thoughtless of me!' I exclaimed. 'Let me help you inside.'

'Dr Jolly was a little rough,' she said, shifting her weight and wincing with pain. 'Leave the bike against the wall, would you?

Thank you for coming. Bye, dear.' She turned, as if to disappear into the house.

'Wait!' I said. 'I'm stuck in a love triangle with Topaz and Dave Randall and don't know what to do.'

Barbara swung around, her face alive with curiosity. 'A love triangle?'

'I desperately need your advice.'

Clearly torn, she asked, 'Can it wait until tomorrow?'

'In fact, I'm so upset, I think I'm going to faint.' I began to sway from side to side and deliberately dropped the bicycle to the ground.

Barbara darted forward and grasped the handlebars, giving me a chance to duck under her arm and race inside.

Like most terraced houses of the period, the front door opened directly into the living room with a tiny kitchen and bathroom beyond. To the right, a staircase led upstairs to the bedrooms above.

I was immediately drawn to the gateleg table on my left, piled high with scraps of material and an open needlework box. There, devoid of his battledress, lay a naked GI Joe doll wearing an eye patch and smoking a pipe. *Bloody hell!* How blatant can Barbara get! No wonder she tried to stop me coming in.

'It's for the window display,' Barbara said, wheeling her bicycle indoors. 'I'm going to make a little suit. What do you think?'

Her attitude towards these killer dolls took my breath away. It was as if we were discussing knitting patterns. 'It certainly looks like Wilf,' I said, wondering what our editor had done to deserve such treatment.

A loud crash sounded above our heads, followed by a string of expletives ending in 'Bollocks!'

We both froze. Barbara had company.

'You'd better leave, dear.' She looked nervous.

Suddenly, heavy footsteps thundered down the stairs, and I came face-to-face with the man with the shaved head and handlebar moustache. My heart practically stopped. Any doubts as to Barbara's coven connection vanished.

'Freddy?' Barbara stammered. 'This is Vicky. We work together.'

'Hullo,' I said.

Freddy just scowled. Dressed in dirty jeans and sleeveless T-shirt, Freddy had a naked woman tattooed on his upper right arm – SADIE. Up close, he was even more intimidating.

'Freddy is my nephew.' *Nephew? Nice one, Barbara.*

'Where the hell did that come from?' Freddy declared, catching sight of Barbara's bicycle.

'Vicky found it at The Three Tuns.'

'The Three Tuns.' Freddy's eyes bored into mine. 'Fancy that.'

My stomach was churning. He was no fool. 'Well, I'd best be off,' I said quickly. I'd have to ask about the coven another time.

'Why don't you stay for a cuppa?' Freddy said. 'You can help me make it.' It was a command, not a request.

Barbara sat down heavily in the armchair, her face creased with worry. No doubt wondering if he would betray her.

I trooped after Freddy into the kitchen. He shut the door and whirled round, pinning me against the wall. 'What the hell is your game?' he snarled.

'I don't know what you mean!'

'You think I'm *blind*?' Freddy said, jabbing his finger into my shoulder. 'It was *you* in the woods last night! Give me the camera. I want those photographs.'

'You must be confused. It was Annabel Lake,' I said, crossing my fingers behind my back.

'Aunt Babs told me this morning that Annabel Lake was in the hospital,' he snapped. '*You* hot-wired that car.'

'Oh *that*!' I said wildly. 'Annabel said I could borrow it. I had a tryst with Dave Randall and, on my way back to the car, heard all the commotion. I suppose I panicked.'

'And stole my aunt's bicycle.' Freddy glowered.

'I thought she'd get a lift home,' I said.

'Aunt Babs has *nothing* to do with this,' Freddy declared, lowering his voice to a whisper. 'And don't you tell her or else you'll be sorry.'

It seemed rather odd for a grown man to be afraid of his aged aunt. Unless . . . in a flash I suddenly knew where I'd seen Freddy's face before. It was on the wall of Gipping police station: WANTED FOR FAILURE TO APPEAR IN COURT, DRIVING WITHOUT A LICENCE – hence the bicycle – AND DISTURBING THE PEACE.

Freddy was on the run.

'Does your aunt know you're a wanted man?' I said casually.

Freddy stepped back, shocked. 'What the hell are you talking about?'

'Let's make a deal,' I said. 'Why don't you tell me all about your little group, and I'll keep your secret.'

'You're wasting your time,' Freddy said. 'That lot couldn't organize a piss-up in a brewery. They're amateurs.'

I didn't believe him for a minute.

'Are you two all right in there?' Barbara called out.

'Be right out in a few!' Freddy yelled. He stomped over to the countertop and put the kettle on the stove.

'At least give me some names,' I said. I retrieved my notebook from my pocket and took out my pencil. 'Who's Barry?'

'Only met him once before.' Freddy shrugged. 'Runs the organic Pick-Your-Own Farm Shop over on Pennymoor.'

'And the others?'

'Don't know and don't really care,' Freddy said. 'I only joined for a laugh.' *A laugh?* Freddy might appear tough, but he had no idea what he was up against.

'Look, we know for a fact Lady Trewallyn is involved,' I said.

Freddy gave me a strange look. 'Of course she is.'

'I need some help.' I knew I was breaking one of Dad's rules,

260

but time was running out. Pulling my wallet out of my jeans pocket, I looked inside. 'This is all I've got.' I handed him a five pound note. 'I don't get an expense account.'

Freddy snatched it. 'Barry told us old Rawlings had been after her assets for months. Even offered her a ton of money. Then, suddenly, she drops him like a hot potato. Typical woman.'

This was interesting. Rawlings had wanted to join the coven, too, but Lady Trewallyn had refused. Why?

'Can you get a photograph of her in action?'

Freddy laughed. 'She's gone.'

'Gone?'

'One of my mates runs a car service,' Freddy said. 'He took her to Heathrow Airport.'

Damn! Not the answer I was hoping for and definitely not worth five pounds.

The kettle began to whistle on the stove. 'Pass the tea bags, will you?' Freddy said.

Catching sight of the kitchen clock, I realized hospital visiting hours would soon be over if I didn't get a move on. 'Thanks, but no thanks for the tea. If you hear anything, call me.'

Leaving Freddy in the kitchen, I went to bid Barbara goodbye but found her fast asleep in the armchair, snoring gently. I was so glad she wasn't involved.

Operating the coven under the guise of the Eco-Warriors was sheer genius. What's more, someone had warned Lady Trewallyn I was hot on her trail. Yet there was still the unanswered question. Who killed Sir Hugh – and, why?

42

I set off for Gipping Hospital with Annabel's BMW keys and even stopped at Tesco to buy her a bunch of grapes and box of Cadbury's Milk Tray chocolates. Knowing I would be the harbinger of disappointing news, I thought it might help soften the blow.

A male nurse with a pierced eyebrow, dressed in green hospital scrubs, directed me to the patient common room overlooking a neglected walled garden.

Annabel was the youngest of several elderly patients by about fifty years. She sat by the window in a wheelchair engaged in animated conversation on a two-way radio. She wore a peacock blue silk robe embroidered with dragons. I half expected her leg to be in a cast but only her ankle was lightly bandaged. *All that fuss for a sprain!*

Annabel waved me over, finishing her conversation with an affected, 'Roger, I read you. Over and out.'

'I brought your car keys and some treats,' I said.

'Leave them there.' Annabel gestured to a plastic side table next to a very uncomfortable-looking upright chair.

I did as I was told and sat down.

'What happened to your face?' she asked.

'I walked into a door.'

'You should look where you're going,' Annabel said. 'Thank God I've got this radio. Belongs to one of Pete's kids so he can keep me up-to-date with news.'

'How are you?'

'Fine, until I saw *this*.' She picked up today's copy of the *Plymouth Bugle*. 'I see you missed a hot story.'

I took the newspaper and gasped with dismay. Splashed over the tackiest tabloid ever were the headlines:

GIPPING BLACK WIDOW!

LADY BY DAY, TRAMP BY NIGHT:
SORDID SECRETS OF KANDI KANE

'I LOVED HER,'
SAYS BROKENHEARTED PIMP IN PORSCHE

Naturally there was a photograph of Chester in sunglasses looking forlornly off-camera. There was even a full-length snap of Lady Trewallyn in full showgirl regalia, complete with a towering sequined headdress and exposing plenty of naked flesh.

It turned out that Chester Forbes and Kandi Kane had been running a scam for years. He'd earmark wealthy, elderly pensioners for Katherine to seduce; marriage would be brief – thanks to her sexual appetite – and they'd split the proceeds. Only this time, it seemed, she had genuinely fallen in love.

'Pete is furious. I *knew* I should have gone to the church.' Annabel clicked her tongue with disapproval. 'Instinct, Vicky, instinct! I would have spotted there was something fishy about him a mile off and, of course, I always guessed she was an imposter.'

Blast Annabel! Blast Pete! Blast Chester!

'She's done a bunk, of course,' Annabel went on. 'Mrs Evans told me. Eloped with old Sharpe to live in Spain.'

So much for Mrs Evans being *my* informer.

'Oh, and Ronnie Binns's little chicken sensation is on page eleven,' Annabel said. 'Instinct, Vicky! I told you his story was not for us.'

I turned to page eleven.

ALIEN CHICKENS!

A GARBOLOGIST'S NIGHTMARE!

A photograph of Ronnie in his waders looking scared was accompanied by a close-up of what looked more like E.T. than a chicken. Ah! The wonders of Adobe Photoshop, I thought. It certainly explained Ronnie's convenient attack of amnesia. But I wasn't fazed. Annabel could think what she liked, but I knew better.

Annabel grabbed the bag of grapes, fastidiously pecked at a few, and put them back on the table. 'I don't like pips.'

'When can you be discharged?' I asked.

'I have a slight concussion, and they won't let me out unless I stay with a friend. Oh . . .' Annabel's scowl changed to a sugary smile. 'Vicky, I wondered—'

'My landlady would never agree,' I said quickly. 'Can't Walter look after you or pay for a nurse?'

Annabel made a strange gulping sound. 'We've broken up.'

'Broken up? Poor you!'

'Yes, poor me. I can keep the car but . . .' Her bottom lip quivered, and I swear I saw a tear in her eye. 'I have to move out of the lodge by Christmas.'

'To be honest, I'm not surprised,' I said.

'What's that supposed to mean?'

'There were rumours about Rawlings and Lady Trewallyn,' I said, recalling Mrs Evans's comment. 'I'm afraid you were replaced.'

Annabel turned pale. 'He told me they were just good friends.'

'And you fell for that old line?'

'That woman has slept with half of Gipping!' Annabel cried.

'It's not too late,' I said. 'She's in Spain now. You can easily win Walter back.'

Annabel shook her head miserably. 'Not now that I've told his wife.'

'You silly thing!' I cried. 'Married men don't like to be nagged. That's what their wives are for. That's why sex sirens like Lady Trewallyn make perfect mistresses.' I pointed to her photograph. 'No offence, Annabel, but look at her. She's hot.'

Annabel sniffed and pulled a tissue from her robe pocket. 'Walter's wife was vile and called me all sorts of names. Of course she *denied* breaking into the lodge.'

'That's because she didn't,' I said, adding casually, 'I popped into the Pavilion the other night for a chat with the Eco-Warriors. Barry told me one of them had put a doll on your bed as a practical joke. Got the idea from *Voodoo Vixens*.'

'You spoke to Barry?' Annabel said with disbelief. 'I've been trying to get to him for weeks.'

'I shouldn't bother now,' I said. 'With Lady Trewallyn exposed as a fraud, the Folly isn't hers to sell anymore. That story's dead.'

With a pathetic whimper, Annabel reached for the chocolates. Ripping off the wrappers, she picked out two chocolate caramels and stuffed both into her mouth.

For a moment I felt a tiny bit sorry for her until I remembered how she hid my wristwatch in her glove compartment. 'I'll ask my landlady about the spare room if you like, but don't hold your breath. Best be off. I've got a scoop to write.'

As I stood up, a distinguished-looking man in hospital whites, swinging his stethoscope, sauntered towards us. He was the spitting image of Bill Clinton.

'Oh goodness.' Annabel turned scarlet and quickly spat out the remains of her chocolate caramels into a tissue. 'It's Doctor Frost!'

She handed me the soggy clump. 'Quickly! Take it. Take it. And don't bother about asking your landlady, Vicky. I'm perfectly happy here.' Tucking her hands beneath her silk robe, Annabel rearranged her breasts and turned to give the doctor a dazzling smile.

As I strolled back to Rumble Lane, I tried to keep calm. It was unfortunate about Chester going to the *Bugle* but there wasn't time to cry over spilt milk.

My story was due in twenty-four hours and as yet, I only had theories, not proof. Thank God Annabel hadn't guessed the Eco-Warriors were just a smokescreen for the coven, whatever Freddy might say.

If Barbara wasn't involved in the coven and Lady Trewallyn had bolted, then there was only one person I could think of who could be High Priestess.

Mrs Poultry.

43

That evening, after eating a Tesco cheese and pickle sandwich sneaked into my room, I took out the coroner's reports once again.

It was clear to me now. Sir Hugh had been murdered in the woods; Dave Randall had found him but Lady Trewallyn had paid for his silence with torrid sex, unaware that Brian had already slipped the coroner's report with the true verdict to the *Gazette*. So as not to arouse suspicion as to her dubious past, Lady Trewallyn then seduced Sharpe who forged a *new* report stating Sir Hugh died from a heart attack – which of course, the *digitalis purpurea* had caused him to have anyway. They had a fling and promptly ran off together.

Brian's shenanigans would have completely supported my story had his brakes not been deliberately cut. True, I had seen Lady Trewallyn and Sharpe leave the morgue only minutes before Brian bolted – but I had also noticed Mrs Poultry in the area, too.

Enter Chester – spurned ex-lover-cum-pimp from Las Vegas – to put a spanner in the works. I'd always wondered why Chester hadn't told the *Bugle* about Lady Trewallyn dabbling in the occult but now I knew. Quite simply, she hadn't.

Was there a connection to Sir Hugh's death and Topaz's claims that her aunt was murdered because of 'something she'd seen' in the woods? The Folly was definitely a love nest, and I was quite sure Mrs Poultry had been one of Sir Hugh's lovers. Didn't Barbara mention that Henrietta had been shocked at Sir Hugh's new nuptials? I hadn't connected it at the time, but I was positive Mrs Poultry's first name was Henrietta. When Topaz's aunt died, perhaps Mrs Poultry believed he would marry her? It would explain her bizarre behaviour at Sir Hugh's funeral when she hid under that hawthorn bush.

I thought back to the early hours of the morning where Mrs Poultry had uncharacteristically brought a man home. And then, today, there was a padlock on the basement door. Maybe, just maybe, whatever had been stored on the ground floor of the Folly just might have been shifted into her basement.

I looked at my watch. It was not quite six in the evening. I knew it was risky. I'd wait until Mrs Poultry was tucked up in bed and go and take a look.

44

Fortunately, Mrs Poultry went to bed early. I picked the padlock and put it in my pocket, not wanting to risk being locked in.

Closing the door quietly behind me, I felt my way down the stairs in the darkness. It was hot and stuffy with an overwhelming smell of dampness.

At the bottom, I switched on my flashlight and swept the room. The walls were covered in black mildew. On my left stood a large freezer. I opened it immediately and peered inside. There were the usual catering supplies – cartons of frozen vol-au-vents, salmon pinwheels, and sausage rolls. I delved deeper, and there, to my delight, discovered a plastic bagful of chicken claws. Ha! *Excellent!* I closed the lid and turned my attention to the rest of the room. What I really needed was occult equipment – a cauldron, instruments of torture, something *witchy*.

Behind me stretched an old pink sheet covering what looked like a mini Loch Ness monster – all lumps and bumps. I lifted up a corner and jumped back in astonishment.

There, caught in the beam of my flashlight, sparkled that Georgian tea urn with a nicely turned spigot. I whipped off the

sheet to find boxes and boxes piled high with silver treasures –
tankards, platters, candelabras, and various knickknacks.

Good grief! Not only was Mrs Poultry a witch, she was the
notorious Gipping Cat Burglar, too! It made total sense. Who
else had access to people's homes without question? Whilst the
family was paying their respects in church, Cradle to Coffin
Catering was doing more than laying out the finger buffet.

Yet, this was no ordinary burglar. Mrs Poultry probably had
psychic powers. She might even sense that I was down here right
this minute.

Suddenly, there was a blinding flash. The entire basement lit
up as if by a nuclear explosion. I screamed and dropped my
flashlight.

'Victoria!' Mrs Poultry, dressed in her tartan nightgown,
limped down the stairs clutching an iron poker. 'What are you
doing down here? How did you get in?'

Keep calm, Vicky! 'Oh, hello, Mrs P,' I said in a friendly
voice, as if being caught with my fingers in the pie was the most
natural thing in the world.

Mrs Poultry stood at the bottom of the stairs blocking my
exit. She had a peculiar glint in her eye. For a horrible moment,
I thought she might strike me.

'Well?' she demanded, taking out her lace handkerchief and
dabbing at her nose. I noted it was red raw.

'I'm researching an article about cellars, particularly
Stachybotrys,' I said wildly. 'I noticed the door was ajar and just
couldn't stop myself.'

'I'm sorry?'

'You've got mould down here.' I retrieved my flashlight and
switched it back on, playing the beam over the black walls.
'That's why you have that runny nose and nasty cough. It's not
an allergy. It's mould.'

'Mould.'

Warming to my theme, I chattered on, thanking Dad for one
of his favourite stories on how to gain access to scope out an

underground vault by pretending to be a building inspector. '*Stachybotrys* is particularly lethal. You need to do a home test. Would you like me to get one?'

An odd smile – more a grimace, really, appeared on Mrs Poultry's face. 'How thoughtful of you to think of my welfare, Victoria. What's your article called?'

'TOXIC MOULD: KILLER SPORES,' I said quickly. 'Didn't you hear about Alice Potts? She had mould in her basement and sued the council for thousands.'

Mrs Poultry nodded, and her mouth smiled again yet her eyes remained cold. 'How fascinating, Victoria. Why don't you tell me more about it over some hot chocolate? And perhaps, I can take a look at that nasty bruise?'

Relieved she'd fallen for my story, I followed her back to the kitchen. Mrs Poultry disappeared into the walk-in pantry – supposedly to retrieve her medicine chest. I sat down at the table surprised to find a well-thumbed copy of *Voodoo Vixens*. Several pages were dog-eared.

Mrs Poultry emerged with a tin of hot chocolate and a vile smelling paste. 'I only use herbs,' she said. 'None of that man-made filth.'

After administering the concoction to my face, she busied herself heating up milk in a saucepan and carefully measuring one level teaspoon of Bourneville. She even gave me a plate with one Cadbury's Chocolate Finger before taking the seat opposite me.

'You've got some wonderful silver,' I said innocently. 'Some looks quite valuable, especially that beautiful tea urn. I'm not surprised you would want to keep it in the basement – what with the Gipping Cat Burglar on the prowl.'

'Silver plate is not worth stealing,' Mrs Poultry declared.

Silver plate? My eye! A curious silence fell between us. I took a sip of hot chocolate. It tasted bitter.

'I heard on the grapevine you know where Salome Steel lives,' I said, pointing at the book.

271

'That's right,' she said pleasantly. 'Perhaps you'd like me to show you where?'

'Now?' I said, surprised. 'Won't she be asleep?'

'Goodness, Victoria, it's only ten thirty.'

Tonight was proving to be utterly astonishing. Not only was the stolen loot from the Gipping Cat Burglar downstairs in the basement, I was soon to find out exactly where Salome Steel lived as well as her identity.

Now that I had wooed Mrs Poultry into a false sense of security, it would only be a matter of time before she invited me to join her coven. I was fairly bursting with excitement. Pete was going to have a shock. Instead of my one scoop, I'd have three!

45

Five minutes later we were in the car. Mrs Poultry had brought a tartan blanket 'in case you get cold' and a fresh thermos of hot chocolate 'in case you'd like more'.

My landlady's new attitude towards me was so warm and caring I began to wonder if I'd misjudged her all these months. Didn't my father have a similar trade? Did it *really* matter that she had stolen all that silver? Good for her! With her acute arthritis, she wouldn't be able to manage Cradle to Coffin Catering forever. With no family to look after her, surely she needed to make provisions for her old age? As for being a witch, not *all* were bad. Some even cared about the environment and global warming.

Ten minutes later, we had left Middle Gipping and crossed Plym Bridge. It would appear that Mrs Poultry's view of 'around the corner' was quite different from my own.

'How did you find out where Salome Steel lives?' I said, surprised that the words coming out of my mouth sounded slurred and far away. I couldn't hear Mrs Poultry's answer. There was a peculiar ringing in my ears. I felt tired. Perhaps I'd close my eyes. Just for a second.

I was awoken by the sound of tearing paper and a strange sipping noise. I opened my eyes. My head felt like cotton wool; my tongue, thick and furry. I was freezing.

With a jolt, I realized I was still in the Morris Traveller but the car had stopped. It was dark outside with a full, bright moon that shone through the windscreen illuminating my landlady. She was drinking from her thermos and eating a sandwich. A ripped paper bag lay open on the tartan rug that was tucked around her legs. She looked as warm as toast.

Had I been *drugged*? The idea seemed far-fetched – yet, Mrs Poultry *had* disappeared into the pantry to retrieve her medicine box, giving her the perfect opportunity to slip a Mickey into my hot chocolate. I should have known her generosity was too good to be true.

I stole a sideways glance at my landlady who was carefully unwrapping a second sandwich. I could easily overpower her, throw her out of the car, grab the keys, and go for help. I'd never physically tackled a senior citizen before – the idea didn't seem right somehow.

Perhaps I was overreacting? A lifetime of inherited suspicion made me mistrust everyone. *Don't be silly, Vicky!* If she'd meant to do you harm, you'd be bound and gagged by now – even dead! This little jaunt was about the coven, I was sure of it. I decided to play along.

'I must have nodded off,' I said, luxuriating in a catlike stretch. I peered out the passenger window and could just make out the undulating shapes of moorland that stretched to the horizon.

'Wow! Does Salome Steel live out here?' When Mrs Poultry didn't reply, I went on, 'I'm really thirsty. Is that hot chocolate?'

'This is tea.' Mrs Poultry drained the last drop and replaced the plastic cup on top of the flask and put it on the floor behind her seat along with the carefully folded paper bag. In silence, she reached over to my side and tried to unlatch the glove compartment with her arthritic fingers.

'Here, allow me,' I said. The latch popped open to reveal a small object wrapped in a piece of cloth. I gave her the bundle. She put it on her lap.

'I'm afraid I brought you here under false pretences.' Mrs Poultry turned to face me, her expression deep in the shadows. 'Tell me about your friendship with the gel from the cafe,' she demanded.

'*Topaz*?' I was stunned. Why would she care about *Topaz*? I racked my sluggish brain but could not remember even mentioning Topaz to Mrs Poultry. I shrugged. 'She's a bit odd but I hardly know her. Why?'

'Don't lie,' Mrs Poultry hissed. 'When I telephoned the Gipping Constabulary on Monday night to report you missing, Detective Constable Probes suggested I call The Copper Kettle.' Mrs Poultry paused, before adding nastily, 'The police officer implied that you and she were . . . *intimate*.'

Blast Probes and his big mouth! Mrs Poultry wanted to know if I was still a virgin. Everyone knows coven initiates must be virgins.

It certainly explained her horror when she spotted me canoodling with Dave on Sunday evening. Then there was that business of how angry she was when I spent the night with Annabel and ended up accepting a lift from Chester in my pyjamas. Hadn't she demanded to know if he'd 'compromised my purity'?

'Don't worry Mrs P. I swear I am still a virgin,' I said brightly. 'I know how important it is for the coven.'

'Coven? What coven?' Mrs Poultry snapped.

'Aren't you a witch?' I stammered.

'Certainly not! What an outrageous suggestion.'

A peculiar feeling began to settle in the pit of my stomach. If this fabricated trip to see Salome Steel was not about joining a coven, why had I been brought here and where, exactly, were we?

'I was joking,' I stammered. 'Actually, Topaz thought you were a witch but I told her she was imagining it.'

'Is that what she's calling herself these days?' Mrs Poultry snorted with disdain. 'I recognized Ethel immediately in Tesco this morning. Ridiculous disguise.'

As the full import of Mrs Poultry's words hit me, I realized Topaz had been right about her aunt being murdered, but wrong about the killer.

Not only did Cradle to Coffin Catering take advantage of the occasion for theft, it provided the perfect opportunity to poison the guests!

I was in deep trouble.

'You think I don't know what you two are up to?' Mrs Poultry's hands clutched the bundle on her lap tightly. 'You left the coroner's reports in a very obvious place, Victoria.'

'Oh *those*!' I said, flippantly, despite my stomach doing somersaults. 'Old news now, of course. With the Lady Trewallyn scandal splashed all over the *Bugle,* there's no story now. Who cares if she murdered her husband? She's left the country and that's that.'

Mrs Poultry began to unwrap the bundle.

'Between you and me, it's good riddance to bad rubbish,' I gabbled on. 'I'm told Sir Hugh was quite a womanizer. Used to have love trysts in that Folly in the woods and slept with half the women in Gipping – Barbara Meadows, Mary J. Larch—'

'That's not true,' Mrs Poultry cried, whipping out a Beretta 92FS. She pointed it at me. 'He only loved *me*!'

'Don't shoot!' Even though it was hard to tell if this was a real Beretta or a BB gun, Dad always said to assume the worst. 'I won't say anything. I don't like the cops.'

Mrs Poultry slipped her free hand inside her coat and pulled out my two precious postcards from Spain. 'I believe these are of great importance to you, Victoria,' she said as she released the Beretta's safety catch. 'I suggest you get out of the car.'

Oh God! This was far worse than I expected. Miserably, I scrambled out.

The Morris spluttered into life. After an eleven-point turn, Mrs Poultry forced the car into first gear and kangarooed away over the uneven moors.

Numb with shock I watched the taillights vanish from sight just as a thick mist descended. I was utterly alone, but I was alive.

46

I went after the Morris Traveller at a trot. The ground rose steadily towards one of the many massive granite outcrops that littered the moors. The full moon was bright enough to light my way, so I was pretty sure I'd get a good view and find my bearings from up there.

How could I have been so stupid? So naive! Mrs Poultry was simply a straightforward murderess and thief. There had never been a coven. All that devil chicken and poppet palaver was just a ruse exploited by my landlady who had sworn she'd never even read *Voodoo Vixens*. The Eco-Warriors had jumped on the same voodoo frenzy and must have thought sending Annabel a poppet a hilarious joke. And to think I'd fallen for it, too!

It was too late to get a front-page scoop now. Mrs Poultry – anonymously of course – was bound to tell the cops my parents lived in Spain. I was stranded on the moors and would probably die of hypothermia. A feeling of self-pity swept over me. Perhaps it was for the best. Without warning, a thick, impenetrable mist descended and completely enveloped me. I had to stop. I couldn't even see my own feet.

Bloody hell! It's the killer fog! Like everyone, I'd heard of these dreaded mists that come out of nowhere. I'd also pooh-poohed ancient folklore that says it's summoned by pixies in order to lead hapless travellers into bottomless mires. Now I wasn't so sure.

I walked on very carefully. It was like playing a horror version of blind man's buff. Hot tears stung my eyes. I started to whimper and began to pray to God. I hadn't had a chat with Him since the break-in at the *Gazette*. I reminded Him that Mrs Poultry had broken at least five of the Ten Commandments and I hadn't broken any. I even resurrected the virgin deal if it would get me back to Gipping safe, and protect Mum and Dad from the law.

As if by magic, the mist vanished. The sky was bright with stars once more. But the rocky outcrop I'd been heading for had vanished. I was hopelessly lost. I didn't even know which of the three moors in southwest England I was actually lost on. How long had I been unconscious?

What if I were in Cornwall! Only last week the trashy *Bugle* had reported that the Beast of Bodmin Moor had savaged a hiker from the Ramblers' Association. We'd all had a laugh about it at the time but what if it were true?

Stop it, Vicky! Get a grip! A surge of hope filled me. When we'd set off, I'd noticed Mrs Poultry's fuel gauge was only a quarter full. When we'd stopped, the needle had hardly moved. Bodmin lay to the northwest and Exmoor to the northeast. Both were 120-mile round-trips. We'd left Rumble Lane shortly after ten. It was now midnight. Mrs Poultry drove at twenty-five miles an hour, meaning it was highly unlikely I was anywhere but Dartmoor. This thought was surprisingly comforting.

Annabel may well have scoffed at my Girl Guide past, but hadn't I snagged the Star Tracker badge at first go? I knew Gipping was to the southeast of Dartmoor so all I had to do was find the Polaris and then I'd find north.

Turning in a slow circle, I studied the starry sky and managed to locate the Plough. I drew an imaginary line upward and . . . there it was!

Blast! I'd been walking completely in the wrong direction – farther away from civilization and closer to the treacherous bog and swampland that surrounded the notorious Dartmoor Prison from which the very terrain acted as an escape deterrent.

I turned to my right and, glancing continuously over my shoulder, made sure the Polaris was always at my seven o'clock. I made my way over a high, grassy knoll and down the other side towards a bank of tall, majestic cypresses in the distance – not wild trees like hawthorn or mountain ash. *Cypresses, Vicky! Human life!*

I broke into a run . . . and that was when I stopped paying attention and stumbled straight into the bog.

It only took three steps before the ground began to quake. It happened so fast that I didn't have time to leap aside. I was sinking. Being dragged under. The oozing mass of peat and stinking vegetation reached my knees, then thighs. Desperately, I struggled to free myself but only sank deeper, horrified by the strange seething hissing sound the bog made.

I began to scream for help. The thick, glutinous muck sucked me farther in. I was waist-deep. Then chest. Oh God. I really was going to die.

I screamed until my voice went hoarse and then, miraculously, my feet found firm ground. But what did it matter? I was still stuck in thick, cold mud.

Suddenly, I heard the sound of a dog barking. It was coming closer. A fat English bulldog waddled into view. It stopped on the edge of the bog, woofed twice, and promptly sat down on its haunches.

'Ahoy there! Ahoy!' A tall man in his early sixties came striding into view. Over his red and white striped pyjamas he wore a greatcoat and, to my utter joy, carried a walking stick and a life belt.

'By Jove, young lady. You're in a bit of a pickle.'

Pulling me out wasn't easy but the man was extraordinarily strong. I clutched the life belt – HMS *Dauntless* – and was

280

dragged facedown across the stinking mire to safety. Exhausted and miserable but so happy to be alive, I just sat for a moment in shock.

'Admiral Charles Gunn. Retired. Dog's Horatio,' said the man, retrieving a hip flask from his inside pocket. 'This'll have you shipshape in no time.'

'Vicky Hill,' I said. 'Pleased to meet you.'

The admiral gestured to the cypress trees. 'Live down there, what,' he said. 'Not far. Get you cleaned up.'

As the admiral used his walking stick to pick our way through several more bogs, he told me he liked to work on his 'little hobby' at night and that as Horatio had 'bilge problems', they were often outside.

The admiral had seen a car drive past his cottage at approximately twenty-three hundred hours.

'At first, I thought it was two lovers going off for some nooky,' he said. 'But when only one person came back, I smelled a rat.'

'You saved my life,' I said shakily.

'These bogs are death traps,' he declared. 'Even the locals never venture there in broad daylight, let alone at night. I bought the cottage for that reason. Keep people ashore.'

I felt sick as the full horror of my ordeal began to sink in. Mrs Poultry was a local. She had known about the danger of these moors and had deliberately chosen this spot.

Her intention had been to kill me.

47

The admiral lived in a picture-postcard thatched cottage next to a little stream.

I did my best to clean up my appearance in the bathroom – or 'head' as the admiral called it. I smelled dreadful – even Horatio gave me a wide berth. Fortunately I was able to rinse off most of the stinking mud from my cagoule in the handheld shower.

The admiral gave me some cream long-john thermals, which I had to roll up, and a heavy wool sweater. It was far too big but clean and warm. My shoes were another matter as the admiral's feet were twice my size. In the end, I borrowed his massive Wellington boots.

All I could think about was finding my landlady.

As the daughter of a professional thief, I knew Mrs Poultry would not leave Gipping without her silver. As her arthritis was so severe, I felt sure she had to have an accomplice. An idea began to form in my mind.

Back in the low-beamed kitchen, Horatio slept soundly in his basket next to the Aga. The admiral handed me my third hot toddy, and said, 'We must call the police.'

'There isn't time,' I said. 'I must get back to Gipping immediately.'

'Nonsense.' He walked over to the oak desk in the corner and picked up the phone by his computer. 'You're not going anywhere, young lady. You've had a dreadful shock.'

'You don't understand. I'm a journalist.' I darted towards him and took the receiver out of his hand. 'No police. Yet.'

'Journalist!' The admiral expression changed from concern to fury. He pushed me aside and stepped in front of his computer, shielding the screen behind him. 'How low and desperate do you people get?'

I was confused. 'I don't understand.'

'You're from *Paparazzi Razzle*!' He fumed. 'Don't try to deny it.'

'No, the *Gazette*,' I said. 'Why . . . oh!' My mouth dropped open in astonishment as I took in reference books on Africa stacked on his desk. A ream of paper scribbled with Post-its. A dry-erase board propped behind the computer. In red marker were three names: Susu, Kisi, and Fatu – the infamous Voodoo Vixens.

'Good grief! *You're* Salome Steel?' I was stunned. 'But you're—?'

'A man,' the admiral said with resigned irritation. He gestured to the receiver I still held in my hand, 'Go ahead. Call your newspaper, but let me tell you one thing,' he said. 'I served in Her Majesty's Navy for forty years. I received the St John's Bravery Award from Queen Elizabeth herself. Your scandal-mongering will destroy my reputation.'

'I'm not that kind of journalist.' This was true. Everyone had a right to privacy. I replaced the phone. 'I'll keep your secret, if you can help me get back to Gipping.'

I gave a brief account of events that led to my rescue but decided against telling him about the silver. After all, I hardly knew him and besides, a man who calls himself Salome Steel and writes steamy sex novels wasn't necessarily normal. Who

283

knew how the admiral would react at the prospect of all that loot?

'All hands on deck!' he exclaimed, striding to the back door.

Horatio, sensing excitement, struggled out of his basket and gave a deep woof. 'No room for you, old boy,' cried the admiral, stopping to give the old dog a pat.

The admiral handed me a motorbike helmet. 'Pop that on, young Vicky. It's battle stations!'

48

The ancient Ariel Red Hunter motorbike was surprisingly fast. Wearing helmet and goggles, I clung tightly to the admiral as we flew along the heather-covered moorland tracks, over a cattle-grid, and towards the distant lights of Gipping.

It was exhilarating. No wonder men got addicted to these machines. The freedom, the speed, the wind in my face, and the power throbbing between my legs – I could easily become a biker's moll.

What would have taken forty minutes by a car driven at twenty-five miles per hour, we accomplished in under fifteen minutes.

The admiral had wanted to go straight to the cops but I persuaded him to drop me home to change my clothes and shoes. I insisted that Mrs Poultry was long gone and I was in no danger. The admiral would find Probes and they'd call an all-cars alert on Mrs Poultry's Morris Traveller.

He seemed puzzled as to why I wouldn't want to give the news myself but I knew how the law worked. I'd be 'helping police with their inquiries' whilst they got all the glory.

I wanted my scoop. I'd earned my scoop! Yes, it was dangerous, but I was determined to catch Mrs Poultry red-handed.

Dad said the element of surprise was often worth more than any weapon so I asked the admiral to drop me off at the top of Rumble Lane.

I was too late. There was no Morris Traveller outside number 10. The house was in darkness.

Bitterly disappointed, I kicked off the admiral's Wellington boots and let myself in through the downstairs bathroom window. Up in my bedroom I took off the long johns and was just about to pull on my jeans when I realized the door to the water tank cupboard was open.

I'd been so preoccupied with Mrs Poultry having my precious postcards, I'd forgotten about the most incriminating evidence of all. She must have taken the coroner's reports, too! She might even try to blackmail me. 'Perverting the course of justice,' rang in my ears, or worse: 'An accessory to murder!'

I took a deep breath. It was vital I checked the basement. Perhaps she hadn't even started to shift the silver yet? I tore downstairs and, to my joy, the padlock was still clasped firmly to the basement door.

I picked the lock once more, switched on the light, and thundered down the stairs. 'Damn and blast it!' I shouted. The boxes had vanished. The silver was gone. I threw open the freezer. Empty.

'Mmmm!' came a sound from behind me. I froze. 'MMMM!'

Slowly, I turned around. There, behind the door, tied with duct tape to the central heating pipes, sat Dave Randall.

He was bound and gagged, his face red with sweat and eyes bulging with fear.

I stared at him in surprise.

He wasn't that handsome at all.

49

'You were her accomplice all the time,' I said, helping Dave to his feet. 'She was at your house the other night. That's why you wouldn't let me in.'

Dave gingerly touched the back of his head. 'She hit me!' He seemed both dazed and incredulous. 'She offered me some hot chocolate and when I said I didn't like it, she just hit me.'

'You do realize, Dave, you can go to jail for this?' I said severely. 'You can say good-bye to your Olympic dream.'

Dave looked scared. 'The old bat made me do it,' he whined. 'I was just shifting the stuff from the Folly for her. It was just a favour, like. She didn't even pay me. I swear to God.'

'Receiving stolen goods is the least of your problems,' I said. 'The cops are far more interested in you finding Sir Hugh's body.'

Dave turned white. 'How do you know?'

'You had a motive,' I said. 'Everyone knows you were having an affair with Lady Trewallyn.'

'We only did it once,' Dave cried. 'Said she'd give me a lap dance and a night to remember if I kept my mouth shut about finding her old man.'

Men are so easily bought, I thought with disgust.

'If this gets out, my career is over.'

'Not if you do as I say,' I said. 'If you help me, I'll persuade the cops to view your case kindly. You might even get a suspended sentence.'

'But I don't know anything,' he wailed.

'You must know where she's gone.'

'Somewhere up north,' he said. 'We'll never catch her now.'

But we could. Mrs Poultry couldn't get far on a quarter tank of petrol and the only place open at this time of night was the motorway service station five miles away at Barrington Cross.

'Where's your Land Rover?' I cried.

50

Dave's Land Rover was parked out of sight at the end of the cul-de-sac. As we turned out of Rumble Lane, a panda car with a blue flashing light, followed by the admiral's motorbike, flew by.

We sped through Middle Gipping, past The Grange, and out into the open countryside.

'I swear I had nothing to do with Sir Hugh's death,' Dave insisted. 'He was with Mrs Poultry at the Folly the night he died.'

'She must have known you saw them together,' I said. 'My guess is that Chester left the photograph on your bed to warn you off Katherine. He was jealous. Then, Mrs Poultry turned up afterwards with the chicken, saw the photograph, and realized it was perfect for her plan.'

'Plan?'

'To frame Katherine for Sir Hugh's death,' I said. 'And, of course, you helped her by not reporting it to the police.'

Dave bit his lip in anguish. 'Oh bugger.'

'Indeed,' I said. 'Katherine doesn't go to the police, either. Instead, she enlists Sharpe to write a *second* report. Same diagnosis. Heart attack. Perfect.'

'I bet she gave him a lap dance, too,' said Dave mournfully.

Dave went on to explain that Mrs Poultry had started the silver scam. He'd helped her move the stolen goods until he turned professional and wanted out. But Mrs Poultry wouldn't let him, and threatened to damage his hedge-jumping sponsorship chances with the Plym Valley Farmers. By then, Sir Hugh had muscled in on the deal. After that, all Dave would say were things got complicated.

Ahead, a yellowish glow rose to greet us – the lights of the motorway. We crested the hill and there below stretched the six-lane motorway and Barrington Cross service station nestled in a dell next to the motorway slip-road.

Mrs Poultry's lone figure stood at the self-service petrol pump, struggling to replace the nozzle in the cradle, which seemed to have a life of its own.

'She's there!' I yelled with excitement. 'We've got her!'

Dave thrust his hand down hard on the horn. *PAARPP!* We peeled into the forecourt and screeched to a halt a whisker away from the front bumper, blocking her escape.

Startled, Mrs Poultry dropped the nozzle and promptly tripped over it. Staggering to her feet, she yanked the driver's door open and made a grab for her handbag on the back seat. *Move, Vicky! Fast!* She's going for her gun!

I leapt out of the Land Rover, grabbed Mrs Poultry round the waist, and hurled her against the side of the Morris Traveller. Grasping her arms firmly by her sides, I screamed at Dave, 'Call the cops! Hurry!'

'I've got a signal!' cried Dave, waving his mobile. Thank God, we were in government-owned West Country Wireless territory.

Mrs Poultry didn't even flinch. Her eyes stared coldly into mine.

'I want those postcards,' I whispered urgently. '*Now*!'

'I posted them to the police station.' Mrs Poultry gave a nasty smile. 'And those reports, along with a nice little note explaining where I found them.'

'I don't believe you.' Surely no one carries stamps in their handbag – let alone the right postage.

As I glanced into the back of her car, Mrs Poultry saw her chance. She stamped hard on my right foot, deftly kicked my left shin, and as I buckled over with pain, delivered a strong uppercut to my chin. I keeled over, falling in a dirty puddle of greasy water.

I really did see stars. I felt dizzy. Sick. Tried to clear my head. 'Dave! Help!' I stumbled to my feet conscious of Dave circling the scene with his mobile phone camera like a professional photographer.

Mrs Poultry was half in the car, reaching over the back seat. I grabbed her ankle and pulled with all my might. She tried to kick me off but I clung on, even when blows from the *Automobile Association Travel Guide* rained down on my head. *So much for arthritis!*

Dave continued to snap away, shouting, 'Look over here, Vicky! Yep! Nice one. Aaaand just one more.'

With one last supreme effort, I let go of Mrs Poultry's foot, launched myself into her lap, grabbed her coat sleeves, and hauled her out of the car and onto the ground.

Straddling her, I pinned her arms above her head. We were both panting, hard.

Dave hurried over with some binder twine from the back of the Land Rover and the two of us trussed her up like a chicken.

'I got some great photos,' Dave said, beaming.

As Dave stood guard, I rummaged through Mrs Poultry's handbag. Thankfully, the two coroner's reports were inside along with my precious postcards. I tucked them into my safari jacket. Now it would only be a case of her word against mine.

A fleet of panda cars poured into the service station, followed by the admiral. By now, a handful of stragglers from the twenty-four-hour Little Chef – WE NEVER CLOSE – had trickled out to see what all the fuss was about.

Mrs Poultry and Dave were bundled into the separate patrol cars.

As I stood gazing in wonder at the amount of silver stashed in the back of the car, I experienced a twinge of guilt. True, I'd apprehended a serial killer but I'd also captured a silver thief. I hoped Dad would understand.

'Well done, Vicky,' said Probes, slipping by my side. His voice was warm with approval. 'You've got your front page, I'd reckon.'

Despite my scraped knees and nasty bruises, a warm glow filled my heart. 'Yes,' I said. 'A Vicky Hill exclusive!'

51

'Oh, Vicky, you are so brave,' Topaz declared. She cupped her chin in her hands and gazed at me with adoration. 'I wish I were like you.'

'I was only doing my job,' I said modestly. It was Saturday afternoon and the cafe had finally emptied. Business had never been so good. Topaz was taking a well-earned break and had joined me at my usual table overlooking the High Street.

The *Gazette* was spread out before us.

A CRIPPEN IN GIPPING?

SILVER THIEF'S SHOCKING ROAD TO MURDER

POISON! POULTRY! AND ME!

True to his word, Wilf had given me a six-page spread, promotion to staff writer, *and* a laptop. Newspaper sales were at an all-time high. Pete had been pleased to write: YOU READ IT HERE FIRST.

Topaz had even hung a large banner that read ORDER YOUR SUNDAY NATIONAL PAPERS TODAY along with a sign reading

'Here at The Kettle tomorrow! The reporter who single-handedly apprehended celebrity caterer turned thief and serial killer after being heavily drugged, abducted, and held at gunpoint on Dartmoor'.

Topaz was predictably jealous of Dave's part in the high-speed car chase even when I pointed out that without his graphic photographs, the front page would have definitely lacked punch – literally.

I was glad to hear Dave agreed to take my advice and turned witness for the prosecution. The *Gazette* even gave him a little publicity to help with his legal fees:

BLACKMAIL!
EVERY OLYMPIC ATHLETE'S NIGHTMARE!

'How did you know those flowers could induce fatal heart attacks?' Topaz said, pointing to a photograph of a bank of foxgloves I'd snapped in Rumble Lane suitably captioned: BOUQUET OF DEATH. 'I have *so* much to learn.'

'It was an easy guess.' I still had the original coroner's report in my drawer. With Brian dead, and Sharpe abroad, there were some things the police were better off not knowing. Besides, as long as justice was done, did it really matter?

'Then, of course, traces were found in the wine bottle left at Hugh's Folly,' I went on. When confronted with the evidence, Mrs Poultry confessed to poisoning Sir Hugh and Topaz's aunt. Their bodies were to be exhumed on Monday.

'I could have sworn Lady Trewallyn was the killer,' Topaz said.

'That's exactly what Mrs Poultry wanted people to think.' Under intense interrogation, Mrs Poultry admitted she knew of Katherine Vanderkamp's marriage to a famed African anthropologist, so seized upon the idea of using voodoo to frame her. Unfortunately, my landlady hadn't bargained on the Salome Steel phenomenon where it seemed every man and his dog were making poppets and mutilating chickens.

'I suppose you'll be giving up the cafe now,' I said hopefully. Lady Trewallyn's marriage had been annulled, leaving Topaz to inherit the country estate.

'Oh no! I'm going to rent The Grange to a farmer.' Topaz reached across the table and squeezed my hand. 'Don't worry, Vicky. My place is right here at The Kettle. I *love* being undercover.'

'But surely it's too dangerous?' I said horrified. 'Whatever will your cousin say?'

'Colin thinks it's a frightfully good idea,' she said. 'Funny about *her*, though.' Topaz gestured to the *Gazette* across the street. Barbara stood in the window replacing her *Voodoo Vixens* banner with a stuffed life-size horse. 'I could have sworn she was up to something with that large pot and scary-looking man.' Topaz giggled. 'Perhaps he was her toy boy!'

'Don't be ridiculous,' I said, embarrassed that I'd thought the same.

I'd let slip that I'd heard Salome Steel had moved to Cornwall. Like all locals, no one was interested in an event south of the River Tamar. Fortunately Barbara perked up when Wilf approved her new window proposal – the Gipping Bards' Christmas production of *Equus*.

A silver Saab 9-3 convertible pulled up outside The Kettle. Doctor Frost got out and went round to open the passenger door. Annabel emerged, dressed in a rust-coloured Juicy Couture tracksuit with Ugg sheepskin boots. She wore dark sunglasses and leaned heavily on a walking cane. *Blast!* I should have known my day was going too well.

'Oh look! It's Annabel Lake!' squealed Topaz, rapping smartly on the window. Annabel peered in our direction and grimaced. In a flash, Topaz darted off in the direction of the front door, leaving me to witness the repulsive spectacle of Annabel giving Doctor Frost a deep French kiss.

To my dismay, Topaz reappeared in the High Street, grabbed Annabel's arm, and made her wave it in my direction.

Seconds later, Annabel – wincing with pain – was propelled towards my table and forced to sit down.

'Here's Vicky!' cried Topaz.

'Glad to see you're up and about,' I said, marvelling at how Annabel turned being an invalid into a fashion statement.

'Doctor Frost is giving me his summer cottage until next May,' said Annabel. 'It's got an Aga.'

'Oh, who cares about Agas?' Topaz exclaimed. 'Isn't Vicky clever? Catching a serial killer! Solving the biggest silver mystery ever!'

'Frankly, Topaz,' Annabel snapped, 'I can't believe Vicky didn't suspect her landlady in the first place. For heaven's sake, the silver was in the basement.'

'Actually, it was kept in the Folly,' I said, pointing to page four where a photograph of Hugh's Folly was accompanied by the caption: LOVE NEST OF LOOT. 'Mrs Poultry mistakenly believed Lady Trewallyn was selling the Folly to Devon Satellite Bell,' I went on. 'She had to move it *somewhere*.'

Annabel went quiet. A peculiar look came over her face. 'Damn! I should have guessed! You *idiot*, Annabel!'

'Bad luck,' Topaz chipped in, throwing me a triumphant look. 'Vicky got there first.'

Annabel turned on me, eyes flashing. 'And I bet I know what else you got to first!'

I felt my face redden and tried to change the subject. 'Topaz, how about some more tea?'

'Coming right up, *boss*.Topaz fluttered away as Annabel rose unsteadily to her feet. She was trembling with rage.

'I *know* there were two coroner's reports!' she cried. 'You stole from me! This scoop should have been mine!'

I recalled my hidden wristwatch, Annabel's patronizing manner, and nasty, snide comments.

'It's just business,' I said with an apologetic smile. 'As you said, journalism is tough, tough, *tough* but we can still be friends.'

'You've got some *nerve*!' And with that, Annabel hobbled out of the cafe.

Topaz returned with a mug of tea. 'Where did she go?'

Suddenly, my mobile rang. Thanks to Devon Satellite Bell merging with West Country Wireless, Gipping now had crystal clear phone reception – and Sky TV. Topaz snatched the mobile out of my grasp.

'Vicky Hill's office,' she said, listening intensely to the chirping on the other end of the line. Covering the receiver with her hand, she rolled her eyes and whispered, 'It's that dreadful Ronnie Binns. Says he's found something at the tip. Shall I take a message?'

'Tell him I'll be there in fifteen minutes.'

Topaz gave him the message and said good-bye. She turned to me in surprise. 'Didn't he sell that stupid alien-chicken-garbologist-nightmare story to the *Bugle*?'

'An investigative journalist must always have an open mind and explore every lead,' I said firmly.

I left The Copper Kettle with a spring in my step. The future had never looked brighter. I had a promotion, a front-page scoop, and informers galore. In a few months I'd even be able to buy a car.

My smile faltered a little – there was still the issue of my inconvenient virginity but perhaps that was for the best. As an investigative reporter on a quest for fame and fortune, the last thing I wanted was to be tied down.

My thoughts turned to my parents in Spain. Lucky me to have reaped the benefit of their experiences – from Mum's insights on love and relationships to Dad's philosophies on business ethics.

Dad always says the world doesn't owe anyone a living and it was up to me to make mine, which was exactly what I planned to do. Gipping was full of secrets just waiting to be discovered. Somehow, I just *knew* I was a whisker away from my next VICKY HILL EXCLUSIVE!